Distant Moon

David Galbraith

MENTOR

This Edition first published 2000 by

Mentor Books
43 Furze Road,
Sandyford Industrial Estate,
Dublin 18.

Tel. (01) 295 2112/3   Fax. (01) 295 2114
e-mail: admin@mentorbooks.ie
www.mentorbooks.ie

ISBN: 1-84210-024-6

A catalogue record for this book is available
from the British Library

Cover Illustration: Slatter-Anderson
Typesetting, editing, design and layout by
Mentor Books

Printed in Ireland by ColourBooks

Dedication

This book is dedicated to my wife, Christine O'Brien, a fine woman from County Wicklow, and to my son and daughter, Mathew and Patricia.

Prologue

It is April 1779. Nineteen-year-old Kate Brennan is leaving her family cottage in County Wicklow to take up a position in the house of Mistress Delamere of Enniskerry, as teacher and nanny to her three children. She is entering a different world.

In these Georgian times, society in England, Scotland, Ireland and Wales is largely rural. London is by far the largest city, with a population of around 700,000 people. Norwich is the next largest, yet has only 30,000 inhabitants. No other city or market town has a population greater than 10,000. And the cities are dangerous places to live. Lord North, the Prime Minister has just been robbed by a highwayman in London, while Horace Walpole has been fired upon while out riding in Hyde Park.

Duels are commonplace, with William Pitt exchanging shots with a parliamentary opponent, George Tierney. The schools are no less dangerous, with the Riot Act having to be read at Winchester School, while at Rugby the pupils have mined the headmaster's study with gunpowder.

But developments in communications are changing the social structure. Turnpike roads are being laid between London and the other main centres of population, greatly reducing the time taken to travel around the country. Fifty coaches are leaving Birmingham every day for the thirteen-hour trip to London. At the same time, a fortune is being spent in constructing canals and waterways to link London, Bristol, Birmingham, Hull and Liverpool .

In England, more and more people have access to the better things of life. Although at the beginning of the century only the aristocracy could afford luxuries like wallpaper, by now almost 2,000,000 yards are being sold in England every year. Everyone is going to the burgeoning horse-race meetings to watch the St Leger, the Oaks, and the Derby. In London, the theatres are booming, with Drury Lane able to accommodate almost 4,000 people in the audience. Tea is drunk constantly by the entire population, accompanied by hot-buttered white bread for breakfast. And while they are enjoying their tea, the public can choose to find out the news from fourteen different morning newspapers in London, and over thirty-five provincial papers throughout the country.

And wonder of wonders, Joseph Bramah has just patented the first superior ball-cock WC, soon to be installed in houses all over the country.

But in Ireland things are somewhat different. While the richer classes have similar tastes and access to the same luxuries as those in England, for the vast majority life is a much more desperate existence. Acts of Parliament have been passed forbidding Catholics from buying land. As a result, more than 95% of the country is owned by non-Catholics, who make up less than 10% of the population. In addition, Catholics have been forbidden to carry arms, vote in elections or sit in Parliament.

Outside of Dublin, many people live in hovels with little or no furniture, often sleeping on straw. The formal education system has failed dismally, but many children are being educated by the clergy, by Irish men and women who have travelled abroad, and by a number of individuals who have devoted themselves to raising the educational standards of an oppressed nation. Yet although poor in worldly goods, the people have a rich treasury of folk culture, much of which is handed down from mother to daughter. In addition, illicit stills are commonplace throughout the country and whiskey is plentiful and cheap.

However, in the Irish Parliament, an opposition group is increasingly advocating an end to British interference in Irish affairs. This is being counterbalanced by the militant Protestant Ascendancy in Dublin which is horrified by the stance of the government in London, as it has begun to take a more sympathetic attitude towards the Catholics in Ireland. Meanwhile, the war of American Independence is accelerating matters, and when France declares war on Britain and rumours begin circulating about an invasion and an uprising, the British government decides to force the issue of Catholic relief on the grounds that the security of the empire demands it.

Not that Kate is too interested in these matters. She has her new position to look forward to . . .

Chapter 1

'Lachlan! Jossie!'

The dogs had obviously got the scent of a rabbit, disregarding her cries as they bounded up the hill. Breathless, Kate chased after them, trying to avoid getting her feet tangled in the heather.

It was the Sunday after Easter, and the first really warm day of the year. The sky was a cloudless blue, while all around her a multitude of green shades contrasted with the dark brown of the heather, twinkling with thousands of tiny flowers. It was such a beautiful day that after Mass in the village church the two women had decided to walk along the hillside, away from the familiar crowd of people and up into the clean air.

At the top of the hillock Kate caught up with the dogs where they were casting around for another scent. Two hundred yards below, her mother was taking it slowly and steadily up the slope with her young brother

Eamonn. Beyond the path, she gazed at the view over the village. In the distance, a cobalt sea sparkled, while over on her left a haze of smoke from the peat fires in the fishermen's houses hung in the air. Turning around, she looked back up behind her to the big house in the distance, surrounded by trees. Further on she could pick out another church steeple, dwarfed by the hills and the massive grey mountain brooding over the countryside below.

Down in the valley, she could barely see Cormack's alehouse at the crossroads. No doubt her father was there, drinking and gossiping with his cronies. She had tried all she could but she had been unable to coax him into coming, despite using all her daughterly charms.

'Sure, it's a grand day, right enough,' she shouted to no one in particular, as her mother and brother clambered up the rock-strewn path.

'Kathleen Brennan, what are you thinking of, picking up you skirts and running like that,' her mother puffed and panted, trying to scold her daughter and catch her breath at the same time.

'Don't you be worrying, Mam. You'll see me next week, after I've been up to Mistress Delamere's. I'll be all prim and proper.'

They stood for a few minutes, taking in the scene. Their little cottage, clinging to the other side of the valley, was so tiny that Kate could barely pick it out.

'My, it's always a grand view from here,' her mother remarked finally. 'But we better be getting back. I've got so much work to do, never mind planting the potatoes. And we need to rouse your Father out of Cormack's or he'll be no use for the rest of the day.'

Turning reluctantly, the two women set off back down the hill, with the dogs racing on ahead. As they reached the village, Kate was surprised to see her father standing outside the alehouse, in a huddle with three or four other men. Seeing them coming, he edged in their direction, half stumbling, an ashen expression on his face.

'We've had a letter from Patrick Nolan,' he muttered. 'He's talking about our Declan – seems he's in a hospital in London, and they say he's dying of consumption.'

For a moment Kate could not trust herself to speak. But then clutching at his arm she burst out, 'What does it say?' Immediately, she was reminded of the day her older brother had left to find work in England. He had been gone for three years, and all she had to show for it was a few letters he had sent at the beginning.

'Only that Declan hasn't been able to find a job, except for unloading the barges down on the riverfront. But the damp and the fog has made him ill. He's been coughing badly, and last week he collapsed. They've taken him to some type of hospital in Grays Inn. But I don't think people get well there – from what young Nolan says I think it's more a place for the dying.'

Pressing her hands to her ears, Kate tried not to listen, a rush of tears stinging her eyes. Her mother had not said a word, but she could see her shock mirrored all too clearly in her face. Only last year, her little brother had died of the cholera. It had been a terrible time and they had still not got over it – and now this.

'What will we do?' she pleaded with them.

'What can we do, child?' her father retorted brusquely. 'Your brother wanted to go to England, and now he'll die there.'

9

With that, he jammed his cap firmly on his head and stamped off across the road towards the cottage. Reaching out blindly, Kate put her arm round her mother's shoulders, trying to console her.

'Come on, Mam, let's get back to the house, and I'll put on a fire and make some tea.'

It was a forlorn, unhappy group that wound its way up the hill. Even the dogs seemed to recognise something was wrong and stopped their mad dashing to and fro. All afternoon Kate tried her best, but she could not get her mother to express her feelings. All she wanted to do was sit in the old rocking chair, fumbling with her rosary beads, muttering her prayers sadly to herself. In the other room, her father had taken to his bed and was not to be disturbed.

By six o'clock, Kate could not take the silence any more. Slipping out of the house, she dashed along the side of the hill towards Lord Jesmond's estate. Not far from the main entrance, a lodge barred the way to unwelcome travellers. Nearby were some farm cottages, huddled together and facing into the prevailing south westerly wind. Even at a distance, she could pick out Cathal behind one of the houses, repairing the dyke that kept the foxes out of the garden.

For a moment, she watched him working, trying to draw strength from his calm, deliberate movements. Then she whistled low, in a way that only they both knew. Recognising the sound immediately, he looked up. Seconds later, he was clambering over the wall and running towards her. Searching for some crumb of comfort, she fell into his arms.

'It's Declan, it's Declan,' she kept sobbing.

'What about Declan? Tell me, for God's sake,' he insisted.

'We've had a letter from Patrick Nolan. Declan's sick and dying in a hospital in London. I've not seen him for three years and now I'm never going to see him again.'

Holding her tightly, he murmured quietly against her hair. His kisses were gentle, brushing against her skin as she burrowed her face into his shoulder.

'Let's go down by the stream,' he whispered, taking her by the hand. 'We can talk about it there.'

Normally, the stream was a beautiful place, set in a secluded valley amongst the woods and surrounded by steep hills. There was even an old stone cottage built at some time in the distant past. Kate had stumbled across it by chance one day out walking with the dogs. It was their special place to get away from other people, to be on their own.

She was glad she had Cathal to comfort her. For a few minutes she pressed herself against his chest, drawing strength from his kisses against her cheek and his fingers smoothing her hair. Listening to his voice, low and insistent against her shoulder, she could feel the depths of despair slowly beginning to pass. His arms felt strong against her back and around her waist. They kissed again, lingering passionately this time. Slowly, his hand slipped over her breast, her nipples responding immediately. Without thinking, she pushed back hard against him.

'What is it, Kate?' he protested. 'Why are you pulling away from me?'

'I'm sorry, Cathal,' she replied quickly, 'But I can't think of us hugging and kissing at a time like this.' It was only half true. Although she had known him for years, the attraction between them had grown stronger over the past few months. Yet while she enjoyed his attention and the strength of his body when he kissed her, it always seemed as if something was missing. Despite his protests, she had resisted all his attempts to make love.

'Just hold me, I want to be comforted, I need to talk about what we can do,' she begged.

'But what can be done? Your father can't go to London, he's got too much work to do here. And for sure, none of us has the money in any case.'

For a moment, she looked up into his plain honest face, desperate for an answer. But all he could do was shake his head, his mouth turned down grimly. God almighty, she thought to herself, had everyone given up hope already? Her brother might as well be dead for all it seemed she or anyone else could do for him now.

The next morning she had to be up bright and early, although she had not slept well. Mistress Delamere was sending a horse and trap at eight o'clock to pick her up and she wanted to be absolutely certain she was ready. Frantically, she bustled around the cottage, making sure she had not forgotten anything.

Her father stood next to the window, drinking a cup of tea. She could tell he was watching her, although he was trying not to turn his head and show it. He was getting on now, she realised. He had always been slightly hazy about when he was born, but according to Mammy's calculations he was close to being forty-six years old. Her father and mother had known each other for almost all their lives, so he said, although they had come from families completely different in outlook. He had grown up alongside eleven brothers and sisters. Mind you, there were only three left – with his father and mother dead for many years now.

And then there was Mam, bent over the fire. She had been a grand woman, all these years, or so Dad kept saying. It was true enough, he often remarked when he had a drink in him, having a wise woman is a sight better than having a bit of land. They had never had much, but with her father being the blacksmith it had been more than most of the other people in the village, and she had never heard her mother complain. Except for having children, that is. Kate knew he had always expected to have a big family like his own, but somehow her mother had kept that from happening. And now it appeared as if two of their children were gone already.

As far as she could tell, her father had never complained about the smallness of their family, and Mam had always said it was in her upbringing. Her family had been different from Dad's, being three sisters, and they had all been fond of learning, reading and writing, and talking about other places. Mam had told her what was happening in parts of the world her father had barely heard of, in France and in Austria, and now in what they were calling the United States of America. Somehow or other, Mam was able to keep up with the news in Dublin, and in London and Liverpool.

According to Dad, it had to be all those years working in the Newcourt's house. Her mother had tended that family for years, long before Kate had been born until she was almost twelve. Daddy reckoned that the Newcourt's daughter, now the Mistress Delamere, looked upon Mam almost like her own mother. He had always blamed those two families for the thoughts in his wife's head. Or maybe it was the other way about, he sometimes said, with a wink and a smile when he came out of Cormack's in the evening.

And now he seemed to have accepted Kate taking a position at the Delamere's as well. At first he had been totally against the idea, unable to understand why she could possibly want to work when she could be married. He had to learn that she would make up her own mind about that – sometimes he treated her as if she was still a baby. And he was going to find it strange with her not being about the house; who would get him his tea now, or make sure he had his pipe filled?

But for all that Kate loved her father dearly. When she was younger, she could remember him telling her how much he cared for his little girl. But nowadays, he couldn't seem to bring himself to say any words like that any more. Aye, he would miss her all the same. He did not realise it now but he would some day. As Mam always said to him after Declan had gone to England – your sons are yours for today, but your daughter is yours forever.

But now she was going to Enniskerry, with the Delamere's. She had heard her mother talking to her father when they thought she had been asleep. It would be good learning for her, her mother had said, with the three little ones, and it would keep her out of mischief with that lad over at Jesmond's. How had they known about her and Cathal? But her father seemed more concerned about what mischief she would learn in the big house, from people who were always travelling to England. And Mister Delamere was apparently mighty friendly with people in the government in Dublin, and he was not sure he wanted his only daughter to hear about what went on there.

The sound of the church bell striking eight wrenched Kate from her daydreaming. If she didn't get a move on the trap would be there to collect her before she had everything packed.

'Eamo,' she screamed at her brother. 'Don't just stand there, do something useful for once in your life and take those bags outside so they're all ready.' Pulling at her arm she tried desperately to get her mother's attention. 'Mam, Mam, do I look all right? Is my hair tucked in?'

'You look beautiful,' her mother sighed, 'but it's work you're going to, not some fancy shenanigans up in Dublin. It's three little ones you're going to be looking after. They'll not be interested in how well you're looking. Have you brought everything you'll need for giving them lessons?'

Before she finished speaking the horse and trap arrived, and her father went outside.

'Morning to you, O'Brien,' Kate could hear him calling.

'And a fine good morning to you, Mister Brennan,' came the answer. 'Do you think that your girl might be anywhere near ready?'

Her father laughed. 'By some miracle, I think she nearly is. But she's had the whole house up nearly half the night, by God. She's taking enough with her to emigrate to America. I hope you've got plenty of space up there at the house.'

Through the window, Kate saw O'Brien getting down from the trap to help pick up the bags.

'Did you hear about our Declan?' her father continued.

'No,' came the reply, 'no more than he's still in England. I heard he's working there now.'

'It's bad news, I'm afraid,' her father continued, shaking his head sorrowfully. 'Patrick Nolan sent us a letter saying he's sick and near to dying somewhere in London.'

'That's terrible news, right enough,' agreed the other man. 'And London being so far away.'

'The worst is the waiting, without knowing what's going on.' Her father rubbed his forehead, thinking she could not hear him, but he did not realise how loud his voice was. 'And Kate's taking it bad, for sure. You won't see it this morning, because her mind is filled with thoughts about the children and her new job, but I know she's feeling it badly. If you get the chance, perhaps you could let Mistress Delamere know quietly what's happened, in case my little one is not herself and the Mistress is wondering what's wrong.'

'I'll surely do that, Mister Brennan,' replied the trap driver, heaving the bags up onto the luggage rack. 'And I hope you'll have better news next time I see you.'

They were kind enough words from her father, Kate decided, although she was sure she would be able to look after herself. But there was no time to dwell on these thoughts; she had another bag to get through the door.

'What the devil have you got there this time, daughter?' her father demanded, raising his eyes to heaven. 'Is it the bed and the curtains you've got there, and the sacks of turf in case it gets cold?'

'Listen, Dad, I'm making sure that I don't have to

come all the way back here every two hours, simply because I've forgotten something. I'd be wearing out a pair of boots every week.' The thought jolted her memory. 'Mam, Mam, have I got the boots and shoes packed?'

'Yes, yes, get off with you,' scolded her mother. 'You'll never get out of here at this rate.'

As O'Brien took hold of her last bag, she turned and gave her mother a big hug. 'I'll be back almost two weeks from today, Mam. I'll come to Mass in the village with you and Eamo. And thanks for getting me this chance with Mistress Delamere.'

'Go on with you or you'll be late, and what will she think on your first day! And be careful. I know how impetuous you are. Always remember what I've told you, a look before is better than two behind. Now be off, and keep safe!'

Her mother gave her a final squeeze, before pushing her away. Kate turned to Eamonn, her younger brother, planting a big kiss on his cheek.

'Don't be grabbing or slobbering at me,' he warned. 'It's about time you were doing some decent work.'

'Thanks for those kind words, my loving brother,' she replied, unable to stop herself smiling.

Slowly, she turned to her father. For a fleeting moment, her past life at the cottage was visible in her mind's eye, all the way back to when she had been a baby, with him telling her stories and carrying her around on his back. Now she was older, although she was sure he loved her, he always kept something back. He was a strong man, she reminded herself, although he had never been anything other than gentle with his family.

All at once, she could feel the tears coming, as she stumbled and fell into his arms. For a few precious seconds, he held her close. 'Kate, my little daughter. We all love you, so you take care. I'm sure you'll be fine up at the Delamere's. But if you're not, I'll be up there asking your man O'Brien here the reasons why.'

She sensed him looking over her head at the trap driver. 'Right, it's time you were going. Some people have got work to do today, and we can't be standing about the entire morning.' Giving her another quick hug, he took her hand and helped her up the step.

'Off we go, then,' shouted O'Brien, as he got the horse started, and the trap set off down the road. Kate half turned and looked back at the three figures standing outside the cottage, silhouetted against the green hills and the sky. They were all waving, Eamonn waving with both arms. Even the dogs, her beloved Lachlan and Jossie, they seemed to be watching her leaving them behind.

She bit her lip and waved back. Just the once. After all, she would be back almost before they knew she had gone. Taking a deep breath she turned away, staring out beyond the road stretching in front of her.

As they approached the big house, once again she marvelled at its magnificent appearance and the wonderful sweep of the driveway. Although she had been there innumerable times before, the setting and the surroundings never failed to impress her. In the past, however, she had always come with her mother to visit Mistress Delamere or else to see the children, usually to help them with their reading and writing. But now that they were getting older, it had been decided they needed regular schooling every day. And who else could be employed as their nanny and teacher, other than Kathleen Brennan? At least that was what the Mistress had said.

And she was going to be paid a guinea a week and her keep. A whole guinea – she could scarcely believe it.

O'Brien took the horse and trap past the main entrance and round into the courtyard at the back of the house. As soon as they stopped, he helped her get her bags down.

'I expect this is all very exciting, Miss Kate,' he remarked politely, while they were offloading.

'It is, Mr O'Brien,' she replied, trying to keep her nervousness from showing in her voice. 'It's a great opportunity, and I'm looking forward to seeing the children again. I only hope I can keep my mind on them and not be thinking of poor Declan all the time.'

All of a sudden the door opened and the children rushed out, squealing and screaming. Beatrice was the youngest at five years old, then Rachel, who was seven, and finally, hanging back a little, came Bernard. He was the eldest, eight years old and big for his age. He was the Delamere's first-born, the apple of their eye. Kate's mother had been at the births of all three as well as the birth of their second son, who had been still-born.

The excitement was too much, even for Bernard, as they competed with each other to welcome her the most. As she listened to them chatting happily and felt them clutching at her hands, she sensed the load on her mind beginning to ease slightly.

Drawn by the noise, Mistress Delamere appeared at the door. 'Kate, hello and welcome. Now, hush up you children. Bernard, you help O'Brien take Miss Brennan's bags up into the house.'

Every time they met, Kate never failed to admire how well this young woman looked, and how easily she seemed to command every situation. If only she could be like that herself some day. Not likely, she muttered quietly to herself.

'Follow me, Kate, I'll show you to the room where you'll be sleeping. Then we'll sort out our routine for the week. Don't worry about that big bag – O'Brien will bring that up.'

Immediately, they all trooped off through the house to a small bedroom at the back overlooking the courtyard and the gardens.

'Well, how will this suit you?' Mistress Delamere enquired.

'It's lovely,' murmured Kate, who had never had a room of her own before. She was more accustomed to sharing a two-roomed cottage with four other people and various animals from time to time, and simply making a little space for herself. To have a room of her own, however tiny, with its own bed and a wardrobe and a table and chair, was like heaven on earth.

'It's lovely,' she murmured again, as the Mistress regarded her quizzically.

'Are you feeling yourself, Kate?' she asked, getting a quick nod for an answer. 'Very well,' she continued. 'Normally you've got so many questions, but today you seem more subdued than usual; I expect it's the thought of being away from your mother and father. You'll soon become accustomed to that, and at least you're with people you know here.'

With an effort, Kate managed to smile. 'I'll be fine. Everything's so nice, and I'm looking forward to starting work. And I have to thank you for giving me this opportunity.'

At that, the woman shooed the children out of the room. 'Right, you settle in here, and I'll see you in half an hour in the study. We'll have some tea and work out your duties.'

She left and closed the door behind her. After the bedlam of five minutes before, the room seemed blissfully quiet. Walking over to the window, Kate gazed at the scene outside. It was truly a wonderful sight, with the gardens coming into bloom, stretching out towards the woods that surrounded the house on three sides. If only she could enjoy it more. She had been looking forward to this day for weeks, but now her brother was so much on her mind. How could she find out whether he was still alive? Who could tell her what was going on in London? She had to know – it was driving her crazy.

Pulling herself together, she turned away and examined her reflection in the little mirror. This was another luxury, she thought idly, as she tucked her hair in and made a face in the glass. If only she were taller and more commanding. And if only she didn't get so many freckles every time the sun shone. But there was nothing that could be done to change that, unfortunately. Shrugging her shoulders, she made some final adjustments to her appearance. Right, she reminded herself firmly, it was time to get started. Please God, that would take her mind off all her other worries.

Making her way through to the study, she found Mistress Delamere sitting at a large table, leafing through some papers.

'Ah, Kate, come here and sit beside me,' she called,

glancing over her shoulder. 'Pour yourself some tea, and tell me how you're going to plan the teaching.'

For a moment, she offered up a silent prayer. Thank God, she had planned the lessons in advance. Nervously she cleared her throat and began to describe what she intended to do. Within minutes her nerves disappeared, and her enthusiasm and preparation soon had the Mistress won over.

The following morning Kate threw herself into the lessons. This was all she had thought about for the last month. And almost before she realised it, her first day was over. While it proved to be more demanding than she had expected, she soon discovered she possessed the knack of being firm and pleasant at the same time. Her students were going to settle down to an established routine, of that she was determined.

The early days went past in a whirl, with so much to do that she had little time to miss her parents, or think of Declan's plight. And as a further distraction, she had discovered the Delamere's library. It was a mystery how the books had got there or who was interested in literature, for she rarely saw anyone else in the house reading. But for her it was a revelation, and every evening she read for hours, everything from William Shakespeare to Jonathan Swift.

At the end of the first week, Mistress Delamere decided they would sit down together and review progress.

'Young children are never happy at learning,' Kate was saying. 'They would be much happier playing or chasing each other around. I can remember doing lessons myself when I would have much preferred to be doing something else. But my mother always made me work, and I can see the benefit now.'

'Of course, you are right,' the Mistress agreed. 'So I'm pleased at how you've got things organised so quickly. But how about yourself? Are you adjusting to being here? Aren't you missing being with your family?'

'Not as much as I thought I might,' Kate replied quickly. 'I'm fine. It's a beautiful place here, and it's rewarding to be working with the children. Sure, I'm missing the others, but I don't have much time to sit around feeling sorry for myself. And I'll be seeing them again next week anyway.'

'That's good,' the Mistress confirmed, nodding her head. 'I'm glad you're settling in. I've been a little concerned because I want to see you the way you are normally, bright and sparky and beautiful. Perhaps it's all this responsibility you have now.'

And then she asked a question that took Kate off guard. 'You know, I've not seen your older brother for a long time. I believe he's over in England. How is he keeping?'

Unable to answer, Kate stopped for a moment. Just when she thought she had managed to get her thoughts in order, these few words from her employer had brought all her worries flooding back. Turning her head, she swallowed hard, afraid to speak in case her voice would give her feelings away.

'Kate, I'm sorry. Am I asking you something that I shouldn't? Forgive me, I'm not meaning to pry. Let's talk about other things, perhaps.'

'No, Mistress Delamere,' she managed to reply. 'It's not your fault. But last week we had terrible news about

Declan. I've been trying not to think about it, but for a minute it all came back to me.'

'What terrible news have you had? Do you want to tell me about it?'

Kate looked up, her eyes bright but unblinking. 'Only that he's taken consumption or the like, and they think he'll not recover. To tell you the truth, I'm afraid I'll never see him again.'

Mistress Delamere reached out towards her. 'But Kate, that's awful news. And who's with him now? Who's looking after him, and who's going to bring him back, if need be?'

'Patrick Nolan might be there with him,' Kate whispered. 'But none of us can go to London. It's too far, we don't know anyone there, and we don't have the money to pay for the journey.'

The Mistress stared blankly, a frown creasing her forehead. 'I know so many Nolans, but I'm not sure I know a Patrick about your brother's age. But I'll wager he's useless at taking care of anybody.' She thought for a minute. 'Is there no woman there in London that can take care of him?'

With a helpless shrug of her shoulders, Kate turned away. 'I don't think so. He had a sweetheart once who lived near here, but that was before he went to England. For sure, she didn't go with him.' Without realising what she was doing, she banged her fist down on the table, making the cups rattle. 'The answer is I don't know, and the frustration of not knowing only makes it worse.'

For a moment, Mistress Delamere paused, clearly taken aback by the fierce outburst. But without further preamble, she looked Kate straight in the eye. 'The answer is obvious. You must go to London.'

Astonished, Kate stared at the other woman, trying to work out whether she was joking. But she appeared to be serious enough. Yet how could she say something like this? Had she no idea what life was really like?

But the Mistress would not be put off. 'Wait, hear me out,' she continued quickly. 'O'Brien can take you to Dublin Quay, and from there you can travel on the mailboat to Liverpool. My husband has an agent there, and he'll arrange your travel to London.'

She stopped to think, rubbing her forehead with the back of her hand. 'We'll say you've recently lost your husband – that will explain you travelling on your own – and you'll not be bothered while you're wearing widow's weeds. You can stay with my cousin who has a house in Bloomsbury. I'll write to her immediately to let her know you're coming.' And she got up from the table to find paper and a pen and ink.

But Kate was still unable to come to terms with what was being proposed. 'Why would you do this for me?' she murmured quietly.

'I can't believe you of all people would need to ask me why. Don't forget what your mother's done for me: she helped me to bring three fine children into this world – and almost a fourth, too. I'll never forget that.' Turning slowly, she studied Kate's expression. 'It's yourself you need to question. Can you do it? Perhaps it's too much, perhaps you're too young. It's simply that when I saw how upset you were, and I know that I can help . . .' Her voice trailed off.

Her eyes suddenly blazing, Kate jumped out of her chair. 'I can do it – I can go there. But what about the children, and what will I tell the parents?'

'The children will be fine. It will postpone their schooling for a few weeks, that's all. I'm positive they'll not complain about that. And I'm certain you'll leave them a programme of work, and I'll make sure they do something every day. As for your parents, it'll be a question of catching your fish and keeping your feet dry at the same time. You'll have to find an approach that will convince them, for I'm sure they'll not want you to go. And now I'm beginning to think that I shouldn't have mentioned the idea – perhaps I've been too reckless.'

By this time Kate's mind was racing. 'I must go, I must go!' she cried. 'Please don't put these thoughts in my head and then try to snatch them away! If you write that letter to your cousin, and give me another to your agent in Liverpool, I could leave after I talk to Mam and Dad next Sunday. I'll decide before then what I'll tell them.'

Mistress Delamere smiled at her obvious determination. 'So be it,' she agreed. 'We shall see what fate brings.'

Back in her room, Kate tried to calm down and get some rest. Truth to tell, she felt physically drained, but some inner excitement would not let her sit still. She paced the room, thinking, planning. How would she do this? What would she take with her?

Catching sight of herself in the mirror, she stopped and gazed at the glass. It was impossible to believe she was looking at her own reflection. Her hair had escaped from its pinning and her breast was heaving with excitement. As she took a few deep breaths, suddenly she was aware of her body. An extraordinary sensation swept

through her, leaving a hollow ache deep in her stomach.
If only Cathal was here now, she thought immediately. If
only she could feel the strength of his body and the
urgency of his kisses. And his arms, holding her,
protecting her.

She shook her head violently; what kind of thinking
was that? These thoughts were a new experience and she
was not sure they were something she wanted to indulge
in. Crossing over to the table, she poured out some cold
water and splashed it over her face. Drying her hands
slowly with her towel, she felt herself calming down, the
tension gradually draining out of her body. Undressing
automatically, she climbed into bed, her eyes beginning
to close immediately.

Suddenly she sat up, a sense of guilt flooding her
mind. She had almost gone to sleep without saying her
prayers. When had she ever done anything like that
before? Throwing back the covers, she knelt down and
gave her thanks to God. Her conscience satisfied, she
crawled back beneath the blankets and fell fast asleep.

Throughout the following week, time seemed to drag
interminably. The letters were written and taken to Bray,
to be collected by the mail coach on its way from
Wexford to Dublin. O'Brien had been despatched to
book a passage from Dublin to Liverpool. All the black
clothes and accessories she would be wearing had been
brought out and were being aired.

Each day she found it more difficult to concentrate on
her work and keep the children fully occupied. In her
head she kept rehearsing what she could say to her father
and mother when she went to see them on the coming
Sunday. But whatever approach she used, she was certain

her father would be furious and forbid her to go. However, she knew that would simply make her all the more determined. The outcome was sure to be harsh words said quickly in anger, and regretted for God knows how long afterwards.

On the Sunday morning, she set off to meet her mother at Mass. Despite her good intentions, she had not been able to decide how best to broach the subject. Inside the church, she knelt down and prayed fervently, hoping to find the right words to say. But inspiration was not forthcoming. With a heavy heart, she took her mother's arm after the service and led her up the hill, away from the other people milling around.

'Mam, there's something I want to talk to you about,' she began. 'Please listen to me for a few minutes.'

'What is it, child, are you not happy up at Enniskerry?' her mother asked anxiously.

'No, it's nothing like that,' she replied hastily. 'Mistress Delamere has treated me more than fairly, and made me very welcome. No, it's something different. I'm very worried about Declan, as you and Dad are too. And I want your blessing to go to London and find him. And if he's still alive, I'll look after him and help him get well.'

Her mother stared at her in amazement. 'Are you mad? Have you lost all the senses that God has given you? How can you go to London? Where will you get the money? Who will protect you? You're still a child, don't forget.'

As she drew breath to launch another onslaught, Kate spoke quickly and quietly. 'Everything's been arranged. Mistress Delamere has employed her husband's agent to organise a passage to London for me.' Her voice rose.

'She's doing it, Mam, because she's concerned about our family and our wellbeing. And so am I!'

'Don't raise your voice to me, my girl,' her mother replied icily. 'Your father and I have more concerns about our family than any outsider. Have you thought through the consequences of your actions? What if you're attacked, what if you're killed? What if you get to London, and you find that, God forbid, Declan is already dead? And even if he's still alive, what do you know about helping people to get well?'

Frantically, Kate shook her head. 'Mam, what you're saying is all if, if, if! Don't you think that I've not thought about these things endlessly? Don't you realise that if we do nothing, then we'll spend the rest of our lives regretting it?' She clutched at her mother's hands. 'Please, Mam, I don't want to go without your blessing.'

'And what about your father? You say you've thought this idea through. So, what have you decided we should tell him?'

'I don't know the answer to that. I was hoping you might talk to him.' Turning her head away, she watched her mother out of the corner of her eye.

'Aye, I thought you might say something like that,' came the sarcastic reply. 'You know fine well your father will be beside himself over this. And you expect me to calm things down and keep him sweet. Is that it?'

Unable to reply, Kate hung her head. Her intentions had been read all too clearly.

'I don't know,' her mother continued. 'It's always easy to use your whip if the horse belongs to someone else. Are you telling me your mind's made up on this?'

'If you absolutely forbid me, Mam, then I won't go.

29

But if you give me your blessing, I'll go this week coming. We have to find out what is happening!' she cried.

Unable to hold herself back, her mother took her in her arms. 'My sweet child, I want to know about Declan as much as you do, but this notion of you sailing to England, it's difficult for me to grasp.'

It was only a slight change but Kate detected it immediately. Her mother was coming round to her side – all she had to do was reassure her a little more.

'And I'm so afraid for you,' her mother continued. 'You're such an impulsive thing, but you know nothing of the world. There'll be people who'll try and take advantage of you at every turn.'

Responding to the show of affection, Kate pressed her forehead into her mother's shoulder. 'If Declan hadn't got sick, I wouldn't be contemplating anything so extreme. I'd be more than happy at Mistress Delamere's.'

Pushing her away, her mother gave her a sideways glance. 'So you say – but I'm not so sure. Perhaps all that reading has given you too many ideas, or perhaps it's all that teaching of Mister Hutchinson. I always fancied he was putting ideas into the children's heads which we'd all come to regret some day.'

'Mammy, it's not like that at all. Mistress Delamere has been to London many times, she knows what it's like, and she's planned out the journey for me. Their agent will make all the arrangements and I'll stay with her cousin in London. She's even made a drawing to show me how to get there.'

'Kate, you make it all sound so plausible. You've got a silver tongue in your mouth and it'll get you into trouble some day, of that I'm sure. I can see I'm going to have to explain this to your father. But one thing I insist on: when you get to London and you find out Declan's condition, whatever that turns out to be, you must write to Mistress Delamere immediately and let us know. And also how long you plan to be there. Look at me, my child,' she demanded. 'Will you do this?'

'Yes, yes, Mam, I promise!' Kate cried, almost dancing up and down with excitement. 'And you'll make it right with Dad?'

'Yes, I expect I'll have to. I should have known all along it would end this way,' her mother replied, a resigned look in her eyes.

'Let's go back to the house and meet up with Dad and Eamo,' Kate suggested, feeling a lot happier.

Her father eventually placated, the rest of the day passed far too quickly, and soon it was time to go. But she had one last task to get through, a task she was dreading. Somehow, she had to tell Cathal. And he would not be very pleased either.

With mixed feelings, she walked down the path, reluctantly waving her goodbyes. Looking back, she could not believe how small the cottage seemed. Had she really spent nineteen years of her life there? Or had she merely become accustomed to her new surroundings too quickly?

The arrangement with Cathal was to meet at five o'clock at the gate to the estate, giving herself time to get back to Mistress Delamere's. He was there, waiting, throwing a stick to one of his dogs. Forgetting for a moment what she had to tell him, she picked up her skirts and tiptoed along the side of the hill, intending to surprise him. But the dogs saw her immediately, attracting his attention.

Immediately, he swept her up in his arms. 'Katie, my little beauty, trying to sneak up on me, were you? Aren't you looking wonderful?' He kept kissing her as he spoke. 'And I swear you've grown taller. You have certainly grown, eh, fuller,' he hesitated.

Kate laughed. 'Fuller? Are you sure, Cathal?' She pirouetted in front of him.

'I'm absolutely convinced,' he replied. 'Without doubt you're taller and definitely more of a woman.'

'Cathal, it's just that you've been starved of my company for so long. You've forgotten what I was like!'

The young man looked at her with a serious expression on his face. 'I could never do that. Everywhere I go I have a picture of you in my mind.' Taking her in his arms again, he held her close. Gently, he kissed her, but then more passionately, his hands reaching for her. At first, she felt herself responding eagerly. After all, she had thought about them being together so often when she was alone in her room in the big house in Enniskerry. Somehow, though, it did not feel the same as it did in her dreams. Perhaps he was pushing her too hard.

'Cathal, give me a second to breathe,' she pleaded.

'Please don't pull away from me, Kate. I hardly ever see you, I want to hold you, I want to touch you, I want to caress you.' There was a longing in his voice.

'I know, Cathal, I understand. And I feel the same way. But you put me off sometimes when you grab at me like that. Let's just take it easily and slowly. Come with me over towards the headland so that I can smell the sea air. And I have to tell you something anyway.'

Taking his hand, she pulled him along after her.

'Right, I'm coming with you. And what's this story you want to tell me?' he asked.

'Cathal, you know my brother is very ill in London.' He nodded in reply. 'Well, he's got nobody to look after him, and I fear he'll not get the care he needs to recover. And he's sure to have spent any money he has on drink, which means he'll have no food, so he'll not have the strength to get well.'

'It seems that you're more than familiar with your brother's inclinations,' Cathal replied dryly. 'He'd go to Mass every morning if the holy water were whiskey. But what's the point you're making?'

'I've made a decision to go to London to find out where he is. If it's possible, I'll try to look after him and help him get well. And I've managed to get my mother's blessing to go. Now I'd like to have yours.'

Cathal was speechless. 'How could you think of such a thing?' he asked finally. She could see his thoughts written all over his face. 'I know you well enough, Kate Brennan,' he continued. 'If you're telling me you're going to London, you must have worked it out thoroughly. And you must have found a way to get there. What is it?'

'Mistress Delamere has offered me the support of her husband's agent in Liverpool,' she explained hesitantly, 'and the hospitality of her cousin in London. And she'll ensure that I don't want for sufficient money to pay my way.'

'She must be a very generous woman, this Mistress Delamere,' Cathal growled.

'Not at all,' she corrected him immediately. 'She's a

very genuine woman, and she's concerned for my mother and her family. My mother was her nanny when she was a child, and later she was the midwife at the birth of her children. There's a bond between my mother and the Mistress that will never be broken.'

Cathal's head drooped miserably. 'I knew when you went to work in that house that they'd change you, that things would never be the same again. Now you're going to England till God knows when, perhaps you'll never come back.' He was almost in tears.

She reached out, taking his hand. 'Don't think like that,' she begged. 'I won't be away too long. I have to hope I can help Declan enough so he can come back with me to Ireland. Patrick Nolan has said in his letter that he wants to do that. You'll barely notice I'm gone.'

'I notice every minute you're gone from me!' he cried. 'I love you, Kate, I want you to be with me, I want you to become my wife someday.' With a muffled sob, he buried his head on her shoulder.

Patiently, she held him tightly in her arms. 'There, there, Cathal, it's not as bad as all that,' she whispered quietly. If only she could tell him she loved him, that would comfort him for sure. He was a good man, all right, and she would always be fond of him. But somehow she knew she could never love him, that she would never spend her life with him. For a moment she experienced a pang of guilt, painful and bittersweet, before it dissolved into regret.

'Come on, Cathal, let's walk on a little bit further. When this business is over, I'll be back, that's a promise, and we'll see each other again.' She turned to face him, steeling herself. 'But I'm sorry, Cathal, I can't marry you.

There's a yearning in my heart, which is not from working for Mistress Delamere. It's always been there, I realise it now, and I have to find out where it's going to take me.'

Letting go his hand, she stood up on tiptoe and kissed him. 'Please pray for me, Cathal, as I will pray for you,' she whispered.

As she walked away, she knew he would be watching her disappearing down the path. It was impossible to believe it had all happened so quickly. The temptation to turn round was overwhelming. Gritting her teeth, she carried on. In her mind's eye, she could see him waving, praying for her to turn back. Forcing herself to keep going she stumbled on into the gathering twilight.

Sleep did not come easily that night. Meeting Cathal and telling him what she planned to do had been a dreadful experience. But at least the way was now clear for her to leave. Comforting herself with that thought, she dragged herself out of bed the next morning and prepared herself to face the day.

Outside, it was a pleasantly warm morning, so she decided to take the children out into the garden and conduct the lessons in the open air. Weather permitting, she intended to do this as often as possible, as it brought back memories of her times at the hedge school, and of her teacher, old Mister Hutchinson.

When she closed her eyes, she could still hear his rich, full voice. 'You must pay attention, Kate! God has given you the gift of a brain, but you have to use it!'

He always seemed to be shouting at her, pushing her hard. For some reason, he was more demanding of her than the other children. Even now, he visited the cottage regularly on Sundays, and he and her mother would sit outside and talk about the ways of the world. Watching her father on these occasions was always amusing, as he professed to be totally disinterested in what was happening anywhere other than Wicklow. Whenever Mister Hutchinson appeared, her father would invariably start banging around the house, complaining about the amount of work needing to be done. But eventually he would get out his pipe and sit outside with the two of them. Not that he joined in much of the conversation, but he would sit and listen to what they had to say, nodding his head from time to time.

Her daydreams were rudely shattered by the sound of Mistress Delamere's voice. 'Kate! Where are you? Are you out in the garden?'

Standing up, she stretched for a moment and walked towards the doorway. 'Yes, Mistress Delamere, we're outside enjoying the sun.'

Quickly, she turned back to the children. 'Look as if you're working hard when your mother appears. Or else we'll all be in trouble.' She had to smile as they bent their heads industriously to their books.

'Ah, Kate, there you are.' The Mistress looked around. 'And is everyone behaving themselves?'

'They're all doing well, Mistress Delamere. It's such a lovely day; they can do their lessons just as easily out here, and it's more healthy for them,' Kate replied.

'I think it's an excellent idea.' For a moment, the woman glanced up at the sun. 'Now, when you're finished here, come and find me and we'll talk about you travel arrangements.'

'Thank you, Mistress Delamere, it won't be long

before we'll be finished for the day.'

An hour or so later, she found the Mistress in the kitchen talking with the cook, Mrs Dempsey. 'Ah, there you are, Kate, sit down with me and have some tea. All the details are in place for your journey. You will need to leave on Thursday.'

'You've finalised all the arrangements?' Kate asked in surprise. 'But you knew I still had to tell my father and mother, and they might have forbidden me from going. All your preparations could have been in vain.'

The Mistress gave her a knowing look. 'I think, Kate, that I understand you well enough to be sure you'd find the right words to convince them. You left me in no doubt you were determined to go, and I was convinced that nothing would stop you.'

Kate smiled ruefully. 'I suppose I shouldn't be so obvious. But you know my reasons for going.'

'Yes, let's not go through that again. The only thing I wasn't sure about was how strong your feelings were for that lad over at Lord Jesmond's estate.'

Kate's head dropped for a moment before she could answer. 'Cathal's a friend, no more than that,' she whispered.

'You poor girl – you really are determined. But for once you should listen to what your mother has to say. I can remember her cheering me up many years ago. "A young man's love," she said, "is just like a turf fire – none of them last for long." I'm sure he'll soon get over his hurt feelings. Now, listen to me closely. I'm going to tell you where to go and who to ask for.'

Chapter 2

———— ◆ ————

By the time the Thursday morning came, Kate was in a fine state of excitement. Mistress Delamere had insisted she take as few clothes and belongings with her as possible, because of the length of the journey and her experience of the regularity with which bags and luggage seemed to get lost along the way.

'And anyway,' she remarked with a twinkle in her eye, 'you might come across a highwayman in Loughlinstown who'll take everything from you at the point of a pistol, and you'll end up having to walk back here before you've even begun.'

'Is it true, Mistress Delamere? I've heard there are such men between Bray and Dublin,' Kate asked anxiously.

'Don't worry. I'm sure if you were confronted by a highwayman you'd have him eating out of your hand after two or three minutes. A few flutters of those eyelashes will do.' She laughed at Kate's worried face. 'And you'll have O'Brien to take you all the way to

Dublin quay.'

For a moment she paused, a serious expression on her face. 'It's a new world you're going to see, Kate. Make sure you have your eyes open but keep your wits about you. Don't go breaking your shins on any stools that aren't in your way. And remember, you're a widow – you're grieving for your dead husband. No one will try to engage you in conversation or otherwise bother you as long as you act like a woman in grief. Now good luck, and go with God.'

As she clung to the unfamiliar bonnet with one hand and the side of the carriage with the other, O'Brien started up the horses and they set off down the drive. Waving to the group gathered outside the door of the house, Kate tried to keep a grip of her emotions. Now they had set off, she had to admit she was terrified. Was she really going to be able to get there all by herself? Never before had she ever been further from her home than the strand at Bray.

Unaccountably, she found herself remembering her father and mother taking her there with her brothers and the dogs in the summer, and how her mother always bathed in the sea whenever she had the chance. At first it had been so embarrassing because of the set of thin clothes which her mother wore specifically for going into the water. Other women went bathing, but they always wore their normal clothes. Eventually, however, they had all become accustomed to this strange habit, and her mother's ideas had even seemed much more sensible after a while. Needless to say her father never went in the water, spending all his time lolling on the sand and smoking his pipe.

And more recently she had walked along the strand with Cathal, but that was too painful to contemplate. With an effort she forced her mind back to the present, looking around her at the village, marvelling at the number of buildings huddled together.

'Aye, I know what you're thinking, Miss Brennan,' O'Brien replied. 'Every day, there's more and more houses being built here. It's all those people moving here who want to get away from the smoke and the dirt in Dublin.'

Urging on the horses, he continued speaking over his shoulder. 'This is the most difficult part of the journey. After we cross the Dargle at the bridge here, we have to get up the Bloody Bank, and it's a steep climb for the animals. I'm glad there's nobody else in front of us to slow us down.'

Every sight was a new sensation. The bridge over the river Dargle was as far as she had ever ventured in the past. Crossing this bridge was taking her somewhere beyond all her previous experiences. The excitement was so intense that it was an effort to sit still.

'Why do you call this the Bloody Bank, Mister O'Brien? I'm sure my mother doesn't refer to it by that name.'

O'Brien laughed. 'I'm sure she doesn't. Hundreds of years ago, the O'Byrne clan left their lands in Glenmalure and came rampaging throughout the countryside. This is the spot where they were stopped in a fierce battle by an army of citizens from Dublin town, led by the Lord Mayor himself, a man called John Drake.'

As he replied, he looked around from side to side.

'We're coming to Loughlinstown soon, Miss Kate. Keep your eyes open. Mistress Delamere was only half-joking when she was talking about thieves and ruffians being afoot.'

Kate did as she was told and scanned the countryside ahead of them. Truth to tell, the thought of being accosted by a highwayman was so terrifying yet at the same time so exciting she scarcely knew what to think. But their journey proved to be uneventful, and before long they reached the outskirts of Dublin itself. At first, she was disappointed to see so many run-down shops selling liquor and cigars, with only the occasional tailor's or milliner's establishment in between. Turning round, she remarked on this to O'Brien.

'That, young miss,' he replied, 'is because this road also leads to Dunleary pier. There you'll meet seamen from every nation in the world, and you can bet none of them have ever taken a vow of temperance.'

But by this time her attention was caught by the sight of some handsome houses and parks bordering the road and facing out towards the sea, with fine lawns and driveways and surrounded by thick woods. Country estate houses were not an uncommon sight in Wicklow, but she had never seen so many in such a short distance and displaying such obvious wealth. Look at the size of some of these houses, she mused to herself. And what size army of gardeners and labourers must be required to keep so many flowers and plants looking their best?

Almost before she knew it, they arrived at Dublin quay. In every direction, she could see ships discharging cargo, coal-carts loading, seamen shouting and cheering, and herring women bawling out the attractions of their baskets. It was impossible to absorb the scene in one glance. And overlooking the harbour, she could make out row after row of huge buildings. Beside her, O'Brien pointed them out, calling them by their names.

'Look, Miss Kate, over there. That's the courthouse on the left, and further on you should be able to see the Custom House. I've heard that those buildings are to be rebuilt in a much grander style, if such a thing could be possible. And over there, that's the Corn Exchange, where you might find the Lord Mayor, if he's at home. And here, look Miss Kate, that's the Carlisle Bridge, the most beautiful prospect in all of Europe. Over there is Sackville Street, and to the side is Gresham's and the Imperial Hotel. They say the chef there is the finest in all of England and Ireland, although I can't testify to that myself.'

'I fear it's all too much for me, Mister O'Brien,' she replied in a small voice. 'Everywhere's so huge, and so dirty, and so noisy. Do you think I'll be able to see this journey through?'

'I can understand why you feel strange,' the man replied. 'I used to think the same way myself. But now, Mister Delamere has so many visitors coming over from England that I usually come here two or three times every week. And now I've become accustomed to the city. Mind you, I wouldn't want to live here myself – I prefer to be in the country, where I can see the Wicklow mountains, and the rain on my face is clean and soft. And where I can get a glass of stout at Cormack's with no man to bother me.'

Kate had to giggle at the seriousness of the expression on the man's face. 'I'll give you two more minutes, Mister

O'Brien, and I swear you'll be writing a poem about the Dargle river and the lost loves of your youth.' For a moment they both laughed.

Immediately, she felt better. The initial fear had been overcome, at least for the moment. Now she was ready to carry on. Shading her eyes, she squinted along the quay.

'So where's this boat that I'm supposed to be sailing on?' she enquired.

'I think you should be calling it a ship, Miss Kate, otherwise you'll be offending the master and his mate. This is it here in front, where they're loading the mail.' Stopping the gig close to the gangplank, he helped her down.

'Now, don't forget you're a widow woman,' he hissed. 'Keep that veil over your face and compose yourself in grief. Don't be staring at people or asking them questions, or it will all be up with you.'

Taking a deep breath, she adjusted her clothing and looked around. Now that she was next to the ship, the noise had intensified. Beside her, other coaches were discharging their passengers. It was clear that not everyone had been as frugal as she with their luggage, as great numbers of trunks, carpet bags, hat boxes, band boxes and bonnet boxes were piled up on the quay. And the children – was everyone travelling with fifteen of their offspring? Somehow she had to get on the ship before the great mounds of luggage were manhandled aboard, or else she was sure to find that her space had been taken.

Not far away, she could see O'Brien talking to a small man wearing an enormous black woollen coat festooned with a remarkable display of brass buttons and ornaments. After a moment or two, they both came over towards her.

'This is Mister Slocum. Sir, this is Mistress Brennan.' O'Brien introduced the man to Kate. 'He's the steward on board this ship and he ensures the passengers' comforts as best he can. He's aware of your bereavement and he's reserved a place for you on board according to Mistress Delamere's instructions. Follow him up the gangplank and I'll bring your bag.'

Gingerly, she tiptoed up the steep incline. As she reached the deck, the ship seemed to be lurching heavily although they were still tied up securely to the harbour wall. It had to be her imagination, but she was sure she could detect the boards moving under her feet. Without warning her stomach began to heave unpleasantly. God, could she not cope with anything new?

Frantically, she hurried to catch up with Mister Slocum, who appeared to be descending a very steep flight of stairs. Somehow she managed to follow him below decks and along a narrow passage into the saloon. As O'Brien stooped behind her, the steward turned back to face them. 'We've only two cabins aboard this ship, and unfortunately none could be made available for you, Mistress Brennan. However, I'll ensure that you have a space here in the saloon where you can make yourself comfortable. Look, you settle down here, and put your bag in this place under the seat. Now, if there's nothing else, I've many more things to attend to before the ship sets sail, but I'll come back to make sure you're comfortable.'

'Thank you for all your attention, Mister Slocum. I'm

sure I'll be able to accommodate myself here.' Squeezing past them, the man set off back up the stairs.

Kate took stock of her surroundings. Already the saloon was crowded; at least ten or twelve children were shouting with excitement and running up and down. And there were still more passengers on the quay waiting to board. She glanced up at the ceiling, so low that O'Brien could not stand upright. Not a major problem for her, perhaps, but the enclosed space and the thick smoke issuing from so many pipes, that was different. The thought of being cooped up in that room for six or seven hours started the panic rising in her chest.

'Mister O'Brien, I'm not going to be able to stay here throughout the voyage,' she declared. 'I'll die of suffocation before we get halfway over. I think I'd prefer to be on the deck in the open air.'

'But Miss Kate, what if it rains? And what about the cold? There's always a keen wind on deck.'

'Mister O'Brien, need I remind you it's only five minutes or so since you were telling me how much you enjoyed the rain on your face out in the country. I must go on the deck. Please bring my bag up for me.'

Struggling back up the stairs, they reached the deck and the open air. What a relief, she told herself, she would have hated it down below.

'Over here, Mister O'Brien, there's a space on this bench here. Put my bag underneath. I'll be far more comfortable here.'

'I have a blanket in the trap which comes in useful when it's cold or wet,' the man remembered suddenly. 'I'll go and get that for you.'

As he disappeared, she looked around. From the crowds on the deck, it appeared that almost everyone on the quay had managed to get on board. Someone was tolling a bell while one of the officers stood on the bridge of the ship, shouting at the top of his voice.

'Now, gentlemen, please!' she heard him calling. As she wondered about the announcement, O'Brien came rushing up the gangplank and thrust a great heavy blanket into her hands.

'Miss Kate, ringing that bell means they'll be casting off soon. Do you have the letters in a safe place? And you know who you're meeting? Don't forget it's Mister Flynn in Liverpool. He'll come on board and ask for you.'

'Would you ever stop fussing, Mister O'Brien. Of course I have everything safe, and I have all my instructions written down. I'm only surprised that you haven't tied a label with the address to my skirt and packed me up with the luggage.'

He looked down at her. 'Then go with God. I've a lot of respect for what you're doing for one so young. Journey safe and well, and I hope you have good news when you reach London. Make sure you write to Mistress Delamere when you get there, or else all our lives will be a misery. And you know that I'll not be able to look your father in the eye till you return. I'm not even sure he'll forgive me then.'

'Now, gentlemen, please!' The officer called once again. O'Brien waved back, as he took his place among the bag-carriers, barrow boys, newspaper sellers and people taking leave of their families being ushered down the gangplank.

And now the ship was moving. With a rush of alarm,

she dashed across the deck to the rail and waved frantically at O'Brien on the quayside. Suddenly, she remembered her guise as a widow woman, and tried to walk sedately back to her bench, hoping that no one had noticed. She could feel the breeze in her face, even through the veil; it was cool and refreshing. The omens were good, she whispered under her breath, as she composed herself for the voyage.

Almost before she knew it, the bell was tolling, over and over again. She gazed around, rubbing her eyes. This time it seemed to be indicating they were getting close to their destination, if the people coming out on deck were any indication. At first, the voyage had kept her interest, as had the habits and appearances of her fellow passengers. Nevertheless, her guise as a widow had seemed to work well, as nobody had approached or tried to speak to her. That was, except of course Mister Slocum, who had managed to find her and served up a fine dinner of beef stew and potatoes. Shortly afterwards he had arrived with a glass of brandy and some water. She regarded the glass with suspicion.

'Mister Slocum, I must tell you that I'm not in the habit of drinking brandy,' she declared firmly.

'This is not for your pleasure, madam,' he replied, unabashed. 'This should be regarded as medicinal, to settle your stomach against rough seas. I'll leave it with you, and you can decide for yourself if you wish to partake of it.'

Shortly afterwards, he had reappeared with his boys, each of whom carried a number of round tin vases, which they distributed amongst the passengers.

'And what would you be handing to me this time,

Mister Slocum?' Kate asked.

'Only to be used should you start to feel ill, Mistress Brennan. We are standing well off from the land now, and you may not have brought your sea legs with you.'

Before she could reply he rolled off in time to the movement of the ship, ready to attend to the other passengers' needs. Kate tucked herself into her corner and covered herself with her blanket. Her stomach had been heaving slightly, but thank God, it had not turned out to be too bad. However, the fleeting thought of the saloon below made her shudder; imagine how she would have felt if she had been cooped up in that airless cabin, with the smoke and the drink, children crying and people being sick. She was glad she had decided to spend the night on deck. Whatever the weather, that was her place. With these thoughts running through her mind, the rhythm and the movement of the ship started to make her feel drowsy. And despite trying to look forward to what her journey might bring, she soon felt her eyes beginning to close.

The bell was tolling again. Blinking against the light, she shook her head. As she tried to stand up, her legs were so stiff, she almost feel over. How could she have forgotten she was tucked up in a corner of the deck? Stretching awkwardly, she managed to pull herself upright using the handrail for support. Where were they now? she wondered, leaning out to see ahead of the ship. Suddenly she could see the land ahead! That had to be England. Despite herself she felt the excitement building up. And now Mister Slocum and his boys were coming round again, this time with hot tea.

'Ah, Mistress Brennan. I see you're awake. Are you

well?' he enquired. 'I came past two or three times during the night, but you were sleeping the sleep of the dead, so I left you in peace.'

'Thank you Mister Slocum,' Kate smiled. 'Other than a little stiff, I feel remarkably well, and wonderfully refreshed. It must be this sea air I'm breathing. How long do you think before we reach Liverpool?'

The steward sniffed the wind. 'Blowing from this direction, no more than thirty minutes. Do you have someone meeting you there?'

'I believe I have. I'm expecting a Mister Flynn to meet me. He's an agent here in the Port of Liverpool and he's aware that I'm travelling on this ship.'

The man nodded his head. 'Then no doubt he'll come on board and ask for you. If you remain here I'll direct him to you. Now I must see to the other passengers.' Bowing theatrically, he shuffled off across the deck.

Having rearranged her clothing and folded up her blanket, Kate took the opportunity to have another look around. Clearly, many of the other passengers had made the journey before. As she watched, she could see them leaning against the handrails and pointing at the rather flat-looking English countryside, which by now was not far away at all.

So far so good, she whispered under her breath. It was difficult to believe she had set out with O'Brien only the previous day, and now here she was, almost in England. It made her dizzy just thinking about it: England and the English. Had she ever met an English person before? Sure, there was Mister and Mistress Delamere, and they had many English customs, but they were Irish; they might be of the gentry but they were still Irish. Then there was Mister Hutchinson; some said that he might have been English at one time, but now he was more Irish than a native.

As the ship veered in towards the harbour, she found herself thinking again about her old schoolteacher. He even spoke the old Irish language which almost no one else did. Mind you, her mother knew more about ancient Irish history, about Fionn MacCumhail and Cuchulainn and the others, than anyone else in the village. In her mind's eye she could see her mother telling her stories, every night she used to tell them, stories that had been told by her mother and her mother before that. Did the English have their own stories? Still musing quietly to herself, she was aroused by a great jolt accompanied by a sudden noise and shouting.

They had arrived. Slowly, she walked towards the handrail which by now was overlooking the quayside. And what a sight met her eyes. It might have been busy in Dublin, but that was nothing compared to the comings and goings in front of her. As far as the eye could see, lengthy queues of wagons were drawn up, with hordes of men loading and unloading goods and cargoes of all kinds. Among all this, there was a continuous movement of coaches, traps, gigs and hansom cabs, disgorging and picking up passengers and their great mounds of luggage. Along the edge of the quay, long lines of people were waving energetically up at the ship, while beside her Kate could see many of the passengers waving in return and calling out to some of the people below.

As soon as the gangplanks were manhandled into position, a great rush of people swarmed across the deck.

Ridiculously, it seemed that half of them were trying to get off while the other half were trying to get on. Crossing her fingers and hoping that one of them was Mister Flynn, she examined the other people crowding the deck, and pushing and elbowing their way down the gangplanks. And there, thankfully, was Mister Slocum, once more dazzling her with his huge greatcoat and its glittering buttons. Behind him, she could see another man hastening in his footsteps.

'Mistress Brennan,' the steward announced, 'it gives me pleasure to introduce you to Mister Flynn, who has come on board asking for your whereabouts.'

For a moment, Kate had to force herself not to burst out laughing at the little man's self-important appearance, and his obvious relish at his position as being the fount of all knowledge. But she was a widow woman. She had to focus her mind on her grief.

'Good morning,' she stated as solemnly as she could. 'I've a letter of introduction in my possession from Mister Delamere of Stephen's Green in Dublin.' Pulling the letter from her handbag, she handed it to the man Flynn.

He scanned it quickly before looking up. 'Yes, this seems to be all in order,' he smiled. 'I'm sorry about your recent loss, but I'll do everything I can to comply with Mister Delamere's instructions.'

Kate felt herself frowning. Recent loss? What the devil was the man talking about? Suddenly, it dawned on her– he was talking about her imaginary dead husband! Thank the good Lord she was wearing the veil which disguised the expression on her face.

'Those are kind words, Mister Flynn,' she replied,

trying to keep her voice even. Before she could say any more, Mister Slocum interrupted. 'Good, good, that seems to be fine. I'll leave you now to make your own arrangements and I'll see to the others.'

As he made to depart, Flynn turned to the steward. 'Thank you very much for looking out for Mistress Brennan on the crossing. Here's something for yourself, and also a shilling for the cook.' The little man gave his thanks and made his way up the deck.

For a moment, the agent looked around with a baffled expression. 'Madam, have you any luggage with you?'

'Only this bag under the bench here,' she replied, gesturing with her hand.

Without waiting, Flynn picked it up and heaved it up over his shoulder. For a moment, he stared at her in surprise. 'It's most unusual, Mistress Brennan, for a lady to travel without a great pile of luggage and other appendages. But can I say most welcome? When Mistress Delamere comes to England, she takes over almost the entire ship to herself.'

Despite her nerves, Kate decided he was not going to get off lightly with this. 'Be careful, sir,' she spoke firmly. 'You're referring to my Mistress, and I'm sure she rewards you well for your efforts.'

'Oh, indeed, indeed,' the other replied quickly, wringing his hands. 'I didn't mean any criticism whatsoever by my comments.'

All of a sudden she found she was starting to enjoy herself. It was rather fun to be in a position of such power that she had these men all bowing and scraping in front of her. But she was thankful for the veil. If they had known they were talking to a nineteen-year old girl, God knows what they might have said.

By this time Mister Flynn was directing her down the gangplank. 'Make way there! In front, kindly make way!' she heard him shouting behind her.

As he led her through the crowds, they reached a large coach with four immense prancing horses in front. In all her life Kate had never seen a coach so huge, perched as it was on high springs and with enormous painted wheels. Was this for her? Sure enough, as they came closer, the baggage boy jumped down and lowered the step for her.

For a moment, the agent stood by the open door to ensure that she had made herself comfortable. 'Madam, this coach will take you to the house of Mister Boulton. I'm afraid it will take six or seven hours, but you'll be able to rest overnight when you get there. From there you should be able to catch the mail coach onward to London. Mister Boulton is expecting you and will see to all the arrangements. I wish you Godspeed and a safe journey. And please, give my best regards to Mister and Mistress Delamere when you're next in their company.'

Thinking about what Mistress Delamere might say in this position, Kate waved her hand imperiously in the man's general direction. 'Fear not, Mister Flynn. You've worked extremely hard to make my journey as effortless as possible. You can be sure that Mister Delamere will be made aware of your good work. And thank you once again.'

'Right, driver, be on your way, and stop for no man until you reach your destination!' Flynn shouted, as he slammed the door. The coach surged forward, and Kate stifled a scream as she was thrown back in her seat. They were off and no mistake. Fortunately the speed was only temporary, as the driver had to pick his way though a mass of coach traffic, pedestrians, people pushing handcarts and others carrying great baskets of goods over their shoulders. Even more so than Dublin, the streets were lined with huge black buildings, interspersed with dirty liquor-shops, alehouses, eating-places and what looked like marine store establishments. However, within thirty minutes they had managed to navigate their way through the worst of the throng, and the coach settled down to a steady rhythm.

As the horses stretched out, Kate gazed through the window. Although interested in everything she could see, what amused her most was the number of people stopping to stare at the coach as they passed through a succession of small villages.

So far, England appeared to be little different from Ireland, except in one major respect – the road was much smoother than those she was accustomed to in County Wicklow. But there seemed to be no less number of small children and street urchins, mixed in with stray dogs and wild looking goats. Every few minutes, one or two ragamuffins would rush out into the road and chase after the coach, just like they did back in Bray, screaming at the tops of their voices for tips and small coins and the like.

And she could see them playing games and singing, no different to the village back home. Even the melodies and the words sounded familiar, as she strained to listen above the rattle of the coach wheels and the horses' hooves. 'Bobby Shaftoe's gone to sea, silver buckles on his knee, when he comes home he'll marry me, bonny Bobby Shaftoe.'

For an instant she was nine years old again, playing with the other children. And then the moment was gone.

As the coach rattled on through the countryside, her mind turned to the prospect of meeting Mister Boulton and his lady wife. She knew nothing whatsoever about them, except that Mistress Delamere had inferred that he was a business associate of her husband, and that they had invested capital together in some major venture. If nothing else, it was going to be interesting to learn more about how the English people lived, and to find out how their house compared to the Delamere's.

It was a fine evening as the coach made its way towards Birmingham. Leaning forward, she peered out of the window, watching the sun dipping towards the horizon. Although it was mainly houses they were passing, her eye was taken by a number of unusual structures. As far as she could see, they appeared to be pouring huge clouds of thick black smoke into the sky. But it was their height which was more amazing than anything else. These were the tallest buildings she had ever seen, other than the church steeple back in the village. Not having a clue as to their purpose, she resolved to ask Mister Boulton if she were given the opportunity.

Without warning, the coach turned sharply into a driveway. Clinging desperately onto the seat covers, she tried to catch a glimpse of the house, but the view was obstructed by a copse of trees. Before she knew it, the driver was shouting at the horses and the coach was pulling up to a halt. Suddenly she was gripped by an attack of nerves, her stomach churning wildly. Who were these people she was going to meet? What would they be like? Would she make a complete fool of herself in front of them?

At the back of her mind, she remembered old Mister Hutchinson's advice: if you're feeling nervous, whatever happens, don't rush at it. Take five deep breaths and then you're ready to give your best.

Easier said than done, she thought ruefully. Closing her eyes, she counted slowly to five. Almost before she had finished, the door was thrown open with a crash and a number of faces peered in.

'Mistress Brennan?' a man's voice enquired.

'Yes, I am she,' she forced a reply in a high-pitched squeak. I must do better than that, she thought desperately.

'Just take my hand and I'll help you down the step,' the voice continued. Adjusting her veil for the hundredth time, she took the proffered hand and stepped as daintily as she could down onto the driveway.

'Thank you, kind sir,' she answered automatically. As he let go of her hand, she glanced nervously at the two people standing in front of her.

'My name is Burton,' the man announced. 'I look after the house for Mister and Mistress Boulton, and this is Jenny, the housemaid. I trust you've had a pleasant journey?'

'Yes, thank you,' she replied, somewhat repetitively. Could she not think of anything more substantial to say?

As the man called to the driver to move the coach round to the courtyard at the side of the house, the housemaid stepped forward.

'Good evening, madam,' she said quietly, curtsying at the same time. Kate realised in a sudden panic that they were both about the same age, and this is what she did whenever she met Mistress Delamere.

'If you follow me, madam, I'll show you to your room.' The girl continued. Stepping forward, Kate was able to get her first full view of the house. For an instant, she struggled to catch her breath. In front of her stood a huge building at least two or three floors high, constructed from massive wooden beams, the like of which she had never seen before. Ornate windows overlooked the drive, fitted with what appeared to be hundreds of tiny glass diamonds held together by strips of metal. Trying to look as if she did this sort of thing every day, she walked through the hallway past the enormous wooden door, studded with great iron bolts and thick black hinges. Everything seemed so much larger than life, from the paintings hanging on the walls, to the staircase sweeping upwards from the hallway, to the sumptuous curtains and furnishings adorning every room.

Realising that Jenny was waiting, she forced herself to stop staring around like an idiot, and followed the girl up the stairs.

'This is your room, madam, just here,' the housemaid said, holding the door open. 'There's water in the bowl, and some clean towels. And Mistress Boulton has instructed me to ask you if you would like to have a bath?'

Leaning forward, the girl placed her hand to the side of her mouth and whispered, 'The Mistress has had these new-fangled taps installed and she likes everyone to see them.'

Immediately, Kate was intrigued. 'Show me this bath

and these taps, if you would, Jenny. I'd like to see them.'

'Through his door, madam. Look, here they are here.'
As she watched, fascinated, the girl turned the tap and
water ran into the bath.

'That's amazing,' she cried, forgetting herself. 'I've
never seen anything like this before.'

'If you rest for a short while, madam, Burton will
bring up some hot water, and then you use the tap to put
in cold and adjust the heat to what suits you.'

Thirty minutes later, she was lying back in the
greatest luxury she had ever experienced, her first really
warm bath. And there was no shortage of soaps,
perfumes and ointments for her own personal use. At last
she felt clean, and it was a wonderful feeling. Enjoying
the moment, she let her mind wander; so far, so good – at
least she had reached Birmingham without incident.
Absent-mindedly, she picked up a piece of the soap in
one hand and massaged it against her stomach. It was so
pleasant, so comfortable, so difficult to believe. Getting
carried away, she squeezed her knees together and then
opened them repeatedly, laughing to herself as the water
gurgled between her legs. Her hand slipped down across
her belly, and almost without her realising it, crept
between her thighs.

Suddenly she sat bolt upright, pulling her hand away.
This bath idea was wonderful – so wonderful it was
sinful. She had to get out of there. And Mistress Boulton
would be kept late if she was not careful.

Jumping out of the bath, she picked up a large towel
and started drying herself brusquely. On the other side
of the room, she noticed a long glass on the wall which
enabled her to see a reflection of her entire body. This

was something else she had never seen before. For a few seconds she peered closely at the face looking back at her. It did not appear all that bad when it was nice and clean. Without thinking, she looked down at her breasts. Could these have been what Cathal was talking about when he had said she was getting bigger? Giggling, she pirouetted a few times, and then she caught sight of her bottom. Oh no, it must have been this he was referring to. Twisting herself this way and that, she tried to get a better view, but whichever way she looked it seemed all out of proportion to the rest of her body.

All of a sudden the ridiculousness of her posturing struck home, and she collapsed on the bed in a fit of laughing. If the people in the village could see her now, she told herself, shaking her head in disbelief. But she had to stop enjoying herself; she had to get organised for Mister and Mistress Boulton.

Picking up the black stockings she had been wearing, she stuffed them into the soapy water in the bath. Waste not want not, she thought, that should at least freshen them up. Thirty minutes later she was dressed in her only change of clothes and ready to meet her hosts.

Chapter 3

—————◆—————

'Mistress Delamere seems to have a great care for you, Kathleen,' the man was saying as they sat at the dinner table. 'In her letter, she expressed her concern that your journey would be too demanding.'

Kate studied him. He was around the same age as her father, but what a difference in appearance and circumstances. Mister Boulton was a large figure in stature and in girth, with a very florid complexion. And his wife, while not so tall, certainly matched her husband in circumference. And they were clearly a couple of considerable means.

'There's a strong bond between Mistress Delamere and my mother,' she replied. 'My mother has known the Mistress since she was a child. She was her nanny and her first teacher.'

'You know, to us over here that seems really unusual. I'm sure it's because we don't really understand the situation in Ireland.'

'What do you think is so unusual, Mister Boulton?' she probed gently.

The man turned to his wife. 'It seems to us in England that what they call the Protestant Ascendancy is trying to get rid of all the Catholics in Ireland, what with the penal laws and the like. And I know that Mistress Delamere is a Protestant, and I believe you to be from a Catholic family, yet you all appear to be on very good terms?'

'Well, Mister Boulton,' she replied sweetly, 'I can only answer that in the way I know my mother would.' She put on an exaggerated accent and placed her hands on her hips. 'And how would an Englishman ever be capable of understanding the Irish?'

For a moment she looked around the table with a twinkle in her eye, before dissolving into laughter along with the other two.

'One thing I can be absolutely sure of, Mister Boulton: I'm not the one to give you the answer – in fact I can't even define the question. My teacher has told me that a mood of change is sweeping through Europe and in America. And I'm beginning to understand that there are people in Ireland who have been caught up in that mood, and who would want to use force to achieve their ends. There are complex relationships between many of the people, and there's no common unifying objective. At least not that I've heard.'

As she finished speaking, she breathed in deeply. It had to be the wine. She had drunk no more than one glass, but then it was almost her first experience of drinking alcohol. That had to be why she was talking too much about things she knew nothing about, and it was going to get her into trouble if she was not careful.

Mister Boulton nodded his head thoughtfully. 'You know,' he began, 'there's another thing I find interesting. So many Irish people come over here, looking for work, as do thousands of people from other countries. But the new thinking, the inventions, the great changes we're seeing in our society here in England, most of this is coming from the Scots. They seem to have an educational system up there which appears to be open to everybody, and as far as I can see, the universities are a hotbed of ideas.'

Before going on, he looked at her carefully, as if trying to assess her reaction. 'But the Irish people who come here, most of them can't read and write, never mind go to university. Are there any such places in Ireland?'

'Of course there are, Mister Boulton,' she cried indignantly. 'Some of the oldest and the most celebrated universities in the world are in Ireland.'

'Well, I don't know what they're teaching,' the man grumbled, 'but it doesn't appear to be anything that anyone can use to any effect.'

'I think that's enough about Ireland and the Irish for today.' This was Mistress Boulton speaking. 'You've persecuted poor Miss Brennan all evening, especially after her long journey.' She turned sympathetically to Kate. 'You must be exhausted, my dear. I think you should go to bed and rest. Then tomorrow you can have all your arguments prepared in advance. For certain, my husband has the most curious mind and he'll no doubt wish to discuss all kinds of matters with you before you leave.'

Without waiting for an answer, she clapped her hands.

'Now, be off with you. We'll see you in the morning.'

Sometime later Kate was awakened by a knock at the door. Lord, what time was it? How had she slept so long? 'Yes, who is it?' she called, struggling to open her eyes.

'It's Jenny, the housemaid, madam. I've brought you some tea and breakfast.'

In a panic, she burrowed under the sheets. She had not brought any proper night-clothes, only an old bodice and a pair of pantaloons. Instantly, she could remember her mother's words; if you must be in rags, at least make them tidy rags. If the maid saw what she was wearing, it would be too embarrassing for both of them.

'Thank you. Please bring it in.' Quietly, she peeped over the edge of the sheets as Jenny bustled around, opening the curtains, pouring the tea. 'What time is it? Have I slept in?'

'It's after nine, madam. Mister and Mistress Boulton have had to go out, but they'll return this afternoon. They've suggested you rest and walk in the garden.'

That was very nice of them, she thought to herself. 'And what about the coach to London? Do you know anything about that?'

'Yes, madam, that's all arranged,' the maid replied. 'You'll be departing first thing tomorrow. Now, if there's nothing else I'll leave you in peace.'

'No, thank you Jenny, that will be fine.' After the maid had gone, she poured herself a cup of tea, and lay back on the bed. A woman could get used to this, without a doubt. But she was going to have to get up; if they knew back in Wicklow that she had become slothful in her ways and was still in bed at nine in the morning, they would be offering up prayers for her at Mass. Shaking her head, she struggled out of the bed and went over to the toilet room. For a moment, she looked longingly at the bath. She was not going to be able to trust herself in there for a while! Instead, she turned towards the window and looked out. From what she could see, it appeared to be a beautiful garden, but it was a dull grey day, and being outside did not immediately appeal.

After breakfast, she decided to go downstairs. The house was quiet and no one seemed to be around, so she wandered from room to room, admiring the paintings and the furnishings. More by luck than judgement, she found her way to the library, to be instantly enthralled by a huge collection of books, many by authors she had never heard of.

Picking one at random, she read a few chapters. Then she found another book, and then another after that. There were so many to read, but she had so little time. Even the grandfather clock chiming two o'clock failed to distract her, and she was alerted only by the footsteps coming into the room behind her.

'Good afternoon, Kathleen.' She almost jumped in the air with fright. It was Mister Boulton. 'I'm sorry to alarm you, my dear. You're clearly fully engaged in whatever you're reading.'

Immediately, she felt a twinge of guilt – should she be in here at all? 'Mister Boulton, good afternoon. I was intending to go for a walk in the garden, but it wasn't a very pleasant day outside. And when I found the library I got diverted, and I didn't realise the time.'

The man waved his hands. 'Don't worry – you read whatever you want.' As he spoke, he came over to the table where she was sitting.

'Let me see what you've been perusing,' he demanded, picking up some of the books which she had piled up on the table.

'You have an interesting taste in authors,' he remarked dryly. 'Henry Fielding, Oliver Goldsmith and Adam Smith?' He raised an eyebrow in her direction.

Blushing with embarrassment, she turned her head away. Why was this? Had he touched upon something about her which no one else had noticed?

'I've not had time to read much of any of those, Mister Boulton,' she stammered, nodding at the collection he had picked up. 'I'd never even heard of Adam Smith before today. And I've only glanced at his book – but he's expressing some ideas which I've never known the like before.'

'Haha, Miss Brennan,' the man declared in reply. 'He is one of those Scotsmen I was telling you about last night.' He waved the book in his hands. 'This has been published only recently, but the ideas in here are going to come to pass, you mark my words.'

'Mister Boulton,' she replied in the haughtiest voice she could muster. 'You may be absolutely correct, both about the ideas and the nationality of the author. But I must point out that you're also holding another book which was written by one Oliver Goldsmith, an Irishman no less, educated at Trinity College in Dublin, one of those universities in Ireland that I was telling you about last night.'

Mister Boulton looked at the book in his hand and then at the girl across the table, who was trying unsuccessfully to keep the defiance out of her expression.

'Well said, young lady,' he replied with a smile.

'Without doubt, the youngest thorn is often the sharpest. I've been getting carried away, and I'm pleased you've been able to put me in my place.'

For a moment he laughed, shaking his head at the same time. 'You know, it didn't occur to me that Goldsmith was Irish.' He looked at her, smiling again. 'And I must remember next time we are debating that you're a more than worthy opponent.'

As he spoke, the room suddenly became brighter as the sunshine streamed in. Mister Boulton looked out the window for a moment, before stretching out his hand. 'Come with me, Kathleen, the clouds have disappeared, let's walk in the garden and talk about other things.'

Standing up, she took him firmly by the arm. 'There never were two people who could light a fire together without having an argument,' she remarked airily. 'At least that's what my mother always used to say.'

For the next hour, they walked lazily around the garden, arm in arm, while Mister Boulton pointed out various different plants and flowers. He seemed proud of his handiwork, she noted to herself. But it was enjoyable keeping him talking, asking him questions and admiring the way that the garden had been laid out.

'And where is Mistress Boulton this afternoon, may I ask?' she enquired eventually.

The man glanced up at the window above their heads. 'She's gone to take a little nap. I believe that last night the excitement and the discussion quite exhausted her. I think she wants to have some rest and get ready for this evening.'

'Oh no, Mister Boulton, not the Irish and the English again, for pity's sake,' Kate begged, rolling her eyes in her best theatrical style.

'No, no I promise, no more of that,' he replied, laughing at her antics. 'But I've been thinking about what you were saying last night, and then seeing you reading Adam Smith today made me realise some things.'

By now Kate was listening avidly. It was the first time in her life that any man, let alone a fifty-year-old gentleman, had ever admitted that he was thinking about something she had said.

'You mentioned this mood of change which is afoot in the world. It's more than a change, it's a revolution. That's what's happening in America, that's what's going to happen in France, and that's what some people hope will happen in Ireland. But you know, there's a revolution going on in this country right now, which is going to have more significance for the population of England, and probably the rest of the world, than the overthrow of any government could ever achieve.'

Immediately, she was intrigued. What revolution was going on in England? 'I don't think I understand you, Mister Boulton. You're going to have to tell me more.'

Stopping abruptly, he gazed out across the neatly trimmed lawns. 'What we're seeing now is nothing less than the start of a complete change in the lives of the people in this country. What's happening, Kathleen, and I can't tell you why it's all at the same time, but we're seeing huge developments in the way that farmers use the land, and also in what we choose to call industry. Think for a moment about the way that most people work and earn their wages. You're either a labourer and you work for a pittance, or else you have a skill and you earn a little more – but then you work by yourself or with a few other people in a small workshop somewhere. Now, as a result of the work done by people like James Watt, we're able to build engines which will drive huge machines which will do the work of hundreds of men.'

As he waved his arms to illustrate his point, she could see he was becoming more passionate about these developments.

'I know nothing about these inventions, Mister Boulton, but does it mean there'll be less work, if the machines are doing it all?'

'On the contrary, young lady, it'll mean more work – but a different type of work. If we're going to maximise the benefit from the power generated by these engines, we'll need to arrange the machines to operate side by side in giant workshops, or factories. What that means is that instead of people working in their homes or in little rooms somewhere, they'll have to come to the same place to work together in large numbers to tend the machines.'

'But, Mister Boulton,' Kate interrupted him in mid flow. 'That doesn't seem feasible to me. How would all these people be able to travel to these places?'

'Exactly, my dear Kathleen, that's the point. They can't all travel from where they live now, so they'll have to move to where the factories are, and whoever owns the factories will have to build houses for them to live in.'

For a moment, she could feel herself being caught up in his enthusiasm. But before she could comment, he was off again.

'But don't think that travelling and transporting things around the country is not going to go through a similar revolution. Already, we've got these large cabs which run on rails around various parts of the country. Right now they're pulled by horses, in the same way that horses pull the barges along the canals. But we'll find a way to replace the animals with one of these engines, and then we'll be able to set up great lines of communication throughout the country.'

As she tried to ask another question, he put up his hand to hold her back. 'Mark my words, this is not going to happen for many years. If I'm lucky, I might see this come to pass in my lifetime, but I've no doubt that you certainly will.'

'Mister Boulton,' Kate tried to get a word in edgeways. 'Was that one of these factories as you call them that I saw on my way here yesterday? It had large chimneys and huge clouds of black smoke billowing everywhere.'

He paused for a moment. 'I'm not sure which route you took to get here, but it could have been the ironworks at Coalbrookdale or at Bradley that you saw. But a little bit of smoke, Kate, surely that's a small price to pay in exchange for the advantage that England will secure in terms of economic power and probably military stature as well.'

'I would have thought they had enough of both already,' she snorted indignantly.

The man laughed heartily, his huge belly wobbling under his waistcoat. 'You may well be right about that. But the thing is, there's not going to be any choice. They're going to have that power, whether or not there's any form of central planning or direction. Go and read what Adam Smith says.'

'And what about the rest of us? Will we have to run along behind? Will there be any crumbs for us from the rich man's table?' she demanded, tossing her head in indignation.

'Nothing stays a secret for long in this world, but it will be catch-up for everyone else, wait and see. Mind you, some Irishmen have recognised this. Mister Delamere, for example, has invested heavily in these new mechanical inventions.'

'Now that's an interesting development . . .' She thought for a moment. 'Mistress Delamere, do you know that she has some workshops in Wicklow, where she employs women in making lace. Is that something which is going to have to change?'

'My goodness, are you two still at it?' an exasperated voice floated down from above their heads before he could answer. Immediately, they both looked up. It was Mistress Boulton. Either she had rested sufficiently, or more likely, she had been awakened by the noise of the debate outside her window.

'Kathleen,' she continued. 'You must have had your fill by now of listening to my husband.'

'Oh, not at all, Mistress Boulton,' she replied. 'It's all very novel and interesting, although rather a lot to take in.'

'Well, I think it's enough. Come inside and we'll have some tea, and you can tell me what you're going to do in London.' The Mistress closed the window firmly, while Kate looked over at Mister Boulton.

'I have to thank you, first for your hospitality, and then for telling me all about this industrial revolution of yours. Believe me, I've found everything you've been saying so intriguing. I'll be particularly curious about the effect it will have on Ireland, whenever that might happen.'

'It has been entirely my pleasure, madam,' he replied, bowing theatrically in front of her.

It had been another interesting day. Her first night in England had passed without disaster, she had met her first English people, and somehow she had managed to survive. Admittedly, she had been hard-pressed on some subjects, and some amazing new ideas had been discussed, most of which she had never heard of before. But now it was time to get going – she was impatient to reach London and to find out what had happened to her brother.

Earlier, Mistress Boulton had advised that it was still a long coach trip to London, taking almost fourteen hours. That would be another day wasted, she complained bitterly to herself. But then again, as they said, a bad cow was better than none at all, so she was going to have to put up with it. If only the morning would come, then she could be on her way.

Although she had slept like a log after the first part of her journey, she found it impossible to get to sleep on the second night. One minute she was too hot, the next too cold. For hours, she kept being haunted by horrible dreams, where Mister Boulton's huge machines were out of control and running amok through the countryside. Black smoke belched and billowed and filled the air, covering everything in sight with thick layers of soot and dirt. It was like some vision of hell she had heard the priest talking about when she was a child at church on a Sunday. Through it all she was being chased by Cathal, barely managing to keep out of his reach. In turn, she kept seeing her brother in the distance, but she could never get close enough to speak to him.

At long last, the dawn filtered through the curtains and she was able to get up. Sadly, she did not feel refreshed at all. Why on earth should that be? It had been a quiet evening, at least compared to the first night, and she had gone early to bed. Unable to work out what her dreams meant, she washed quickly in cold water, dressed, and tiptoed quietly downstairs.

In the kitchen, Burton, Jenny and the cook were all up and waiting.

'Good morning, Mistress Brennan.' This was Burton, in a voice far too hearty for Kate's comfort. 'Good morning,' she murmured quietly in return.

'We need to be leaving within the half hour. I'll be taking you over to the inn where the coach leaves for London, but it's best to get there early in case there's a lot of people waiting to travel.'

'Thank you, Burton. I'm ready to leave now. If you would bring my bag downstairs, that will be fine.' She really was beginning to get good at this, she told herself; Mistress Delamere would be proud to see her now. Realising that she was about to get going at last, she began to feel slightly better.

'Aha, Kathleen!' She heard the voice in the doorway. 'You can't leave without saying goodbye.' It was Mister Boulton.

'I wouldn't dream of doing that,' she declared. 'But it's still very early and I didn't want to wake you.'

'No matter, the whole house is out of bed now, and pleased to be so.' He turned to his wife who had just appeared. 'Kathleen is just leaving, dear.'

The woman appeared, swathed in a nightgown. Coming over to Kate, she swept her up in a full embrace.

'My dear girl, it's been so nice to meet you. I wish you a safe journey and good fortune when you get to London. Our house is always open to you, so come back and see us, and please give our regards to Mistress Delamere when you see her.'

Kate could hardly reply, being almost suffocated between the woman's ample bosoms. Eventually, she managed to extricate herself and turned to Mister Boulton.

Leaning forward, he kissed her on the cheek. 'May God go with you, dear,' he whispered, squeezing her hand at the same time.

All of sudden, she began to feel tearful again. How could she be so much in control one minute and then be acting like a child the next? Maybe because they were friendly people and they had shown her great hospitality, and in some ways she was sorry to be going so quickly.

'Thank you again for showing me such kindness,' she replied, her voice trembling slightly. 'Whatever happens, you'll remain in my thoughts.'

Giving them a quick wave, she turned away before they could see her crying. On the way to the inn, she sat in the carriage with tears streaming down her cheeks. Why was she feeling so emotional? She had enjoyed meeting the Boultons, but not so much that she was desperately unhappy to be leaving. Was it the knowledge that she would be in London soon and she was afraid of what she would find there? It did not bear thinking about. The cab surged forward as she sat in the dark, alone with her thoughts.

Mistress Boulton was right about the coach journey, it did seem to take forever. And although a place had been found for her in the corner which was reasonably comfortable, she could do little more than sleep and think. What was more, through her veil she could see the man opposite her eyeing her at the slightest opportunity. Every time the coach lurched over a pothole, he found a reason for touching her or brushing against her skirt. By any standards he was a loathsome piece of work, and she longed to give him a piece of her mind. But she had to remember she was supposed to be a widow, so she gritted her teeth and kept herself to herself.

After a while, even the view became monotonous, as the coach rattled along through unrelenting flat green countryside. The only interest or excitement came at the few stops they made throughout the day, mainly for refreshments and to change the horses.

By the time she noticed the scenery starting to change it was early evening. Now they were passing through streets with houses and gardens and the occasional shop. The road was also becoming increasingly congested with other traffic, and it was not long before the coach was reduced almost to a walking pace. Twisting round in her seat, she tried to find some landmark which would let her identify where they were.

'Aye, it's always the same once we get to London,' the man across from her complained. 'The last two miles takes as long as ten out in the country.'

So this was her first glimpse of the city. Breathing deeply, she looked outside again. The road appeared to be reasonably wide, with narrow alleyways on both sides leading off to God knows where. Every available space was crowded, with groups of people standing around, and others walking, carrying great baskets of wares, pushing carts, riding horses, or dodging in and out of the unending lines of cabs and carriages. It seemed amazing that anyone could get from one place to the next.

And the noise and the smells! She could hear what sounded like a continuous shouting and cheering, interspersed with the clattering of coach wheels and horse's hooves, and an overall babble that ebbed and flowed as the coach slowly inched forward. Between the houses, she could see washing and laundry strung up everywhere she looked. Underfoot, the streets appeared to be filthy and stinking, with horse droppings piled up in places, and dirty water slopping around in the gutters. The buildings themselves were all an unremitting dirty black, which might have been grime but she was too far away to tell for sure.

Finally the coach turned into a courtyard and came to a halt. Immediately, the other passengers jumped up and began pushing and elbowing their way through the door. Outside, the bedlam was greater than ever. Hesitating for a moment, she gripped the edge of the seat, praying for inspiration; terror seemed to have seized every muscle in her body. This was something she had not expected. Everything had gone so easily, so smoothly so far, but now she had to get out into this cauldron of noise and humanity, and somehow find her way to Bloomsbury. Where in the name of God was Bloomsbury? Where exactly was she now?

It had all appeared so straightforward when she had been discussing the arrangements back in the peace and quiet of Mistress Delamere's house. 'Get off the coach in London, Kate. It's a place near the City called Cheapside. From there, you ask a hackney cab driver to take you to

St Thomas' Street. Make sure you ask him the price first. It should cost about a shilling.'

That had seemed simple enough. But she had not considered being in this huge courtyard, with other coaches coming and going, passengers getting off and on, and everywhere porters and commissionnaires shouting and screaming at the tops of their voices. Once more she looked out of the window – if she was going to see this through, she had to do it now. The longer she sat there the more difficult it was going to be. Counting slowly to five, she caught hold of the side of the door and threw herself into the heaving throng outside. Instantly, she was surrounded by a mass of people, thrusting cards into her face, shouting in her ears.

'This way, madam, for the Hotel Victoria! Madam, the Hotel Bristol? Here, over here, for the Regents Hotel! How much luggage have you got, madam?' A thousand voices babbled around her.

'Stand back from me!' she screamed shrilly. 'Can you not see that I'm a widow!' For a moment, the hubbub reduced marginally, enough to allow her to elbow her way to the front of the coach where the driver and his mate had unloaded the luggage. As soon as she saw her bag, she lunged forward, trying to wrench it free from the pile. The driver's mate saw her struggling and came over to offer his assistance.

'Madam, here let me help you.' Disentangling her belongings from the others, he turned and smiled at her. With some relief, she noticed he had a slight resemblance to O'Brien, Mistress Delamere's man, and was also of a similar age. For some reason this made her feel slightly more comfortable.

'Is there always such bedlam in this place?'

He laughed this time. 'This is not one of our busy days. You should come here just before holydays or celebrations. It's like hell on earth. But we have to earn our keep.'

Kate considered for a second, before deciding she had to trust him. 'I have to make my way to Bloomsbury, and I need to find a hackney cab to take me there. But I've never been here before, and I don't know what to do.'

He squinted at her for a moment. 'It's a difficult journey you're making, all this way for a woman on her own.' Then, making up his mind, he nodded his head. 'Come with me, and keep close behind.' Picking up her bag, he shouted something over his shoulder at the driver, who replied with a string of curses. But the bagman merely grinned. 'He thinks I'm avoiding the work and trying to impress a lady.'

Again, he shouted across the yard, this time to a younger man and a boy who were lolling against a rickety-looking coach. 'There you are, madam, they'll take you where you want to go. I think you'll be safe with them.' Without further ado, he threw her bag into the back of the cab. Rummaging in the pocket of her handbag, she searched for something to give him for his efforts.

'Madam, it's of no account. I couldn't stand by and see a poor widow woman in trouble. Have a safe journey.' A moment later, he disappeared into the crowd.

Kate turned to the hackney cab driver. She felt much better now she had managed to get through the masses of people. 'I'd like to go to St Thomas' Street in Bloomsbury. Do you know of that place?'

'Yes, madam.' The driver's response was brief.

'And how much will you charge for this journey?' she demanded, trying to make her voice sound stronger.

'I think that one shilling and sixpence would be fair, madam,' the man replied, a little cautiously.

'Are you sure about that? I've been told that one shilling is the price, and that I should not be concerned because no cab driver would ever try and cheat on a widow woman.' She spoke firmly, but inside she was trembling; she could hardly believe what she had said. What if he decided not to take her? What would she do then?

But the cab driver shrugged his shoulders. 'Then a shilling it is, madam. I don't want to be accused throughout London as the hackney cab driver who robbed a widow of her money.'

As soon as she climbed up into the back, they set off. Sitting back on the cushions, she started to feel a little bit proud of herself. It had been a terrible start to the day, but she had survived. She had managed to control her fears. And now she had negotiated with a London cab driver: that had to be some kind of achievement for a girl from Wicklow on her first trip to England.

Feeling more confident, she looked around. Whatever route they were taking, the road was not as congested as those she had travelled earlier. She could see fine houses on each side, many in a style similar to the Boulton's house, and some very large and fancy-looking shops with grand signs outside. But everything still appeared grimy and dirty. Even the leaves on the trees looked limp and bedraggled.

However, she did not have much time to think about

her surroundings. Almost before she knew it, the hackney cab pulled up and the driver jumped down.

'Here we are, madam, St Thomas' Street in Bloomsbury, just as you asked.'

Kate was not ready – she had not been expecting the journey to be so short. Searching furiously through the contents of her handbag, she eventually found the directions and the letter of introduction. She scanned them quickly, while the driver was lifting her bag down from the cab.

'Take a hackney cab to St Thomas' Street in Bloomsbury,' she muttered to herself. 'Yes, I've done that. Then keep your eyes open for Connaught House.' She looked around. All the houses seemed to be surrounded by high walls with massive gates, but none of them was obviously the place she was trying to find. She read on. 'They are putting house numbers up on the streets in London now, and I believe the house is number two.' Again she looked from side to side, but she could see nothing to indicate a house number.

By now the cab driver was becoming impatient to find another fare. Kate decided that it would be better to get out and pay him his money, without letting him see that she did not know where to go next.

'Thank you very much for finding this street for me,' she said as she handed over the shilling and trying to maintain a confident air.

The man lifted his cap, jumped back up on the cab and was on his way, leaving her standing on the pavement, the letter in her hand and her bag at her feet. It was beginning to get dark. Just keep calm, she told herself firmly, it must be here somewhere. Uncertainly she walked towards the nearest gate, which was fashioned from huge wrought iron railings. Peering through the gaps, she tried to see what was inside, suddenly letting out a piercing scream and jumping backwards. A man's face was staring at her, only a foot or so away.

'God, sir, but you frightened me,' she said sternly when she had managed to compose herself.

'I'm sorry,' he replied. 'I heard the noise outside and I was merely looking out to see what was going on.'

Again, she approached the gate. 'Perhaps you can help me. I'm looking for Connaught House, for Mister and Mistress Jardine.'

'And who are you to be looking for such a house, might I ask?' came the demand.

Impatiently, she brandished her letter of introduction. 'My name is Kathleen Brennan and my sponsor is Mistress Delamere of County Wicklow in Ireland. I'm looking for the house of her cousin, Mistress Jardine.'

The man took the letter through the bars of the gate and scrutinised it closely. He was clearly not the best of readers, having to point to each word and repeat it out loud. And his lips were moving so slowly that he was not making much sense.

By now, Kate was starting to feel more and more worried. She looked around nervously. Night was drawing in, and she had to find the house soon. This strange man was exasperating her.

Snatching the letter from his hand, she drew herself up to her full height. 'Do you know where Connaught House is or don't you?' she demanded in her strongest tones.

'This is the house, madam,' the reply came grudgingly. 'My name is Reynolds, and I'm employed by Mistress

Jardine.' He started to open the gate with much clanking of bolts. Within seconds, Kate had pushed her way through; for a moment it seemed she might have been left on the street for the night.

'I'm sorry, madam, but Mister and Mistress Jardine are not at home this evening. They'll be returning tomorrow. Mistress Jardine has had a letter from her cousin and we've been expecting you. You can't be too careful, you know – London is full of murderers, thieves and prostitutes, and there's been many cases of houses around here being ransacked.'

'And which were you taking me for?' she demanded. 'Or was it perhaps all three?'

'Begging your pardon, madam. But if you've not spent much time in London you'll not be aware of how dangerous it is on the streets of the city at night. I'm not sure what it's like in Wicklow, but I can't believe it's as bad as it is here.'

Kate smiled to herself. Perhaps he was right. He knew better than her what it was like in London, that was for sure. But at least she had arrived. Thankfully, no more travelling, no more coaches, at least for a short time, and no more confined spaces with foul-smelling men leering at her. Tomorrow she might be able to find Declan, at long last.

Reynolds lifted her bag and closed and barred the gate behind her. Inside the house was cold and dark. Moments after he showed her to her room, she lay exhausted on the bed, thinking back to how pleasant it had been at Mistress Boulton's compared to here in Bloomsbury. Welcome to London, she thought to herself, as she drifted off to sleep.

The next morning, she awoke at first light, determined not to waste a single hour of the day. She had to find Declan as soon as possible. Downstairs, she found the cook in the kitchen, drinking tea.

'Good morning, I am Kathleen Brennan, and I'm a guest of Mistress Jardine,' she announced, making absolutely sure there were no misunderstandings about her identity. 'And that looks like a lovely cup of tea you're drinking.'

The cook smiled. 'Good morning, madam, my name is Mrs. Simpson – we've been expecting you. However, it's not often that we have guests rising at this hour, so I haven't quite got everything ready. If you give me ten minutes I'll arrange a table for you in the breakfast room.' She directed her into a light and airy room with large windows overlooking a garden.

Kate walked over to the window. Like that of the Delamere's and the Boulton's, this house possessed a fine outlook. The main difference was the high wall which was now fully visible, surrounding the house and the garden on all sides. The only break in the wall was a small gate, which even from a distance she could see was heavily barred and bolted.

The cook came in with the breakfast tray and set it on the table. 'Here you are, madam, some porridge and a nice pot of tea.'

'Thank you Mrs. Simpson, I'm ready for that. But first, can I ask you a question? I have to try and find my brother today. He's ill and I believe he might be in a house in Grays Inn. Tell me, do you know that area? Is it far from here?'

'Yes, madam, I know Grays Inn all right. It's not far

from here by hackney cab. In fact you must have passed it last night on your way here from Cheapside.'

Kate thought for a moment. It had not been all that far, even from Cheapside. 'And could I walk there, do you think?'

'I'm sure you could, madam. Except that there are all manners of strange and dangerous people abroad on the streets. From here, walking along Holborn would be the best way. There's always the chance of catching a cab driver, although they don't always stop, even when you stand out in the street and wave.'

'Is it dangerous even at this hour of the morning?' Kate was slightly incredulous.

The cook laughed. 'Madam, it's dangerous at all times of the day. Especially, if I may say so, for a woman who speaks the way you do. They'll suspect you're not from around these parts. If anybody takes you for one of these frog-eating Frenchwomen, you're liable to be threatened or pushed about.'

'I'll speak very little, and keep myself to myself,' she resolved solemnly. Without a doubt, the woman seemed to have taken against the French. Was this unusual, or did all English people feel the same way?

By now, Mrs. Simpson was fully into her stride. 'And don't go down towards the river either. All you'll find there are alehouses, barber shops, laundries and God knows what else; that's no place for a lady. And along Cheapside and through the City to the east is Aldgate and Spitalfields. God help any woman who goes east of the City of London.'

Kate frowned. 'And what of Grays Inn? Is a woman safe to travel there?'

'As you travel east on Holborn you'll find Grays Inn on your left hand. There are many legal establishments there. At the end of the street close to Holborn, a woman will be reasonably safe, if anyone can be from the lawyers. Anywhere further north, and you stand the chance of getting involved in all manner of trouble.'

'Why is that, Mrs. Simpson?' she demanded, eager to find out more, but concerned at the same time. This Mrs. Simpson was a fountain of knowledge.

'Not far from where I'm talking about, madam, is Smithfields, where the meat market is held. Every morning, farmers bring their herds of sheep and cows through the streets just to the north of here. This causes terrible congestion, as you can imagine. And it's not unusual to find stray animals wandering around, which some people steal and slaughter in the street. Blood and filth is everywhere. And that gets followed by uproar when the farmers find out what's happened.'

'Ugh, that sounds disgusting,' she sniffed in reply. 'I don't think I want to go anywhere near there. I'll walk along Holborn and perhaps I'll be lucky and find a cab. If Mistress Jardine returns, please convey my compliments and let her know where I've gone. Tell her that I'll return this evening by six o'clock.'

Ten minutes later, she was walking along the streets of London. Everything she had seen and heard the previous day was now so much closer. The filth at the sides of the road was deeper, the stink was more abominable, the open drains at the edge of the pavement more putrid. How could the people live in such houses, all leaning at different angles, with so many floors, and with what appeared to be half the windows blocked off?

As she stepped gingerly along the street, she looked up some of the alleyways. Filthy water seemed to be running everywhere, laundry flapped lazily in the breeze, and every so often she would hear a bellow from someone up above, before a bucket of water or God knows what else was discharged on to the ground below.

Amongst all this were the people. Bell-ringers, chimney sweeps with dirty faces, knife sharpeners, women selling everything from fish to medicines, strolling musicians, and on every corner, groups of people singing songs. But more than any other were the beggars, men and women of every description, jostling the pedestrians as they went past.

Despite the crowds and the noise and the abhorrent smells, the variety and style of the shops was truly amazing to behold. Bakers and butchers she had seen before in Bray, but now she was confronted by shoemakers, tailors, buttonmakers, drapers, buckle-masters and God knows how many others. Some day, she decided, when she had more time and perhaps some money, she would come back and look in these shops. But not now – she had more important matters to attend. Without delay, she pressed on through the crowds of people thronging the pavement.

Grays Inn was easy to find. 'Walk along Holborn and you will find it on the left hand side.' Those had been Mrs. Simpson's directions, and they turned out to be absolutely correct. At the corner, she pulled Patrick Nolan's letter out of her handbag to check the name of the place she was searching for. She knew it well enough, since she had studied the scrap of paper probably fifty times or so. But she wanted to read it again once more, to be absolutely sure. And perhaps to calm her nerves a little as well.

The Sanatorium of St John was the name, according to Patrick Nolan, and established by the Holy Sisters of Jerusalem, to help people who were ill and had nobody else to turn to. Feeling slightly apprehensive, she crossed into the lane through Grays Inn, clutching the letter in her hand. Away from the main road, there were fewer people around, which was comforting in a small way. At the end of the lane, she looked around, trying to catch a glimpse of any sign that would tell her she had found the place, but there was little to be seen.

She walked further up the road, but she could find nothing that resembled the sanatorium. By now she was getting some distance away from Holborn, and it was becoming obvious that the houses and even the people were looking shabbier. From the amount of filth and dung piled up on all sides, it appeared that she might even have reached the area that Mrs. Simpson had suggested she avoid.

And she was starting to feel concerned at the level of attention she was attracting. A few small and extremely dirty children had started chasing after her, shouting and screaming and snatching at her skirts. She tried walking faster, but still they followed her. Suddenly, she noticed she had passed the last of the houses and had reached a open green area. Further on there were more buildings to be seen, but even from a distance away it was clear that these were more impressive and better kept than those she had just passed.

Somehow she must have walked past and not seen it, she told herself. Stopping to retrace her footsteps, she turned round and caught a glimpse of a nursing sister entering the last house. Without hesitation, she dashed after her.

'Sister!' she shouted at the top of her voice. 'Sister! Please wait a moment!'

The woman stopped in the doorway, a suspicious look on her face. Kate dashed up to her. 'Sister, my name is Kathleen Brennan, I think my brother may be here. His name is Declan, and he's very sick. And I've come to find him.' All of this came out in a mad gabble of words.

The sister held up her hand. 'Slow down please, madam, I didn't understand half of that. How did you find this place, and what makes you think your brother is here?'

Gasping for breath, she tried to compose herself: count to five before anything else. 'I'm sorry, Sister,' she began carefully, 'I've been travelling for days to get here, and I wasn't sure of the location. And there's no sign either. I'm looking for the Sanatorium of St John. I've a letter in my possession which says that my brother is or was here not very long ago.' She handed the letter over to the sister.

The other woman glanced at it quickly. 'You've travelled a long way, you say?'

'Yes, I've come from County Wicklow in Ireland, although it feels like I've come ten thousand miles,' she sighed. 'Please tell me, have I come to the right place?'

'Come with me and we'll speak to the matron,' the woman replied, beckoning to her to follow.

Chapter 4

Inside, although it was gloomy, Kate could see a long row of beds huddled closely together. Although someone was lying on every bed, she was surprised at the silence, particularly after the bedlam out in the streets. No one seemed to be speaking – in fact, most of the occupants of the beds appeared to be asleep. But as her ears became better attuned, she realised there was some noise after all, the distressing sound of different people coughing weakly and even crying.

Hurrying along, she caught up with the sister, who turned off into a side room. Through the door, she could see more beds, with a tall imposing figure of a woman working alongside one patient.

'Sister Mary Francis, this is Kathleen Brennan. She tells me she's come from Ireland to find her brother – she thinks he may be here.'

The woman turned around. She must be the matron,

Kate thought to herself.

'And what would your brother's name be?' she enquired, raising an eyebrow in Kate's direction.

'His name is Declan Brennan,' she burst out. 'He has a friend called Patrick Nolan – he wrote the letter telling us about Declan.'

'And you're from Wicklow, you say. We don't get many visitors here, least of all from Ireland.'

Impatiently, Kate shook her head. What was wrong with the woman? Why all these questions? Why could she not tell her whether Declan was there or not?

But the matron must have been reading her thoughts. 'We have to be very careful. We're tolerated by the people outside, but they've no liking for priests or nuns. We have to be sure about our visitors. Some have come here in the past who've tried to murder the sick and the dying in their beds. As if they couldn't wait another few hours for them to die naturally.'

'Please, Sister Mary Francis,' Kate begged. 'Is my brother here, or isn't he? Or has he died? I have to know.'

'Yes, he's here. And he's still alive.' Her heart leapt. 'But only just. Sister Agnes will take you to him. But first, I must ask you. Do you know what kind of place this is?'

Kate could only shake her head – the news about Declan had left her speechless.

'We've no shortage of patients here,' the matron continued. 'But we don't have any surgeons and we've precious little medicaments. The majority of the people who come here are poor and they've no one to look after them. Instead of dying alone in a hovel somewhere, or worse, in the gutter, we give them a place where they can get some peace, and where someone will pray for them. Very few of our patients survive for long. And it's dangerous for the sisters to be working closely with them. It's easy to catch an illness with so many sick people in one place, and three sisters have died already this year.'

Carefully, she looked at Kate, obviously trying to assess her reactions. 'I'm saying this because I don't want to build up your hopes about your brother, and also because it will be dangerous to be near so many other sick people.'

'I understand, Sister,' she replied, trying to keep her impatience under control. 'And thank you for telling me the truth. But I've not come all this way to find out that my brother is still alive and then leave him to his own devices.'

Spreading her arms in an appeal, she turned to the other woman. 'Sister Agnes, please take me to him.'

With a helpless shrug of her shoulders, the woman led her through the sanatorium until they reached a bed situated at the rear of the building.

'This is Declan Brennan,' the sister stated abruptly, gesturing to a scrawny figure huddled under a thin blanket. 'Be careful, he's very weak. He's been coughing heavily, and we've not managed to get him to eat very much. I don't think he has much strength left, but I'll leave you with him. If you need any help, please call me.'

Apprehensively, Kate stood at the side of the bed. It took a few moments before she could force herself to lean forward.

'Declan,' she whispered. 'It's me, Kate, your sister.' There was no response from the figure on the bed.

Leaning forward again, she touched the man on the shoulder, pulling him gently towards her. God, he was so thin, his body felt like bone covered with loose skin. Clearing her throat, she tried again.

'Declan, can you hear me? It's Kate come to see you.'

His strength almost gone, the man on the bed coughed weakly. Painfully, he turned over on to his back. For a moment, Kate could barely believe her eyes. It was her brother, she could see that, but he was so emaciated she could barely recognise him. His face was gaunt, covered in two-week old stubble and his skin was white, almost without a trace of colour. Again, he coughed, opening his eyes. She could see him staring at her, an almost sightless gaze, as if he was unable to see her.

'Declan,' she repeated. 'It's me, your sister Kate.'

Finally he spoke, so quietly she had to lean forward again, just to hear him.

'Is it true? It's not a dream? You're really my sister Kate? Give me your hand and let me feel it. I want to know that you're real.'

Without thinking, she grasped his hand. Suddenly she realised he had not seen her for four years. Even if he had been healthy, he might not have recognised her, she had grown so much in that time.

'It's true, I'm real, I'm your sister, and I'm here.' She smiled at him as she squeezed his hand.

'It's unbelievable, my little sister. You look nothing like you used to look.' Straining every muscle, he tried to push himself up off the bed, but he did not have the strength.

'Don't strain yourself,' she whispered. 'Just lie back and rest. Dad and Mam are safe and well back in

Wicklow. So is Eamonn – but we lost Joseph last year. He got sick and then he just got worse and worse. It was terrible. But I'll tell you all about these things when you're stronger.'

Anxiously, she scrutinised him as he lay back on the bolster and closed his eyes. God, he looked awful, and it looked as if he had not eaten anything solid for weeks. But at least he was not coughing as badly as she expected. Hearing footsteps behind her, she turned around. It was the matron, obviously coming to find out how she was getting on.

'Sister, Sister Mary Francis. I can't thank you enough. It's my brother, and he's well enough to speak. We talked there for a minute or two. He didn't recognise me at first, but that's because I was still a young girl when he left Ireland. But he knows me now, well enough.'

'Stop, stop, stop, young lady!' The matron put her hands up. 'Will you ever let me speak?' But Kate could see her smiling slightly. Perhaps her relief had been so obvious that the woman's mood was lifting a little.

'Now look, this man's been at death's door for weeks. I know it's exciting for you, but you must let him rest. It would be too awful if he survived until you arrived and then the excitement killed him.'

Realising she was probably being too eager, Kate bowed her head. 'I'm sorry, Sister. I had forgotten myself for a moment. I'll let him rest now. But is there anything I can do? His nightgown is in tatters. Can I get him something better to wear? And he looks as if he is emaciated. Do you have enough food here? Can I go and get him anything?'

In response, the sister pulled her away from the bed

by the arm. 'In the name of God, girl, how are we going to be able to keep up with you and all these questions? The answer is probably yes to everything. We don't have enough of anything here, no, not even prayers. Yes, if you can get him something better to wear, go and get it. If you can get any soap, bring that too. We need soap for the other people in here as well. And yes, we don't have enough food. And what we have doesn't provide much nourishment.'

She looked hard at Kate. 'But remember, he's very ill. We've not been able to get him to eat anything, but maybe you'll have better luck. Now leave him in peace for two hours, go and get him some food, and say some prayers for him.'

As the sister left, Kate tiptoed out behind her. If she went back down to those shops, it might be possible to buy some bread, and perhaps a bowl with some soup. That would be a good starting point. Beside the door on her way outside, she noticed a tiny altar situated to one side, with two candles burning low in front of it. Quickly, she knelt down, whispering a few prayers of thanks. At the same time she added a few candles to her shopping list. In the state Declan was in, he was going to need his fair share of heavenly intervention.

Two hours later, she had found everything she needed. This time she was much more purposeful as she strode back up through Grays Inn. She didn't notice the squalor quite so much, and the children and the dogs did not bother her as they had before.

As she reached the sanatorium, she was in a more positive mood than she had been for some weeks. In her head, she could see a plan forming, of how she would help Declan to recover and when they would be able to return to Ireland. She was almost humming a tune as she swept past the lines of patients towards the bed where she had left Declan sleeping.

At the rear of the building the light was bad, and she had to peer into the gloom to make sure she was going in the right direction. Ahead of her, she could make out the bed, she was sure of that, but she could also see two men standing close by. Feeling slightly concerned, she quickened her pace without making it obvious she was in a hurry. As she got closer, she could see that one man was big and heavy looking, while the other was equally as tall, but cut a much more elegant figure. Moments later, she reached the bed without them hearing her coming.

'Yes, is there something wrong here?' she called as loudly as she could, trying not to disturb all the other patients nearby. Both men turned round, startled at the interruption.

'No, I don't think there's anything wrong at all,' the heavy-set man replied. 'We're simply visiting this friend of ours to see if there's been any change in his condition. And who might you be?'

'I'm this man's sister. I've come here to tend to him, to help him recover if I can,' Kate responded as firmly as she could.

'What? His sister? Declan Brennan's sister?' He was shaking his head. 'I don't believe you. Declan's sister is Kate Brennan, but she's only a young slip of a lass.'

'I'll have you know that young lassies, as you describe them, they grow up, especially when you've not seen them for four years or more.' Kate glowered at the two men. 'And I would have said that you were Patrick

Nolan, except he was a slim, handsome looking individual the last time I saw him.' She turned and nodded at the more elegant of the two men. 'I'm sorry, but you have the better of me. I'm sure that we've never met before.'

He responded by bowing in her direction. 'Madame,' he began in a heavily accented tone. 'I too am sure that we have never met. I would never have forgotten such a beautiful and charming woman as yourself.'

Despite herself, Kate smiled. He was foreign without a doubt, she decided immediately, was he French perhaps? One of these frog-eaters, as Mrs Simpson described them? He was dressed rather more elegantly than she was accustomed to seeing, and his clothes looked clean, which was also unusual.

But he was continuing. 'My name is James Lavelle, and this is my colleague, Patrick Nolan. So you were correct after all. And are you indeed the sister of Declan Brennan?'

Placing her basket on a chair, she walked round the bed. 'Yes, I am Kathleen Brennan,' she replied, flashing a look at Nolan. 'And I have your letter here in my bag which you sent telling us about Declan's illness.' She put out her hand to Lavelle. With a firm grip, he looked down at her, holding her eyes in a steady gaze. For a second she was mesmerised, until she forced herself to look away. Before she could remove her hand, he kissed it, at first incredibly gently, and then rather more theatrically.

'Madame Brennan, or is it mademoiselle perhaps, it's a pleasure to make your acquaintance,' she heard him say. He was bowing once again, but for some reason his voice seemed to be indistinct, as if it was coming from somewhere in the distance.

Patrick Nolan's voice brought her back to the present. 'So it is you after all, Kate. Well, you certainly have grown. And don't listen to this man Lavelle, he's merely a silvery-tongued Frenchman, that's all.'

Kate turned to look at Declan, who had been half-awakened by the conversation. As far as she could see, he still looked wretched. But she had managed to get some soup and bread, and a cloth and soap. She would try and get some nourishment into him, and then clean him up. And if she could get a razor from somewhere, she thought, she would try and give him a shave and make him more presentable looking. But now these other two men were getting in her way.

For a few minutes, she fussed around the bed, wishing they would go. Taking hold of the edges of the pillow to push it further under her brother's head and neck, her arm rubbed against something cold and smooth. Pulling back the covers, she saw at once what it was – an old stoneware jar, like the one her father kept at the house out of reach of the children. She snatched it up and shook it violently. It sounded as if it was half-full.

'What's the meaning of this?' she turned, screaming at Nolan. 'Have you lost all of the sense that God has given you? No wonder the man is near to dying. You're killing him by giving him poteen. Is that what it is you're trying to do?' She hurled the bottle to the ground, smashing it in a thousand pieces.

'It's not like that at all,' the man protested. 'It was to try and ease the pain for him when he was at his worst.'

Kate bristled at him. 'It's food the man needs, not drink. Now, get out of my sight, the both of you.' She realised she was brandishing her finger in his face.

But Nolan turned and looked at the man Lavelle. 'Come on, James, we better get out of here. I can see that Declan's not the only one in this family that has a temper.' But the Frenchman looked at Kate and smiled.

'Mademoiselle, that was beautiful, fantastique! I look forward to meeting you again soon.' He bowed once more and disappeared through the door after Nolan, leaving Kate alone in peace with her brother.

For the rest of the afternoon, she spent her time trying to get Declan to eat something, and cleaning up his bed. Tomorrow, she thought methodically, she would start by trying to wash him, and if she could find that razor, then she would try her hand at shaving. She was sitting quietly by the side of his bed when Sister Mary Francis appeared.

'And how is your brother faring now?' she enquired.

Kate jumped up at the sound of her voice. 'I'm sorry, Sister, I didn't hear you coming. He's very peaceful, and he's barely coughing at all now. I'm determined that he'll recover soon. And I'm praying for him as well,' she added as an afterthought.

'Well, that's more than many of the other people in here are receiving,' the sister declared with some feeling.

Kate looked around. 'Sister, can I ask you something?' She carried on before the other woman could answer. 'I don't think that this spot is the best place for Declan to rest. There's too much chance of him catching an illness from somebody else because they're all closely packed together. Could I move his bed outside into the hall near the door, where he can get some fresh air?'

The woman rubbed her chin thoughtfully. 'When

we're overflowing with patients we sometimes put them there. It's fine at night because the door's always locked and barred. But if someone forgets to shut the door during the day, there might be a draught coming through there.'

This was what she wanted. 'I think that we could cope with that, Sister. I'll be here most of the time during the day to make sure that doesn't happen. Could we do that now? Could you help me to move the bed?'

The sister laughed. 'You're an impatient lady, Kathleen Brennan. You're only here a short while, and you want to change everything. But all right, let me help you.'

With a struggle the bed was manhandled into the new position near the door. As they stood back to look at the results of their efforts, the sister remembered she had come only to see her for a few moments and that she should really be somewhere else.

'Kathleen, that will have to do. Do you know what time it is? It's after five o'clock. You had better be making your way back to Bloomsbury. We'll be locking everything up here at six. I'll speak to you tomorrow.' And she rushed off.

Kate glanced over at her brother, who seemed to be still sleeping soundly despite the pushing and pulling his bed had received. She really did have to start walking back, she thought to herself. Being caught anywhere near this part of the world after dusk would be terrifying. Giving Declan's arm one last squeeze, she tiptoed quietly out through the door.

Outside in the street, she looked up and down quickly, making absolutely sure nothing unusual was going on.

Out of the corner of her eye, she noticed the figure of a man lounging against the wall across the street. Jesus, Mary and Joseph, it was James Lavelle. A tingle of excitement swept through her, leaving her breathless. What was he doing here? Who was he waiting for? Had Patrick Nolan come back? Or was he waiting for her? If he had come to see her, what was she going to say to him?

As these questions whirled around inside her head, the man looked round and saw her standing in the doorway. Immediately, his face broke into a smile, before he waved and hurried across the street.

Again he took her hand and kissed it with a flourish. 'Mademoiselle Brennan, it is I, James Lavelle.'

'I can certainly see that, Monsieur Lavelle,' she replied, in as haughty a voice as she could muster.

'You're not still angry, I trust?' He looked at her, his eyes round and innocent. Kate could not resist the expression on his face.

'No, no, Monsieur, I'm not angry. I was a little upset this morning, probably because of the strain of the travelling, and then finally finding my sick brother. I'm truly sorry for shouting at you and Patrick; he must think really ill of me.'

'On the contrary, Mademoiselle, he thinks you've shown fantastic courage to come here all by yourself.'

Kate shrugged her shoulders. 'It was not so difficult. But tell me, why are you here, Monsieur Lavelle?'

This time his smile was wider than ever. 'Why, I'm here to escort you back to your residence. And you must be less formal. Please call me James.'

Taking both her hands, he looked down at her. For some insane reason, she felt her knees go weak.

Suddenly, it was difficult to breathe properly. It had to be the way he was looking at her, as he had earlier in the day; almost mesmerising. Forcing herself to breathe deeply, she counted up to five. This is ridiculous, she told herself sternly. Here she was, standing in the street with this stranger, people around going about their business, and she could barely form two words to say to him.

'And you must call me Kate,' she replied eventually, although it came out more as a croak. But that was better, she had managed to say something, instead of merely standing with a foolish expression on her face.

'I'm staying some distance from here,' she managed to say. 'In Bloomsbury, in the house of a cousin of my Mistress.'

'That will take us no time at all, and it will be my pleasure to accompany you there, Mademoiselle Kate.'

He pronounced her name so beautifully, and the sound of his voice seemed to flow gently over her. Shivering slightly, she set off down the street, the man falling into step alongside her. All too soon they reached St Thomas' Street.

'So this is the residence? Are they Irish, these people?'

Kate looked up at the house. 'Mistress Jardine is, for sure. I'm not certain about her husband. Why do you ask that?'

'This is a big house with very expensive upkeep. I imagine the Mistress is a rich woman?'

Kate rubbed her forehead. 'I expect so. To tell you the truth, I've never thought about it much. In fact, I've not met them yet; they weren't here when I arrived last night, nor when I left early this morning.' Was it only last night she had arrived? So much seemed to have happened since. Fleetingly, she thought of Mister Boulton. It felt like years had gone by since they had stood in his garden, instead of a few days.

But James was speaking again. 'Kate, I've truly enjoyed your company this evening. I thought this morning when you were angry how beautiful you were, with your wonderful green eyes flashing and your breast heaving. But now I've had the pleasure of a few more moments of your company, I see you're even more beautiful than I first thought.'

Kate felt herself blushing furiously. He was clearly using all his considerable charm, but he did make it sound good. And he was taking her hand and kissing it again.

'Goodnight, Kate, I'll go back to my hovel and dream about you. And perhaps I'll see you tomorrow. Goodnight, once again.' And he disappeared into the gathering gloom.

Shaking her head, she took a deep breath. He had so completely taken all her attention that she had forgotten what she was supposed to be doing next. But now she had to be ready to meet with Mistress Jardine. Taking another deep breath, she pulled hard on the bell that Reynolds had shown her earlier in the day.

Mistress Jardine turned out to be just as striking as her cousin, having perhaps an even more positive attitude than her cousin, if that were possible. For once Kate was confronted by someone with more questions about things than she had. The Mistress wanted to know about everything – her brother, Mistress Delamere, the journey, what was happening in Ireland, what did she think of the weather, her impressions of England. But thankfully, she was not going to have to answer immediately, as the Mistress was about to leave for the theatre.

'Kathleen, listen to me,' she was saying. 'Please make yourself at home. Mrs Simpson has prepared a dinner for you. I'm sorry you have to eat alone, but I promise that tomorrow night we'll sit down together and have a good discussion.'

For once, Kate was thankful. In the last few minutes, she had begun to feel dreadfully tired. 'Mistress Jardine, thank you for your hospitality,' she replied quickly. 'And don't worry about me – I feel absolutely exhausted. I expect I'll take to my bed very shortly indeed.'

'Fine, that's settled then. Now I must rush or I'll be late. The carriage is already at the door. Good night and sleep well.' Without further ceremony, she dashed out of the room in a whirlwind of perfume and lace.

Within the hour, Kate was stretched out on her bed, fully dressed. Although she was half-asleep, the memories of the last few days were still spinning round in her head. Not far away, she could see James Lavelle's laughing face, so clearly she could reach out and touch him. He had such wonderful white teeth, and such a dazzling smile. It was warm and pleasant to be lying there, his hand stroking her back. Eagerly, she stretched her body up towards him, as he leaned forward to kiss her.

Swearing at herself, she awoke and struggled to her feet. She had known the man for less than five minutes and already she was dreaming about him. What was the matter with her? She had more important things to consider. She had to get undressed, wash her face and say her prayers before she fell asleep. And she had to write a letter to Mistress Delamere, so she could pass on the news of Declan to her parents, otherwise her life would be a misery when she got back to Ireland.

Thankfully, the following day at the sanatorium passed uneventfully. She managed to get Declan to take two bowls of soup and some of Mrs Simpson's home-made bread. Now that he had company, he spent less time sleeping during the day, and they were able to have something of a conversation. That was still a little one-sided with Kate doing most of the talking, but her brother seemed to enjoy lying back on the bed, listening to her familiar accent.

Every hour or so, he would fall into a doze, giving her time to get up and stretch her legs. Each time she looked around, she was amazed at how many other people were in the sanatorium yet how few sisters there were to tend to them. Not a single patient had received a visitor while she had been there, at least not as far as she could see.

It did not seem long before five o'clock in the afternoon came round. For a moment, she glanced at her brother, by now sleeping peacefully. She had fed him, managed to clean the top half of his body, and tomorrow he was going to be shaved, like it or not. He had hardly coughed all day, and he was definitely looking better. Even Sister Mary Francis had agreed that he was improving when she had come round earlier.

Collecting the bowls and cups and utensils that Mrs Simpson had provided, she placed them safely into her basket. After smoothing her brother's forehead one last time, she slipped out the side door, ready to make her way home. Immediately, her mind turned to James

Lavelle. She had not thought about him all afternoon – well, scarcely at all. She had not allowed herself the luxury of daydreaming, especially about a man she barely knew. There was too much work to be done. However, he had said the previous evening that he might see her today. Apprehensively, she closed the fastenings on the door, turned around and looked up. And there he was, waving across to her as before. Instantly, she felt her spirits soaring above the street. What was happening? she muttered fiercely to herself. Pull yourself together, practise your breathing, pretend you don't see him, and don't rush in his direction.

For a few moments, she adjusted her bonnet and straightened her skirts, before looking up again. Now he was standing right in front of her.

'Why, Monsieur Lavelle, where did you spring from?' she demanded, posing the question in the coolest tone she could muster.

The man smiled broadly. 'Why, Mademoiselle Kate, I'm here again to see you, as I said I would last evening.' Grasping her free hand, he held it firmly between his.

Warily, she glanced around. 'It's nice to see you again. But we can't stand here. We're blocking the entrance to the street.'

'I don't intend that we stand here. I've come to ensure your safe passage back to Bloomsbury. Come, let's go in that direction now.'

Taking her by the elbow, he directed her to the side of the street. As he let her go, some other people brushed past, and he placed his hand on her back for a few moments, holding her firmly in the circle of his arm. Involuntarily, she felt herself shivering. She could not bring herself to look up into his face, only a few inches from hers.

'Have you had a good day?' he murmured, dangerously close to her ear.

'Yes.' That was as much as she could trust herself to say. For a moment she looked up into his eyes before wriggling free.

God, he had been so close to her. She had felt the strength in his body and the warmth of his breath against the side of her face. And it had left her feeling completely helpless. Had she ever been like this when she had been close to Cathal? Furiously, she racked her brain, but she could not remember; it was already a lifetime ago. Alongside, she could see him watching her, smiling. With a struggle, she managed to find her voice.

'I can't be standing here all evening, watching the people go by. I have to meet with Mistress Jardine later and I need to get myself ready.'

He laughed gently. 'Well, what are we waiting for?' And he put out his arm for her to take. Nervously, she put her arm in his, and they set off along the pavement.

Again it seemed like no time at all before they reached St Thomas' Street and Connaught House. It scarcely seemed possible that it was already half past six, and that she had to be ready for dinner at eight. Outside the house, they stopped, still arm in arm. Drawing her into the shadow of the gate, he turned her towards him.

It was amazing, she muttered to herself. Walking along together, they had enjoyed a wonderful conversation, yet now she was starting to feel helpless again. Dreamlike, she sensed him taking the basket from her hand and placing it on the ground beside them.

Again she saw him looking down at her, as she ached to stretch out towards him. He was going to kiss her, she thought panic-stricken, but she could not move a muscle.

Instead, he took her hands in his, in the way that he had done before. This time he brought both of them up to his lips. Looking at her steadily, he kissed them gently. This time there were no flourishes, no French theatricals. She could feel a tightness in her chest that was making it difficult to breathe. As she was about to lean towards him, he stepped back and let her hands fall.

'My beautiful Irish mademoiselle, I can keep you no longer. Enjoy your soiree with Mistress Jardine, and sleep well. I'll be thinking about you.' And then he was gone.

For a few moments, she stood in the same position, rooted to the spot. Mechanically, she bent down and picked up her basket. With a sigh, she walked over to the gate, but she was not thinking about what she was doing. Her thoughts were most definitely elsewhere.

Half an hour later, when she should have been getting ready to meet Mistress Jardine, she was still lying on the bed. She could feel herself floating above her body again, able to watch her reactions, but without being involved personally.

Over and over, she could feel the strength of his arm encircling her body, and the touch of his hands on her back. She imagined his fingers caressing her as he whispered quietly in her ear; toying with the fastenings of her bodice, slowly, gently. Now he was kissing her shoulders, his lips were burning, searing against her skin. She could hear herself murmuring something, but the words were too indistinct to make out. There was a pleading note about her voice. Somehow her bodice had become undone, and she could feel the cool, night air fluttering against her breasts. His hands were caressing her, teasing her nipples, while she reached out blindly, aching to wrap her arms around him.

Turning over on the bed, she thrust her face into the pillow until she could hardly breathe. What was she lying here thinking about? In all the time she and Cathal had hugged and kissed, she had never experienced a single feeling anything near to this. Please God, she begged, help me banish these thoughts from my mind.

With a superhuman effort, she managed to roll off the bed onto her knees to pray for help. Racking her brain, she tried to remember the words, but they seemed so difficult to find. She struggled through her prayers, but she was unable to concentrate. Why could she not remember something so simple, something she said every night ? It was so irritating, everything was so difficult, being so far away from her parents and Mistress Delamere. She could feel tears coming as her thoughts strayed back to the village, and the children up at the big house.

Unexpectedly, a knock sounded at the door. 'Yes, who is it?' she called, her voice shaking.

'Madam, it's Jenny, the maid. I'm knocking in case you need anything.'

Kate jumped to her feet. 'No, I have everything here; I was merely having a short nap. I'll be ready in twenty minutes. Please give my compliments to Mistress Jardine.'

Dousing her face in cold water, she gave herself a shake. What a snivelling wretch she was, lying there indulging herself in idle and wicked thoughts. One would think she was still a child, instead of a woman out travelling the world.

A few minutes later, she stood in front of the glass, looking at her reflection as she towelled herself dry. Pausing for an instant, she found herself thinking again of James Lavelle. He had probably made love to countless numbers of women, she decided. And now he was turning his attentions to a little Irish girl. Or was he simply having some fun? Did he know that she had never really been with a man? Or could that be the attraction? Perhaps a man could tell if a woman was a virgin, when he kissed her or looked into her eyes. Who could tell, she sighed to herself.

A few hours later, she was sitting in a massive overstuffed armchair, sampling her first ever glass of port. Dinner had turned out to be a slightly formal affair, with the two women being joined by a distant relative of Mistress Jardine's, who was studying to become a vicar.

The man had since retired for the evening, or gone elsewhere to continue his studies, she was not sure which. Once they were alone, the Mistress had suggested they move to the drawing room, where they could relax and enjoy a convivial drink.

'I enjoy a brandy myself,' Mistress Jardine was remarking, pouring herself an extremely large measure. 'And how about you, Kathleen, or can I call you Kate? Will you join me? A brandy, or perhaps a gin, or possibly a nice glass of port?'

Faced with that sort of choice, and particularly after two or three glasses of wine at dinner, she felt she could hardly ask for tea.

'I think I'll try the port, Mistress Jardine,' she decided, trying to sound as if this was something she did every day. 'And, yes, please call me Kate.' The first mouthful or two almost made her choke, but gradually it became much more palatable.

'So, Kate, if the gentlemen were with us now, if I can refer to my husband as a gentleman, they would be lighting their fat cigars and polluting the house with their stinking smoke. So we are blessed to be escaping that.' Leaning back in her chair, she gazed across at Kate. 'Now tell me, you've been in London for a few days, what do you think of it?'

Kate thought for a moment, while having another sip of port. 'You know, Mistress Jardine, I've been here such a short time and I've seen so little of the city. I don't think I know enough yet about London and its people.'

Mistress Jardine poured herself another large brandy. 'Now, now, you must have formed some opinions. Tell me, I'm interested in knowing. And let me top you up there.' Stretching over, she refilled Kate's glass.

'I have to confess that on my arrival at Cheapside I found the place to be more dreadful than I ever imagined. Even driving through the streets in the coach, I couldn't believe the noise and the smells and the dirt. I'm sorry, Mistress Jardine, but I find everywhere so filthy.'

'Aha, that's because we burn the coal here, morning, noon and night in some houses. It's always smoky, even in summer. In winter, sometimes it's impossible to see more than a few yards at a time, the air is filled with so much smoke.'

The Mistress sat back again in her chair, stretching

herself luxuriously – like a sleek cat, Kate mused.

'I wasn't prepared for the bustle on Cheapside, either. While there were much goings-on in Dublin and Liverpool, they were nowhere near as rowdy as I found coming to London.'

The other woman stood up, slightly shaky on her feet. 'I must go and powder my nose,' she announced. 'I'll be back in a few minutes. Please carry on without me.' A little unsteadily, she wobbled across the room.

The woman was the worse for wear from the brandy, Kate realised. She had better not drink too much port or she would end up in the same state herself. For all that, it did not seem to have had much effect so far. She felt warm and comfortable, her head seemed to be clear enough, and she did not appear to be saying anything particularly stupid.

Moments later, the Mistress returned, throwing herself down in her chair. 'That feels a lot better.' she declared. 'Now I'm ready for another.' Taking hold of the brandy decanter, she filled her glass, her hand shaking only very slightly. 'Go on, Kate, tell me more. And have another port while you're at it. It's not often that I get the chance to relax without men leering or trying to paw me. I know that can be flattering now and again, but it's nice to have some time without them, to be away from their shouting and cursing, their disgusting stories and the way they keep threatening each other with violence all the time.'

Kate arched her eyebrows in amazement. Just what kind of circles did Mistress Jardine move in, she wondered.

'Where was I?' she asked, deciding it was much safer

to continue. 'Yes, it was such bedlam at Cheapside and I wasn't really expecting it. But now I've become accustomed to being here, I don't feel quite so terrified every time I have to leave the house. But another big difference is the fashions in which people dress; so many women wear these enormous hats, I sometimes think they'll topple over. And every time there's a gust of wind, it's a real comedy, with so many women screaming and bonnets being blown through the air. And it's the same with parasols – it hasn't rained once since I've been here, yet every woman of style carries a parasol. Sometimes I think I could stand all day long at the corner of Holborn and Chancery Lane just watching the people go by.'

Stopping to get her breath back, she took another sip of port. It really tasted quite pleasant now, so she decided to have another. As she was filling her glass, she was amazed to see Mistress Jardine stretch herself out in the chair, hitch up her skirts and throw one shapely leg and dainty foot up and over the armrest. My God, she was a languorous one indeed, thought Kate, and obviously had no truck with any rules about sitting up, or being prim and straight-backed.

'If I was not living in Bloomsbury, and a woman of some means, with a position to maintain, I swear I would smoke a pipe this very minute,' she exclaimed suddenly, much to Kate's amazement. 'So, what about my house here? How do you think that this compares to that of my cousin, over there in deepest Wicklow?' Slyly, she looked over the top of her glass.

Kate opened her mouth to reply, when for some reason she realised that this was a dangerous question. Cautiously, she began to speak.

'I believe they are both very different in their own way. You must remember I'm not very knowledgeable on this subject.'

Not very knowledgeable on this subject? Almost all her life had been spent living in a two-roomed cottage! A room of her own was something she had enjoyed for no more than a few weeks. And now she was about to discuss interior design with a woman she barely knew, who kept a fashionable house in one of the best parts of London! It did not bear thinking about. Choosing her words carefully, she continued. 'I think the reason is the complete difference in appearance, perhaps there's a town style and a country style. In your house here, everything looks new and clean, which gives the rooms a bright and spacious feeling; it's such a contrast to the hustle and bustle outside in the streets. Mistress Delamere's house back in Wicklow is much more ornate, everything seems heavier, and the rooms are more cluttered. But I think that both houses are wonderful.'

Kate looked sideways to see how she was taking this response. It must have sounded perfectly acceptable, as Mistress Jardine was leaning forward unconcernedly, pouring herself another drink.

For some reason, Kate felt a mad desire to giggle. It was ridiculous for her to be sitting in this room discussing such matters, especially with a woman whose every move involved so much flouncing, preening and other extravagant gestures. And the style of her clothes – even Mistress Delamere's attire would look dowdy beside her cousin's exotic creations.

Earlier that evening, in preparation for dinner with a vicar and a young Irish country girl, Mistress Jardine had chosen a full skirt with scarcely any top to it whatsoever. Kate took another quick peek over the top of her glass while the Mistress made herself comfortable. How did the bodice stay in position? Her neck, her shoulders and her arms were bare. And the front of her dress was cut so low that every time she leaned forward for the brandy decanter, her breasts were almost in full view. And it had been the same the previous evening when they had met briefly as she was about to leave for the theatre. It was impossible to imagine herself wearing such clothes. What would her mother say if she were to come home dressed like that? Now she had the giggles again.

'Kate, you're sitting there, laughing away to yourself,' Mistress Jardine interrupted her thinking. 'What's so funny?'

Still smiling, she shook her head. 'It's nothing. It's simply that I'm enjoying the evening, Mistress Jardine.'

'Changing the subject,' the other woman continued, 'how is your brother keeping? I understand he's recovered somewhat.'

'Yes, indeed,' Kate responded eagerly. 'I'm very pleased at the progress he's making. He's now able to eat soup and bread, but I'm going to try and start him on potatoes in the next two or three days.'

'Aha, that's good news,' Mistress Jardine exclaimed. 'And of course, the Irish must have their potatoes.' She laughed uproariously as a thought occurred to her.

'Do you remember this, Kate? 'A bag of potatoes and a ha'porth of lard, makes a mighty fine meal for an Irish Pat." We used to sing that when we were children.'

Kate looked at her in astonishment.

'Don't forget that I'm Irish too. I might have lived

here for nigh on fifteen years, but I still remember Dublin and Wicklow. Drink with me, I give you a toast.' Jumping to her feet, she raised her glass. 'To the Hill of Howth!' she exclaimed, taking a large gulp of the brandy.

Inexplicably, Kate felt compelled to do the same. Before she knew it, she was on her feet, shouting. 'And I give you an ancient toast, Mistress Jardine. To Cuchulainn, the hound of Ulster!' Together, they drained their glasses and crashed them down on the table.

'Ah, but I enjoyed that,' the Mistress gasped. 'It just proves we can have as much fun without having men around all the time. God is good, right enough, but the devil is not bad either.'

As she was refilling the glasses, she looked slyly across the table. 'Speaking of which, who's this young man you appear to have found, who's walking you back to the house each evening?'

Involuntarily, Kate's hand flew to her mouth. How did the Mistress know about this? What was she going to say in reply?

'He's merely a friend of my brother's,' she swallowed nervously. 'I met him the first day I went to the hospital. But I barely know him.'

'Well, I think it's admirable. You've been here scarcely five minutes, your brother is recovering, and you've found yourself a young man into the bargain.'

Kate felt she had to protest, but the Mistress waved her hand, cutting her short. 'You don't need to explain – I was only joking. But another thought occurs to me. If your brother's getting well, you must have a little more time to see London. I'd like you to come to the theatre with us later this week.'

Oh no, Kate groaned inwardly; this was too much. She had read about the theatres in London, and Mister Hutchinson had told her about Drury Lane, encouraging her to read some of Goldsmith's plays. But to actually go there?

'Oh, Mistress Jardine, I don't think I could. It would be too much for me, and I don't have any clothes to wear,' she pleaded desperately.

'Don't be ridiculous! You'll really enjoy it. It will be a new experience and you might not get another opportunity while you're here. And everyone will be wondering who this beautiful young lady is – we'll have men of all ages showering us with invitations.'

She scrutinised Kate. 'I have a friend who's of a similar build, what I can see of you anyway. I'll have some of her skirts sent over and you can wear one of those for the evening. She'll not mind – she has hundreds more to choose from.' Clapping her hands, she lay back comfortably in her chair. 'Good, that's settled, then. We've something to look forward to.'

Kate looked at her glass of port, which at some point in the conversation had been emptied again. How could she drink another drop? And this idea of going to the theatre; it was madness, without a doubt, but it was exciting as well. And to be wearing one of those expensive dresses like Mistress Jardine's? The thought was intoxicating.

Taking a few deep breaths, she glanced at the other woman. who looked as if she had fallen asleep; she could hear her snoring gently – and with such a lack of propriety! Her hair had come loose and fallen around her shoulders. Her mouth was open, and she was reclining, her legs apart, one foot resting on the table, the other on the floor, with her breasts almost falling out of her bodice.

Thank God she had not drunk so much; she would not want to end up in that condition. Pushing herself up out of the chair, she decided to go to bed. As she set off towards the door, somehow or other her foot got tangled up in her skirt, making her fall over on her side, jarring her knee and elbow. How could she have done that, she giggled to herself, as she lay on the floor. At least it did not feel too painful, so she managed to struggle up and set off again.

Strangely enough, she had forgotten where her room was located. Ah, that was it, she remembered – up the stairs and to the right. But there seemed to be so many stairs, she had to stop halfway up. She could not remember the staircase being as long as this, she could hear her voice saying. By now she was having a good conversation with herself. Around the corner and then the second door on the right. For a minute, she had confused the layout with Mister Boulton's house. How could she do anything like that? Finally she found her room.

Immediately, she fell sideways across the bed, struggling to drag herself face first into a more comfortable position. She had not washed her face or said her prayers but it did not seem to matter. In any case, it was too much like hard work to get up again. Rolling over on to her back, she sprawled out comfortably on top of the blankets. This was how Mistress Jardine had been reclining, she giggled again to herself.

Throwing out her arms, she pulled up her skirts and lay back on the pillow, her legs stretched out luxuriously towards each corner of the bed. Within seconds, James was in her thoughts and there beside her. This time, he was kneeling between her legs, removing her shoes. Now his hands were on her knees and her thighs. Without waiting a moment longer, she hooked her feet around his waist and pulled him down towards her.

Some time later, she awoke with a start. Bleary-eyed, she tried to get her bearings, but it was still dark outside. Something, however, was seriously wrong with her stomach. For some reason it was heaving violently, as if she was back on board the ship. And her head had been affected as well. When she looked at the ceiling it appeared to be revolving, around and around and around. Desperately she rubbed at her eyes, but it made no difference. The whole world seemed to be turning, faster and faster.

Oh God, she could hear herself saying, over and over again. This is terrible, please help me. Gripping the headboard behind the bed, she dragged herself into an upright position to try and clear her head. Every muscle in her body was so painful, as if someone had been pounding her for hours with a giant hammer. And her elbow, it was hurting so much; why should that be?

After a while time became meaningless, as she lay on top of the covers, tossing and turning, her stomach rumbling and gurgling, her head spinning. At some stage she must have fallen into a sleep of sorts, and when she awoke the sun was streaming through the windows. Her head was now achingly painful. Forcing herself to get up and get moving, she rolled off the bed and stumbled into the bathroom.

Slowly, mechanically, she got undressed. Perhaps a

cold bath would help her to feel better. Plunging into the water brought almost instant invigoration, but it was too cold to linger for long, and as well as the mysterious pains in her elbow and her knee, the mental gyrations in her head were becoming a worry. Every so often, short memories of the previous evening's events kept flashing through her mind. But for some reason, she could not piece them all together.

'Oh, God,' she offered up a silent prayer. 'Please make me feel better, and I swear I'll never touch the port wine again.'

Being as quiet as she could under the circumstances, she crept down the stairs to the kitchen. Her head was still throbbing, but thankfully her elbow and her knee were giving her less concern.

In the kitchen, Mrs Simpson was polishing away furiously, surrounded by pots and pans. 'Good morning, Miss Brennan,' she remarked cheerily. 'And how are you this lovely morning?'

Why was this woman shouting and bellowing so much? Kate muttered under her breath.

'I'm fine, Mrs Simpson,' she whispered in reply. 'At least I will be after a cup of tea.'

'And would you like some porridge and fresh bread, Miss Brennan? I know you like to start the day with a good breakfast.'

The thought of porridge made her stomach start to heave again.

'No, I don't think that would be a good idea, Mrs Simpson,' she grimaced. 'A cup of tea will be sufficient.'

Sitting down at the table, she rested her head in her hands. Never again, she promised herself, would strong drink pass her lips.

Wearily, she knew she had to get through the day somehow. All afternoon her headache persisted and by early evening she felt completely exhausted. Needless to say, everybody she spoke to was full of cheer: Mrs Simpson, the sisters at the hospital, and even Declan, and the noise from the crowds on the streets was almost unbearable. By five o'clock, she had seen and done as much as she could.

Outside in the lane, she was half-expecting James to be there waiting for her, but he was nowhere to be seen. In some respects she was thankful for that. His light and friendly manner was normally so attractive, but today she was sure she would not be good company. And while it would be pleasant to have him walking alongside her, feeling the touch and the strength of his arm, it was probably for the best that she was alone today.

By the time she reached St Thomas' Street, her headache had almost disappeared, although she was still dreadfully tired. That evening, Mister and Mistress Jardine were nowhere to be seen, so she retired early. As soon as she reached her bed, she fell immediately into a sound sleep, without any thoughts of anyone else – neither Declan, nor Mistress Jardine, nor even James Lavelle.

Chapter 5

Early next morning, Kate was sitting in the breakfast room discussing her plans for the day with Mrs Simpson.

'Miss Brennan,' the cook was saying. 'You're keeping me back, talking about your brother and all. I've got a long list of things to do, and I must get on.' Still complaining, she bustled off into the kitchen.

Feeling a little lethargic, Kate decided to have a second cup of tea. Outside, the garden was sparkling in the early morning sunshine. As she was admiring the view, she heard footsteps behind her. Immediately, she turned round in her chair, thinking it was Reynolds, or even Mrs Simpson coming back for something or other.

But it was neither of those. Instead, it was a large, powerful looking man, with a strong nose, iron grey hair and huge sidewhiskers. With her first glance, Kate could see that as well as being a striking individual, he was dressed in an immaculate black jacket and breeches, set off by highly polished boots and a wonderfully white starched shirt.

Apprehensively, she stood up and pushed back her chair.

'Good morning, madam,' he intoned, his voice remarkably deep and quiet.

'Good morning, sir,' Kate stammered in return. Who was this? Was this Mister Jardine, the husband that the Mistress was always referring to?

'You must be Miss Brennan,' he continued, extending his huge hand. Nervously, Kate brushed it with her fingers.

'Yes, I am she. And you, sir?'

His touch turned out to be incredibly light for such a powerful looking individual.

'I've heard so much about you, Miss Brennan, I was not sure what to expect. But as you seem to be on good terms with my wife and her cousin, I expect that you're another one of these scheming Irish women who get their pleasure from twisting men around their little fingers.'

What was she to make of this? 'Are you Mister Jardine, sir?' she repeated lamely.

'Yes, that's me, young lady. I'm the husband of that woman Jardine who also lives in this house.'

It was impossible to tell whether he was joking or not. But one thing was sure: the mental picture she had formed from Mistress Jardine's comments about her husband was completely wrong.

'Sit down, sit down,' he insisted. 'I haven't come to disturb your breakfast. In fact, I would never normally get up at this Godforsaken hour, but this morning I've some important people to see and I must get to my office in good time.'

Before he could finish, he was interrupted by Mrs Simpson rushing out of the kitchen with a fresh pot of tea.

'Here you are, Mister Jardine. I hope this is to your liking. Is there anything else I can get you?'

Kate looked on, amazed to see so much bowing and scraping from the cook. She had never seen her do that before with anyone else.

'Just some hot bread and butter will be sufficient for me, Mrs Simpson,' he said, in that low, deep voice. Turning again to Kate, he studied her from under his bushy eyebrows.

'I understand you will be joining us on our next evening to the theatre?'

Although his voice was low and his tone was pleasant, for some reason Kate felt as if he would brook no refusals. And his presence seemed to dwarf everything else, including her. Merely sitting next to him, she felt small and almost overpowered. But his question reminded her of the arrangements that the Mistress had mentioned a few days earlier.

'I think so, perhaps, I'm not sure, Mister Jardine.' She began stammering again. How could she say something so pathetic?

'Well, I'm told it has all been arranged. Even as we speak, special boxes are being organised, people are being invited, catering is being laid on.' Without warning, he leaned forwards, his huge face looming over her. 'You wouldn't be thinking of changing your mind, would you, Miss Brennan? Once the Mistress has decided that something is going to happen, then by God it happens in style.'

Half-terrified, half-fascinated, she shrank back in her

chair. God, what was she letting herself in for?

'Mister Jardine, would you ever be quiet and stop bothering the poor girl, and at this time of the morning as well.' The Mistress swept into the room, beautifully coiffured. 'Good morning, husband, I'm glad to see you're awake and afoot.' She kissed him on the cheek. 'And good morning to you, Kate,' she said sweetly. 'You're looking lovely this morning. Are you ready for your day at the hospital?'

Kate could scarcely believe it. In a matter of a few seconds, the atmosphere in the room had changed completely. One moment the man had seemed huge, almost menacing in appearance, the next he had shown himself to be completely under the spell of his wife. Whatever form of magic she was using, it was working most effectively.

'Yes, Mistress Jardine.' Kate replied, her voice stronger as she took her cue from the other woman. 'I'm just about ready to leave.'

'That is exceptional timing. Mister Jardine is also ready to leave, aren't you, darling? You can go with him in his carriage. As for me, I have some purchases to make today.'

For a moment, the woman fondled her husband's neck before leaving, blowing kisses to all and sundry.

A moment or two later, Mister Jardine finished off his tea and stood up. 'If you're ready, Miss Brennan?'

Outside the front gate, Reynolds was standing by an absolutely magnificent carriage. The bodywork was a deep green with cream trimmings, set off with elegant designs painted on the doors. In front, two matching black horses waited impatiently, pawing the ground. On a word from the driver, they set off towards Holborn at a ferocious speed, scattering pigeons, children and pedestrians in all directions. As they swung into the lane through Grays Inn, she was reminded instantly of her trip from Liverpool to Birmingham, when the people at the sides of the road had stopped and craned their necks to see who was travelling past in such style

Within a few minutes they had reached the sanatorium. Throughout the journey, Mister Jardine said nothing, contenting himself by sitting comfortably in the corner, watching her with an enigmatic smile on his face.

'Mister Jardine, can you stop the coach, please?' Kate shouted suddenly, as they reached the sanatorium sooner than she had been expecting. 'This is where I have to get off.'

The man called over his shoulder to the driver who brought the coach to a dramatic halt. Stepping out into the road, Mister Jardine looked around, disregarding the stares from the passers-by.

'Are you sure this is the place you're going to?' he asked, as if she had made some mistake.

'Yes, Mister Jardine, this is where I go every day when I leave your house. There's over eighty sick and dying people in there, and only a handful of nurses to look after them. While I'm here I'm more than happy to help.'

Without waiting for any assistance, she jumped down from the carriage and walked towards the door of the hospital. But something made her stop and turn to face him. 'And if I seem a little concerned about going to the theatre with you and your wife, that's because I sometimes get tired after a day here, seeing so many people suffering and dying.'

She turned on her heel and pushed her way through the door. That was better, she thought immediately. At least she had been able to leave him in no doubt about what her real purpose was in being there.

As she peeked through the window, she could see him outside in the street, looking around and rubbing his chin thoughtfully. Beside him the horses continued to paw the ground and flick their tails, while the passers-by gawped at the splendour of the carriage. But as far as she could see, he did not seem to be taking the slightest notice of them.

Inside the hospital, she walked slowly between the beds. Some of the people she recognised now, and it seemed to cheer them up a little if she stopped to say a few words to anyone who was awake. By this time, most of the sisters had become accustomed to seeing her there, and she usually tried her best to keep their spirits up as well.

On that Monday, however, she was still thinking about her encounter with Mister Jardine. Had he been serious or simply pulling her leg? It was difficult to be sure. And what about the relationship between Mister Jardine and his wife? That was difficult to work out as well. And did they share the same bed? They must have done at one time, since they had three children at boarding school. But their offspring rarely came up in conversation. By all accounts, Mistress Jardine had an aversion to having any more children; perhaps that was why her husband spent so many nights at his club.

Still pondering, she found herself at Declan's bed. Or at least the bed where she had last seen him. But, of her brother there was no sign.

Overcome by a sense of foreboding, she dashed back down the ward to find the nearest nurse. Calm down, calm down, she told herself. There must be a simple explanation.

'Sister,' she forced out in as controlled a voice as she could muster. 'Have you seen my brother today? He's normally in the bed in the hallway by the door, but I can't see him anywhere.'

The woman looked around with a puzzled expression on her face. 'I don't understand it,' she replied. 'I passed him about an hour ago and he was in bed and wide awake. He told me he'd been able to go and relieve himself without our help, so I went off to attend to some other people more in need of my attention.'

Kate felt tension rising in her chest. 'Do you think he may have tried to go somewhere by himself?' she whispered, her voice strained. That could be the answer, she decided, before the other woman could reply. Could he have walked out in the street? Normally he wore a nightgown when he was in bed, with his clothes lying on a nearby chair. Immediately, she dashed back to the alcove in the hallway. Sure enough, the chair was empty. Pulling back the covers on the bed, she found the crumpled night-gown, discarded under the sheets. Where had he gone? Without waiting, she opened the door and rushed out into the street. Even though it was not yet mid-morning, the usual crowds of passers-by, hawkers, children and dogs were milling around. Desperately, she looked up and down. And although she could not see very far in either direction, there was not the slightest sign of Declan to be seen anywhere.

By this time the sense of panic was overwhelming.

Her chest was growing tighter, and she could hear her breathing, rasping in her throat. 'The stupid bastard,' she muttered under her breath. Instantly, her hands flew to her mouth. My God, that was the first time she had ever spoken such a word. For a moment she regretted what she had done. But that was what he was – a stupid bastard, and God forgive her for saying it.

Frantically, she tried to fight her way through the people on the pavement, but it was impossible. There were too many, and she was too small to see any distance. This was ridiculous. All she was doing was running aimlessly up and down the street. What was she expecting to find? Stop and think, she told herself, and remember what Mister Hutchinson had always said.

Leaning back against the window of a nearby shop, she breathed deeply and counted up to ten. Think, woman, think, she muttered wildly. If she was Declan, where would she be trying to get to ?

For a few moments, her mind raced furiously. Food? No, it could not be that. He would have known she was coming and that she would get whatever he wanted. Clothes? No, he had his clothes, so that was not the answer either. Immediately, his whereabouts dawned on her. Yes, she knew where he had gone – it had been obvious all along.

Retracing her steps to the hospital, she rushed around until she found Sister Mary Francis. 'Sister, Sister, please tell me,' she cried, bursting through the door into the matron's room. 'Where is the nearest alehouse, or brandy-shop, do you know?'

The sister looked up, speechless for a moment. 'Kathleen, indeed. I did not take you for a drinker, especially at this hour of the morning.'

Biting her lip, Kate forced herself to speak slowly. 'Sister Mary Francis, my brother has disappeared from his bed and there's only one place he would go. So I would be grateful if you would tell me the location of the establishments near here where they sell strong drink.' By the time she finished the sentence, she was almost shouting.

The sister's expression did not change. 'You certainly have an interesting life, Kathleen. I personally have little experience of drinking places near Grays Inn, but I do believe I've passed a number not far from here on the left-hand side as you go towards Holborn. He must have gone in that direction, as there's only common land in the other for three quarters of a mile or so.'

Before the woman could finish, Kate had rushed off. Right, she knew what she was looking for. Across the street she went, dodging between the horses and the cabs. Within a few yards she found it, a drinking shop where they sold brandy. This seemed an unlikely place for Declan, but who could tell what a man desperate for strong drink would do?

Putting her hand on the door handle to push it open, she realised suddenly what she was about to do. What in God's name might there be on the other side of the threshold? What nature of people would be drinking brandy in the middle of the morning? For a moment, she wavered. Then she closed her eyes and thrust her arm out. Immediately, the door swung open, so easily she almost fell over. Regaining her balance, she had a quick look around, but it was such an anti-climax. The room was completely empty except for one old man reading a newspaper, and another, presumably a serving-man, cleaning the tables. For a moment, they both looked at her in astonishment. 'Sorry, this is not the place,' she hissed under her breath, as she backed into the street.

Outside, she cursed again. Please God, he had to forgive her for using such language, but she was sorely tested. Then she remembered. Only a few hundred yards away stood the Lord Chatham, where she had passed every day.

Again, she fought her way through the pedestrians and the street traffic. Outside the door, she took a deep breath, collecting herself. Across the threshold it was very gloomy, but she could pick out a number of people sitting at various tables. Looking around quickly, she noticed some women as well as men. Thankfully, almost everyone ignored her. For a moment she stood motionless, uncertain what to do next, until a girl who had been leaning against a nearby table came towards her.

'Yes, madam, what can we do for you here?' She put her hands on her hips and fixed Kate with a brazen stare. 'Are you sure that you've come through the right door? Or have you lost your way?' She turned and laughed with some of the people sitting close by.

Inexplicably, Kate found her hands clenching into fists. For the first time in her life she succumbed to a rage, the blood pounding in her head. She was on the point of raising her hand to strike the woman to the ground, when some half-forgotten voice of common sense whispered in her ear. This was not the way to solve this problem. Somehow she had to get this woman on her side.

Out of the blue, she found the inspiration. 'I think

perhaps that you're not from around these parts?' she murmured, keeping her voice as low as possible.

'For sure, madam, that I'm not. I'm from County Wexford and proud of it.' The woman put her hands on her hips and dared Kate to reply.

'Then you'd not be coming between a Fenian brother and his sister, would you?' Kate put on her broadest Wicklow accent.

The other woman stared at her in amazement, a bewildered expression on her face. Before she could reply, Kate went on. 'I've come from the sanatorium further up the road. My brother has been sick and I've been caring for him. But he's too fond of the drink, and he's gone wandering off somewhere. Now I'm trying to find him, before he does himself an injury.'

'Madam, please forgive me. You should have told me before.' The woman's voice had taken on a pleading note. 'Please don't tell Sister Mary Francis that I've spoken rudely to you. She can be hard enough on me as it is for working in this place, but I have to earn something to keep myself and my child.'

'For God's sake get a hold of yourself,' Kate hissed. 'I'm not about to go off telling tales to anybody. Just tell me, is my brother here or not?'

'I think he might be, madam,' the woman replied. 'There's a man here drinking by himself and he doesn't look all that well to me.'

'Take me to him,' Kate commanded. But already the woman was walking around the counter between the tables. And there he was, leaning forward over the table, almost unable to support himself.

'Declan, you stupid bastard.' This time Kate

whispered the words, as her brother looked up through watery eyes.

'Kate, I'm sorry, I didn't mean to be so much trouble.' His voice was so weak she could barely hear him.

'Declan, I'll swing for you some day, that's for sure.' She ran towards him, the tears running down her cheeks, catching him around the shoulders as he slumped forward.

Glancing behind her, she realised that the other woman was still watching. 'I have to thank you for bringing me to him.' she began. 'He's not recovered yet, but he's fond of his drink, and I expect he thought he could manage by himself.' She paused for a moment. 'Forgive me for asking, but what's your name?'

'Teresa Ryan,' the woman replied in a low voice, 'from near Gorey, to the north of Wexford town.'

'Well, Teresa, my name is Kathleen Brennan, from Kilcarra in Wicklow, and very pleased I am to meet you. But I would be even more pleased if you could give me some help to get my brother back on his feet.'

Together the two women managed to get Declan upright and walking, if a bit unsteadily.

'He still seems weak,' Teresa pointed out, 'but the drink has made it look worse than it is. If you can get him back into bed and rested you might find it's not had too much effect.'

Kate looked appreciatively at the other woman. 'I've no doubt that you're more experienced in these matters than me, so I'll take your word for it. Thanks again for all your help. And if you have a few minutes during the day, why don't you come in and see me or Sister Mary Francis. I'm sure she'd give you a much easier time if you were to visit her occasionally and say a few prayers for the sick.'

'I'll try, madam, I can't promise, but I'll try,' the Irishwoman replied.

As she pushed her way through the door, still supporting Declan, Kate stopped and looked back. 'And for the love of God, Teresa, don't keep referring to me as madam. Call me Kate, I'm more than happy with that.'

The bar girl smiled warily. 'May God be with you, Kate Brennan.' She turned round and looked wearily at the customers behind her, clamouring for her attention. 'All right,' she cried at the top of her voice, as Kate disappeared through the door. 'Would you ever have a bit of patience and you'll all be served!'

Back at the hospital, Kate helped Declan into bed. 'I'm sorry,' he kept mumbling. 'I thought I was stronger than I was.'

'Just lie down and have a rest – you'll be fine in an hour or two,' she insisted, trying to keep a soothing note in her voice.

Within a few minutes he was asleep, leaving her able to sit down and relax. It was not long before she felt herself getting too comfortable, her head drooping against her chest.

Involuntarily, she sat up with a start. Shaking her head, she rubbed the sleep from her eyes. To stop herself from falling asleep again, she decided to write another letter home. There was so much to tell them – perhaps too much. Maybe she would be better off not relating every little detail that had happened to her. Perhaps she should merely say that Declan's health was improving and they would be returning in a few days. Yes, that would be the best approach, she decided, as she went off to find paper and pen.

By the time she had written her letter and fed and washed Declan, it was almost five o'clock. Packing up her belongings, she leaned over and whispered goodnight to her brother, leaving him undisturbed. A moment later she was outside, about to set off for Mistress Jardine's. As she turned to walk down the street, she almost bumped into James Lavelle, who had appeared like some genie from a bottle.

'Well, Monsieur Lavelle,' she remarked, as casually as she could. 'I was not expecting you, not after last night.'

'Kate, my little Irish beauty. I came here last night, but you were already gone. I tell you, I was devastated. I wanted so much to see you but I had some other things to attend to, and they kept me late.' He gave her such an appealing look that she had to smile.

'I think you're exaggerating a little, Monsieur. But it's nice to see you, and I missed you last night as well.'

'So tell me, Kate,' he began, as they strolled along the street. 'How did you enjoy your evening with Mistress Jardine?'

She paused slightly, remembering, then had to laugh. 'Without doubt it was an eventful experience. Now I know how the people of a certain style in London live their lives. I also received a valuable lesson about the evils of strong drink. Mistress Jardine persuaded me into drinking port – something I'm never going to do ever again.'

This time it was Lavelle's turn to smile, as he took her arm in his. 'Kate, port is a drink for old men. Some day I'll introduce you to the beautiful wines of France, which

133

you'll be able to drink and enjoy without suffering from the after-effects for days afterwards.'

'I think not, Monsieur Lavelle. Strong drink will never pass my lips again.' She looked up at him, a determined set to her jaw.

'Kate, you are so beautiful when you flash your eyes at me. It's too captivating.' Squeezing her elbow, Lavelle guided her around the corner towards St Thomas' Street.

'I missed you too, last night,' he whispered, holding her just above her elbow and gazing intently into her eyes.

'James, James,' Kate laughed, struggling free from his grip. 'You don't know your own strength. I thought you were trying to break my arm there for a minute.'

Leaning forward, he tilted her chin up with one hand and kissed her gently on the lips. Kate was frozen to the spot. Placing his hands on her shoulders, he pulled her close. She could feel herself swaying against him, her arms still down by her sides, her face upturned, her eyes closed. He kissed her again, her lips yielding and responding to his touch. God, it was so beautiful. His touch was gentle, but she could sense the firmness in him, and the pressure of his body against her breasts.

'Kate, Kate,' he whispered, his voice sweet as he stroked the side of her face. 'Something about you is having a dangerous effect on me.' Drawing back, he laughed softly as she opened her eyes. The next moment he was smiling wickedly, and holding her hands in his.

'Kate, we are out in the street. You can't do this in London,' he laughed again. 'I must go and so must you. Sleep well and I'll see you tomorrow.' He quickly kissed her cheek and was gone.

Even though he had disappeared, Kate stood rooted to

the spot, giving herself time to calm down. His nearness had left her hot and flustered, making it difficult to think clearly. Eventually, she managed to stumble into the house. In her bedroom, she stretched out on the bed to rest, but her mind was brimming over, tossing and tumbling, stopping her from falling asleep. Pulling back the covers, she got up and sat in the wicker chair by the window. Despite her best intentions, James seemed to be in front of her constantly, preventing her from dislodging him from her mind. But the panic she had experienced earlier when Declan had gone missing was not far away either. In between, she could see Mister Jardine's powerful face looking at her intently, as if he was trying to read her innermost thoughts. And Mistress Jardine was there too, in her underwear, reeking of perfume and with her chest half-exposed.

For a few moments, she held her head in her hands. It was too much, she told herself sorrowfully. All at once, she remembered the terror and the excitement when Mistress Delamere had suggested she come to England. If she had known then what lay ahead of her, she would never have been able to step on board that ship.

Two hours later, she awoke from a troubled sleep, cold and stiff, still sitting in the chair. Stretching herself, she stood up to take off her clothes. Moonlight streamed through the window and cast shadows across the room. As her dress slipped off, her reflection stood out clearly in the glass on the wall.

With a touch of curiosity, she stood back and looked at her image. It had to be the light, but her breasts were almost as full as Mistress Jardine's. Gently, she touched her nipples with the palms of her hands. Would James

Lavelle ever like this body? she thought idly. He must know so many French girls, and they were supposed to be the most voluptuous in all of Europe. She was sure to be too skinny for him. What if he tried to touch her body or caress her? He was so different from Cathal. Some inner sense had made him easy to deal with. But how would she cope with James? Surely he would be too experienced for her.

Climbing back into bed, she pulled the covers up over her head. It was nice to be in the dark and away from everything, even for a short while. If only she was with her parents now, she would not have to think about these troublesome thoughts. If only she could be out on the hillside again, running with the dogs, she would not have to cope with the pressures of all these people. Really, they were expecting too much. She felt the tears coming, hot against her cheeks. Why, God? she kept whispering, as she wrapped her arms around her body and rocked herself to sleep.

At the hospital the next day, she was in surprisingly high spirits, singing to herself as she sat by Declan. He was really improving, and it looked as if they would be able to go home soon. The excitement of the previous day had been forgotten, and the demons of the night had been exorcised from her mind.

A good night's sleep and then a quick cold bath. That was the trick to get a body started in the morning, she decided, as she chatted to her brother and the sisters who came by every so often.

Late in the afternoon, Patrick Nolan turned up unexpectedly to see how Declan was progressing. As he approached the bed, Kate could see him studying her warily. Stopping abruptly, he put his hands up in a placatory gesture.

'Good afternoon to you, Kate. Before you start, I'm here merely to see how Declan is. Don't go shouting at me for disturbing him.'

Amused, she laughed at the man's discomfort. 'I'm sorry about our first day, Patrick. I was upset, that was all. You're more than welcome, especially now that Declan is doing well. I'll go and stretch my legs and let you talk to him.'

Half an hour later, she returned to find him still there, sitting beside the bed. Hearing her coming back, he looked up with a smile.

'You're right, Kate, your brother is looking grand. It's such a change since the last time I saw him. Sure, if I ever get sick, will you come and look after me? I think I'd like a bit of whatever it is that Declan's getting.'

Kate nodded happily. 'I never did say thanks for getting him here, and letting us know about his condition.'

'Sure, that was nothing,' the man replied, looking at Declan. 'I think he's gone to sleep. I expect I had better be getting off.'

As he stood up to leave, he coughed nervously. 'Kate, I'm going down the road from here to have a glass or two,' he began. 'It's a place where the Irish get together, and I was wondering if you would like to come along?'

'Are you talking about that alehouse near Holborn, I think they call it the Lord Chatham or something like that?'

Patrick raised his eyebrows. 'Oh, so you know the place, then?'

'Not really,' Kate replied. 'But I've met a Teresa Ryan who works there, and she's Irish, from County Wexford.'

As she spoke, she was amazed to see his eyes shining.

'She is a fine girl, that Teresa, right enough,' he muttered. 'It's a hard life for a woman working in that place, but she does a grand job.'

Pausing for a moment, he gave her a sideways look. 'If you were thinking of stopping here to wait for James Lavelle, you'll be out of luck. He'll not be here this evening, at least not at this time. He's meeting some people who've arrived recently from France.'

'In that case, Mister Nolan, how can I refuse? Lead me to the Lord Chatham. But I'll not be taking any strong drink. I had enough of that earlier this week.'

The alehouse was just as she recalled it, except much busier. Despite her protests, Patrick Nolan insisted on buying her a tankard of ale.

'Just to try it out, Kate. You can't be coming to London without being able to say that you have sampled the ale.'

Picking up their drinks, they moved to a large table where six or seven other people were already seated. Patrick made the introductions, but Kate's mind was too full of other things to remember all their names. The others drifted into a conversation about how difficult life was for an Irishman living in London, but after a few moments, she found it did not hold her interest. Trying not to be too obvious, she looked around to see what was happening elsewhere. It was a busy place, that was for sure. There must have been over a hundred people in the alehouse, while three or four serving-women rushed around continuously, shouting and laughing with the customers.

There was something familiar about it all. Yes, that was it, she realised suddenly. It was the same noise she could remember hearing outside Cormack's pub in the village, whenever someone left the door open. That seemed like a thousand years ago, walking with the dogs through the village, or waiting outside for her father, while he imbibed a glass or two.

Lost in memories, her gaze swept around the room again. Over on the other side of the bar, she could see Teresa Ryan, joking with a man sitting at one of the tables. As she looked up, Kate gave her a quick wave. A few moments later, the girl came over to the table.

'Hello, Miss Brennan, I didn't expect to see you back so soon,' she shouted above the noise.

Kate stood up so they could speak more easily. 'Teresa, call me Kate,' she insisted. But she smiled as she spoke, taking hold of the girl's hand. 'I managed to get my brother back to the hospital and he's fine now. You were right, he was simply the worse the wear for drink. But I think he might have learned a lesson – let's hope so anyway. And thanks again for all your help.'

'For sure, that was nothing,' Teresa replied. 'But I see you're here with Patrick Nolan. How do you know him?'

Kate detected a slightly inquisitive tone to the question. 'I barely know him at all, Teresa. He was a friend of Declan's back in Wicklow, and I used to see them together from time to time. But I was only a young girl then and I don't remember him noticing me.' She paused for a moment. 'He did well by us, letting us know about Declan's condition, and I'll not forget that.' Leaning forward, she lowered her voice. 'But I think he's got his eye set on a young Irish woman who's working in this alehouse, or have I got it wrong?'

Teresa glanced at Nolan and then at Kate. 'He's a grand fellow, right enough, and he wants to take me on, and my little girl as well, or so he says. And he's so good with his hands. He's fixed so many things for me and made little toys for the baby, it's a wonder to watch him working.' She looked away. 'But he wants me to go with him back to Ireland. What sort of life would we have there? Certainly, it's not wonderful here, but at least I'm able to work and I've somewhere to live.' She shrugged her shoulders disconsolately. 'I don't know what's the best for us. But I must get on. I'll speak to you later.'

For a moment or two, Kate watched her as she bustled backwards and forwards, bearing aloft great trays of tankards. She felt equally as helpless herself. There was no answer to Teresa's question. It seemed unbelievable that so many Irish people had to leave their country to earn a living, to find somewhere to live, or just to survive. Yet it had to be true, they were all around her in this alehouse. As she pondered over the girl's words, she realised that the tone of the conversation around her had changed. Instead of talking about the plight of the Irish in London, they were now discussing the lot of the people back in Ireland, and what if anything could be done.

Across from her, a young fellow was speaking in a restrained voice, but his eyes were wild with passion.

'We can drive them out of the country for once and for all. The French will help us, possibly the Spanish as well. All we need to do is to rise up together.'

There was a general murmur of support for his comments. Across the table, she noticed another man, older than the others, whose name she recalled as being

James Tandy. He had said very little, and generally only during the gaps in the conversation, as if to rally the others. And he always called upon them by name to speak their views.

Suddenly, she realised what was happening. This was very clever. Without them realising it Tandy was making the others commit themselves to a set of half-formed and ill-conceived ideas. And he was encouraging their support for each other, simply by channelling their widespread general dissatisfaction into a single specific issue. Very clever indeed.

Listening to the others, she glanced sideways at Patrick Nolan, still sitting beside her. 'What are they are talking about, Patrick?' she whispered. 'Who is this man?' But Nolan was concentrating on what the others were discussing, and he put his hand up, as if to get her to keep quiet. Kate, however, was not having any of that. Immediately, she dug her fingers into his arm, until he was forced to respond.

'For God's sake, Kate,' he looked at her with an exasperated expression. 'I'm trying to listen to your man here, about how we could throw the English out of Ireland.'

'So am I,' hissed Kate in return. 'And what he's saying doesn't make much sense to me.'

As she turned back to her tankard of ale, she realised that a hush had fallen over the conversation. Lifting her head, she was taken aback to see that everyone else was staring at her.

'So, Miss Brennan,' the man Tandy spoke slowly. 'So none of this makes sense to you?'

Kate looked again at the faces surrounding her. How

on earth had she got into this? Why could she not have kept her mouth closed, and just sat quietly in her seat and respected her elders and betters, as a young Irish girl should?

Dismissing the thought, she leaned forward and put her hands flat out on the table. For a moment, Patrick Nolan tried to catch her arm but she brushed him off.

'Let me ask you all a question,' she began, as some force inside her took hold. 'How does someone qualify to be Irish?' Looking at the others, she took in the expressions on their faces, some bold, some sullen.

'Do they have to have lived in Ireland? Is that sufficient, or perhaps there is a qualifying period of a number of years residence? Or again, perhaps there has to be five generations of the family living in Ireland? Or is it that they have to be a Catholic? Is that it?'

As she posed the questions, she could see their features changing. Now they were frowning, some were perplexed. But no one was prepared to stop her. 'You've been discussing how to throw the English out of Ireland. Do you really mean the Protestants? Or is it anyone who has an income of more than one hundred pounds in a year?'

Pausing for a moment, she collected her thoughts. How many times had her old teacher forced her over and over again to debate this very point? 'It's not easy to define who is Irish and who is English. We've been bound up with people from this country for over six hundred years, and the Normans before that, and the Vikings before them. When it comes to selecting who can stay and who must go, it's not going to be easy to decide. And who is to be the one who will make that decision?

And if they choose not to leave, will you pick up your swords and your muskets to make them go? And who are you going to turn them against? Perhaps against the Volunteers? Perhaps against you own brothers?'

Kate realised she was spitting out her words and that she was banging the table with her fist at the same time. But, by God, she had their attention. She looked around but no one would catch her eye.

She stood up. At her shoulder, she sensed Patrick Nolan putting out a restraining hand, but again she shrugged him off. On the other side of the group of people, she could see Teresa Ryan looking at her, her hand covering her mouth.

Without waiting, Kate took a deep breath. 'The English Government barely cares a jot about Ireland, and the English people care even less. If you're talking about fighting for equal rights, or the freedom to speak out about injustice, and the right of representation and free trade, and against victimisation and patronage and absentee landlords, then if we stand together throughout Ireland, we can convince the English Government by the force of our argument of the justness of our cause and the need for change.'

Slowly, she looked around the table, letting her words sink in. 'But an elite group of people in Dublin who call themselves Irish monopolises our society, our legal system and our government. Those are the people that we need to change, and the best way to do that is to get the English government on our side. And we will not achieve that if we frighten them by fighting amongst ourselves or by armed uprisings or by allying with the French.'

Suddenly, her knees felt weak as she sat back in her chair, shaking with tension and with the passion of her words. What had possessed her to be so stupid? Around the table, there was barely a sound. Except for one slow handclap. Twisting her head around, she squinted at the figure silhouetted against the lamps. It was James Lavelle! He must have been standing behind her, listening to everything she said.

'So, Miss Brennan. I leave you alone for a few hours and already you're trying to change the course of a glorious revolution.' Coming over towards her, he squeezed her shoulder. 'I see you're every bit as passionate in expressing your views and defending your country as you're in looking after your brother,' he remarked quietly. 'Come with me and let's talk about this away from the others. And in any case you need to be getting back to Mistress Jardine's house.'

Taking her by the hand, he led her out through the door. She felt herself following him, almost obediently. The effort of her unplanned oratory had left her spent.

'Was that your true opinion you were expressing back there, Kate?' he asked as they strolled along Holborn.

'I'm not sure,' she responded blankly. 'I've never given these things much thought before, except in the class at the school. But I've seen and heard so much in the last few weeks that I don't know what to think. And my views probably don't matter much anyway.'

'On the contrary, Kate, it seems to me that what you think might be more important than you realise. You seem to know so many people, some of whom are capable of wielding considerable influence. The people you were belabouring back there, the sans-culottes, they don't have the opportunity to influence anyone.'

For a moment, Kate mulled this over. 'James, I can't take you seriously. A few weeks ago, I spent most of my time up to my ankles in an Irish bog, helping my mother. I don't think that anyone is the slightest bit interested in anything I have to say. Anyway,' she continued, 'enough of this boring talk. Tell me about France, and where you used to live.' And she took his arm in hers, and dragged him along the road.

By the time they arrived at Mistress Jardine's house, it was a much later hour than usual. Outside the gate, it was almost fully dark, and they had barely seen anyone else since turning off the main street. Whatever had got into her earlier in the evening when she had stood up and spoken so forcibly appeared to be still with her. She had found herself teasing and flirting with James all the way back to the house, and although it was late, she did not want to let him go.

Now she was standing in front of him, her face open and smiling, belying the sense of excitement tingling through her body. Drawing her into the darkest shadows, he took her in his arms. This time she reached for him, pulling his head and shoulders down towards her. Now the feeling of wanting was so intense in the pit of her stomach. Taking his face between her hands, she kissed him, softly at first, but then more firmly, as she felt the pressure of his arms and his body increasing around her.

After a few seconds he broke off, gasping for breath. 'Kate, you're driving me mad. You're so beautiful and your kisses are so intense.'

As he spoke, his fingers stroked her cheek tenderly, while his lips burned against her neck.

'I want to make love to you,' he whispered slowly, his hands slipping down to her breasts, so gently, so easily. His touch was incredibly light, yet had the most arousing effect on her body. She could feel her skin glowing as he looked at her, his fingers caressing her nipples through the material of her dress.

'I want to make love to you too, James.' She could not stop the words coming out. She could feel his body, hard against hers, and his hands, massaging her breasts. God, it was incredible. Shyly, she turned her head to one side. 'But I've never made love before to any man. I don't think I even know what to do.'

For a long moment, the Frenchman kissed her fully on the lips. 'Kate, you're such a beauty, and so high-spirited. And a virgin as well! It's really too much for one man to take.'

Putting his arms around her waist, he smiled at her and rubbed her nose. 'But I'm absolutely sure you don't want to lose your virginity in some back alleyway, so I think your honour is safe, at least for tonight, unfortunately.'

Reluctantly, he kissed her cheek. 'Go into the house and dream about us making love. And I'll see you tomorrow.'

All of a sudden, she remembered the planned outing. 'I'll not be there tomorrow. What I mean is, I will be there but I'll have to leave very early. I'm going to the theatre apparently, with Mister and Mistress Jardine.'

Lavelle looked at her closely. 'I thought you were joking about that. Do you mean you're really going up to Drury Lane, all dressed up in fashionable clothes, like one of the gentry?'

'I believe that is the plan,' she replied evenly.

'So where are your principles now, Kate Brennan? In a few hours you'll be spending more in one evening than many Irish families earn in a year, yet not long ago you were talking about standing together and arguing for what is right?' His voice grew cold.

For a moment or two Kate was confused by this change of attitude. But not for long. 'Just stop there, James Lavelle. Don't talk to me like that. I've not put myself forward as some paragon of Irish virtues. I may have told you that I don't know what I'm talking about much of the time, but don't start trying to force your ideals upon me. I'll form my own views, and I'll not have someone else putting words in my mouth.'

Stepping back quickly, she glared furiously at the Frenchman. 'And if that is going to be your attitude towards me, Monsieur Lavelle, then thank you and good night.' Turning abruptly, she marched through the entrance to Mistress Jardine's house without looking back to see his reactions.

A few moments later, she flounced into her bedroom in very high dudgeon indeed. One minute he wants me, she snarled to herself, and the next he wants to tell me what to think. If that was going to be the price of making love, she could see herself remaining a virgin for some time to come.

Then she realised she was pacing up and down the room. This time the absurdity was too much, making her collapse in a fit of giggles. Slipping off her clothes, she washed her face and hands in cold water.

Despite her fine words, it was impossible to get the man out of her mind. His kisses still burned against her skin, while his fingers fondled and teased her breasts. The same knot of desire gripped the pit of her stomach, while the tremor of excitement she had felt when they had talked about making love still coursed through her body. Unsteadily, she walked towards the bed. For a crazy moment, she could feel Lavelle taking her by the hand, with her following obediently, just as she had earlier in the evening when they had left the alehouse.

Taking hold of the bolster, she wrapped her arms around it, hugging it fiercely as she tried to get off to sleep. She tried to think again about the Frenchman, but for some reason now, her thoughts kept coming back to the Lord Chatham, and Teresa Ryan and Patrick Nolan.

Why had she stood up in front of them like that? She had never behaved like that in her life before. And the passion she had felt when she was speaking had been almost more exciting than the feelings she had for James Lavelle. But she had to be right; those people in that alehouse were grasping at ideas that did not make any sense. Thank God they had only Patrick Nolan or perhaps Declan to rally them. Those two would never be able to lead any functioning organisation. That man Tandy was a different matter, but he seemed more of a plotter than a leader.

All night long, she tossed and turned, but she could not get to sleep. Her mind had taken hold of something and would not let go. Maybe someday it would be different. Maybe someday there would be a cause that that everyone across Ireland could identify with. Perhaps then an uprising would work. But surely there had to be other ways worth trying first. God help them all if they found a leader before they found a cause.

There were so many things she still had to learn. About England, about Ireland, about other people, and about men, especially men.

Chapter 6

At breakfast the following morning, Kate had the dubious pleasure of Mistress Jardine's company. As usual, the woman was dressed to the nines, despite the early hour.

'Now, Kate,' she was saying. 'Don't forget to be back here in plenty of time. The performance normally starts at half past six, but tonight it will be an hour later because the weather is so warm. I'm having three different dresses sent over, and you can try them all. And we may have to get Mrs Simpson to take in a few tucks here and there. Then we need to see to our hair and to our faces. That may be five minutes for you, but it needs much more time to make me beautiful.'

With an affectionate gesture, she squeezed Kate's hand. 'Try and be back here for three. That should give us enough time to get ready. I'll see you then.' Without waiting for an answer she flounced out, leaving Kate to her breakfast.

At the hospital, the day passed uneventfully, and it seemed no time at all before she was threading her way through the crowds towards St Thomas Street. As the house came into view, all at once she began to feel distinctly apprehensive. What in God's name had she let herself in for now? Keeping pace with the Mistress was difficult enough, but what was to be made of Mister Jardine? How would he react through the evening? And what about these other people the Mistress had mentioned?

Gritting her teeth in determination, she made her way into the kitchen, where she found Mrs Simpson among the pots and pans.

'Ah, Miss Brennan, I trust you'll enjoy your evening out. Mistress Jardine always makes such a big commotion but everyone generally has a good time.'

'I hope you're right, Mrs Simpson,' Kate fretted. 'But I must confess I'm feeling rather nervous.'

'Don't you worry, Miss Brennan. Reynolds has set out a lovely hot bath for you. That will help you relax, and I've smuggled you up a large brandy. Have that while you're in the bath, and you'll be ready for anything.'

Lying in a warm bath drinking brandy at four o'clock in the afternoon! What a delicious idea, Kate thought to herself.

'And Miss Brennan, the dresses are laid out on the bed. I'll help you if you need anything, but I'm sure that Mistress Jardine will be in, fussing about as usual.'

Upstairs in her room, she found the promised bath, beautifully hot and almost full to the brim. And there, laid out on the bed, were the three fabulous creations awaiting her approval. She inspected each in turn.

Without doubt they were all beautiful and made from the finest materials, but they all had one thing in common. Each possessed no more than the tiniest bodice, with almost nothing to cover her shoulders or her arms, leaving half her chest exposed as well. God in heaven, she muttered desperately, how was she going to wear one of these? And how was she to keep herself decent and covered up? Again, she could feel her nerves fluttering wildly in her stomach.

Beside the bath, she could see an enormous tumbler of brandy. Perhaps a sip of that would calm her nerves. It had a horrible taste, but at least it made her pleasantly warm inside.

A few minutes later, she was lying comfortably in the bath, having finished off the brandy. Soaping herself luxuriously, her mind wandered back to her first experience at the Boultons. She was drifting off nicely into a pleasant daydream, when the door opened noisily behind her.

'Kate, hello, are you there?' It was the Mistress.

She found herself panicking; how could she cover herself up? 'I'm just having my bath, Mistress Jardine,' she called loudly, in the hope that the other woman might leave her enough time to get herself decent. But there was no chance of that. And a moment later she was standing by the side of the bath.

'Ah, that's what I like to see. A bonny, clean-smelling young Irish colleen.'

Fearfully, Kate crossed her legs and covered her breasts with her arms, but the Mistress carried on regardless, pulling over a chair and sitting down beside her.

'Now, Kate, don't forget to do your hair. Once we get

it dried, I'll put it up for you. And I hope you like the dresses I've had sent over.'

Cowering in the bath with embarrassment, Kate tried to keep as much of her body as possible under the water. With some difficulty, she managed to twist her head around to look at the Mistress while she was talking. She was sitting there, as nice as ninepence, in her drawers and with a scrap of material just about restraining her breasts.

'I think I'll be just another few minutes, Mistress Jardine. And I'll wash my hair as well,' she stammered in a small voice.

'Fine, fine, Kate, while you're doing that I'll go and refill our brandy glasses. I see yours is empty.'

As soon as she had gone, Kate leaped out of the bath, dried herself furiously, and slipped into a huge nightgown. By the time the woman had returned, she was sitting on the chair beside the bed, brushing her hair.

'Here you are, a little snifter to put us into a fine mood for this evening.'

Kate continued to brush her hair, saying nothing. But she could see the other woman out of the corner of her eye, watching her movements.

'You really do have beautiful hair, Kate,' she declared suddenly.

'Thank you, Mistress Jardine,' she replied, 'but I fear it's getting too long. I'll need to have it all cut off soon.'

'I think it's wonderful as it is. All you need are a few more combs and pins to tie it and hold it in place. Here, let me do it for you.'

Before she could protest, the hairbrush had been snatched from her hand and her hair gathered up and arranged into position. Although not unpleasant, it felt strange having someone else tending to her hair. No one had ever done that before except her mother, and that was years previously. But Mistress Jardine was obviously enjoying the task, scrutinising her efforts from a variety of angles before fixing the arrangement with an assortment of clips and pins.

For a moment or two, she was standing directly in front, intent on what she was doing. As she leaned forward, Kate could feel her senses being assaulted by a cloud of perfume. It was a powerful, heady scent, almost compelling her to lie back and close her eyes, letting it drift over her. With the brandy still warm inside, and the touch of the other woman's fingers in her hair, it was very pleasant indeed sitting there.

'Right,' the Mistress announced gaily, 'I've finished. Look at yourself in the glass and tell me what you think.'

Standing up a little unsteadily, Kate inspected her reflection. At least her facial expression appeared normal, she noticed thankfully. But her hair was wonderful, framing her face, yet exposing her ears and her neck and shoulders.

'Mistress Jardine, it looks marvellous. You must have a skill for this sort of thing.'

'It's nothing,' the other woman was obviously delighted. 'I'm glad you like it. I'm off to get myself dressed and you must do the same – we've no more than an hour to get ready. I'll be back to inspect you at six.'

Turning to the dresses, Kate set about trying to find the one she could cope best with wearing. None of them did much to cover her chest, but one fitted her particularly nicely, and had shoulders and huge frills on the sleeves. Apprehensively, she looked at herself in the glass. Staring back at her was someone she did not recognise. In part, it was because the dress was so closely fitted that it showed off the line of her body, in stark contrast to her own clothes which were so voluminous that it was impossible to detect any sort of shape underneath.

Twirling this way and that, she was examining her reflection when the Mistress returned.

'Why, Kate, you've been transformed! Every man in London will swoon at your feet tonight.'

Turning her head, she glanced at the Mistress, who was dressed in her finest and dripping with jewellery.

'I think, Mistress Jardine, that if I can get through it all without swooning myself I'll be more than happy.'

With a flick of her head, the woman dismissed her doubts immediately. 'Look at this, I've brought over a necklace for you to wear, and some nice shoes with heels, which should make us about the same height. And here's a shawl to drape over your shoulders.'

Side by side, they stood together in front of the glass. 'Now Kate, shoulders back and chest out, and stand up as straight as you can. God, what a fine pair we make,' she exclaimed. 'With any luck they'll think us to be sisters. Let's have a toast before we leave the house.'

Immediately, she produced another two brandies. 'Here's to us!' she shouted, throwing the neat spirit down her throat. 'Here's to us,' Kate echoed weakly.

After that send-off, the evening disappeared into a haze of half-remembered experiences. First of all, she had to cope with the carriage and sitting with Mister Jardine. All day long she had been worrying about his presence, but his mood could not have been more different to that

155

she had seen previously. He was outgoing and charming, giving the impression of being as pleased as punch to have two fine ladies on his arm. Then there was the theatre itself. Drury Lane was sheer bedlam, with hordes of people seemingly determined to force their way through the doors. Outside, hawkers and traders were shouting and screaming, as they each tried to outdo the other in selling their wares. For some reason which she could not fathom, oranges were being sold on every corner, with no shortage of buyers, and so many people had sticks in their hands, and cushions under their arms.

Despite the crowds, Mister Jardine managed to obtain entry to the building through a heavily protected side door. Once inside, Kate was totally unprepared for what she found. It was like a huge amphitheatre, illuminated by thousands of candles, with seats and boxes rising steeply on three sides surrounding the stage. Every nook and cranny appeared to be crammed with people, most of whom were banging their sticks against the floor or the nearest wall. With the noise levels at such an intensity, they were forced to shout at each other to make themselves heard. Down below, the musicians huddled together in a pit in front of the stage, while the audience amused themselves by lobbing the occasional orange in their direction.

As she stood with the others in Mister Jardine's box above and to one side of the stage, she silently thanked God for not having been thrust into the tumult that surrounded them. Beside her, Mistress Jardine was in her element, chatting and shrieking continuously, and forever bringing over yet another young man to be introduced. After a while, and another few brandies, all the men began to look the same. At first, she had been sorely embarrassed by the variety of bold looks she had received and by the number of men who were clearly leering down the front of her dress. However, it was some consolation to observe that the Mistress was receiving the same treatment, the difference being that she was revelling in the attention and the proximity of so many men.

During the performance itself, she began by trying to pay attention so she could perhaps understand what the play was about. Mistress Jardine had told her that the famous actress, Sarah Siddons, would be taking one of the leading parts, and she wanted to see what she looked like. Unfortunately, there was so much interplay between the audience and the cast, with great shouts and cheers every few minutes, huge bursts of laughter, and so much whistling and catcalling that she found it too difficult to keep track. Even while the play was being performed, there were continuous comings and goings and movements in the crowd. Mister Jardine's box was no better, with a variety of people constantly arriving, being introduced, and then moving on elsewhere.

During all the hubbub, the Mistress found a moment alone with Kate.

'How are you enjoying this experience, Kate? Isn't it exciting? It's the same every Mayday. There are always crowds celebrating everywhere. Have you ever seen so many people dressed in such finery? And I was right – every man wants to know who you are. You could dine out in London for the next year on the invitations you'll receive after tonight.'

Kate shuddered at the prospect. 'I can't understand

that, Mistress Jardine; there seems to be no shortage of beautiful women around. Everywhere I look I'm dazzled by their appearance, not to mention the colours of their dresses and their jewels and perfumes.'

'What you have to realise is that not all these ladies are like us. Many of them are women of the night, and the men are all aware of that.'

Kate frowned. Women of the night? What on earth was she talking about? And ladies like us? If only the men who were being introduced were more interesting; if only they were more like James. She had to see him again. Why in the name of God had she shouted at him? If he did not come round to the hospital to meet her, how would she find him? If only he were here now, she would be able to enjoy it all so much more.

For a moment, she looked out of the corner of her eye at Mister Jardine standing beside her. He seemed to be taking an intense pride in showing her off, even outdoing the Mistress from time to time in the number of introductions being made. Despite that, his presence was reassuring. Whatever the noise levels, he continued to speak in the same low commanding voice that Kate was familiar with, and no matter the crowds and the shouts and the screams, he did not have any problems being heard. At the same time his powerful and domineering appearance was a rock that no other man would want to go up against. Sitting by his side was probably the safest place to be.

Perhaps that was what he really wanted from a wife, Kate decided. A woman who would stay by his side; a beautiful lady that he could show off. Mistress Jardine was anything but that – beautiful certainly, and a poised and confident woman, she was clearly enjoying herself meeting and greeting people. Despite England being such a strange country in some ways, the two of them made such an unusual pairing, never mind being a world away from her parents.

Before she realised what had happened, the play had finished and their party had left the theatre, eventually finding their way round to some rooms nearby, where she was delighted to see food being laid out on buffet tables for their enjoyment. Almost dizzy from hunger and the effect of the brandy, the food gave her the excuse to eat rather than drink, at least for a few minutes. The last thing she wanted to do was faint or fall over, especially in a borrowed dress, and make a complete fool of herself in front of all of London.

The next thing she knew, a group of musicians had struck up, and various men and women started dancing in a manner completely unlike anything she had ever experienced. Terrified that she might have to get involved, she hid behind the figure of Mister Jardine, who was standing foursquare beside one of the buffet tables. But she could not conceal herself for long, as one after another the young men who had been introduced earlier came and searched her out.

The first few dances were easily the worst moments of her life, as she tried to hang on to her shawl, her shoes and her dignity, and somehow keep up with her partners, all of whom seemed to be incredibly energetic. It was all so different to the Irish dancing she was familiar with. She was accustomed to a more formal approach, where partners rarely touched, and much of the dancing was individually performed. Now a succession of young men were clutching her around the waist, grabbing at her hands, and gloating at her breasts. For some moments she thought she would not be able to cope, but then she remembered the Mistress's words earlier that evening: 'shoulders back and chest out'. If they were going to leer at her, then by God, they were going to get an eyeful. They would not forget the night they danced with Kathleen Brennan.

However, the spirit was stronger than the flesh, and after a series of particularly energetic turns around the floor, she began to feel herself flagging. Without warning, the huge shape of Mister Jardine loomed into view, blocking himself between her and her latest partner.

'Miss Brennan, I've come to rescue you,' his deep voice boomed out across the room.

Immediately, she felt herself being swept up in his grip, her feet almost lifted from the floor.

'Thank you, Mister Jardine,' she heard herself gasping in a small voice. 'I was beginning to think that these men were trying to exhaust me.'

For one amazing moment, his face broke into a smile. 'Mistress Jardine has the best description for them. She likens them to a set of bagpipes – they never make a noise till their bellies are full.'

There was nothing she could say to that, except to marvel at him chuckling away to himself, his great body shaking with good humour. After a few more minutes in his fierce grip, he directed her over to the side of the room where his wife was standing, shaking her head in appreciation.

'Kate Brennan, you're a wonder, I don't know how you do it. You've managed to dance all these men to a standstill, yet you still look cool and composed. Look at me, I'm so hot and bothered.'

Kate looked closely at the woman's appearance. What was she talking about? As far as could be seen, she still looked absolutely stunning, with barely a hair out of place. On the other hand, perhaps this really meant she was thinking of leaving, or could be persuaded to leave if she were to think she was not quite looking her best.

'For sure, Mistress Jardine, it's very warm in here, and not good for the complexion.' Kate looked sideways to see how she was taking this. 'Perhaps a breath of evening air on our way back to Connaught House would refresh us?'

'That's such a good idea, Kate. In any event you've conquered half the young men of London by now. I couldn't bear to see you captivate all my devotees in one evening and leave me friendless for ever after. Come, let us depart.'

Briefly, she glanced in her husband's direction. 'Are you happy with that, my darling?'

'Whatever you say, madam,' Mister Jardine replied. 'I'm ready when you are.'

As their carriage set off towards to Bloomsbury, Kate lay back on the cushions and let out a huge sigh of relief. How had she managed to get through that night? It was such a pleasure not to have to worry any longer about tripping over her skirts, or keeping her hair in position, or making sure that her breasts were still contained within the bodice of her dress. Every man she had danced with seemed determined to shake them loose from their restraining material. But she had coped with that and everything else so far. And she could not remember spilling anything on the dress, or tearing it in any way.

Stretching out luxuriously, she found herself copying the Mistress's sitting position, lounging back against the carriage cushions with her legs splayed apart and her skirts drawn up to let the cool night air play around her knees. Without a doubt, this was the way for a lady to travel.

Looking over at the other woman, she giggled with the sheer pleasure of it all. Immediately, Mistress Jardine returned her glance with an uproarious laugh of her own. All the way back to St Thomas' Street they carried on, neither one nor the other able to stop giggling and laughing, while Mister Jardine looked on in bafflement at such idiotic behaviour. What had happened to the two fine ladies he had set off with earlier that evening?

A little later, as she was getting ready for bed, her thoughts drifted over the events of the evening. At first, all she could remember was how much fun it had been. But then she kept seeing the figure of James Lavelle, his voice ringing in her ears, asking her again and again whether she was satisfied with her night's work. All at once, she could see Teresa Ryan in her mind's eye, working her fingers to the bone every day, trying to earn enough to keep herself and her baby out of the poorhouse. For sure, Teresa would never experience the excitement of going up to Drury Lane, or dancing the night away with the idle rich.

And then there were those people she had been abusing in the alehouse. Was it any wonder that they felt the way they did? They had no work, no money, no education, no future. The devil always dances in an empty pocket, that was for sure, and all they were doing was striking out blindly in the only way they knew how. How could she come into their lives for a moment or two and lecture them on what they should be doing, about what was right and what was wrong?

Why did she always have to be opening her mouth? What must James be thinking of her now? And Teresa, and Patrick, and the others?

Slipping to her knees by the side of the bed to say her prayers, she begged God to help her be more considerate to the other people around her. But no matter how hard she tried, she kept stumbling over her words, until she was almost in tears with frustration. How could she feel so good one minute, and then so desperate the next?

The next day was a deeply painful experience. This time it was not mental agonies or an over-indulgence in strong drink to blame. On the contrary, her head was fine and her complexion clear, but every muscle in her body was protesting at her efforts at dancing the previous evening. As she walked along Holborn, she realised for the first time just how much physical effort it took to navigate her way through the crowds of people, never mind avoiding the horses and the piles of dung and refuse at the sides of the road.

It was a blessed relief to be able to sit down at the hospital and rest her aching body. Even speaking was painful; it must have been all the shouting to make herself heard. But that was her finished. No more drinking, no more wild dancing. How did Mistress Jardine keep up that sort of life? And how did she always look so well? And did she never feel tired in the middle of the day?

Lost in thought, Kate sat half dozing in the chair. From time to time she managed to waken up and chat a little to her brother, but then she would drift off again. Late in the afternoon, she was sitting back comfortably with her eyes closed when she sensed the shadow or the presence of somebody else standing over her. Opening her eyes lazily, she jumped to her feet with shock, letting out a shriek at the same time. It was Lavelle, half-sitting on the edge of the bed.

'My God, James,' she gasped. 'You really frightened me. Where did you spring from?'

The Frenchman rewarded her with his most dazzling smile. 'My beautiful Kate, forgive me, I didn't mean to scare you. But you looked so peaceful sitting there, with your eyes closed, and your breast rising and falling so prettily.'

'I swear, James, you could have been an Irishman, you have so much blarney. But it's nice to see you. I wasn't sure whether I would again after the other night.'

Lavelle waved his arm with a flourish. 'I've forgotten about that already. But tell me, how is your brother keeping?'

Kate glanced at the figure on the bed, resting comfortably under a blanket. 'He's almost fully recovered. He still gets a little tired and sleeps a lot, but every day he's getting much better.'

'I see,' replied Lavelle thoughtfully. 'So that means you'll be leaving here soon?'

This was an awkward question. How was she going to answer?

'I think it does, James,' she spoke in a small voice. 'I

have to. I promised I would stay here only until Declan had recovered – and he wants to go back to Ireland. I have to go back, James.'

'Does that mean that we'll never see each other again, Kate?' He put his hand out and touched her cheek.

'James, please. This is very difficult for me. I don't want that to happen but I don't have any other answer.'

Slowly, he edged closer to her. 'And what you said the other evening, that you wanted to make love to me. Do you still feel the same way?'

'Oh James, please.' All of her aches and pains were forgotten, but she could not look at him directly. She turned her head to one side. 'Of course I do, James,' she whispered, so quietly that he had to lean forward to hear the words.

With a hint of a smile, he ruffled his fingers through her hair. 'It's a lovely thought, Kate Brennan, but I don't know where we could be alone.'

Turning her head carefully, she studied his expression. All at once, the temptation was overwhelming. 'I know where we can go, James.' She had spoken before the thought and the words had formed in her head.

Glancing over her shoulder, she studied her brother's features. 'He's sleeping peacefully. I think I can leave him safely for the evening. The Sisters will come round to lock the door and they'll keep an eye on him.'

Taking him by the arm, she looked at Lavelle from under her eyelashes. 'If we leave here now, James, we can walk back to Connaught House. I know a place where we can go.'

It was almost six in the evening when they arrived back at St Thomas' Street. Her mind seemed detached, as if she was floating gently above her body. She could see herself, walking along the street with the Frenchman beside her, holding his hand while he whispered in her ear. It was a strangely light-headed feeling, mixed with excitement, anticipation, even apprehension. They were going to make love! Everything she had thought about, the doubts and fears, the concerns about her body, everything was centred on this moment.

She was still moving automatically as she rang the bell for Mrs Simpson to open the gate.

'You go round the side, James,' she instructed him, now she had worked out her plan. 'Mister and Mistress Jardine have a dinner engagement this evening and Reynolds will be with them in the carriage. I'll go into the garden to read for a few hours, and I'll open the side gate. You can slip in and we can go into the summer house.'

For a moment, Lavelle gazed at her with an admiring expression on his face. 'You have planned this, Kate Brennan. You must have been thinking about it for some time.'

Trying not to let her excitement show, she smiled shyly. 'On you go, quickly. Here comes Mrs Simpson.'

It took no more than a few minutes to get a book from the library and make a show of going into the garden to read in the late afternoon sun. Sliding the bolts on the gate and letting James slip through was easy. Seconds later, they were facing each other in the front room of the summer house. Kate had been there only once before, but it was still the same, furnished in the modern style that Mistress Jardine favoured, with a long low table and several stuffed armchairs and a large couch.

Wondering what would happen next, she stood uncertainly, the book clutched in her hands. Reaching out, he took one step towards her and she fell into his arms, the book slipping between her fingers and dropping to the floor.

His kisses were so sweet, so intense, so beautiful. He was so close, so tender, so gentle, but at the same time so firm. Closing her eyes, she let his presence sweep over her. She sensed him turning her round until he was standing behind her, while she pressed her back and her bottom against his body. His lips and his tongue were searching out her neck and her shoulders, while all the time he kept whispering softly in her ear. It was so beautiful that it was almost agonising. Slowly his fingers picked with the fastenings of her dress. She could feel him slowly working his way down, undoing each button one after another from her neck to her waist. Her dress slipped easily off her shoulders and down over her arms, as she felt his lips burning into her skin. Inside, she could feel a knot of desire spreading through her stomach and into her chest; her breasts and her nipples seemed to be pushing against the material of her bodice. Carefully, Lavelle eased her bodice off her shoulders and down across her stomach. God almighty, he was going to touch her bare breasts.

'Oh Kate, you're so wonderfully beautiful,' she heard him whispering, as his lips brushed her neck again. Gently, he tantalised her nipples with his fingers, fondling her breasts in the palms of her hands. It was an exquisite sensation. Slowly, his hand slipped across her stomach and under the waistband of her petticoats.

'Oh God, please God,' she heard someone whimper,

unable to recognise the sound of her own voice. Fearfully, she squeezed her thighs together.

'Kate, my little baby,' she heard him speaking softly in her ear, 'don't be so tense. Lean back against me, and let your legs relax. Just move your thighs apart a little, that's a good girl, so my hand can slip in between.'

Oh heavens, he was going to touch her between her legs. Obedient to his every command, her legs parted slightly. By now, her whole body was trembling as his hand slid gently across her belly. The shock and the pleasure was unbelievable as his fingers caressed her and the urge to twist round and take him in her arms was almost overwhelming, as his kisses captivated her lips and his fingers worked their magic against her body.

'James, James, please make love to me,' she heard herself whispering. Beside herself with tension, she felt his hand on her shoulders motioning her towards the couch. And then she heard it. A voice, far away in the distance.

'Kate, Kate, are you there?' It had to be some sort of dream. It could not be real. But it was.

'Kate, where are you?' The voice was closer now. My God, it was Mistress Jardine. What was she doing here? She was not due back for hours.

She wrenched herself out of Lavelle's embrace.

'James, it's the Mistress. What on earth is she doing here? Listen to me, she can't find us here like this.'

As she was speaking, she was pulling her bodice and her dress up over her shoulders as fast as she could.

'Quickly, fasten me up at the back. And keep out of sight, for God's sake. I'll find out what she wants and get her back into the house. You go back out through the gate ;

before Reynolds finds you and I'll bolt it up later. Hurry up, go now!'

She looked over her shoulder at Lavelle, concentrating furiously on trying to do up her dress. The situation was just so ridiculous she could not stop herself from giggling. Even James found her merriment infectious, and before long he was laughing too. This had been her big moment. She had been all ready. She had planned it, everything was going so beautifully, and now this. At least she had got her dress fastened up .

'I'm here, Mistress Jardine,' she called as loudly as she could. 'I was reading and I must have fallen asleep.'

Turning to the Frenchman, she kissed him swiftly on the lips. 'Don't linger here, James. As soon as we're out of sight, go out through the side door. I'll see you tomorrow. Maybe we'll be able to try again.' With a saucy look, she picked up the book and rushed out of the door.

'Aha, Kate, there you are.' The Mistress had almost reached the summer house. Kate had waylaid her just in time.

'Mistress Jardine, I was not expecting to see you. I thought you had a dinner engagement this evening.' As smoothly as she could, Kate took the other woman's arm and led her back towards the house. Please God, she prayed fervently, make sure that James has fastened everything up properly, and that she did not look too dishevelled. And while he was at it, please make her body stop trembling. How close had they been to being discovered? The thought was too terrifying to even contemplate.

'It was a very early evening engagement. I didn't

really want to go, especially because I was so tired after last night. But I had to be there because it involved business for my husband. Such are the trials of being a wife.' Despite her words, Kate observed, the Mistress did not look particularly put out.

But she was continuing onto another topic of conversation. 'Do you remember what I said to you last night, Kate? That you had conquered half of London? Well, I was right, you know. All day long messengers have been arriving at the house, presenting the cards of their masters.'

For a moment, Kate was nonplussed. 'I'm sorry, Mistress Jardine, I don't know what you mean.'

'Kate, these are the men you were introduced to last night. Now they're sending you their cards with invitations to all manner of events. Let's go and look through them and I'll show you what I mean.'

As they made their way into the house, Kate crossed her fingers and prayed fervently. Please God, make sure that James has managed to get out without being discovered. Gritting her teeth, she followed the woman through the hall. But it was no use. It would not be possible to relax until she had seen the side gate locked and barred.

'Could you get hold of the cards, Mistress Jardine?' she asked quickly. 'I need to dash back to the summer house. I think I've left a book behind that I was reading. It will take me no more than a moment.'

Without waiting for an answer, she rushed back down the garden path. Thank God, James appeared to have gone. With a struggle she succeeded in swinging the gate closed and forcing the bolts into position. The sense of pure, unadulterated relief was unbelievable. If she was ever going to try and make love again, it was going to be in a place where there was no chance whatsoever of being disturbed. She could not possibly go through all that performance a second time. But as she remembered the expression on James's face when they had heard the Mistress's voice, it was impossible to stop giggling. How could they have been so stupid?

Feeling much better, she strolled back to the house, ready for whatever else the Mistress was preparing to put her through.

'In here, Kate, I'm in the drawing room.' Sure enough, the older woman had her usual glass of brandy close to hand, and was sifting through a small pile of cards. There must have been about fifteen to twenty in the pile.

'Look at this, Kate. "Mister Sanderson sends his compliments and requests the company of Miss Kathleen Brenann.' Look, he's spelt your name wrong. Throw him out. He's a very weedy young man in any case. Look, here's another one. "The Honourable Mister Trevelyan sends his compliments and is delighted to invite Miss Kathleen Brennan to a fete in the gardens of his country house.' And here's one from someone whose name I don't recognise.'

Picking up the card, Kate looked at it idly. 'I remember him,' she exclaimed. 'He was the very small man who insisted on dancing with me.'

'I recall him now,' the Mistress replied thoughtfully. 'I saw you having a long conversation with a veritable shrimp of a young gentleman, while the entire company stood looking on with their mouths hanging open.'

Again, Kate could hardly speak for laughing. 'He was

indeed a very small man – probably the only one in that place who could not see down the front of my dress. Mind you, that did not deter him from trying. He might be little but he is extremely lively, and he's a better way with words than even a Kerryman, that's for sure.' This time it was Mistress Jardine's turn to laugh.

'William Wilberforce,' Kate announced as she scanned the card in her hand. 'He told me he's about to take up a position as a Member of Parliament. Mind you, we had a terrible argument when we first spoke and I said I was from Ireland, and somehow I got to talking about the plight of the people in the country.'

Mistress Jardine frowned slightly. 'But why should that cause an argument?'

Kate smiled ruefully. 'He didn't believe I could know anything of these things, what with being dressed like a lady and dancing the night away at the most fashionable establishment in London.' She pressed her lips together firmly as her mind went back to the previous evening. 'I had to correct him there, but I think I left him in no doubt about my background or how I came to be here. He seemed to accept that, and then became marvellously interested in everything I had to say about Wicklow and the rest of the country.'

'Are you sure, Kate?' giggled Mistress Jardine. 'Was it really the Irish who had caught his interest, or was it standing next to you? Look, there's so many other cards to read! I told you, you'll have to stay here and drive all these men mad with passion.'

For the next hour, the two women had great enjoyment reading through the cards while Kate heard all about her suitors' shortcomings. It was difficult to resist the temptation to join the Mistress at the brandy, but she managed to restrict herself to one glass. Despite the promises, it was so easy to slip back into bad habits. But it was clear from Mistress Jardine's demeanour that the evening could easily develop into a session, and she was determined to resist that at all costs.

In any event, she had to explain her plans for going back to Ireland. 'Mistress Jardine,' she swallowed nervously, not sure how to begin. 'As you know, my brother is almost fully recovered, thank God. By that, I mean he'll have to leave the sanatorium in the next few days. They need the bed for other people who are really ill.'

As she was speaking, the Mistress stopped riffling through the cards. Without looking at Kate she asked the dreaded question. 'And what does that mean? Are you saying you're planning to go back to Ireland?'

Kate swallowed again. 'I must, Mistress Jardine. I've promised my parents, and your cousin Mistress Delamere. I've told them I'll be returning when Declan is well again. I have to look after Mistress Delamere's children, and they'll be missing their lessons.'

'Why can't she send them to boarding school like everyone else, and then you could stay here?' The woman turned with a mournful expression on her face.

Putting on her best smile, Kate shook her head. 'She'll be doing that soon enough, but not till next year or the year after. They're still too young, and in any event Mistress Delamere wants them to learn something about Ireland as well. That's why I need to be there.'

The Mistress took Kate's hands in hers. 'And then what will you do? Come back to London?'

'I've not given any thought to coming back here. Mistress Delamere knows half the people in Dublin, and there are many with small children. If everything goes well with what I'm doing, then I hope she'll provide me with references that will help me find another position.'

Without replying, Mistress Jardine stood up and walked over to the sideboard to find another decanter of brandy. She tried to pour it out but her hand was shaking so much that the liquid kept spilling.

'Here, let me help you.' Kate jumped up and took the glass out of her hands before she dropped it.

But the woman caught her roughly by the arm. 'And does that mean, Kathleen Brennan, that we'll not be seeing you again in London?'

'It's impossible to be sure about anything, but it seems most unlikely to me,' she replied quietly.

'And what if I gave you some references? I know more than half the people in London. You could easily find a position here.'

Pausing for a moment, Kate turned away slightly. 'Mistress Jardine, this visit to London, and to England for that matter, has been the most extraordinary experience of my life. I've seen so much and learned so much in such a short time. And you've been so generous I can hardly believe it. But I don't think that I could live in London, while I still had a choice. When I was coming here, a man called O'Brien drove me up to Dublin, and he was telling me how much he enjoyed the Wicklow rain in his face and the wind in his hair. I thought he was simply getting old, but now I know what he meant.'

Bending over, she pulled up her skirts a little. 'Mistress Jardine, when I go back they'll think I've become English in my speaking and my manners. I'll have to steep my feet in a peat bog for about a week to find my Irish accent again.'

At last, the woman smiled faintly. Thank God for that, Kate thought. It had begun to get difficult for a moment or two, and she had not been sure she was going to get away. What an evening. Almost making love to James Lavelle and now trying to comfort a woman who appeared to be really unhappy at her going. If this is what the Mistress was like, what would happen with James when she had to leave? For a moment, she felt unable to cope with the thought of all these emotions.

Although the Mistress was unusually quiet, Kate could see her watching every movement over the rim of her glass.

Without realising what she was doing, Kate reached forward and took the glass from the other woman's hand and put it down on the sideboard. Impulsively, she put out her arms and the Mistress fell forward into her embrace. God, she had to be very careful – she seemed to have become extremely vulnerable. Kate felt the Mistress clinging to her, her tears wet against her cheek.

'There, there,' Kate whispered. 'It's not as bad as that. We'll see each other again, I'm positive about that. And you can always come to Dublin. I'm sure your cousin would be delighted to see you.'

Very slowly, she moved her hands to the Mistress's shoulders, and pushed her gently away.

'Kate, I don't know what you'll be thinking of me, crying like this. It's just that it's been so much fun having you here, and I've enjoyed your company so much.' She wiped the tears away from her eyes and laughed a little.

'At least you'll have some good memories of London. But it looks like we have to put all of that behind us. In that case, I expect we must talk about how you're going to travel, so I can make the arrangements.'

Kate sighed heavily with relief. For a few minutes she had scarcely been able to breathe, but now the Mistress seemed back in control of herself again. Discussing her departure was always going to be difficult, but at last she could concentrate on what had to be done to organise the journey. And now that she could relax, perhaps she could be tempted by one more small brandy.

Chapter 7

———◆———

Remarkable as it seemed, Declan had reached the stage where he was fully capable of getting up and moving about without assistance. Although he still tired easily, it was obvious that it was almost time for him to leave. For sure, somebody more unfortunate needed his place more than him.

Sitting beside the bed, Kate was watching him absentmindedly while he stretched his legs. At the same time she was going over the arrangements in her head for the journey back to Wicklow. Without warning, Patrick Nolan walked in, carrying a baby girl and accompanied by Teresa Ryan.

'God almighty, Patrick, I can't believe it,' Declan shouted from the other side of the room. 'I need to get back into bed before my legs buckle under me with shock.'

'I think it's a grand sight indeed,' Kate countered with a smile. 'A fine example of domestic bliss, right enough.'

Patrick Nolan smiled ruefully and put his arm around Teresa's shoulders. 'The woman has worked her scheming way with me. She's forced me to take her on, and her child, and all her personal possessions, which, by the way, amount to absolutely nothing.' He looked tenderly at the woman by his side. 'But I'm completely beside myself with happiness. I never thought such a fine girl would ever fall in love with me, and agree to be my wife.'

Appreciatively, Kate clapped her hands. 'It's a grand thing to see, right enough. But does this mean you'll be staying here, or are you going back to Ireland?'

Nolan glanced again at the woman beside him. 'I think we're going to be staying here. I'd never find enough work in Ireland to keep those two going. Have you ever seen how much they eat?' They all laughed. For a fleeting moment, Kate could see Cathal standing beside her, telling her how much he loved her. The image was so intense, so bittersweet, that she had to close her eyes and indulge herself for a few seconds. She could almost reach out and touch him. Shaking her head, she pushed the thought to the back of her mind. That was then, this was now.

With an effort, she forced herself to concentrate on what Teresa was saying.

'I'll be back in a few minutes. I'd like to find Sister Mary Francis and say hello. That'll be a nice shock for her, seeing me here.'

As Nolan stood awkwardly by the bed, holding the little girl in his arms, Kate jumped up out of her chair. 'Here, Patrick,' she begged, 'let me hold her for a few minutes.'

Stretching out her arms, she took hold of the little girl and started rocking her to and fro. At the same time, she scrutinised the man under her lowered eyelids. This was a big commitment for him to take, she mused quietly to herself, especially as he did not appear to like being in London very much. But it seemed to be the only place where they could make enough money to keep body and soul together. Very slowly, an idea began to form in her head.

'Patrick, tell me now, I want to ask you something.' But the man was muttering something to Declan and was not paying her much interest. 'Patrick, would you ever listen to me? Have you heard of a man called James Watt?'

For some reason, that did catch his attention. He looked over at her. 'Yes, I've heard something about him. He's working on making these steam engines that they say are going to be used to drive carriages and the like without using horses. But what would you understand about anything like that?'

'Never mind about me,' Kate replied testily. 'And tell me, do you know anything about these engines as you call them?'

'I've seen some drawings, and I suppose I understand some of the principles of how they operate. But there's too much science involved for me. And these are strange questions you're asking me, Kate Brennan. You're an unusual woman sometimes, you've got so many sides to your character it's difficult to keep up. I'm sure you're going to make some poor man miserable one day.'

Kate laughed. 'Don't be trying any of your Irish blarney on me, I'm well up to that, thank you very much.

179

But back to these engines. Forget the science, do you think you could learn how to make all the parts that are involved, or how to assemble them all?'

'For God's sake, Kate, what are you driving at? How should I know? I think I could cope with the assembly, but I'm not sure about the techniques involved in the making of the parts. It's not something we get much experience of in Ireland, don't forget.'

She could see him studying her in exasperation. 'The reason why I ask, Patrick, is because I've met a Mister Boulton who lives a fair way north of here, near a place called Birmingham, and he's involved in the making of these steam engines. And I think that Mister Delamere over at Enniskerry might be involved as well. They employ a number of Irish people as labourers, but most of those who oversee the work are Scottish. But if I wrote a letter of introduction he might be interested in an Irishman who could read and write, and who knew something about the engines he's trying to build.'

By now, Patrick Nolan was hanging on to her every word. 'Are you suggesting that there might be work to be found with this Mister Boulton, not a labouring job, and that you might have some influence with him?' He looked across the room, his disbelief all too apparent on his face.

'You've just asked me one more question than I can answer, Patrick. But I'll write to my Mister Boulton, and if he has any work available I'll ask him to send a reply back to Sister Mary Francis here at the hospital. That's the best I can say, I can't promise anything.'

Slightly uncomfortable that she had raised the subject in the first place, she looked down at the baby in her arms. 'But enough of that, tell me this little one's name.'

Nolan looked at her pensively for a moment. 'You're a deep one, right enough. It's not what I expected from a skinny little girl from Kilcarra village.'

He shook his head again. 'The baby is called Marie. I'm not the father, as I'm sure you know, all that happened long before I knew Teresa. But she's a beautiful little girl, right enough, and I'm really fond of her.'

For a few minutes Kate paraded up and down, humming an old Irish lullaby and rocking the baby in her arms. From the other side of the room, Nolan continued to watch her, a knowing smile on his face.

'I don't think, Kate, that you had better let James Lavelle see you holding a baby like that.'

She raised one eyebrow in a question. 'Why is that, Patrick? Do you think he doesn't like children?'

'I'm sure he doesn't,' the man declared. 'And I see you're getting very friendly with him. You'll probably not like me for saying this, but be very careful. I said before that he's a silvery-tongued Frenchman, and that's indeed what he is. He's infatuated many girls in his time, broken their hearts, and then left them behind.'

Kate snorted, almost frightening the baby. 'Is that what you think I am, Patrick Nolan? Do you think that I'm infatuated with this man, that I'm just a starry-eyed, innocent young Irish girl, lovestruck at the sight of a fine French gentleman? Is that what you think?'

The man put his hands out to placate her. 'Kate, please don't start shouting at me again. It's none of my business, I'm sure. But do you know who James Lavelle is? What he's doing here in London?'

She gave him a fierce glare. 'We've not talked much about such matters.'

'Perhaps, Kate, if you don't mind me saying so, perhaps you should. The reason James Lavelle is here is because he's a recruiting officer for the Irish Brigade in the French army. Nearly one million Irishmen have given their lives fighting for the French over the last hundred years or so. Lavelle is here to make sure the supply continues.'

Impulsively, she opened her mouth to reply but Nolan put his hand up. 'Just to finish off, he's also a key contact with the French government who would support almost any kind of uprising in Ireland, whether it has any chance of success or not, just to harass the English.'

For a few moments Kate stood motionless, the baby held tightly in her arms, while she tried to grasp the implications of Nolan's words.

'I'm sorry to have said all this, Kate. Perhaps I shouldn't have spoken about it at all. But Teresa and I talked about it this morning and we decided we had to tell you.'

As he finished speaking, Kate looked up and studied him thoughtfully. To be truthful, his words came as no real surprise. She had suspected something like this all along. After all, what was a Frenchman like Lavelle doing in London? He had to be there for a reason, but she had chosen not to think about it. Perhaps Nolan was right, perhaps she was infatuated with the man, perhaps she was not prepared to see anything but the elegant, slightly exotic side of James Lavelle. But what did Nolan care?

'So you and Teresa Ryan are discussing me behind my back, is that it?' she demanded abruptly, trying to cover her confusion.

'Kate, this is clearly a sensitive subject for you, but whether you like it or not, the answer to your question is yes. And not just your relationship with James Lavelle. We've talked about other things as well. What really gave Teresa and me great heart was the way you stood up in the Lord Chatham the other night and spoke out in front of all those people. No one has suggested before that there might be any other way forward except by violence. And as for me, I felt I was being forced to go back to Ireland to fight for something which I didn't really understand. But I'd have lost any chance I had with Teresa if I'd done that. Now I've made the choice, and we'll build a life for ourselves here. But whatever happens, if you find the people who can do what you've said needs to be done, then you can be sure that you'll have our support.'

He stopped, almost out of breath, looking sheepishly at the floor.

Kate was impressed. In the past, she had rarely heard him say more than a dozen words at a time, and suddenly he comes out with this speech. What he was attempting to say was not particularly clear and his logic seemed awry in places, but for sure it sounded as if it had come from the heart.

Smiling broadly, she tried to take the awkwardness out of the moment. 'I don't know whether to take all that as a compliment or not, Patrick. But it's good to know that somebody is looking out for me. Now take your baby back, and go and find Teresa. I know she should be starting work soon and she'll not want to be late. You'll probably find that Sister Mary Francis is giving her a lecture on the pitfalls of taking up with an Irishman in London.'

As Nolan disappeared, Kate looked over at her brother to see how he was faring through all this. He had climbed back into bed, but now he was lying back on the pillows, eyeing her suspiciously.

'What have you been up to, Kate Brennan, while I've been lying here in a sick bed? I heard most of that conversation there and I'm not sure that I understand it. And I'm not sure that I care for it much either.'

Pulling the blanket up to his chin, she pushed him back on the bed. 'Don't get excited, Declan, you'll make yourself ill again. Nothing unusual is happening, except that your little baby sister has grown a lot older, and has started to get thoughts of her own in her head. And come on now, would you expect anything else from the daughter of Mrs Brennan of Kilcarra?'

Without waiting for an answer, she turned down the edge of the blanket and tucked it in around the bed. 'Just you lie there and get a little rest after all that excitement. I'll find us something to eat – I'll be back in half an hour or so.'

On her way out, Kate went round to find Sister Mary Francis, who she found sitting in her little cubby-hole with her head in her hands. Even though she knocked as gently as she could on the table, the woman jumped up with a start.

'Kate Brennan, I didn't realise you were there.'

'I'm sorry to disturb you, Sister,' Kate began. 'But I wanted to let you know that we're planning to leave in three days from now. My brother Declan is well enough by now, and Mistress Jardine, is making the arrangements for us to travel up to Liverpool on the mail coach.'

The sister stood up. 'We'll be sorry to see you go. You've been a great tonic for the patients and the other sisters. And your adventures in London have been truly amazing, by all accounts.'

Kate looked quizzically at the sister for a few moments. Had somebody been telling her about James Lavelle? Or perhaps they had been talking about her down at the alehouse? She shrugged her shoulders. Who could tell? It seemed that she could barely put a foot outside the door here in London without someone noticing it.

'I'll come and say goodbye to everyone before we leave, Sister Mary Francis. And once again, thanks for everything you've done for us.' As she turned to go, she hesitated for a moment. 'I couldn't help noticing, Sister, but you weren't looking very happy when I came in. Is everything all right? Are you feeling ill?'

The sister sighed. 'When is everything all right when you're engaged in work like this? I'm fine, but I've let myself get a little depressed. Every day is a struggle here to make ends meet. And seeing you leaving to go back to Ireland doesn't help.' She looked up and smiled. 'I'll have to say a few more prayers to God, that's all, Kate. I'm sure he'll help me to keep going.'

Later in the afternoon, Kate sat reflecting on the sister's words. Since the moment she had spoken to James Lavelle about making love, she had not been able to say any prayers at all. After listening to Sister Mary Francis, all she felt now was a profound sense of guilt. For a moment she thought about going down on her knees, but she knew it would be impossible. If Lavelle were to walk through the door she would be flirting with him, teasing him, hugging and kissing him within minutes. Whatever it was, infatuation, love or whatever, somehow it had to be kept separate from her thoughts about God, otherwise the guilt would become too much to take.

And what if James were suddenly to appear? Would he want her, or would he think it too much trouble? Had that been her high moment of passion or would she be ready to try again? Her thoughts drifted back to the few minutes they had spent in the summer house together. All she could remember was the intensity of the feeling, and the sheer unadulterated excitement of his presence. Every sense in her body had been taken to a new height. She could smell the scent of his skin, hear every whisper, feel every caress. It had been beautiful, but thinking about it now, it had been so frightening.

What would he have done if they had not been disturbed? Would he have taken off all her clothes? And then what? And what would have happened after it was all over? God, if they had not been disturbed, she would not be a virgin today. How would that feel? Would she be any different? Would she have been able to speak to Sister Mary Francis? It did not bear thinking about.

Suddenly, Kate realised that it was almost time for her to go. She stood up and had a quick look outside in case James was standing in the street, but there was no sign of him. What a pity, she had been so looking forward to seeing him again. But at least the problem of what she would do if she saw him did not have to be resolved today. Never mind, she consoled herself, he would probably be around tomorrow. Picking up her belongings, she made sure her brother was comfortable before setting off back to St Thomas' Street and Connaught House.

The next few days were a strange mixture. On the one hand, there was the frenzy of excitement as the letters were written and sent off to Mr Flynn in Liverpool and to Mistress Delamere in Enniskerry. On the other, the time was dragging on interminably now that the decision to leave had been taken.

Kate had thought she might have to keep out of Mistress Jardine's presence, to avoid any more emotional scenes. But the woman seemed a lot happier now that Kate's mind was made up. James Lavelle, however, was still a problem. Or more so his non-appearance. Almost continuously, she found herself daydreaming, where she and the Frenchman would be talking together, or walking along by the sea, hugging and kissing. Sometimes her dreams were so intrusive that she found it difficult to concentrate on what other people were saying. She was so desperate to see him again. What on earth was he doing? Why was he not coming round to see her? He knew she was leaving soon, surely he must come to say goodbye at least.

Perhaps Patrick Nolan was right after all. Perhaps Lavelle was simply a fly-by-night, with a string of girls on his arm at the same time. She was probably another one in the queue. The best thing to do would be to forget him, get back to Wicklow, and concentrate on her work with Mistress Delamere's children. She was only nineteen and didn't have to fill her head with stupid thoughts about men at her age.

Giving herself a shake, she looked round to see how her brother was faring. It was amazing how well Declan was looking now – and so difficult to believe he was the same man she had found a few weeks previously. Shuddering quietly, she remembered how she had found him, huddled under the sheets, looking like a bag of skin and bones. What was less encouraging was how animated he had become in his manner of speaking, much as he had been in the cottage back in Wicklow.

'I'm telling you, my little sister,' he began as soon as he saw her looking at him, 'the world is changing. The order of things is going to be different. Look at what's happening in North America. Samuel Adams and Thomas Jefferson are leading the way. Have you heard about Lexington and Bunker Hill? It's a revolution, I'm telling you. The Sons of Liberty and the Minutemen are throwing the British out. They're going to claim that country for their own, don't you understand?'

'Calm yourself,' Kate hissed at him. 'You'll be giving yourself palpitations if you keep on, not to mention disturbing all these other poor people around us.'

'But there's so much going on and I'm lying here in a sick bed. Look at France, for God's sake. It's in turmoil over there – the old order is being overthrown. And think what it must have been like when John Paul Jones sailed into Dublin Bay and sank that English ship. God almighty, what a day that must have been. I'm telling you, our opportunity will come and we must be ready – even if it means taking up the sword and shield. That's the only language they understand in London.' He gasped for breath, but only for a moment. 'And we know that whatever happens, the French will come to our aid if they think there's any chance whatsoever of defeating the British. There's even French soldiers helping in North America right now. And here, in England, they almost caused an overthrow just thirty years ago.' He looked at her fiercely, but Kate pushed him back down on the bed.

'I told you to calm down. If you bring on a coughing fit, it will set you back.' Now was not the time to get into a debate with him about how to cure the ills of Ireland. 'You've got to be ready to leave in a day or two, so don't be straining yourself,' she pleaded. Eventually, he lay back on the bed, still too weak to resist her for long.

As she watched him drifting off into sleep, her attention was caught by what sounded like men shouting. The noise appeared to be coming from outside. Getting out of her chair, she walked across the room to see what was happening. Tentatively she reached out to grasp the handle, when the door was thrown open violently in her face. Jumping back in fright, she was confronted by two men, one staggering under the weight of the other.

'Help me,' one of them called hoarsely. Without thinking, she rushed towards him, catching hold of the man who was being supported. Instantly, she was horrified by the stain across his chest and the scarlet mess under his arm. As she reached out, the two men stumbled against her, saturating the sleeve of her dress with the injured man's blood.

'Hold him up,' she screamed. 'Let's get him through the door, there's a table in a room nearby that we can lay him on. That will have to do, there are no empty beds here.'

Forcing the door open with her shoulder, she dragged the semi-conscious man towards the table, while his companion tried to hold him upright. Desperately, she attempted to manhandle him into position, acutely aware of his breath against her cheek, and the soft rhythmic moaning sound in his throat.

As they got him up on the table, the other man staggered backwards. Without looking round, Kate tried to see the extent of the wound, ripping at his shirt and swabbing away the blood.

'What has happened here?' she demanded.

'He's taken a ball in the shoulder,' the other man croaked. 'He's been in a duel and been hit.'

By now, she could see the raw edges of the wound. 'The ball will need to come out,' she snapped. 'Otherwise he'll die. And he may die anyway.' Turning abruptly, she glared at the man leaning against the wall. 'There's no one here who can do that. You'll have to find a surgeon or else you'll have to remove it yourself.'

The man shuddered. 'I can't. I'm sorry but I can't even look at a wound. I'll faint myself if I have to. Please, there must be someone here who can take the ball out.'

Her temper boiled over. 'Are you completely useless?' she shouted in his face. 'There's no surgeon here, this is not a hospital, this is a place where the Sisters of Jerusalem tend to the poor and the sick and the dying.'

Kate thought furiously. 'Do you have a knife in your possession?'

The man nodded dumbly. Reaching inside his coat, he pulled out a long slim blade.

Impatiently, she snatched it from his hand. 'Right, that will have to do. Now, what I need you to get for me – what's your name?'

The words came out in a gabble. 'My name is Henry,

the man on the table is called Edward,' he managed to say.

'Right, Mister Henry,' she snapped. 'You're going to have to get up off your backside and help me, or else your friend Edward will die.'

'What do you want me to do?' he asked meekly.

'First of all, get me a candle,' she ordered. Peering at the wounded man's shoulder, she pressed gently around the edges of the wound. Beneath her fingers, she felt his body jerk involuntarily, while beads of perspiration stood out against his brow.

To her inexperienced eye, he seemed to be far gone. Studying his face, she could see his skin drawn tightly across his cheekbones, a deathly pallor behind the tanned features. His hair was jet-black but loose, not drawn back in the fashionable bow style. Without thinking, she brushed it back from his forehead. His flesh was cold and clammy to the touch. Wiping her hands on her dress, she looked across the room. All of a sudden, she realised she had forgotten the other man, who was still waiting to be told what to do next. How did she know what to do next?

'Get the candle,' she ordered. 'And I also need whiskey, or gin.'

He looked at her helplessly. 'Whiskey? In God's name, woman, where will I get that in a place like this?'

Again, she thought hard. 'I know where. You get the candle and I'll be back in a moment or two.'

Instantly, she rushed back into the sanatorium. She knew where she was going – her brother. Sick or not, and despite her best efforts, he was sure to have whiskey or poteen hidden somewhere. As she reached his bed, he was still sleeping. Immediately, she caught him around the shoulders and shook him awake.

'Declan! I need some whiskey! I know you've got some here somewhere. Where is it?'

Her brother was thrust into wakefulness. 'What is it, whiskey? What do you want whiskey for? I've no whiskey here.'

But Kate was in no mood to argue, pulling at the covers and the sheets. 'I know you've got some here,' she shouted.

Pushing with all her strength, she forced him to roll over. While he tried to resist, he was still too weak, and right now Kate seemed to have the strength of five women. Frantically, she threw the bedclothes to one side. Behind the pillow she found it, another flat stoneware bottle like the one she had smashed previously. Despite her vigilance, Nolan had managed to smuggle some in. Perhaps this time it was just as well.

Snatching the bottle, she pulled out the stopper. As she put her nose to the brim, the smell reminded her of her father; this was the 'medicine' he had given her when she was young, to ease the pain when she had a toothache. With a shriek of triumph, she ran between the beds with the bottle, Declan's curses ringing in her ears.

By this time, the other man had returned with the candle, but he was hanging back, unable to stomach the sight of the blood.

'Get that candle lit,' she shouted. In one glance, she could see the wounded man's body trembling uncontrollably. If he was to be saved, whatever was necessary had to be done quickly. Wiping the blood from his shoulder with another scrap torn from his shirt, she took a deep breath, and splashed half the poteen into the wound. Gasping in agony, his body arched violently above the table. Somehow she pushed him back, forcing the rest of the contents of the bottle between his lips, calling to his companion to hold him down.

With the other man unable to look, she picked the knife up carefully by the handle, brushed her hand across her brow, and thrust the gleaming steel into the wounded man's flesh. In a trance of concentration, she turned the point of the blade into his shoulder. Suddenly she felt the ball. Pressing lightly on the edges of the wound with her left hand, she manoeuvred the lead weight to the surface with the tip of the knife. She could hardly bear to listen to his cries of agony, but she had to get the task finished, no matter what.

'Henry, look,' she cried triumphantly. 'We have it. See it here, I've managed to get it out.'

'Do whatever you have to do,' the man gasped. 'I can't watch any of this.'

'For God's sake, pull yourself together,' she shouted in reply. 'Give me the candle.' With the blood seeping from the wound and the perspiration running into her eyes, she could scarcely see what she was doing. Gently, she wiped his shoulder with the back of her arm. Sighing heavily, the man slumped against the table, slipping into unconsciousness.

Out of the corner of her eye, she noticed Henry placing the lighted candle by her side. For a moment, she held the blade to the flame.

'My God,' he whispered. 'What are you going to do next?'

'I have to stop the bleeding,' she replied matter-of-factly. 'The ball is out, so he will not die from that. But I must stop him bleeding to death.'

Suddenly, she felt a strange calmness settling over her, as if her actions were being guided by some unseen force. Carefully, she turned the blade of the knife over in the flame, contemplating the injured man sprawled across the rough wooden surface. He was older than she had first thought, she realised now. Even in the poor light, she could see clearly the lines on his forehead and around the sides of his eyes, as if he laughed a lot. Please God, she prayed for the umpteenth time, please God don't let him die.

Gritting her teeth, she extracted the blade from the candle flame. Without hesitation, she pressed it, hissing and spitting, against the wounded man's shoulder. He screamed once, and she heard a clatter. It was his companion, collapsing in a faint on the floor.

Still, she held the scalding hot knife to the wound. A moment or two passed before she realised that the blood had stopped and that the man was deathly still. All of a sudden, the enormity of what she had done struck home. Gripping the edge of the table with one hand, she pressed the other to her mouth, trying to stop the bile rising in her throat. Overwhelmed by the sequence of events, her legs began to buckle as she fell back against the wall.

'What is going on here?' a voice boomed out, cutting through the tension in the room. 'I demand to know what is happening!'

Kate shook her head. Was she dreaming? Looking up, she stared blindly into the outraged face of Sister Mary Francis.

'Sister, please,' she wailed, 'I think I've just killed a man. I didn't mean to do it.' As her inner strength ebbed away, she fell to her knees on the floor.

'Please God, forgive me, I didn't know what I was doing.' Her tears were hot, stinging her eyes.

Perplexed, the sister looked around, at the tear-stained girl, her dress saturated in blood, at the man lying on the table with a severe wound in his chest and another collapsed on the floor.

'Aye, that's some sight, right enough,' she declared firmly. 'Let's take a look at this fellow you've killed.' Putting her ear to his chest, she inspected the wounded man closely. 'I think, Kate, that he has a little more strength than you give him credit for. He looks to me as if he'll live for a bit longer yet. But how about this other one on the floor? I'm not so sure about him,' she chortled briefly.

Turning, she looked at Kate. 'My God, child, you're in a sorry state. Look at you, covered in blood, and tears and red eyes. Come on, up you get. It looks to me as if you might have saved his life rather than killed him. With any luck this man will pull through, and the other will come to presently.'

Sure enough, Henry stirred and slowly struggled to his feet. Holding his head in his hands, he tried to recognise his surroundings. 'What happened?' he asked. 'Is it all over?'

'Yes, it's finished,' Sister Mary Francis replied. 'Your companion's life has been saved, at least for the moment, that's for sure.'

Leaning against the table, Henry looked down at his injured friend. 'It's a miracle. All we can do is thank God for delivering him.'

'Not at all, young man. It's true that God must be thanked, but so should this young girl here. Thank her,' the sister declared.

He looked around at Kate on the other side of the room. 'We'll never forget the service you've given us this day.' Unable to reply, she stood with her back pressed against the wall.

Brushing himself down, Henry carried on. 'I'll need to find a horse and carriage to take Edward back to his house. I'll return as soon as I can.' He turned to the sister. 'Please look after him just a little longer.' With that he slipped out of the door and was gone.

Sister Mary Francis took Kate by the hand. 'You poor child. What have you been through? And look at your clothes. You must change out of that dress so it can be washed.'

'I've nothing else to wear, Sister,' she whispered dully.

'Then we'll get you something from one of the other sisters, while we get you cleaned up.' With a quick glance, she gestured at the man lying unconscious on the makeshift bed. 'Leave him and come with me. I'll make sure his shoulder is washed and bandaged.'

Kate was still in a trance as they found an old sister's habit about the right size. Wearing this, and slowly rubbing her dress clean in a bath of cold water, she felt herself slowly coming back to reality. All of a sudden, she realised she had forgotten about her brother. By this time, he would be convinced she had deserted him.

Sure enough, he was in a grumpy mood. 'What's been happening here today? And why are you dressed like that?' he began by complaining. 'You've been disturbing me, stealing my whiskey. I hope you had a good reason for that.'

'I had reason enough,' she replied quietly. 'A man was

dying and I felt I had to do something to help save his life.'

'What could you do?' her brother scoffed. 'And he was probably an Englishman.'

'He was simply a man,' she replied, a little more strongly. 'I didn't have time to spend in idle chatter, or to find out his full name, never mind his country.' Suddenly weary of the conversation, she stood up. 'You have some rest now, Declan, I'll see you're not disturbed. Later on I'll be back with something to eat.'

Kissing him on the forehead before he could object, she tiptoed across to the other end of the room. By now it was starting to get dark. Making her way back to the room where the injured man lay, she saw that the sisters had bandaged his shoulder and covered him with a blanket.

It was strange, she mused to herself, he was clearly much older than her, yet he had a boyish look to him when he was sleeping. As she watched, he stirred restlessly in his sleep. Unable to resist the temptation, she crept across the room.

'Please get well,' she whispered. 'I didn't mean to put you through so much pain.' For a moment, she stroked his brow with the back of her fingers. Without realising it, she began to hear words and a melody in her head, a song she had not heard for years, a song her mother had sung to help her fall asleep. She could hear herself whispering softly, in time with the rhythm of his breathing. The urge to take him in her arms and cradle him was almost overwhelming.

'I think he's going to survive,' a quiet voice beside her murmured. It was Sister Mary Francis. 'But you have to get some sleep yourself. You look exhausted, and it's too late to go to Mistress Jardine's house. One of the Sisters will look out for him through the night. If there's any change in his condition, we'll call you.'

Standing up slowly, Kate grasped the other woman's hand. Until now, she had not realised how tired she was.

'It was a fine thing you did here today, Kate. Not many other people could have done that. This man here owes you his life.'

'I just did what I could. All I'm hoping for now is that Declan will be well enough to travel back to Wicklow.'

The sister mused over this for a few seconds. 'I think you might find Wicklow a mighty dull place after all this, Kate Brennan. However, we shall see. Now be off with you and get yourself some sleep.'

Shortly before dawn, a sharp tug on her arm roused her from an uncomfortable slumber.

'What is it?' she cried, suddenly wide awake. 'Is it Declan – is something wrong with him?'

It was one of the sisters she did not recognise. 'No, no, Declan's fine,' the woman replied evenly. 'He's been eating like a horse and sleeping soundly all night. No, it's the man with the wounded shoulder – he's becoming very restless.'

Kate sat bolt upright. The man with the wounded shoulder? Suddenly she remembered the events of the previous evening. 'Is he all right? Is he awake?' She clutched at the other woman's arm for support.

'I don't know,' replied the sister. 'He was fine for two or three hours but now I think a fever is taking him over.'

Without thinking, Kate jumped up from the chair, almost tripping over. She had completely forgotten she was still wearing the sister's habit.

'I'm not sure I can cope with this. One minute it's the pistol ball, the next it's the fever. Do you think that God is listening to all my prayers for his health and his soul?' she enquired.

'You know better than that, Kate,' the other woman replied. 'God is watching over us at all times. But I'd go quickly to him all the same. I think he may be in some pain.'

When she got to the makeshift bed, she was shocked by what she saw. The wounded man's body was obviously being rocked by paroxysms of pain, his brow was feverishly hot, and his skin was beaded with perspiration.

Ripping another piece from his tattered shirt, she ran outside and dipped the cloth in a rainwater barrel. Gently, she mopped his brow with the cooling fluid. Over a period of an hour he began to calm down, falling back slowly into a more restful slumber.

As she leaned across the bed, she realised he was still wearing the same clothes, even the shoes, that he had been wearing the previous day. But now they were saturated in blood and perspiration. It also went through her mind that he might have wet himself or soiled himself with the stress and the agonies of the day before. She found herself thinking of her father – how would he feel if he awakened to a situation like this? She had to find a way of keeping the man's dignity but keeping him clean as well.

In a rush, she dashed back to her brother's bed. 'Good morning, Declan, are you keeping well?'

'Yes, I think I'm feeling fine this morning,' her brother

replied drowsily. 'I'm looking forward now to leaving, but I'm more than ready for breakfast first.'

'Sorry, but you may have to look after yourself for a few hours,' Kate insisted firmly. 'And I want that nightgown you have under your pillow.'

'For God's sake, woman, what are you playing at now?' he cursed her.

'Just give me the nightgown.' Before he could protest any further, she snatched it out of his reach.

By now the wounded man was in a deep sleep, breathing regularly, lying flat on his back. Tiptoeing up to the side of the bed, she slipped her hands under the blanket and unbuckled his shoes. They came off easily enough. What next, she thought. Pulling the blanket down gently, she looked at the torn shirt and the bandages that the other sisters had applied. The garment was in such a state that it was not difficult to remove it altogether. Fearful that one of the sisters might come up quietly from behind and surprise her, she looked around, but no one else was to be seen. With some effort she managed to get the nightgown over his head and down across his chest. As she pulled at the flannel, it was difficult not to marvel at his skin, so brown, and the black curls of hair on his chest. Her father, her brother, even Cathal, they were all heavy, fleshy-bodied. This man was different. He was tall, for sure, with good shoulders, and his body was strong, but lean, tight, muscular. She tried to stop herself – but somehow her hand slipped into the hollow of his stomach. It was smooth, flat, hard. As she touched his skin, he moved slightly, murmuring in his sleep. All of a sudden, it was becoming impossible to breathe. Help me, God, she prayed, please stop me doing this. Her hands had never caressed a man's chest before, not even with Cathal or James, and certainly not like this.

Somehow, she managed to concentrate. Now she had the nightgown over the top half of his body. But what about the breeches? They had to come off, for sure. But would she be able for it? With her hands trembling she unbuckled the fastenings at his waist and at his knees. Taking one more deep breath, she slipped one hand under his back, and in one mad rush levered all his lower garments down round his knees and off over his feet.

Then he was naked in front of her. She could see his legs and thighs, strong and muscular. But her eyes were drawn to his stomach, to his belly. The black hair on his chest curled down across his stomach and into his groin. For a moment she followed the shape of his body with her eyes before forcing herself to turn her head away. But the sight of his body, his chest, his stomach, his legs, his manhood, seared deeply into her brain.

Pulling the nightgown quickly down around his body, she straightened up, breathing deeply. Her thoughts went back to her mother, far away, a thousand years ago it seemed, telling her about a woman's ways, something she had not really understood back then. Her mother had told her about men and women making love, about how a man's body could thrust its way into a woman's, about fathering babies. But she had never paid much attention; truth to tell, she had been too young and she had not really been listening. The thought had occurred to her for a moment when she had been with James, but the excitement had been too intense to spend much time thinking about where her actions might lead.

But now, as she looked down at this man's face, as she

stroked his brow, as she brushed his hair back, she could not tear her mind away from the memory of his naked body, so close to her, so easy to touch.

'God, please help me,' she muttered under her breath. 'I want to help him but I'm afraid of myself.'

Forcefully, she banged her fist down against the surface of the table. What was wrong with her? What kind of thoughts were these? It was not so very long ago that she had decided not to have anything more to do with men, and to go back to Wicklow and concentrate on her work.

Pushing these thoughts to the back of her mind, she busied herself arranging his gown and tucking the blanket around him. He needed to be left in peace for a while, she decided, as she glanced up to take one last look at his face.

Kate clutched at her chest in astonishment. His eyes were open, clear, blue and steady, and he was watching her, and half-smiling too, it seemed. He started to speak but it came out as a croak. Desperately, she ran to fetch a glass of water, and lifting his head with one hand, poured it gently between his lips.

'Ah, that's much better,' he ventured, his voice low and husky. 'And you're certainly a fine sight to greet a man's eye first thing in the morning. Or is it afternoon?' As he finished speaking, he pushed against the table as if to get up. 'Christ,' he swore as the pain racked through his body. 'What in the name of thunder has happened to me? Or am I dead already and reached another place?' He looked at her squarely. 'Tell me, Sister, where am I?'

'I'm not a sister,' she replied. 'I was here looking after my brother, when you and your companion fell through the door, with you bleeding badly from that shoulder which is now giving you so much pain.'

'I wish it was just the shoulder,' he grunted. 'Although that's bad enough. I feel painful all over.' He peered more closely at her. 'I don't think I've ever seen a sister before without her veil covering her head and half her face.' He paused. 'I never knew they were so beautiful.'

Kate blushed furiously. 'I told you I'm not a sister,' she insisted. 'I've had to borrow these clothes. My name is Kate and I just happened to be here when you staggered in.'

'Kate, is it? And you're Irish. That explains the beautiful green eyes and the wonderful smile.'

Kate longed for a clever response to this but she could not think of one. Instead, for some reason she felt more tongue-tied than anything else. How stupid it was not to be unable to speak to him sensibly.

'Now it's all starting to come back. I remember the duel, and being hit, and then I think I remember talking to my friend Henry. My God,' he exclaimed, looking down at himself. 'Where are my clothes? What am I wearing?'

At last she was able to speak. 'It's my brother's nightgown you have on. Your clothes are on that chair over there. They were wet and covered in blood, and they had to come off so you could sleep.'

'Who took them off?' He looked at her suspiciously.

This time Kate could not prevent herself from giggling. 'I'm not sure that matters. You were in no fit state to know, anyway,' she replied.

'Well, it's not much of a body, but it's the only one I have,' the man grumbled. 'I think you have the advantage of me. What else do you know?' his eyes narrowed, but his smile gave him away.

Feeling slightly more comfortable, Kate managed to laugh. 'I know something of what you look like, but it was dark and I kept my eyes averted.' You liar, she thought. 'I also know your name to be Edward, but I know nothing else.'

'I'll warrant he is a soldier,' a voice boomed out behind her, making her jump. 'He has the mark of the military about him.' It was Sister Mary Francis.

'I see you're awake,' she stated flatly to the man. Bending over, she looked closely at his face. 'And how are you feeling?' Without waiting for any answer, she went on. 'I hope you're better, for you'll have to leave. I can't have any soldiers here, taking up space that poor people could make better use of.'

She dared him to reply, but he kept silent, preferring to look over her shoulder at Kate standing in the background.

'And what have you put this young girl through over the last twenty-four hours? She's saved your life, that one. She got the ball out of your shoulder, and stopped the bleeding. And all the time that friend of yours was incapable of giving any help,' she spat out the words. 'I want to see you gone by this evening. I'll be round again later to make sure. But now I have some real work to do.' And she bustled off.

Edward looked hard at Kate. Again, she felt the numbing sensation deep in the pit of her stomach. For a moment she could feel him looking right inside her mind.

'So, this is my introduction to the beautiful Kate, masquerading as a Sister of Mercy, stripping off men's clothes when they are helpless, and in between times hacking their bodies around like a bloody surgeon.' He shook his head and lay back. 'And now I'm indebted to you for my life. It's all too much for me. I have to rest some more before I can take it all in.' He closed his eyes.

Stepping forward towards him, again she almost tripped over the nun's habit she was still wearing. Before anything else happened, she reminded herself, she had to change back into her dress. As she bent over the bed and gazed at his face, she realised he had already fallen asleep.

'Rest yourself and get well,' she said under her breath. An insane desire to kiss him on the forehead almost overwhelmed her. But somehow she resisted, tearing herself away.

A few minutes later, she found Declan awake and in fine form. 'Yes,' he said to her. 'They've been telling me all about you. I'm sure we'll never hear the end of this story when we get back to Ireland.'

What a relief, she thought immediately. At least he had got over his grumpiness. One thing was certain, however, she had better not tell him it was an English soldier who had been wounded. That would cause no end of trouble, particularly when they got back home. Declan knew so many mysterious people in Wicklow, and she had her suspicions about what he would be doing when he got back there. He seemed obsessed with the idea that somehow they could force the English to leave, but his arguments always seemed so simple-minded. Anyway, at least he appeared well enough to travel.

'Kate, I'm really hungry,' he was complaining. Suddenly, she realised that she had eaten nothing for almost twenty-four hours. Her brother might be hungry, but she was ravenous.

'All right, I'll go and get some bread and soup,' she decided. 'Contain yourself for an hour or so and I'll be back with breakfast.'

Making up her mind quickly, she decided to go to the usual place where the bread was not stale and the soup was more than cabbage water. But first she had to change back into her old dress. For a moment, as she placed the sister's habit down on the bed where she had slept, she took the material between her fingers and wondered about the life of a nun. Could she do something like that? Could she give her life to God and helping other people the way these nursing sisters did? What they were doing seemed so noble, so worthwhile. Then her mind went back to the excitement she had experienced being with James, and her thoughts when she was undressing the man Edward, and the pleasure she had taken from touching his body. My God, how could she even think of being a nun? The way her mind was working, she was almost certainly bound for hell already.

Somehow or other, though, that prospect did not seem to worry her too much, particularly after all she had been through in the last few days. Again, she shook her head. Where were these thoughts coming from? With an effort, she forced her mind back to the present. Food and drink, these were the main priorities, and then a place on the mail coach to Liverpool.

A short time later, she was sitting alongside her brother, having got breakfast for both of them. He was regaling her with tales of his adventures in London before he was taken sick. After fifteen minutes of this, however, she found her mind beginning to wander.

'Declan, stories about you drinking gin all night long and getting dead drunk and singing songs about Irish sailors don't interest me, especially at this time of the day. Have you nothing more interesting to talk about?'

'Well, if you must know,' he replied, 'your man Edward was taken away while you were out. They came and took him in a big carriage.'

Immediately, she felt herself panicking. 'What? Did nobody stop them till I returned? Who knows about this?'

'The sisters know all about it,' Declan replied quietly. 'They told me.'

Without another word, she rushed off to find Sister Mary Francis. 'Sister, they've taken away the man I was tending, is it true?' She gasped, trying to catch her breath.

'Kate, my girl, take hold of yourself. They came when you were out. The man Henry brought a fine carriage with three or four footmen and servants and a surgeon. I don't think they needed a young girl from Wicklow to help them.'

'But what did he say? Did he leave any message?'

The sister took her by the hand. 'He was almost unconscious when they took him away. But Henry asked if you were here. He's left this for you.' It was a leather purse with some gold coins inside. Briefly, she glanced at it before hurling it down on the floor. 'I'm not interested in money,' she cried. 'Did you find out his name?'

'I'm sorry, Kate, I don't know his name. But Henry said he would be eternally grateful to you. I told him to remember Kathleen Brennan from County Wicklow, but I don't know whether he heard me above the noise of the horses.'

As the tears rolled slowly down her cheeks, the feeling of despair was almost overwhelming. 'How could he leave me without saying goodbye?' she whimpered, her face racked with misery. Seeing her plight, the sister was filled with compassion and took her in her arms.

'Kate, you saved him, for sure. But to these people, you're only a child. And you're not from their society. You'll learn that there are huge gulfs between you and them. They'll forget all about you – you have to forget about him too.'

By now, Kate could taste the salt on her lips. How could this woman speak to her like this? Did she not understand anything? This man had been in her thoughts ever since he had been carried into the hospital. Tearing herself away, she walked slowly across to the other side of the room.

'I'm sorry, Sister,' she said flatly. 'I've disgraced myself in front of you. My brother Declan and I will be leaving tomorrow for Liverpool, and a passage back to Ireland. Thank you for all your kindness, and forgive me for all my recklessness.'

'Kate, don't be so unhappy. You've uplifted everybody here by your example and your good spirits. We won't forget you. But you've got a long way to travel. Go with God and journey safely. Write to us from Wicklow, tell us about the life there. It will help us pass some time away from the tedium and despair here in London.'

'I promise I will, Sister Mary Francis,' she whispered, wiping away her tears. For a moment, she looked at the other woman, before turning and walking back to where her brother was waiting.

'Come and visit us when you're back in London,' the

sister called, as Kate trudged between the beds. The words echoed strangely. What was the woman talking about? When would she ever have another opportunity to travel to England?

Chapter 8

Around five o'clock in the evening, Kate said farewell to her brother, arranging to meet him early the next morning. Mister Jardine's carriage was going to transport them to Cheapside where they would be taking the mail coach north, and she wanted to make sure he would be ready when they arrived at the sanatorium.

On her way back, she decided to stop in at the Lord Chatham to say farewell to Teresa Ryan and Patrick Nolan if he was there. All the way through Grays Inn, she kept her eyes open on the off-chance she might encounter James Lavelle, but he was nowhere to be seen. Without doubt, she was going to be leaving without seeing him again. Truth to tell, she could not make up her mind whether that was a good or a bad thing. The excitement of the summerhouse was still fresh in her memory, but it seemed to have lost the edge it had previously.

Strangely enough, the departure of the man Edward from the hospital had left a much deeper impact. Every detail of the night's event stood out in absolute clarity. His leaving without saying good-bye had left her totally numb, but the thought of never seeing him again was even worse – certainly enough to set off the panic in her chest and the constrictions in her throat.

With a heavy heart, she pushed her way into the Lord Chatham. It was still early, and there were no more than a few people in the alehouse. Thankfully, Teresa was standing at the bar, talking with one or two customers. As soon as she saw Kate coming in, she came over in her direction.

'How are you?' she asked immediately. 'I heard about what happened last night after we left. What you did was unbelievable. They tell me that man was going to die for sure.'

Dumbly, Kate nodded her head in reply.

'Are you all right?' Teresa asked, her voice filled with concern. 'You don't look too well to me. Come over here into this corner and sit down for a moment.' Teresa led her to a quiet table out of sight of most of the other customers.

'Physically, I feel fine,' Kate began. 'Although I'm a bit tired after yesterday. But it's my head that's giving me the problems. You know I have been meeting James Lavelle a few times? Well, I've not seen him for four days now and we're leaving tomorrow and I'm never going to see him again. And then that man last night. They came and took him away from the hospital when I wasn't there, and now I'm never going to see him again either.' Without warning, she burst into tears.

Immediately, the other woman reached out her hand. 'Go on, have a good cry,' she insisted. 'It will do you good. I don't know how you've put up with all the strain of the last few weeks, and living in that house as well.'

'Oh, it's not that, Teresa,' Kate sobbed through her tears. 'I don't know what it is. One minute I feel fine and I know what I'm doing, and then the next I fear that I'm making a fool of myself.'

'That's probably because you've been trying to do too much. Don't forget this is still a strange place to you, with strange people.' Teresa took her hands and stroked them 'Sit here a moment, and I'll get you a small brandy. That'll make you feel better.'

Teresa came back with the glass and Kate took a sip. It tasted awful. 'Is this what you sell in this place? It's absolutely disgusting. I'll never complain about Mistress Jardine's brandy again.'

The bar girl put her hands out and smiled. 'This is what happens when you stay with the gentry: you get the taste for expensive things. It's probably the finest French brandy you're drinking at Mistress Jardine's. That's definitely not what you get in here.'

But drinking the neat spirit and talking to the lively girl was beginning to make her feel better. 'Listen, Teresa,' she replied finally, 'I had better get over to Connaught House and you need to be getting back to work. I hope we can meet again someday, and I wish you and Patrick and Marie all the best in the future. If it was not for him, my brother might not be still alive today.'

Impulsively, she stood up and threw her arms around the other girl, giving her a hug. By this time, Teresa had started crying as well. 'Please God, Kate, have a safe journey, and write me a letter from Wicklow.' She turned as if to pull herself away.

'There's something I have to tell you before you go.

It's about James Lavelle. I didn't know this, Patrick told me about it. You've not seen him for three or four days, I know that. And you'll not see him before you leave. The day after the last time you saw him, he had two visitors from France, and the three left almost immediately.'

Kate dried her eyes and looked sharply at the other girl. 'Where did they go to? Do you know?'

'Yes I do,' Teresa hesitated. 'They went to Ireland. God knows what business they'll be up to there. And I wouldn't tell that brother of yours if I were you, or he'll be wanting to join them.'

All the way back to St Thomas' Street, Kate was unable to get the girl's words out of her head. But did they make any difference? Weighing it up, she concluded that this revelation scarcely mattered at all. Lavelle was going to be someone who had merely flitted into her life for a moment and then disappeared. The chances of them meeting in Ireland were so remote as to be unthinkable. If he was everything they said, he would travel to Wexford and Cork, where he would find people prepared to listen to him. Pushing the thought of the Frenchman out of her mind, she braced herself to meet up with Mistress Jardine.

After the traumas of their previous meeting, she was pleased to find the Mistress in good form. As soon as she stepped through the door, she was confronted by a barrage of questions about why she had not returned to the house the previous evening.

'You've not finally been bewitched by this mysterious young man that you keep seeing, have you?' she demanded. 'Did you have an assignation with him last night?'

It was all Kate could do not to burst out laughing. 'My God, Mistress Jardine, if only it were something simple like that.' Trying to stick to the facts, she went on to tell the entire story.

After she had finished, the woman clapped her hands in admiration. 'Why, that's wonderful. And do you think he still believes you to be a nursing sister?'

Screwing up her face, Kate thought for a moment. 'You know, I was in such a daze most of the time, I'm not sure. I believe I told him a number of times that I wasn't a nun, but now I'm not sure.'

'And you say his name was Edward, and that he had a friend called Henry, and that a splendid carriage took them away, and that he was an English army officer?' The Mistress's mind was churning through this combination of facts.

'I'm sure I'll discover who he is, and when I do I'll write to you,' the Mistress declared.

Kate thought for a few moments further. 'He was not like any of the men we met in London the other evening. His skin was tanned, as if he'd spent a lot of time in the sun, and his hair was not cut in the fashionable way, and he was not wearing a wig. And he didn't gush in the way that many of those men did. When he had recovered enough to speak, he was confident, relaxed, amused even, at least as far as I could see.'

'Kate, you have such marvellous adventures, and you're meeting the most interesting men. I have to find out who he is.' And she went off to get herself a brandy. 'So everything is ready for tomorrow?' she called from the other side of the room.

'Yes, Mistress Jardine,' Kate replied softly. Now that

the moment to leave had almost arrived, she had begun to feel tearful again. God, this woman seemed to have an unbelievable effect on her, and her outlook on life. She had opened up her house to a stranger without a qualm, introducing her to a society which she would normally never have been part of, and showing her a style of living which she would doubtless never see anywhere in Wicklow. How would she ever repay her? How would she ever forget her? And of course it was in her summerhouse where She had first experienced the pleasure and the passion and the intimacy of being with a man. It was going to be a wrench to leave London, but there was no going back on the arrangements now.

Struggling out of her room with her bags the following day, Kate was surprised to meet Mister Jardine standing in the hallway. This was not an hour of the morning when he was generally to be seen.

'Ah, Miss Brennan,' he growled, his gravelly voice offset by a benign expression. 'I'm glad to have caught you. I wanted to tell you myself how pleasant it's been with you here as a guest. This house will always be open to you.'

He had such a schoolmasterly appearance that Kate could barely suppress a giggle. Would he be saying this if he had known she had almost lost her virginity in his back garden?

Without warning, he swept her up in a fierce embrace, not dissimilar to the way he had held her when they were dancing. With the breath knocked out of her body by the shock, she was gasping for air when he set her back down.

Snatching up her bags as if they weighed nothing, he

shepherded her downstairs. Outside in the courtyard, he threw her belongings into the carriage, before turning and taking her by the hand.

'We'll not be travelling to Cheapside, but Reynolds will go with you to collect your brother and he'll make sure you've got your seats on the coach. Have a safe journey, Miss Brennan, and come back and visit us.'

Almost in tears, she climbed up into the carriage as he held the door open. In the background, she could see Mrs Simpson waving to her, but all she could do was nod her head pathetically in return. As she pressed herself into the corner of the coach, the Mistress came running out of the house and ran down to the coach.

'Kate, I'm sorry. I couldn't bear to say goodbye again and I was going to stay in bed until you'd gone. But then I couldn't do that either.' For a moment, they looked at one another, bereft of words to say.

'Au revoir,' the Mistress whispered finally. 'Godspeed and safe journey.'

By this time, Kate could not trust herself to utter a word. Dumbly, she waved out of the window, as the carriage made its way out into St Thomas' Street. Thankfully, Declan was ready when she arrived at the hospital a few minutes later. He had precious few belongings to show for his three years in London, other than one small bag. Once again, she had to bear up under the farewells from Sister Mary Francis and the others. Again the tears flowed. Wiping her eyes as the carriage set off along Holborn, she saw her brother watching her curiously.

'Jaysus, you've really got yourself into some state,' he remarked. 'As for me, I'll be pleased to leave London and this country. It's not been a good experience at all.'

As he spoke, Kate tried to stop herself sniffling. That's because you never meet or talk to anybody other than Irish people, she thought to herself. You don't have the slightest idea what the people who live in this country think about anything. But she kept her thoughts to herself. They had a long way to travel and starting off with an argument would not bode well.

Although Cheapside was as crowded and as noisy as the day she had arrived, this time it did not seem such a daunting place. Stepping down from the carriage, she looked around, imprinting the noise and the scene in her memory. It was unlikely that she would ever return to London, and she wanted to remember it, just as it was. But her brother had no time for that, he was already off, making sure they had their seats on the coach.

'Thank you, Reynolds, that will be all.' Kate waved imperiously to Mistress Jardine's man. This was probably the last time she would have a driver and such an impressive carriage, so she might as well make the most of the final moments. Could she ever get used to that life, with servants and carriages? It seemed such an unlikely prospect that it was not worth while thinking about. What she had to concentrate on now was the journey north, finding her seat and making herself comfortable. It was going to be a long trip.

And a long trip it was indeed. Almost two days spent travelling along uneven roads, with an overnight stop at an inn near Coventry. With no hot food available, they had to to share a large room with seven or eight other people, and then she had to try and keep Declan from drinking too much ale. What a nightmare! But what a blessed relief it was to see the dock at Liverpool, and even better to see Mister Flynn waiting to meet them, hopping about from one foot to the other.

As soon as they stopped, Kate got down from the coach and went over to see him. 'Mr Flynn, hello, it's nice of you to meet us here.'

'Excuse me, madam, but I think you're mistaken. I'm here to meet the Widow Brennan and her brother, come from London.'

Immediately, she burst out laughing. She had forgotten completely the guise she had used on her journey across from Ireland.

'Mister Flynn, I'm sorry. It's me, and I am Miss Kathleen Brennan. I was wearing the widow's weeds to keep people away when I was travelling by myself. Most people still respect a woman in mourning and they'll leave her alone in peace. And it worked. I had no trouble at all on my trip from Dublin to London. Thanks in part to your efforts, of course.'

By now, the man looked completely nonplussed. Pulling out a copy of the letter that Mistress Jardine had written to make the arrangements, she thrust it under his nose. 'You have a letter like this from Mistress Jardine in London, yes? That's where I've been staying. She's a cousin of Mistress Delamere, that's why she sent you the letter.'

Trying to come to terms with the sudden change of roles, Flynn shook his head. 'Everything's fine, madam. I know Mister Jardine. I also act for him here at the port of Liverpool. But you look completely different to the woman who took the coach to Mister Boulton's house. I didn't know you were so young.'

'Does that matter in some way, Mr Flynn? Does that change your thinking? I'm sure that Mistress Delamere will be interested in hearing about this.' Employing her haughtiest voice, she began taking great delight in making the agent squirm.

The man started hopping from one foot to the other again, and wringing his hands at the same time. 'Miss Brennan, I have everything in order. The ship sails this evening and you both have a passage booked. I didn't mean to offend you. I'm at your service, of course.'

At this, she smiled to put the man out of his misery. 'Thank you, Mr Flynn. I'm sure that you'll have everything organised perfectly.'

Meanwhile, Declan had been standing back, watching all of this with an incredulous look on his face. 'Honestly, Kate, you sure know how to order people about. The poor fellow was only doing his job, and you started berating him.'

Glancing at her brother, she spoke as sweetly as she could. 'You're not yet fully recovered. I don't want you to have to do anything in case it sets you back. So I'm making sure that we get back to Wicklow with the minimum inconvenience. I'm happy to do that, but you need to let me get on with it in my own way.'

'That's fine by me, Kate,' he replied quietly, putting his hands up to placate her. 'You're doing a grand job so far.' For a moment, he paused. 'And do you think we might be able to get a drink on this ship?'

The journey back across the Irish sea turned out to be uneventful. Again, Kate decided to stay on deck and keep under the blanket that Mr Flynn had held on to for her from her previous trip. It was a little disappointing to find that Mr Slocum was not the steward this time, but the service was equally as good. Having Mister Delamere as a sponsor certainly seemed to help in these matters. In the meantime, Declan set himself up in the saloon below where he was able to buy a drink, but soon enough the smoke and the lack of money drove him up on deck to join her.

'So what will you be doing when you get back to Wicklow, Kate?' he began by asking.

She did not have to think about this at all. 'After I've seen Mam and Dad and Eamo, I'll be back up at the house in Enniskerry. I've been away too long and I have to make sure that the Mistress' children get back into their routine as quickly as possible.'

For a moment, Declan pondered on that. 'And how long do you intend to stay there, doing that job?'

'That's a funny question to ask me, Declan. Sure I'll be staying there until Mistress Delamere's children have all gone to boarding school. That is, of course, if she'll have me there all that time.'

Absent-mindedly, her brother scratched his head. 'Well, if you say so. I was asking only because you're so completely different to the sister I remember. But it's more than that. You're even different to the Irish girls I know. There's so many of them working in London, and I probably know most of them. But in the main they are all quiet, shy and reserved. None of them walk around and talk to every person they meet, and look other people right in the eye the way you do, as if you own the place.'

Instead of replying, however, she started to sing quietly, an old Irish shanty her father had taught her.

Declan looked away, trying to resist the mood she was creating. But he was unable to hold out for long, and within a few minutes he was singing along with her.

'Now that was nice, Declan, I enjoyed that. Come on, we can sing another one together.' She spoke quietly but a little firmly, as she squeezed his hand and leaned her head against his shoulder.

The next day they got off the ship at Dublin quay. It was a soft day, warm and damp. During her trip to England, it had scarcely rained at all, and it was only now that she realised how much she had missed it. Looking up at the slate-grey sky, she let the raindrops fall on her face. Lord, it was beautiful. It felt so good to be back. Now she knew why some people getting off the ship were kneeling down and kissing the ground. It was a wonderful feeling.

And there was O'Brien with the horse and trap, waiting to meet the boat. 'Mr O'Brien!' she shouted at the top of her voice, as she dashed through the crowds, her brother struggling to keep up with her.

'Mr O'Brien, it's me, Kate. Have you come to meet us?' She had to lean against the trap to catch her breath.

The man looked startled. 'Faith, Kate, I barely recognised you. You looked completely different the last time I saw you.'

Kate chuckled in good humour. 'That's because I've had my hair done differently, and I'm wearing a dress that someone has given me. I'm still the same girl you brought here not so long ago.'

Immediately, the man jumped down from the trap. 'Give me your bag and let me help you up into the cab, Miss Brennan.'

This seemed rather formal, Kate noted. He had never done that before. Normally she had to climb up herself. Did he think she was weak perhaps after her trip to London? Putting out her hand for his support, she stepped daintily up into the trap.

O'Brien turned round and saw Declan watching him carefully. 'Hello, Declan, it's good to see you looking so well,' he began quietly, giving him an appraising glance.

'Hello, Mr O'Brien, it's good to be back.' Declan's voice was subdued.

'We weren't sure we were going to see you back again,' O'Brien continued. 'Many people thought Miss Brennan was going on a fool's errand when she set off to London, and that she'd never find you. But from the looks of things it would appear that she's done a grand job.'

'Yes, she has that.' Declan replied, still not his normal self.

As she listened to his mumbling, Kate stared at her brother. What was wrong with him? She was positive he was pleased to be back. Why did he sound so miserable now? Suddenly, she understood his problem. He had been away for three years, with nothing to show for it, except to fall ill, and it had taken his little sister to go there and bring him back, as if he was unable to fend for himself. He had to be worried about what everyone was thinking.

'Sure it was nothing at all, Mr O'Brien,' Kate spoke up loudly to attract the man's attention. 'It was an easy trip to London, everything was arranged, so getting there was no problem at all. And then Declan was not really that bad when I got there. Just a wee touch of fever, like we all get from time to time. He's been champing at the bit to get back for over a week now, but I was so tired I had to rest for a while before we could travel. No, my brother was in fine form in London.'

She could see the emotions on Declan's face. Was it disbelief, and perhaps a little gratitude? Whatever, he picked up his bag and jumped up into the trap. Thank God for that, she thought.

O'Brien climbed up on the other side next to Kate, glancing sideways at her for a moment. 'So that's how it was, Miss Brennan. I should have known it would have been something like that.'

He looked at her again, catching her eye briefly while he untied the reins, before starting them off on the road to Kilcarra.

It was an extraordinary feeling, travelling through the outskirts of Dublin once again. Although away from home for no more than a few weeks, she had become accustomed to the continuous hustle and bustle on the streets of London. Even more strange was the sight of the mountains behind the town, and in the distance beyond Loughlinstown and Bray. In London, the streets were so hemmed in by houses and high buildings that it was impossible to see any distance.

And although Dublin did not lag far behind London for smells and dirt, the same crowds of people were noticeably absent. This lack of congestion meant that O'Brien was able to make good time along the road out of Dublin, and it was not long before they were driving through Bray and up the Wicklow road. Arriving at the village, Kate found herself experiencing an unexpected mixture of feelings. As she stood up in the carriage, she gazed around at the emerald green countryside. The atmosphere was so quiet it was unbelievable. All she could hear was a distant hammering noise, probably her father working at the smithy. A few children were playing in the dirt, laughing and singing songs, but that was all. After the sights of London, it was an incredibly peaceful scene. Nobody barging up and down the streets, no hawkers trying to sell her useless trinkets, no beggars snatching at her clothing or trying to attract her attention.

Yet that had been exciting in a way. Every day had brought so many things to see, so many things to do. Oh well, she consoled herself, she was back now. She had to chalk it down to experience and concentrate on the tasks ahead of her.

By her side, she noticed Mr O'Brien walking round the trap to help her down. He really was getting to be very formal.

'Here you are, Miss Brennan, home at last. Take my hand and I'll help you.' But Kate was already jumping down and running towards the cottage. She met her mother as she ducked out through the door to see who was there, the dogs yelping beside her.

'Kate, my baby, you're back,' she cried immediately. 'Thank God. Come here and let me hug you.'

Without a word, she fell into her mother's arms, her joy and relief preventing her from speaking. After a few moments, she had to push back a little to give herself room to breathe.

'Mam, it's so good to be back, but you're almost crushing me to death. Would you ever let me get some air.' Stepping back, they looked at one another, while Kate fondled each of the dogs in turn.

'Oh, my girl,' her mother exclaimed. 'What have you done with your hair? And those clothes? You're too sophisticated to be talking to the likes of us now, I can see that.'

'Don't be so daft, Mammy. I'm just the same person I always was. But look who else is here.' While she was speaking, she could see her mother's gaze falling upon Declan. Her son, someone she had not seen for over three years, someone she had thought might be dead.

'Declan, come here to your mother.' As she held him in her arms, Kate could see her pinching him to make sure he was real, the tears streaming down her cheeks. For a moment, she felt like crying herself, seeing her mother so happy.

'Oh, it's so good to see you Declan,' she heard her murmuring. 'But why have you not been writing to us? We've heard nothing from you for nearly three years. We've been so worried about you.'

Declan had no answer to that. This is better, Kate decided. One minute he might be the prodigal son returning, but the next he was being told off. That would get him back immediately into the ways of the Irish, and even more quickly into their mother's ways.

But now it was time for Kate to be getting on to Enniskerry. 'I don't want to break up this happy reunion,' she interrupted, 'but I need to go and say hello to Dad and then go up to Mistress Delamere's.' Taking her mother's elbow, she led her to one side.

'How is Dad feeling now about me going to England? Do you think he'll still be angry?'

Her mother paused before answering. 'Your father was not angry at you going. He was desperately afraid that something would happen to his precious little baby. And he didn't think that a good Irish girl should be travelling by herself all the way to London, especially at your age.'

As she was speaking, Kate could see an appraising look in her eye. 'I just hope that when he sees you coming towards him he'll still see his little girl, and not the woman you seem to have become remarkably quickly. Whatever happens, I think your father has got some serious adjustments to make to his thinking.'

Pursing her lips, Kate thought this over for a moment. What was her mother saying? That she had changed in some way? She had been away no more than a few weeks, and she felt the same as she did before she left. And then there was this matter with the man O'Brien. He seemed to be so respectful all of a sudden. Even Declan did not seem to be finding it easy to cope with their relationship. Well, they would have to sort it out for themselves. All of a sudden, she had a fleeting image of Mistress Jardine. Imagine what it would be like if she had come back having picked up her fancy ways – blowing kisses, hugging everyone in sight, shrieking and shouting – God, now that would be something for them to see.

Kissing her mother on the cheek, she gave her arm a squeeze. 'I have to go now. Say hello to Eamonn for me when he comes back. I'll see you all on Sunday.'

Without waiting any longer, she turned towards the trap. 'Right, Mr O'Brien, we have to go now. I want to stop quickly on the way to see my father and then on to Enniskerry.'

Immediately, he helped her up into the trap. 'As you wish, Miss Brennan.'

At the bottom of the hill, they turned towards the smithy where she was expecting her father to be working.

Almost before she had got her thoughts in order, they had arrived. She could see him standing outside, shading his eyes against the light. Although O'Brien got off to help her, again Kate jumped down by herself and ran across the yard. Stopping a few yards away, she walked more sedately towards him.

'Dad, it's me, Kate. I'm back.'

Her father looked her up and down for a moment. 'Hrmmph,' he snorted. 'I can see that right enough.' And then he smiled. 'My little girl is back. Thank God you're safe.'

Thankfully, she fell into his arms. This time, the tears would not stop. 'Oh Dad, I'm so sorry. I didn't want to go without telling you, but I knew I had to. Please forgive me.'

'Kate, you sure know how to twist a man round your little finger. You know I forgive you. I was so worried about how you would cope. But it's good to see you back home again. And it's wonderful news about Declan.'

Pausing, he looked over at the trap. 'And your man O'Brien there. Is he your own personal driver now? Taking you to Dublin and everywhere else?'

As she wiped away her tears with the back of her hand, she tried to laugh. 'I sent a letter to Mistress Delamere so that she knew we were coming, and she sent Mr O'Brien to pick us up. I'll be coming over again to see you on Sunday, and I'll definitely be walking.'

Breathing a huge sigh of relief at having been forgiven, she kissed him quickly. 'But now I must be going. Until Sunday.'

As they reached the village of Enniskerry, the driveway of the house looked every bit as magnificent as she remembered it. Her mind flashed back to the moment when she had arrived with all her belongings to take up her position. Had that been only a few weeks ago? It seemed unbelievable.

At the front door of the house, it was the same as before. As soon as the trap pulled to a halt, the children rushed outside and swarmed around her like bees.

'Miss Kate, we missed you. But it was great not to have to do many lessons.' This was Beatrice, always the loudest. 'And we've someone staying with us, someone else you have to give lessons to.'

Kate had noticed a fourth child, a small boy hanging back by the door. 'Hello,' she shouted over to him. 'What's your name?'

'Arthur,' came the one word reply. Again, Kate could not help smiling. It looked as if she would have to wait till Mistress Delamere appeared before she found out more.

And here she was now. 'Well then, Kate Brennan, you're welcome. I understand you've had a successful journey, and that everything has gone well.'

'For sure it has, Mistress Delamere,' she replied easily. Standing in the doorway, she looked around at the scene outside for a moment. 'But it's nice to be back.'

The Mistress raised her eyebrows slightly. 'Fine, fine. I think we'll get you settled in again, then we can talk. My cousin has written about all of your adventures. You're going to have to tell me everything.'

Chapter 9

It did not take long to settle back into the routine at the house. First of all, she sat down with Mistress Delamere and told her all about her journey. Then at the weekend she talked into the night with her parents back at the cottage. But within a few weeks, the memory of her stay in London began to fade. Sometimes when she lay in bed at night half-sleeping, the journey seemed as if it had been no more than a dream.

But she had plenty of work to keep her occupied. Beatrice was not exaggerating when she said they had not been doing much in the way of lessons, and a lot of catching up was going to be necessary. Not to mention the fourth child she had to look after, young Arthur Wellesley. He turned out to be the youngest son of another cousin of Mistress Delamere's, who lived in Dublin. His parents were travelling to England for a few months through the summer, and had taken up Mistress Delamere's offer to look after the little boy, and to provide him with his school lessons at the same time.

But he was proving to be more difficult than the other children. A year younger than Bernard, he was nowhere nearly as communicative. He was clearly an intelligent child, able to pick up new ideas much faster than the others, but she was never quite sure what was in his mind.

Being as busy as she was, she thought occasionally about James Lavelle, and what he was up to. More often than not, however, she found herself daydreaming about the man Edward, wondering if he had survived, and whether he even remembered the girl who had helped him. But for most of the time she tried to force these thoughts out of her mind, concentrating on her work.

A month after her return to Wicklow, she was sitting in the garden with the children, when Mistress Delamere came out to join them.

'Well now, Kate,' she began. 'How are the children behaving themselves? I hope they are all being attentive?'

'Yes, everything seems to be going fine, Mistress Delamere.' Kate paused for a moment. 'I've been thinking of a way to show you how they are progressing. So, the children would like to perform a little play for you, where you'll be able to watch and listen to them reading and doing a little acting. Would you be happy to sit through that next week?'

Smiling broadly, the Mistress clasped her hands together in approval. 'That sounds wonderful to me. What's it going to be called?'

'I was thinking about a small part of the story about the coming of Fionn MacCumhail and how he saved the great palace at Tara,' she began nervously. Lord, she muttered under her breath, how was she going to take that for an idea? Was she going to be happy about her children learning old Irish fairy tales?

But she need not have worried. 'Kate, that will be marvellous. I've not heard anything of those stories for years, not since your mother used to tell them to me by the fireside when I was a young girl.' Suddenly, the realisation dawned. 'But of course! You'll know all of those stories. Your mother must have told them to you at one time.'

Kate laughed, as much with relief as anything else. 'I'm not sure I know them all, but I can certainly remember some. I wasn't sure you would want your own children to learn about them, that's all.'

'Of course I do,' the Mistress replied indignantly. 'I want them to grow up to be Irish and proud of it, and that's part of their culture. Now you've got me interested, and I'm really looking forward to next week.'

Without warning, she brought one hand from behind her back. 'By the way,' she remarked, smiling at the same time, 'I thought you might be interested in this. It's a letter which has come for you from London.'

Kate jumped up in excitement. A letter addressed to her? She had never received a letter before. And from London?

Her hands were trembling as she picked up the opener. At her side she could hear Mistress Delamere speaking. 'Don't open it here, Kate. Go and sit down in the house with some tea and take your time over it. I'll sit with the children until they're finished what they're doing.'

'Thank you, Mistress Delamere, that's very kind of you,' she replied quickly, rushing off into the house.

The letter was from Sister Mary Francis. As soon as

she began reading, she was transported back to Grays Inn, back to the sanatorium. All the sisters were well, the patients less so. Teresa Ryan was in good health and still coming to see them from time to time. And a remarkable event had occurred without any word of warning – Mister Jardine had arrived in his fine carriage and asked if they would accept him as a sponsor. In one fell swoop, all their worries about making ends meet had been resolved. All those long nights of prayers to God had not been in vain – and perhaps a little support from Kate Brennan had reaped dividends.

This made wonderful reading. But it was the last few words in the letter which seized her attention, transfixing her to her chair. The man Henry had come in to tell them his friend had survived and was recuperating, although it was going to be some time before he had fully recovered. He was still alive, thank God. For a moment, her world was transformed.

Sitting back and making herself comfortable, she cast her mind back over the events of that night. For the first time since coming back home, she allowed herself to linger on his smile, the gentle, humorous way he had spoken, the touch of her hand on his skin, the moment he had lain naked in front of her. The memory sent a shiver down her spine. How could she have done what she did? It was too incredible to contemplate.

On the following Saturday afternoon, she was sitting outside, keeping an eye on the children playing. Mistress Delamere had agreed she would get Saturday afternoons and Sundays to herself, but most Saturdays she spent in the garden at the house. Indeed, where else would she be going?

She was amusing herself, trying to remember the tale of Fionn MacCumhail, and writing it out for the forthcoming presentation to Mistress Delamere. It had been a few years since her mother had told her this tale, and recalling the story was taking a considerable effort of concentration. So engrossed was she in her work that she did not realise she had company.

The unexpected sound of a man's voice startled her, almost causing her to upset her pens and ink over her dress.

'I'm sorry to disturb you, young lady, but I was just admiring your handwriting. It's not often I come across someone who writes as beautifully as you.'

Turning round, she squinted against the light to see who was speaking. It appeared to be a man around thirty to forty years old, well fed by the looks of him, and dressed finely into the bargain.

'You have the advantage of me, sir,' she replied firmly. 'I didn't expect to find someone peeking over my shoulder.' Putting her papers down on the little table beside her, she stood up.

'No, no,' the man cried. 'Don't stop what you're doing. It looks so interesting, and I would like to read some of it when you're finished. Or perhaps you'd care to read some to me?'

Frowning slightly, Kate studied the man more closely. Without doubt he had the touch of a flatterer about him, but he sounded sincere. But who was he, and what was he doing there?

He must have been reading her thoughts, as he stepped forward and put out his hand. 'Hello, my name is Henry Grattan, and I'm extremely pleased to meet you.'

For a moment, Kate stopped to take it in this announcement. Was this Henry Grattan, the lawyer and politician? The one whose views her father did not agree with? The one who was trying to put a declaration of rights before the Irish parliament, for God's sake? It must be the same, because her father had told her he was friendly with Mister Delamere. How on earth was she going to deal with him?

Gingerly, she took his hand. 'Well, Mister Grattan, I'm pleased to meet you. My name is Kathleen Brennan.' She spoke with more confidence than she felt.

'Oh, good, I was hoping that's who you'd be. Mistress Delamere has been telling me she has this beautiful treasure looking after the children and teaching them amazing things.'

Kate tried to stop herself from bursting out laughing. This was too ridiculous to be true. 'I don't think I've heard myself described in those terms before. I believe my mother might express it slightly differently.'

But he was not listening. 'I understand that you've returned recently from a great adventure in England,' he continued, 'not only saving your brother from an early grave, but also conquering all of London with your beauty and your wit.'

This was more than absurd. 'Mister Grattan, I think you're getting me confused with someone else—' she began, but he interrupted her before she could say anything else.

'Miss Brennan, I'm only joking. But I've heard so much about you. And tell me about your writing, please.'

Quickly making her mind up, she decided she was going to have to humour him.

'I'm trying to remember an old Irish tale that my mother told me many years ago. It's a story similar to those you might have read when you were younger, about the Greek and Roman gods perhaps.' She could see him studying her, a question on his lips, but she continued before he could interrupt.

'The children are going to read from it next week for Mistress Delamere. Young Arthur over there, who's here for the summer, is finding it really interesting. He doesn't say much, so I'm never sure how he's progressing, but this is something that's really caught his attention. I expect it's because it's all blood and thunder, and laying waste to the countryside, something which all small boys like, and even some larger ones.'

The man clapped his hands in appreciation. 'That sounds really wonderful, Miss Brennan. I would dearly like to read it when you've finished.'

Kate smiled to herself. Everybody seemed to be interested in these stories. Someday, perhaps, she would find out why. And this visitor was turning out to be not that difficult to talk to. 'Perhaps, Mister Grattan, perhaps. But tell me, what are you doing here, in Mistress Delamere's garden?'

'So Miss Brennan, it's your turn to ask the questions, is it? Very well, Mister and Mistress Delamere are giving a small reception this evening and I've been invited. Most of the people are travelling from Dublin, but I'm living nearby at Wingfield in Bray, so I've come early. And I do enjoy it here in this beautiful place.' As he looked around, he swept open his arms, as if to encompass everything he could see.

'But you'll be coming too, will you not, Miss Brennan?'

'I don't think so, Mister Grattan—' she began slowly, before he interrupted her again.

'But you must. I'll go and speak with Mistress Delamere immediately and make sure there's a space for you next to me.' He turned as if to rush off in the direction of the house.

She had to stop this. Thrusting out her hand without thinking, she grasped him by the arm. 'One moment, Mister Grattan, sir. Mistress Delamere may or may not be of the mood to invite me to this reception, I'm not sure. But I would not wish to attend, whatever that mood. I'm in the employment of Mistress Delamere and we have an excellent working relationship, and I'll not jeopardise that by attending her functions and mingling with her guests.'

Her mind was racing. Was he going to understand her point of view? Or would he tell the Mistress what she had said? 'As a rule, we only discuss the children's work and the ways of the world when we are alone here in the house during the week, and when Mister Delamere is in Dublin.'

But she ended up making a face and softening her expression. 'And in any event, I've nothing to wear to such an occasion.'

Mister Grattan beamed in her direction. 'Well, Miss Brennan, I'll not press you. I can see that you're a very strong-willed young lady. But then Mistress Delamere did warn me about that.' He smiled ruefully, suddenly changing tack.

'Enough of that. I'm curious about something else. I don't meet many Irish girls who know of the Greek gods, nor many who write in such a beautiful style. Where did

236

you learn that, might I ask?'

His words were so patronising that she could not help herself bridling. 'You may indeed ask, Mister Grattan, but should I answer? Some of us might be poor – we might even be Catholics, but that doesn't make us complete idiots.'

But at least he recognised that he had gone too far. 'I'm sorry Miss Brennan, I'm not phrasing my questions in the best possible way. I didn't mean to offend you. I found it interesting, that was all,' he finished off lamely.

Now he sounded so apologetic that Kate decided to turn on the charm. 'Then I'll tell you, Mister Grattan,' she declared, offering him her most devastating smile. 'My teacher was a man who seemingly knew about everything. And when I was young, and didn't know any better, he filled my head with all manner of thoughts. So now I'm a little older, I know very little about a great many things.'

This time the man burst out laughing at Kate's exaggerated posturing. 'And who was this teacher who committed this grave crime?'

'We used to call him Old Mister Hutchinson, but I don't think he was all that old. I see him occasionally at my mother's house on Sundays, and he still keeps telling me things and asking me questions.'

'I think you've said enough, Kate,' the man replied, stroking his chin thoughtfully. 'I believe you're talking about Peter Hutchinson. I remember him as a lecturer at Trinity when I was a student, but he always believed that education should be for everyone rather than for a select few. I knew he had gone teaching in a hedge school somewhere, but I didn't know it was near here. Well,

well, that explains many things to me now. And did you know that he is an Englishman?'

Kate shook her head. 'That I did not, Mister Grattan. And somehow or other, when I was being told stories about Russia and China, and hearing about Torquemada and Saladin, I didn't think to ask whether I was being given the English or the Irish version.'

Carefully, she brushed an imaginary speck of dust from the sleeve of her dress. It was time to get back to what she had being doing or else she would never get finished. 'And now, Mister Grattan, it's been nice talking with you, but I must get on with my work. Enjoy your reception with Mistress Delamere.' She turned back towards her papers and pens.

The man bowed again. 'The pleasure has been all mine, Miss Brennan.'

Two hours went past before Kate felt she had managed to get enough of her story down on paper for the children to start reading. As she was packing up, she saw Mistress Delamere coming across the garden towards her.

'Hello Kate, still working, I see,' she began.

'I've finished now, Mistress Delamere. I think it's time for the children to go in for tea, and I'll have to take a nap,' she replied, stifling a yawn.

'I understand, Kate, that you've been in discussions with Mister Grattan this afternoon.' Immediately, Kate was wary of what was going to come next. But to her surprise, the Mistress leaned forward and lowered her voice.

'I think you've completely captivated that man. He's come back to the house totally under your spell. You must share with me some day what it is you say to these people.'

For a moment, Kate was mystified. What had she said to him, indeed? He had seemed a little on the pompous side, but then she knew of his reputation so that was not a surprise. 'I'm sure I've no answer to that, Mistress Delamere.' she replied, shrugging her shoulders.

The other woman laughed. 'Just be prepared for more regular visits from Mister Grattan. But tell me,' she continued. 'What are you planning to do tomorrow?'

Kate thought for a moment. 'I'll walk down to the village and meet Mam at Mass, and then go out for a walk with the dogs in the afternoon. But I must come back tomorrow evening and start writing letters. I promised everyone in England that I would write to them and I've not even started yet.'

Suddenly, she remembered something else. 'And just one other thing, Mistress Delamere. I've not thanked you properly for sponsoring the trip to London for me. If it wasn't for your support, my brother might not be alive today.' For a moment the memories came rushing back, almost bringing tears to her eyes.

'Away with you, Kate,' the Mistress replied dismissively. 'Sure, it was nothing at all. I get all the thanks I need from watching you with the children. Now take that serious expression off your face before we go back into the house.'

A little later, Kate went up to her room and lay down on the bed. Normally her eyes closed within seconds of lying down but this evening was different. For some reason she felt restless. Yes, she did feel tired, but her mind kept jumping from one thought to another. Perhaps it was the conversation with Mister Grattan. It had been a debate rather than a conversation, and perhaps that had stimulated her mind. After all, there were precious few opportunities to have debates with the children. For a moment, she smiled ruefully to herself. Debating with the great lawyer, Henry Grattan? What an exciting, frightening, prospect. Imagine having to do that every day.

Unaccountably, her thoughts drifted back to London, back to Mistress Jardine. It was so peaceful here in Wicklow, right enough, and being abroad in London had seemed terrifying at times. But there could be no doubt it had been exciting, and there was never a dull moment living in Connaught House. It was a strange world, indeed. When she had been in England, all she could think of was being home in Wicklow. Now she had returned, her mind kept straying back to London.

As ever, her thoughts turned to the letter from Sister Mary Francis and her words about the man Edward, and that fateful evening in the hospital. Closing her eyes, she dropped off into a fitful sleep, imagining kissing his forehead and soothing away the pain from the wound in his shoulder.

The summer months passed in Wicklow and Kate adjusted gradually to the pattern of life at the house. During the week, her hands were full looking after the four children, and she was fully tested in coming up with new ideas to keep them stimulated. The performance of 'Fionn MacCumhail' was received enthusiastically by Mistress Delamere, and the children were so excited by their role-playing that it was decided she would organise something similar every month. The readings and the writing down of more of the old stories kept her very busy indeed.

On Saturday afternoons, she spent most of her time reading or writing letters to the people she had met in England. Mistress Jardine had written with all the gossip from London, but she had still been unable to find out the name of the man Edward. This letter greatly amused Mistress Delamere, as she had assured Kate that her cousin rarely wrote to anyone.

Moreover, Patrick Nolan had been in touch, mentioning that he and Teresa were going to get married although they had not decided when. He had received a message from Mister Boulton telling him he would be made welcome were he to come to Birmingham to discuss a position. So now they had given up drinking ale and were saving their money to pay for Patrick's coach fare.

And Mistress Boulton had also written, expressing their pleasure at Declan's recovery, telling Kate all about her husband's latest ideas, and inviting her to visit whenever she pleased.

From time to time, Mister Grattan would turn up on Saturday afternoons to visit the Delameres, sometimes in the company of a few other men, sometimes by himself. His encouragement kept pushing Kate to put down on paper as many of the old stories as she could remember. Through the summer, their relationship turned gradually into one of mutual respect. Kate found herself being able to see behind the bombast and the oratory, and discovered that the man had a genuine interest in all of the people in Ireland and not just the chosen few in Dublin. And for his part, after he had managed to cope with her smile, her beauty, and her downright stubbornness, he discovered that she was an intelligent, inquisitive woman, with an extraordinary appetite for knowledge about every subject under the sun.

What was particularly interesting was Mister Grattan's perceptions of what was best for the future of Ireland. After all, he was the most celebrated politician in all of Ireland, and one of the most influential men in Dublin. If anyone was to succeed in making changes, he was the most likely. It was obvious that he was closely involved with the elite group in Dublin which Mister Hutchinson had first described, and which she had spoken about less than enthusiastically in the alehouse in London. But he appeared to be supportive of improving the lot of the majority of the population of Ireland, whereas there were many others in that group who were not.

These Saturday afternoon conversations, usually involving Mister Grattan, Mistress Delamere, and another man called Mister Daly, continued through the summer. Rather than being enlightened, however, Kate often found herself becoming more and more frustrated. All they kept talking about was the recent change in the law to allow Catholics to own property if they took an oath of allegiance to King George, as if this was a great success and a major step forward. Did they not realise that this had not the slightest significance for the majority of the population? They would never be able to buy property. And how many would take the oath? It merely proved to her how far removed the people in power in Dublin were from the rest of the country.

Mister Grattan and his friends could huff and puff, and put forward their declarations of rights, and even proposals for an independent Irish Government, but what was going to change for the ordinary people? Who was going to represent them, and to speak up for them, and protect their interests?

Here they were, three people discussing what could be done to help their country. A few miles away, her mother and old Mr Hutchinson, and possibly her father, were probably having a similar conversation from a completely different perspective, and no doubt coming up with a different solution. In the Lord Chatham, and for sure in many other alehouses across London, groups of Irish people were debating yet another viewpoint and arriving at a third conclusion. How could they all be brought together? How could they all start working in the same direction? Who was going to provide the leadership? All she had was more and more questions, with precious few answers.

But despite these concerns, life had to continue. On Sundays, Kate had got into the habit of walking down to the village to meet her mother at Mass, and then taking the dogs out on the hillside in the afternoon. Her worst moment had come seeing Cathal standing outside the church with some other men. Despite her waving energetically, he had turned his back and gone into Cormack's. He could scarcely have made it more plain that he did not want to see her. For a moment, she had toyed with the idea of following him into the alehouse. After all, she had been in far worse places in London. In the end she decided it would probably lead to a confrontation, and if that was going to happen, it would be better in a less public place. But she had not seen him since.

In spite these odd moments, however, life in Enniskerry was generally a peaceful existence, and there seemed to be little that could disturb it. Gradually the memories of London grew further and further away, becoming more and more indistinct.

Each year at the end of July, it was Mistress Delamere's custom to hold a garden party. Everyone in the area was invited, from old Lord Jesmond himself to the local farmers and villagers, and even the girls who were employed in making lace in Delamere's mill over in Bray. And of course, Kate's mother and father always had their invitations.

It was a grand event right enough, with food and drink and entertainment from jugglers and magicians, as well as music and dancing in the early evening. Kate had not been able to attend the party for at least four years, between her younger brother dying, and then being sick herself, or her father being ill. But this year she was in the thick of the organisation, and had been pressed into service by Mistress Delamere to help keep the punchbowls filled up. No one was to be allowed to go thirsty.

As the day wore on, Kate's admiration for Teresa Ryan increased by leaps and bounds. She had never dreamed that a serving girl needed such a strong constitution, to keep running back and forth carrying huge trays of drinks. The patience and tact required was unbelievable, with the guests always wanting their glasses recharged at the same time. And nobody was prepared to wait. By late afternoon, she was hot, tired and flustered. Holding yet another empty tray in her hand, she was contemplating a mad rush into the kitchen, when Mistress Delamere suddenly appeared out of the crowds in front of her, looking as cool as a cucumber as usual, and took her by the arm.

'You must slow down a little, Kate,' she insisted. 'You're rushing around like a madwoman. Don't listen to all these people. They can always wait a few moments longer for a refill.'

'I've never done anything like this before,' she gasped in reply, her hand on her chest. 'It's much harder work than I thought.'

The Mistress smiled. 'Come with me for a moment. Someone has arrived from Dublin who'd like to meet you.'

Kate felt a panic rising in her chest. 'Oh, Mistress Delamere, not a friend of Mister Grattan. I don't think I could cope at this moment with another debate, whatever the subject.'

But Mistress Delamere pulled her by the arm. 'I don't think this is an acquaintance of Mister Grattan. His name is Mister Tilbrook, and he's not from Dublin. Look, there he is standing in the doorway.'

Turning slowly, Kate glanced over towards the door of the house. In shock, she almost dropped her tray, her knees buckling beneath her. It was Edward from the hospital! Thank God, he had not seen her, although perhaps he would not recognise her anyway. Carefully, she put her hand on the table beside her for support.

Mistress Delamere was speaking again. 'Are you all right?' she was enquiring. 'Come with me and I'll introduce you.'

In a trance, she walked slowly towards the door, her head bowed, looking up fearfully through her eyelashes.

By now the Mistress was speaking to the man. 'Mister Tilbrook, I'd like to introduce you to somebody.' Holding out her arm, she beckoned Kate towards her. Before she could say any more, however, the cook came running out of the kitchen.

'Mistress Delamere, come quickly,' she shrieked, 'we have a disaster on our hands. Come quickly!' Without waiting she dashed off in the other direction.

Raising one eyebrow, the Mistress looked round at Kate. 'I'm sorry. I must find out what's wrong. I'll have to leave you to introduce yourselves.' Turning abruptly, she hurried into the house after the other woman.

With every muscle in her body locked by tension, it took a supreme effort not to collapse at his feet. She could hear him speaking somewhere in the distance, and vaguely saw him put out his hand in greeting.

'Hello, my name is Edward,' he murmured, his voice low but not as husky as before. 'And who might you be?'

All she could offer in reply was a mumble. 'I'm Kathleen.' For a second, she touched his hand before quickly letting it go. As yet she had not been able to look up at his face. Although it seemed to take an eternity, eventually she managed to raise her eyes. He was smiling, the face she saw in her dreams nearly every night, the man she had butchered in the hospital all those months ago.

He looked well now, right enough. High cheekbones, long jet-black hair, and twinkling blue eyes. He was clean shaven, which was slightly unusual, and his skin was still brown from the sun. He looked lean and hard, and his clothes were well-made, rather than fashionable. Somehow or other, she managed to take all of this in with one glance. Or had she known what he was going to look like all along?

But the look on his face was so infectious, she had to smile in return. For a moment, they stood facing each other, a few inches apart, smiling like idiots, while all around them hordes of people crowded backwards and forwards.

Had he recognised her? Did he know who she was? Did he remember the name of the girl who had helped him? And what in God's name was he doing here? All these thoughts rushed through her mind, one after another.

'Are we going to stand here in the doorway looking at one another? Or are we going to move to the side and let these people go by?'

Although his voice was quiet, she had no difficulty in hearing him. She could not bring herself to reply, the girl who had been so articulate with so many people over the last few months. She nodded her head dumbly.

Taking her by the hand, he led her outside and slightly away from the others. God, his hand felt so strong, yet his grip was gentle. As they reached a quieter part of the garden, she managed to get her thoughts into some semblance of order.

'Mister Tilbrook, I'm pleased to meet you.' Her voice croaked horribly. Covering her mouth with her hand, she tried to clear her throat, so she could speak properly. 'But I've so much work to do. I'm helping Mistress Delamere by serving the punch. no one is getting any drink while I'm here and they'll start complaining soon. I have to get back to my duties.'

'That's fine by me, Miss Kathleen. Perhaps you could

start by getting me a glass. As you would say over here, I have a terrible thirst on me.' And he put on the most awful Irish accent. Unable to help herself, she had to laugh. But it came out more as a nervous hoot, rather than a pleasant tinkle of laughter. In the name of God, she thought, control yourself. Whether or not the man had recognised her, he was most unlikely to be impressed if he were to think he had encountered a complete half-wit.

But she could not utter another word. All she could do was nod her head and rush off into the kitchen for another bowl of punch. From somewhere, she managed to find a glass and get it filled before dashing back to where she had left him. But when she got there, he was nowhere to be seen. For a moment, she looked around, but with so many people milling about, trying to find him seemed pointless. And on every side she could hear great shouts going up for more drink. With a philosophical shrug of her shoulders, she threw herself back into the fray.

At seven o'clock sharp, the music stopped and no more drink was served. This was Mistress Delamere's strict instructions, as she knew from experience how long it took to get the revellers out of the grounds of the house. For Kate, seven did not come a moment too soon. Exhaustion was setting in as well as disappointment that she had not been able to find Edward again. And now the clearing up had to be done as well.

A few minutes later, as she was wandering around with a tray in her hand, picking up empty tankards and glasses, she felt a hand on her elbow. Turning around, he was there, back at her side – except he had changed his clothes. This time he was dressed much as he had been when she had helped carry him into the hospital, in a heavy white silk shirt and black breeches. He looked so dashing that she could feel her heart leaping, her fatigue slipping away as if by magic.

'Mister Tilbrook, I was looking for you. I wondered where you had gone.' That was better. At least she had been able to speak in something approaching a normal tone of voice.

'Miss Kathleen, another girl came and gave me a drink, and I lost sight of you. There were so many people here, but I didn't know any of them. So I decided to spend an hour or two riding in the wonderful countryside around here. But now I've returned to continue our conversation.'

'So, Mister Tilbrook,' she responded, her voice still unnaturally tight with tension. 'I think you're not from around these parts. What brings you to Wicklow?'

'Miss Kathleen, you're absolutely correct. In fact, this is my first ever visit to Ireland. I've come here because I've heard of the marvellous recuperative powers of the Irish countryside, and County Wicklow in particular.'

Despite his friendly attitude, Kate was still finding it difficult to look directly at him. Did he know who he was talking to? Surely not, he would have mentioned it to her by now. What was she going to say next? Somehow she had to find out if he had recognised her. Taking a deep breath, she forced herself to turn her head in his direction. He was so tall, and broad shouldered; it was an effort to keep her voice under control.

'Recuperative? You don't look very ill to me, Mister Tilbrook.'

'Aha, Miss Kathleen,' he replied immediately. 'That's

because of these fine clothes I'm wearing. You've not seen what's underneath this shirt. If you had, you'd wonder at the fact I'm still alive at all.'

As he gazed at her solemnly, Kate had to turn her head away. But she had to find out.

'Tell me, please, Mister Tilbrook.' All she could manage was a whisper. 'Tell me what happened to you.'

'Well, Miss Kathleen, it's a fearsome story, and I'm not sure it's suitable to be told to a young Irish girl such as yourself. But I'll tell you, since you ask. Some weeks ago I was challenged to a duel in London, the reasons why are not important to this story. I ended up taking a ball in the shoulder, and I was in a very poor state from the wound and losing blood. My dear friend, Henry Browne, God bless him, dragged me, half-conscious, into some godforsaken place which was full of sick people. While I was lying there, with my life ebbing away, some savage woman came up to me and committed the most unutterably brutal act of butchery on my defenceless body.'

As she felt herself flinching at his story, she could see his face out of the corner of her eye, his face mirroring his concern. 'I'm sorry, Miss Kathleen, perhaps it's too fearful for you.'

'No, no, please go on, Mister Tilbrook.' She had to know the truth.

'Well, after that, the woman had the audacity to dress herself up as a nursing sister, and then when I was completely helpless and totally at her mercy, she indulged herself by removing all my clothes and leaving me with nothing but an old night gown to preserve my modesty. Have you ever heard such a thing? And is it any wonder I need to find somewhere to recuperate?'

Apprehensively, Kate stared at him. For a moment, he looked so fierce, she could feel herself wilting under his glare. And then his beautiful blue eyes twinkled.

'That woman saved my life on that fateful day, and I vowed I would find her and thank her in person. And that, Kathleen Brennan from County Wicklow, is why I'm here.'

Her hand flew to her mouth. He had known all along who she was. He must have known even when they were standing in the doorway earlier. For a moment the panic in her chest was so overpowering that she almost fainted at his feet. But then she began to experience a different sensation. All she could hear was his voice, all she could see was his face, and his beautiful, wonderful smile.

Dumbstruck, she stood motionless as he took the tray from her hand and put it to one side. Taking both her hands in his, he looked down at her upturned face, and for a moment, kissed her gently on the lips.

'Thank you Kate Brennan, I'll always be in your debt.' His voice was low and firm, his words were only for her. And then he let her go.

Very slowly, she drifted back to reality. What was he going to do now? Now that he had found her and thanked her, would he be going back to England?

'Mister Tilbrook—' she began.

But he put his hand on her arm and shook it gently to interrupt her. 'Kate, when we are speaking together, please call me Edward. When there are other people around, you can refer to me how you will. You have such a beautiful voice, and it sounds so wonderful when you say my name.'

All over again, the exhilaration flooded through her body. Other people around, when we are alone? It did not sound as if he was intending to leave.

'Mister Tilbrook – I mean Edward,' she corrected herself quickly as he smiled at her. 'Will you be staying in Ireland for long?'

'Well, that depends really on what there is to keep me here. I have a distant relative in Dublin, where I'm staying at the moment. Also, I know Lord Powerscourt slightly, and I spoke with him earlier today when he was here. I've arranged to stay at his house for the next few days. And then my mother was related to Sir Francis Hutchinson, who lives somewhere near here, and I could introduce myself to him as well. I also know Mister Delamere, although I've met his lady wife only today and just for a few moments.'

He paused for a second or two, while her mind raced. He seemed to know so many people – Lord this, and Sir that. What was he going to say when he found out that she was plain Kathleen Brennan, a poor Irish girl from Kilcarra? She could feel the panic starting to come back.

'And then there's Kate Brennan, with whom I have a slight acquaintance. In fact, she knows me much better than I know her. But I would like to get to know her a lot better, and I'm hoping that she'll want that too. And I would like to find out more about Ireland, and I fancy that she's just the person to tell me all about it.'

Kate had to laugh, more at herself than anything else. He was teasing her, that was all. But where had all her smart replies gone? Surely she could not let him away with this completely.

'Well now, Edward,' she began, still nervous about

calling him by his first name. 'I'm not sure about all of that. But what about your shoulder? Is it any better? Can you still move your arm?'

'Despite your best efforts, Kate, it appears to be in reasonable working order. The wound is healing nicely, although I fear I'll never again be the finest swordsman in all of Europe.' He struck up a classic pose and ran her through with his imaginary sword.

Refusing to believe him, Kate grasped his shirtsleeve. 'Show me. Let me see you raise your arm up.'

'I'm telling you it's fine,' he replied, laughing and wriggling free from her grip. 'There's just a slight twinge, that's all.'

But Kate continued to look at him disbelievingly. 'Let me see you do it.'

Slowly, he raised his arm, grimacing slightly. 'Look, Kate, it's fine. I can see that you're a woman who'll brook no refusals in your quest for an answer.'

Closing her eyes for a moment, she offered up a silent prayer. 'Thank God, you are recovering. I've not been able to stop thinking about how I may have injured you.'

Suddenly he was very close to her. For a moment, his hand was touching her cheek, brushing back her hair. 'And is that all you were thinking about me, all these weeks?'

All at once, she could feel herself blushing furiously. Somehow, she managed to look up into his face, only inches away. One eyebrow was slightly crooked, and there was a faint mark that looked like a scar on his forehead, and another one near his left eye. Was he really a swordsman? Desperately, she tried to keep her emotions under control, her attention caught suddenly by a voice beside her.

'My God, I leave you alone for a minute, Kate Brennan, and I find that you have captivated another man.' It was Mistress Delamere.

'She has this way with her, Mistress Delamere,' Edward observed gaily, taking a pace or two back. 'But I fancy she may have been taking lessons from yourself in this regard? What chance do we men have in the company of such pulchritude?'

'Away with you and your blarney, Edward Tilbrook.' The Mistress was trying to be firm but she could not stop smiling. 'I thought you were not supposed to be Irish. You might not have the accent, but you have the words for sure.'

She turned to Kate. 'Are you going to be safe with this man, my dear?'

Again, Kate felt her face turn red. 'I think so, Mistress Delamere,' she replied, stumbling slightly over her words. 'I've met Mr Tilbrook once before, when I was over in London.' Out of the corner of her eye, she noticed that Edward had assumed the most innocent of expressions. He was not going to get away so easily. 'And I think I've found a way of keeping him under control,' she continued. Smiling demurely, she watched him under her eyelashes.

Meanwhile Mistress Delamere looked from one to the other. 'While you two have been billing and cooing, the rest of us have finished most of the cleaning up. What remains we will do tomorrow. So, Mister Tilbrook, are you going to favour us with your company this evening?'

Edward looked at the sky and the sun setting behind the mountains in the west. 'Thank you for your kindness,

Mistress Delamere, but I've arranged with Lord Powerscourt to stay at his house for a few days. And I think I need to be on my way. I don't want to be caught on these Irish roads after dark, and be at the mercy of all sorts of brigands and ruffians.'

He turned to Kate. 'Miss Brennan, will I have the pleasure of your company at some stage tomorrow?'

Kate looked at him, and then at Mistress Delamere, and then back again. What was she going to say now? She desperately wanted to see him.

But the Mistress spoke first.

'I'll leave you two to decide on these important matters yourselves. I have things to do.' And she departed into the house.

Finally, Kate managed to reply. 'I think so, I'm not sure, perhaps.' Her voice was quavering again, and the words seemed so difficult to say.

Edward looked at her, his head to one side, a question forming on his lips.

She sensed herself rushing blindly on. 'Tomorrow is Sunday, you see, it's my day off, that's why I'm not sure, do you understand?' What was she saying? How could anyone possibly understand what she was talking about?

'Kate, just one moment,' Edward was scratching his head. 'Somewhere there you managed to lose me.'

'What I meant to say,' she began, trying desperately to think of the best way to put it. But there was only one way. 'On Sundays I go down to the village to see my mother and father. I go with them to Mass. And then I like to go out with the dogs out on the hillside.' She looked at him sideways to see how he would take this. But she need not have worried – he did not bat an eyelid.

Except he scratched his head again.

'Perhaps I could accompany you on your walk for an hour or so? I would really like that.'

All at once, she breathed a huge secret sigh of relief. 'That would be wonderful, Edward. I'll meet you on the old road above the village, which runs west up into the hills, at one o'clock.'

For one moment, he looked at her again, as if he was going to kiss her. She could feel her knees shaking, while the muscles in her stomach formed into knots. But instead he leaned forward and whispered in her ear.

'That will be lovely, Kate Brennan. I'm looking forward to tomorrow already.'

As he went off to say his farewells to Mistress Delamere, Kate slowly regained her composure. For some reason she had been so worried that when he found out she was from the village and a Catholic as well, that that would be the end of it. Then she realised he must have known all along. The first time he had seen her, she had been wearing a nun's habit, for God's sake. Of course he had known.

Feeling very weary, she trudged back to the house and up to her room. It had been a long day, and all the activity had finally caught up with her. Before getting into bed she knelt down to say her prayers. As she finished, she stopped to think for a moment; it had been a wonderful day, but tomorrow was going to be even better. Jumping into bed, she pulled the covers up over her head. Sunday could not come too soon.

Chapter 10

———— ❖ ————

It was almost one o'clock before Kate managed to get out of the cottage. Her mother had been telling her how Declan was finding it difficult to settle back down in the village. Her father had taken him on to help in the smithy, and there was plenty of work to do. The problem was that the village was simply too quiet. In a way, Kate could sympathise; she had been to England for no more than a few weeks, and even she had found it difficult to settle down on her return.

But despite her concerns for her brother, she could not concentrate on what her mother was saying. She had someone to meet on the hill above the church and she was going to be late.

The sun was shining as she hurried along the path, the dogs running madly beside her. At first she could not see anyone, until she heard the whinny of a horse nearby. As she looked around, Edward appeared from behind some bushes, sitting nonchalantly on a thoroughbred horse, looking as if he owned the entire countryside. He was dressed in similar style to the previous day, in silk shirt, dark breeches and long leather boots.

'Well then, who is this beautiful lady out walking by herself on this hillside?' he called out, nudging the animal over towards her. As he came closer, he seemed to throw himself off the horse and land acrobatically in front of her, the horse's reins still held firmly in one hand.

As he bowed in welcome, Kate clapped her hands in admiration. He obviously knew a bit about horses and riding.

'Isn't he a fine looking fellow?' he asked, slapping the animal on the shoulder. 'Do you know anything about horses, Miss Brennan?'

Eyeing the animal up and down, she shook her head. 'I've seen plenty in my time. My father has a smithy down in the village, so there's always horses about down there. But I have to confess that I've never been on a horse's back in my life.'

Without warning, he smiled, bent forward and kissed her on the lips, all in one smooth movement, before she had a chance to respond. 'Hello, Kate, it's nice to see you again, looking as beautiful as ever. And these are the dogs, presumably. What are they called?'

Still trying to keep her emotions under control, she pointed them out. 'This is Lachlan, and that one over there is Jossie. They don't get out walking much except when I'm around. So they always have plenty of energy on Sundays.'

As she was speaking, Edward peered up the sides of the valley surrounding them. 'So where are you going to take me this afternoon, Miss Brennan?'

For a moment, she racked her brain. 'Up here and to the right, there's a nice little spot where you can get a good view of the countryside. The last part is a bit of a scramble, but you can leave the horse at the bottom.'

'I'm entirely in your hands, just lead me on.' He smiled at her again, that wonderful, dazzling smile.

It was a breathtaking experience, walking up the hill, arm in arm, with the dogs foraging on each side, while the horse plodded along quietly beside them. Her body was tingling with a nervous excitement, but it was a different feeling to the previous day. Then, she had been too tongue-tied speak, whereas today she could hardly stop talking. And while she held Edward's arm demurely all the way up the hill, the urge to grab him with both hands and to press her cheek against his shoulder was almost overwhelming.

Before she knew it, they had reached the top of the knoll. This was the same spot where she had stood that day in April, not long before she started working for Mistress Delamere. Clinging to his arm, she turned him this way and that, pointing out the view and the various places they could see.

'Look there, Edward, that's Enniskerry over there. Fera Cualann, some of the older people call it, in Irish. You can just see Mistress Delamere's house from here. And there, that's Powerscourt, where you're staying. Do you see that valley beyond those trees? They call that the Scalp – my old schoolteacher says it was created by a huge glacier thousands of years ago. They've just built a new road through there to Dublin. And here, this way: that's the sea over yonder, and the village of Bray. And those houses you can make out through the haze, I think that might be Old Connaught. And in front of us is the Glen o' the Downs. Mister O'Brien says they're going to run the mail coaches through there on their way from Dublin to Wicklow and Arklow; that will make a big difference to the village if they do that. And these hills here are the Sugarloaves, and do you see that huge dark mountain away over there behind us with the clouds covering the top? That's called Lughnaquilla. That mountain looks out over all of County Wicklow. On a clear day, some people say that it's possible to see from the top all the way to the mountains of Kerry in the south. I've been up there just once and it's a fearsome, wild country, I can tell you.'

Stopping to catch her breath, she glanced sideways to see if Edward appeared to be interested. He seemed fascinated. 'It's a beautiful view, Kate. It's so green, it's like a garden – the garden of Ireland, you might say. Where I come from, we don't have much scenery like this.' Taking hold of both her hands, he turned towards her. 'You sound as if you love it here.'

More than ever, she could sense how close they were to each other. It was that overpowering sensation again. Looking up, she tried to smile. Somehow she had to try and ease the tension she could feel catching her chest. 'It's lovely here, Edward, especially on a day like today. Sometimes, on a spring evening before the sun goes down, and the moon hangs in the distance over the green mountains, it seems like the most beautiful place on God's earth. But when it's pouring rain and the wind is blowing hard, sometimes I'm not so sure.'

Now he was holding her arms, and his hands were moving to her shoulders. His voice was so low and husky that she had to strain forward to hear him. 'I haven't seen the moon, and it hasn't rained either since I've been here, Kate Brennan.'

And then he kissed her. Not the way he had kissed her the previous evening. Not the way he had kissed her when they had met on the road an hour earlier. This time his arms dropped round her waist, this time he held her firmly, this time his lips explored hers, softly, gently, tenderly, passionately.

Kate lost track of how long they stood there, their arms around one another. His kisses covered her lips, her neck, her cheeks, her forehead. God, it was so wonderful, she did not want him to stop. But somehow they managed to disentangle themselves a little. Embarrassed by the sudden depth of their passion, Kate slowly caught his eye. She could see him smiling a little ruefully. Immediately, she knew he had felt it too.

'How did you do that, Kate?' he whispered. 'That was so beautiful, so incredibly beautiful.' As his hands caressed her back, she felt his arms relaxing slightly. Slowly the tension eased in her stomach and her legs.

But her voice would not work properly. 'Edward, please,' was as much as she could say. Lifting one hand, she touched his cheek gently. 'Edward, tell me please, I don't know what happened there,' she begged, resting her head against his chest, luxuriating in the touch of his fingers running through her hair.

'Kate Brennan, you didn't tell me you were such a dangerous woman. I should have been much more careful about protecting my state of mind. I think we might be safer if we simply make our way carefully back down that hill, and perhaps we'll see what it turns out like at the bottom.'

Walking down the road was like walking on air, except she was barely able to contain herself. One minute she was pulling him by the hand, making him run for a few yards, the next she was ambling along slowly, cuddling up against him. And Edward was every bit as bad, she could see that. He was finding it impossible to stop touching her. He kept holding her hand, then her arm, then he would put his arm around her shoulders, then he would put his hand on her back, then he would brush his lips against her neck. Every so often he would stop and take her in his arms. It was so wonderful, she could scarcely stop herself from laughing and giggling.

But as they arrived at the outskirts of the village, they had to stop. Taking a moment or two to compose herself, she tucked her hair back in and smoothed her dress. It would not look good if she walked back through the houses with her face flushed and her hair undone. As she called the dogs to heel, she glanced again at Edward's expression.

'Mister Tilbrook, I hope you enjoyed your brief introduction to Ireland.'

'I think, Miss Brennan, that perhaps I might need to go through it again. I'm not sure I managed to capture the full flavour of the Irish welcome.' His eyes twinkled. 'Would you be available next Saturday perhaps, if I called for you at noon?'

Leaning forward, she squeezed his hand tightly. They had better not start hugging and kissing again. Somebody would almost certainly see them. 'Mister Tilbrook, I would look forward to that.'

As he mounted the horse, she stood back to give him a

little space. Before she realised it, he was gone, his farewell fading in the breeze.

A few minutes later, she climbed the slope towards the cottage, meeting her mother outside in the garden. Clenching her fists to ease the tension, she tried to speak normally. 'Hello, Mam, I'm back. How are you keeping? Is there any tea in the pot?'

Her mother stood up and looked at the girl in front of her. She took in the ruffled hair, the colour in the cheeks, the bruised lips, and the heaving breast. And above all, the flashing eyes and the laughing face.

'Where did you go with the dogs then, Kate?' she enquired carefully.

'Oh, only up the hill, Mam, behind the church,' Kate replied quickly. 'You know, where I usually go.'

'And did you meet anyone else while you were up there?' her mother asked innocently.

Kate blushed crimson. 'Anyone else, Mam. What do you mean?' she stammered. 'There is never anyone else up there.'

Why was she being asked all these questions? Nobody could possibly know that she had met Edward. Someone might have seen them coming back to the village, but they would not be able to mention it to anyone else until tomorrow. Or did her mother just know these things?

Without another word, Kate rushed into the house. If her mother did suspect something, the last thing she wanted was a cross-examination. She was going to have to keep the conversation to her week at the big house, how the children had behaved, and the news she had heard from Dublin. These would be much safer subjects, and far less emotional.

A few hours later, she was back in her room at Mistress Delamere's house in Enniskerry. Even now, she could feel the excitement and the tension in her body. Lying on the bed, she tried to recall how she had felt when James Lavelle had almost made love to her. Strangely, she could hardly remember; all she could think about now was Edward's kisses, and his fingers caressing her back.

Jumping off the bed, she began to get undressed. As her clothes slipped off she could feel the touch of his lips on her neck. With a long sigh she lay back on the pillows, and deliciously gave herself to dreaming about what had happened that afternoon. As she remembered the passion in their kisses, her hand crawled slowly across her stomach and slipped easily between her thighs. It had been such a wonderful day.

It was almost the middle of the week before she managed to get her emotions under control. On the outside she tried to appear as she usually did, but inside was a different matter altogether. Concentrating on her teaching was such an effort that she went to bed every evening feeling exhausted, and then she spent all night tossing and turning, getting almost no rest.

Normally, after she set the children their tasks, she used that time to look forward and develop the lessons she would be setting later on. But not this week. Each time the children settled down, her mind drifted back to the previous Sunday afternoon. Before long, she would be thinking about kissing and cuddling and how good she had felt. But pleasant as they were, as often as not these daydreams left her hot, flustered and aroused. Three or four times early in the week she had to go upstairs and throw cold water over her face to help her to concentrate. It helped a little but the effect did not last for long.

By Wednesday, after a few days had passed, she was feeling slightly more relaxed and in control. What helped particularly was the interest that young Arthur Wellesley was showing in her teaching. Every day he wanted to ask her questions, especially after the other children had finished their lesson and gone off to play before tea. He was of a more serious disposition than the others, but he had an impressive capacity for learning new subjects. He was interested in all of Kate's stories about Fionn and Cuchulainn and Conn the Hundred Fighter, especially the bloodthirsty parts. He also wanted to know about everything else that went on in the world; his questions forcing her to think long and hard, occasionally having to cast her mind back to Mr Hutchinson's observations, and sometimes having to search through Mistress Delamere's library.

Despite his single-mindedness, it was stimulating to find a child with such a thirst for knowledge, and Kate was reminded sometimes of herself at the hedge school. She must have come across to Mr Hutchinson in a similar way, constantly asking questions, never giving him peace. They had been good times, although they seemed so long ago. And now she was teaching this boy, always so polite, just as she had been. He even framed his questions in the same way. 'Miss Brennan, can you tell me about this?' And it was always, 'Thank you Miss Brennan.' What on earth would he be telling his mother and father when they came back from England? And they were going to be pleased at finding their son's head packed with useless knowledge about the most obscure subjects, leavened with a wide appreciation of old Ireland's heathen ways?

And then she had Mistress Delamere to contend with. She had guessed that Edward Tilbrook was the man in the hospital in Kate's telling of the events in London, but now she wanted to know more. Where did he come from? What was his background? How old was he? Had he been married before? Was he still an English army officer?

These and a hundred more probing questions. Simply listening to the woman brought all of Kate's doubts out in the open. These were questions she should have been asking him herself. Instead she spent all that time kissing him and clinging to him like an idiot. Why could she not have found out more about him first? What if he was already married?

By the time the following Saturday came round, she had worked herself up into a frenzy of doubts. At first, she could not make up her mind whether to stay in the garden until Edward called, if in fact he came at all. Or perhaps it would be better to be in her room when he arrived? Or should she be hovering somewhere close to the door, so she could slip out with a minimum of fuss? Would it be acceptable if she walked down the driveway and caught him outside the grounds of the house before anyone even saw him?

What did one do in these circumstances? All morning, she paced up and down nervously, trying to decide. It was obvious to everyone, especially Mistress Delamere, that she had something on her mind.

'Kate, what on earth is the matter with you today? You're going to wear out that piece of Axminster if you're not careful.'

Her cheeks burning with embarrassment, she hung her head. 'Oh, I'm sorry, Mistress Delamere, I didn't realise what I was doing.' Involuntarily, however, she glanced out of the door and down the driveway, but there was nobody in sight.

'I think you're rather tense today, Kate. Why don't you go into the kitchen, sit down and have a cup of tea? That will help you to relax. O'Brien will call you should anything unusual happen. He's very experienced in these matters, and he knows when to speak and when not to.'

Reluctantly, she decided she had better follow Mistress Delamere's suggestion. A few minutes later she was sitting in the kitchen, drinking her tea, and practising the questions she was going to ask. Without warning, Edward appeared through the door, his smile as broad as ever. She jumped up, almost spilling the tea in her lap.

'My God, you surprised me there.' It was almost a shriek. 'How did you get in here?'

He looked at her, still smiling. Every inch a man who knew how to melt her heart. 'It was not difficult, Kate, not even for an Englishman. Mistress Delamere and her man O'Brien were standing outside the door when I arrived. She said I was expected and that you were in the kitchen. So here I am, with my horse and trap. I thought we could go for a little trip somewhere.'

So the Mistress had guessed all along that Edward was coming to visit her today. So much for keeping all this a secret, she thought wryly to herself. Well, if everyone knew, then she might as well stand up, take his arm, and walk out the door with him. Which she did, although she need scarcely have worried. The hallway was empty, with nobody to be seen in the courtyard either.

Outside, Edward held her hand as she stepped up into the trap. He was about to pick up the reins for the horse when Mistress Delamere appeared at the side of the door.

'Have a nice time, Kate,' she called. 'What shall I tell Mister Grattan if he comes here today and wonders where you are?' Her voice was almost drowned out by the noise of the horse's hooves. Almost but not quite.

'Aha, Kate Brennan,' Edward gave her a sly look as he got the horse started. 'So who is this Mister Grattan who comes to see you?'

She swore under her breath – it was unbelievable: all morning she had been practising her questions to put to him, and now he had managed to put her on the defensive before she had a chance to begin. She was going to need all her charm and her sweetest smile.

'He's a gentleman friend of Mister and Mistress Delamere who comes to call occasionally on a Saturday afternoon. He has a house nearby, and one, I believe, in Tunbridge Wells in England. When he's here we generally discuss politics and current affairs in both England and Ireland.'

'I see,' replied Edward, not in the slightest put out by the self-mocking tone of her voice. 'That is interesting. But much more important, where are you planning to take me today?'

Following her conversation earlier in the week with Mistress Delamere, Kate had been thinking hard about this. They had to go to a place where other people would be around. She was determined to find out all she could, but if they were alone like the previous week she couldn't trust herself to resist if he started kissing and cuddling, and she would never find out the answers to any of her questions.

'I think I'd like to drive down to Bray, and then along the Seapoint Road. We can walk along the strand and take in the sea air.' Despite her best intentions, she could not resist squeezing his arm for a moment. But she had to ask him now, while she was still resolute.

'So tell me, Edward,' she began, as innocently as she could. 'Do you have a house in England?'

'I see, Kate, that today is going to be the day of the inquisition, is that it? No more romance until you know who you're dealing with, is that your game?' His look was stern, but his eyes were twinkling.

But how had he managed to do that? Or was he so experienced with women that he knew what they were thinking even before they spoke?

As he took hold of her hand and kissed it gently, Kate realised that she must have looked a little crestfallen and that he was making up to her.

'Well, Miss Brennan, where shall I begin? Yes, I have a house in London, not all that far away from your Mistress Jardine. But I've been abroad in the service of my country, so I haven't been there very often.'

As he finished speaking, she drew in a deep breath. 'So you've been campaigning with the English army?'

Edward looked at her for a moment. 'I would do if I was called upon to do so, but I haven't seen much in the way of front-line action. My task is to find out who is plotting against us, and what they are planning to do next. That's why my skin is so brown. It's been burnt by the sun in places far away from here, in Africa, India and the Arabic countries. I have the gift of being able to speak in French, Spanish and some Arabic tongues, and my appearance doesn't resemble a typical English gentleman. So often I can find out in advance what is being planned, and I usually try and speak with the prisoners we take, because sometimes they have useful information.'

Again he looked at her, and smiled. 'But I fear it's become a task for men younger than me. I've had enough of conflict and personal injury. Little did I know, mind you, that my greatest moment of danger would be at the hands of a mad Irish woman.'

By this time they had reached Bray, and he stopped talking for a moment to concentrate on guiding the trap along the main street. As they turned onto the path that led down to the beach, he began speaking again.

'As far as my family is concerned, my mother and father are both dead some years from the fever, my brother also, and I have one sister who is in Virginia, in America, and another who is married to a Frenchman, believe it or not. But I don't know the whereabouts of either, and I haven't heard from them for years.'

Keeping the horse under control, he glanced at her out of the corner of his eye. 'And that, Miss Brennan, is me.'

A moment later, they reached the strand at the end of the Seapoint Road, and Edward brought the horse to a halt. Jumping athletically to the ground, he walked round to help her down. Instead of taking her hand, however, he leaned forward and grasped her round the waist. It was so easy to fall forward into his arms. And it felt so good.

Putting her hands around his back, she laid her head on his chest and held him close. The thought of not having any family, of losing a mother and father, it was so frightening. But it was something she had never considered before, something that had never occurred to her to think about. But she had to ask one last question.

'And have you been married, Edward?' she whispered, against his chest.

The man laughed and fondled the back of her neck. 'I've come close to it a few times, but I've always managed to escape.' Looking down at her, he put his hand gently under her chin. 'Don't look so serious. It's only a little joke. No, I haven't been married. There's only one woman in my life and she's standing in front of me right now. There's your answer. Now let me tie up this horse and we'll go for a stroll along this strand, as you call it.'

The walk out towards the headland and back again took almost two hours. By the time they returned to where the horse was, the mood of the previous Sunday had been more than recaptured. Although there were other people walking nearby, and even some swimming in the sea, Kate could not stop herself from taking his hand, or his arm, or from touching his chest. And he was no different. At one point she was convinced he was going to sweep her up and start kissing her in public in the middle of the strand. But he had managed to control himself, more's the pity.

As they were coming back through the village of Bray, on impulse she directed him along the track beside the river where there was some common ground.

'Sometimes they have horse races here,' she explained. 'And I've often seen people riding horses over this common. It might be interesting to see what's going on.'

Sure enough, it wasn't long before they came upon a small group of men with some horses. Some were riding, while others had dismounted and were walking the animals on the bridle. Edward looked around, surveying the scene.

'Let's stop here for a moment, Kate, and watch what they're doing. It looks to me as if they might be training those horses over there; maybe they're getting ready for a race.'

As Edward got down from the trap to have a closer look, Kate watched him anxiously for a moment, before jumping down and going over to join him.

'I don't think you want to get any closer, Edward. The people involved in horse racing have the reputation of being excessively rowdy. I don't want to be associated with any of them.'

But it was too late. One of the men had seen Edward and came sidling over in their direction.

'Good day to you, sir,' he called out, in a broad accent. 'I can see you're admiring the horses. Do you know, you look like a sporting gentleman, sir. Would you be interested in a small wager?'

Immediately, Kate pulled at Edward's arm. 'Come away from here, please' she hissed. 'My mother has always told me that this is not a good place to stop.'

But Edward just smiled. 'Don't worry, Kate, it's only a bit of fun, that's all.'

Before she could stop him, he turned and spoke to the other man. 'I'm not sure about that, my good fellow. I can't see anything here that would make me want to risk my money.'

Kate looked up. She had never heard him speaking like that before – he sounded like an English aristocrat.

Edward continued in the same lofty tone. 'And what were you thinking of, my good man?'

The Irishman nodded at his companions. 'Well, for sure, I have here some of the finest animals you'll see in all of Ireland. And we were thinking we might have a race.'

'I say, sir,' cried Edward. 'Are you expecting me to place a wager on who will win when I don't know the horses or the jockeys?'

'It appears to me that you might be a good judge of these things, sir,' the man replied, giving Edward a sly look. 'I think you might even have been on a horse's back a few times yourself. You might even want to join in the race, sir?'

'I could not possibly do that,' Edward's voice boomed. 'I'm much heavier than any of you. I would be at a complete disadvantage.'

Once more, Kate tried desperately to pull him away. 'Edward, for God's sake,' she pleaded with him. 'Don't get involved in this.'

But again he shook her off. Now the Irishman was bringing forward one or two bigger horses. 'Well, you could be having one of these animals, sir, and then you would not be at a disadvantage at all.'

For a few moments, Edward scrutinised the mounts in front of him. 'And what is this race?' His voice boomed out again in the same excruciating accent. 'Where to, and how long?'

'Do you see that tree down there, sir? From here to there and back is about a mile. How would that suit you? Just you and me. And I was thinking we might have ten guineas on the result?'

By now, Kate had resigned herself to having to watch them race. She was sorry she had ever thought of bringing Edward here. He seemed determined to go through with this madness, meaning she would have to put up with it, but why did he have to keep speaking like this caricature of an English lord?

Edward squinted at the tree, and then at the horse. Stepping to one side, he picked up a large branch of dead wood and thrust it into the ground close to where they were standing.

'If you want a race, my good man, then I'll give you one. From here round that tree and back again twice, finishing at this line here. And let's have a sporting wager of twenty guineas.' He slapped the Irishman on the back. 'What do you say to that?'

The man thought about it for a minute. 'You're on, sir,' he replied, spitting into his palm and shaking hands on the arrangement.

Kate could scarcely believe this was happening in front of her eyes. But she had to watch as Edward went over to the horse, adjusted the stirrups for a moment or two, and then climbed up into the saddle. For some reason he looked strangely awkward compared to the way she had seen him riding the previous weekend. Then she realised the difference. The stirrups were set so short that his knees were bent at a sharp angle high on the horse's shoulders. Before she had time to take this in, the two riders had lined up and they were off. And it seemed to be at an amazing speed, with the horses kicking up huge clods of earth as they went past.

The Irishman was soon a long way in the lead, riding as if his life depended upon it. But although he was lagging behind, Edward did not appear to be trying to catch up. In fact, he looked very strange indeed, riding with his face up against the horse's mane, and his bottom stuck up in the air. As far as she could see, he wasn't sitting in the saddle at all.

At the end of the first lap, Edward was so far behind that she could hear the Irishman's companions cheering, as they began to celebrate a fine victory over the English gentleman. And although she had tried not to get involved, to be truthful she felt a little disappointed. After everything he had said about horses, she had been convinced that he was a good judge of animals and a good horseman, but her assessment seemed to be some way off the mark.

Turning away slowly, she tried not to let the others see her disappointment. As she began trudging back over to the trap, all of a sudden it became noticeable that the cheering had died down considerably. Glancing over her shoulder, she was amazed to see that the race was nearly finished. But somehow or other, Edward's horse had almost caught up on the other. And while the local man was belabouring his mount with his whip, it was obvious even to her that the poor beast was exhausted. Meanwhile, Edward was riding in his unusual position, without using a whip, and apparently without using much effort either. But as inexpert as she was, even from a distance she could see the strength in his knees and his heels, holding the animal straight, pushing it forward. Mesmerised, she watched as his horse seemed to sweep forward and joined the other, the two animals crossing the line together.

As the riders trotted back to the group of spectators, it was obvious they had been in a race, as they tried to catch their breath and wipe the mud from their faces.

The Irishman was the first to speak. 'I would say you can ride a bit, sir.'

With a broad smile, Edward looked over at him. 'That I can. But you're more than capable yourself, I think. Still, you'd want to find out a bit more before you make your next wager, would you not?'

Kate looked sharply at his expression, as did the other man. Gone was the high-pitched English accent. Gone were the foppish mannerisms. In fact he sounded more Irish than anything else.

'I'd call it a dead heat, wouldn't you?' he continued, putting his hand out to the other man.

'For sure, that I would,' replied the Irishman, cocking his head to one side. 'But do you think you might fancy another go tomorrow?' Immediately, they both laughed uproariously, getting down from their horses and slapping each other on the back.

As Edward handed over the reins to one of the other men, Kate went over and grabbed him by the arm.

'Why did you do that? What was all this English way of speaking and then changing to sound like an Irishman?'

'Sure, Kate, would I ever do a thing like that?' He switched back to his normal voice. 'It was just a bit of fun, and I like racing and the challenge. And besides I wanted him to think I was an easy target.'

'But surely you could have won the race in the end?' Kate was baffled.

'That I could have, my dear Kate. I know that and he knows that; but he doesn't have the twenty guineas, and I have no need of the money. So it was a fair result.'

All she could do was shake her head, as she brushed

some clumps of grass and mud from his coat. 'Edward Tilbrook, you're a devious man. I can see I'm going to have to spend all my time watching you, or else you'll be taking advantage of me.'

'Kate,' he replied, 'I can't think of anything else in the world I would rather do. Now come and give me a kiss.' And she fell into his arms, into their own world, just the two of them.

After Mass the next morning, Kate walked back to the cottage with her mother. Eamonn had gone off to see his friends while Declan was nowhere to be seen. As usual, her father had decided to stay in Cormack's and have a few glasses of stout.

'So how are things up at the House, Kate?' her mother was asking.

'I'm still enjoying it, Mam, although it's hard work, especially now with four children.'

Her mother took her arm. 'And I understand you're receiving lots of letters from England. You must have made a big impression on the people over there.'

'Just from a few people, Mam, that's all,' Kate replied briefly. Conversations which turned to her time in England were something she did not care for, particularly since she had told her parents only the briefest details about the trip. With some relief, she heard her mother changing the subject.

'And what are you planning to do this afternoon?'

Again she spoke quickly. 'I was thinking I'd do what I nearly always do. I'll take the dogs out for a walk on the hillside.'

For a moment, her mother looked at her steadily. 'And

would you like one of us to come with you? Why don't you ask Declan along, perhaps. He needs more exercise than the dogs, for God's sake.'

Although she had to laugh, this was a dangerous subject. 'No, no, Mam, I'll be all right by myself. I like to walk wherever I want, and I can only do that by myself.'

Her mother gave her another long look. 'Whatever you say, Kate. Just be careful, that's all I would say to you.'

This was becoming too difficult, she muttered to herself as soon as her mother was out of earshot. Somehow or other, she seemed to have detected that something was going on. They were was going to have to be more careful, or else she would have to tell her. And she was not ready for that yet.

For the next hour or so, she pottered around the cottage, drinking tea, and tidying up places that had already been tidied up three or four times.

'In the name of God, Kate,' her mother said finally. 'I thought you told me you were going out. Look, the dogs are going mad. Would you ever be on your way?'

At last, the time was right, and she set off through the village and up the hill past the church. Although desperate to see Edward again, she still had to pause for a moment and look back down the valley. It was another wonderful day, a miracle really. She and Edward seemed to be blessed with fine weather whenever they were together.

As the minutes went by, she began to wonder where he might be, when suddenly he came up the track behind her, again with the horse and trap.

'Miss Brennan, could I interest you in a lift?' he called

out, as he pulled up beside her.

Laughing, she ran over towards the trap. 'Edward, I've missed you,' she cried, jumping up onto the seat and kissing him all in one continuous movement. 'I've been thinking about you constantly.'

Edward squeezed her waist playfully. 'For goodness' sake woman, you're not supposed to say things like that. And we saw each other only yesterday.'

For a moment she smiled at the memory, before a thought struck her. 'But you have the horse and trap with you. I'm supposed to be out walking with the dogs.'

'Kate, you've been telling me so much about the countryside around here, that I thought we might go right up to the top of the valley with the dogs, and take them out for a walk there.'

Enthusiastically, she clapped her hands. 'That's a wonderful idea, Edward, especially as I've been up there only a few times. It's such a long hard hill to climb. But if the horse can manage it, the view is worth all the effort.'

With the dogs foraging alongside, they took it fairly slowly up what was really no more than a track, with Kate clinging to Edward's arm. After a few minutes of this, she felt him digging her in the ribs with his elbow.

'While the poor horse is dragging us up here, Kate, why don't you tell me one of your tales. Mistress Delamere mentioned to me that you've been writing them all down.'

'They're merely old fairy stories, Edward, but they might have happened a long time ago. Someday I'll let you see them.'

She looked around. 'Look, we're near the top. From

here we can go in different ways. That direction takes us all the way to Glendalough, where Saint Kevin started up his monastery. And if we take this other path, we'll go past Powerscourt where you were staying last week. There's a beautiful waterfall near there and a grassy meadow where we can walk with the dogs. I think we'll go there today.'

Edward encouraged the horse to start up again. 'Whatever you say is fine by me, Kate Brennan. As long as you don't get us lost.'

Again, she took him by the arm. 'I've always wanted to go up to Glendalough. I've never been there, and my schoolteacher has told me all about it. But it takes two hours at least with a horse and trap. Would you take me there next Saturday when we have more time?'

For some reason, she felt shy about asking him about the next week. They had never spoken about how long he would be staying in Ireland. She was not even sure he would still be there next week.

But she need not have worried. 'I can hardly wait, Kate. All I ask is that you do your homework beforehand, so you can give me the guided tour. But now that we're here, take me to this waterfall.'

The afternoon turned out beautifully. Because of the dry weather, the water level in the river was too low for the falls to be spectacular, but it was peaceful in this wooded part of the country. With not another person to be seen, they strolled between the trees, laughing, hugging, and kissing. Kate could feel them being drawn closer and closer together. She knew they were going to make love.

Briefly, her mind went back to James Lavelle. Yes, she

had wanted him, but it had been no more than a moment of passion. With Edward, she wanted to be with him, to listen to him, to feel him touching her, to hold him in her arms and protect him. She was so glad nothing had developed with James. He was a lovely man, but she wanted Edward. He was the one she wanted to give herself to, he was the one she loved. Kate stopped for a moment. What had she just said to herself? Turning half round and glancing upwards, she studied his face carefully. She did love him. That was it, that was why it felt so good, just thinking about it.

Impetuously, she put her hand on Edward's arm to stop him from walking any further. Snuggling deeply into his embrace, she turned her face upwards. 'Have you enjoyed this afternoon, Edward?'

With an easy smile, he nodded in agreement. 'It's always wonderful being with you, Kate Brennan.'

'I never know when you're serious, Edward,' she whispered, catching his eye with hers. 'But I've enjoyed our time together so much.'

Burying her face in his chest, she luxuriated in the strength of his body. 'And I've fallen in love with you,' she murmured, so quietly that he could scarcely hear.

For a long moment, Edward held her face gently between his hands, his fingers stroking her cheeks. 'Kate, my sweet little girl. Are you sure? If you are, we are lost together. I've loved you from the first moment I saw you in the hospital.' Interrupting himself, he kissed her tenderly on the lips. 'But I could see so many barriers between us. I didn't think it right to put those pressures upon you. But now, if you're sure, I think we can try to cross them together.'

As she walked back through the village after he dropped her off, Kate's head was still spinning. Although trying to think about what they would do next, all she really felt like doing was shouting out loud, and laughing, and doing a little jig every few steps. It was the strangest feeling. What was she going to tell her mother? Would she ever be able to explain?

As she arrived at the cottage her mother came out through the doorway. 'Kate, where have you been for so long? Look at those poor dogs. They're absolutely exhausted. I don't know what's got into you.'

Impulsively, Kate decided she had to say something. 'Mam, what did you feel like when you first met Dad? Did you feel strange or different?'

Her mother gave her a long slow look. 'I might have guessed. You've been swooning over some young man. Are you going to tell me who it is? It's not that Cathal, is it? I thought you and he weren't talking to each other.'

'No Mam,' Kate sighed. 'It's not Cathal. It's someone I met while I was in London.'

Her mother sniffed. 'Some drinking crony of Declan's, or even one of Patrick Nolan's unsavoury friends, I presume. Could you not do any better than that?'

Kate looked hard at her mother. She had to tell her. 'No, Mam. It's nobody like that. It's an Englishman I met at the hospital.'

'What?' her mother exploded. 'An Englishman? Are you mad? Have you lost all your senses? These are the people who have raped this country, they've taken everything we ever had, and you have to go losing your head over one? Is an Irishman not good enough for you?'

'Mam, Mam,' Kate wailed, 'He's not like that at all.

And he loves me.' Lifting her head defiantly, her eyes flashed as she stamped her foot on the floor. 'And I love him.'

Without warning, her mother picked up an iron poker, walked across the room, and brandished it in her daughter's face. 'Let me tell you my girl, if I see you out with any Englishman, I'll not be responsible for my actions. And when your father hears about this, there will be hell to pay.'

'I'm sorry, Mam, that you feel that way,' Kate replied, breathing heavily. 'But I'll not be threatened by my own mother over this. When you have calmed down, perhaps we can discuss this matter again.'

For a moment, she spoke coolly, in control of her emotions. But all at once she could hold it no longer, bursting into a flood of tears. Still sobbing, she went over to pick up her bag, and ran out of the house without a backward glance. Her mother took one step forward then stopped, blinded by her own tears and the irrational fury that swept through her body.

Chapter 11

All week, Kate could not stop thinking about her mother's words. Truth to tell, she had expected some form of adverse comment, but nothing as strong as the reactions she had encountered. If this was what it was like just mentioning the word 'Englishman', what was it going to be like when she told them it was an English soldier she had fallen in love with?

It was so unfair. Nobody cared if Declan had been seeing an English girl; nobody worried about that. And it was not as if Kate had been flaunting herself around the village and talking about it to everyone. It could be even worse: she could be pregnant and going to have a baby. What would they have said then? She had not even made love to the man, for God's sake. What if she told her mother she was still a virgin? What would she say to that?

Her mother was a fine one to talk, she was only forty years old and had a grown family already. That meant that Mam and Dad had first made love when she was only seventeen years old, or even earlier. She had no right to try to be putting her foot down. Kate had never thought about her parents making love before now, but they must have done. They must still be doing it, for God's sake! The whole situation was just so unfair. But if they thought that they would stop her seeing Edward, they had better think again. Did her mother not know that she loved the man?

In a state of furious determination, Kate worked her way through the week. The children did more lessons than ever, while she finished off more letters and wrote down more words for her Irish fables than she had previously in any other week. But it did not go unnoticed. By Thursday evening, Mistress Delamere felt she had to say something. While they were having tea together, she decided to speak up.

'How are things going with the children this week? Everyone seems to be very busy.'

Before replying, Kate put down her cup of tea. 'Yes, they're working hard, and I think they're all making excellent progress.'

Pausing for a moment, the Mistress eyed her warily. 'You don't think that perhaps you're pushing yourself a little too hard?'

'I don't think so, Mistress Delamere,' she replied a little uncertainly. 'I've a few things on my mind, and working helps me to concentrate.'

'Kate Brennan, I can see the same look on your face that you had when you came here at first, and you were worried about your brother. Something's concerning you – but if you don't want to talk about it, I won't press you.'

All of a sudden, Kate could feel herself close to tears. 'It's Edward Tilbrook, Mistress Delamere. Well, it's not really Edward. I think I've fallen in love with him, and I tried to tell my mother about it. But she went into a blind fury and wouldn't even discuss it. She even threatened to do him harm yet she doesn't even know the man.'

Mistress Delamere sat back in her chair, taking stock of what she had just heard. 'You think you've fallen in love with him, you say. Well, he's a remarkably attractive man, but he's quite a bit older than you and much more experienced in the ways of the world. Have you thought that you might simply be infatuated with him? That it might be something that won't last?'

Jumping up out of her chair, Kate paced backwards and forwards across the carpet. 'Mistress Delamere, you may think that I'm only a young girl and easily led, but let me tell you I know what infatuation feels like. And I can assure you this is not infatuation.'

For a moment, the Mistress eyed her with a cool detachment. 'All right, I believe you. Now, sit down for a moment and we'll try and see what the problem might be.'

Smiling sheepishly at her outburst, she sat down quietly at the table. 'I'm sorry, Mistress Delamere. But last Sunday I was so happy I felt like singing, and then my mother's words killed it for me.'

The other woman nodded. 'So let me understand this. You've fallen in love with Edward Tilbrook. How does he feel towards you?'

'He says he loves me too.'

'So you love each other.' Choosing her words carefully, she carried on. 'And are you pregnant, by any chance?'

Kate shifted uncomfortably in her chair. 'I don't think so. No, I'm sure I can't be.'

The Mistress scratched her head. 'That's a funny thing to say, Kate. Either you are or you aren't.'

Red with embarrassment, Kate hung her head. 'We haven't made love, if that's what you mean.'

'Well, it wasn't quite what I meant, but it does answer the question.' Mistress Delamere thought for a moment.

'I'm fortunate to know your mother very well, and I respect her for her sincerity and also her forthright manner of speaking. I can understand why your parents would be desperately unhappy at their only daughter taking up with an Englishman. The history of the English in Ireland and especially the redcoats is not a story to be proud of. The Irish have been treated desperately badly by the English, and many people in this country have long memories.'

Reaching across the table, she took Kate's hand. 'However, you're not your typical young Irish girl, Kate. Your parents have provided you with a good education, and your schoolteacher has opened your eyes to the world. In the last year you've met so many people, and you've amazed me by your ability to charm them with your beauty and intelligence. But don't expect your family or your friends to see the world the way that you do, and especially, don't expect them to see an English army officer in a favourable light.'

She stopped to pour out some tea, allowing Kate to ponder over her words. 'I'm sure that you and Edward are in love,' she continued. 'I'm also sure that he'll have to return to England soon to attend to his responsibilities there. What I suggest is that you wait until he's done that, and you've been apart for some time, and then look to see if you're still so much in love. After that, you may have to face up to a confrontation with your parents, but I suggest you wait until then.'

Holding her head in her hands, Kate gazed pensively into her cup of tea. 'I'm sorry to be such a burden. And I have to thank you for your kind thoughts. As ever, I'm sure you're right. Before I do anything else, I'll ask Edward how long he plans to stay here in Ireland.' Without waiting any longer, she stood up from the table. 'And now I must go to bed, Mistress Delamere. All this emotion is so exhausting.'

The other woman laughed. 'It's much better when you get older and things are not quite so intense. Sleep well and remember, don't work yourself so hard.'

That night, Kate did sleep much more soundly. Early the next morning, as she stood in front of the glass examining her face, it was good to see that the black smudges under her eyes had almost disappeared. She was going to take Mistress Delamere's words to heart, and have an easier, more enjoyable day. And Edward would be back tomorrow– the thought of seeing him again added to her mood. Suddenly she felt happy, for the first time in almost five days.

Slipping off her nightgown, she leaned over the washbowl to clean her hands and face. Suddenly she though of Edward standing behind her, holding her around the waist, kissing her back. The feeling was so exciting she had to glance over her shoulder to make sure she was still alone. Having been so unhappy earlier in the week, she had been unable to think much about them being together, but now she felt much better. For a few moments she treated herself by imagining he was still there. Then, towelling herself vigorously, she looked forward to the days ahead.

In very little time it was Saturday, and Edward arrived, as good-natured as ever. Outside the gate, Kate made him stop the carriage and the two horses he had brought this time.

'What's wrong? Have you forgotten something?' he asked her anxiously.

Leaning across the bench seat, she threw her arms around his shoulders. 'There's nothing wrong, Edward. In fact it's the opposite. I just wanted to do this.' And she kissed him again and again, wriggling herself up against him.

With a struggle, he managed to wrestle himself free. 'What's the matter with you? We're just outside Mistress Delamere's house and it's the middle of the day. What if someone sees us?'

'I don't care, Edward. I love you, and I wanted a cuddle.'

Edward shook his head. 'You realise, of course, that you're driving me mad? Have you thought of that?'

Sitting up straight, she rested her hands primly in her lap. 'All right, Mister Tilbrook. Let's be on our way. I'm ready now, and I promise not to distract you again.'

Edward had to laugh at her serious expression. 'Don't forget, Kate, we're going to Glendalough today. I've found out which direction to travel, and you're going to tell me all about it.'

'When you get lost, Mister Tilbrook, you can come to me begging for directions,' she replied, refusing to meet his gaze. 'But until then you lead the way.'

But she could not play the game for long, and after a few moments she took him by the arm, and started her history lesson. 'Kevin, or Coemghen in the ancient Irish, was born in the year 498, when the Romans were still in England. He was ordained a priest in a monastery in Tallaght, which is near Dublin, but he decided to become a hermit and came to Glendalough to live.'

Before he could ask the question, she turned and shook her head. 'Don't ask me why he wanted to be a hermit, I haven't the faintest idea. But he had a way with animals and any cow that he touched always yielded more milk than the others. The people found out about that and he was not able to remain a hermit for long, because they all wanted him to touch their cows. Do you know, we could be doing with somebody like that in Kilcarra right now.'

Giggling at her own joke, she had to stop to let herself recover. 'It's then said that he had a dream in which God told him that a religious place should be established at Glendalough, and scholars would come from all over the world to study there. And that's what happened.'

Edward looked at her out of the corner of his eye. 'Am I expected to believe all this? How do you know what happened all those years ago? Or is this one of your stories?'

'No, it's not a story. This is all true. My schoolteacher studied these matters and he's read some of the writings of the times. After Kevin died, the Vikings came and ransacked the place, but the monks built a tower to take refuge in, which is still standing, so I believe. I'd like to see that, because Mister Hutchinson has told me so much about it.'

As she carried on, she could see that he was losing track of her tales of Coemlug and Coemell, the O'Tooles and the O'Byrnes, shaking his head at the unlikely name of Dermot McMurrough, and pursing his lips when she managed to drag the Pope in as well. Funnily enough, it had never occurred to her before, but almost everyone seemed to have been involved with Glendalough at some time or other.

Her store of knowledge about their destination exhausted, she began to take a greater interest in her surroundings. For all the number of people connected with the place, it was not proving to be easy to find, especially when they had no more than a scrap of a drawing from O'Brien to guide them.

'Mister Tilbrook, do you know where exactly we are at this moment?' she demanded suddenly. 'Or do we need to ask somebody for directions?'

Fortunately, Edward had seen an old building over on their right which they had been looking out for, and which they took to be the Glanmore Castle marked on O'Brien's map. After that it was not too far, perhaps an hour or so. Sure enough, they arrived soon enough at the small hamlet of Laragh, and shortly after that reached a river spanned by a rickety-looking bridge, which Edward decided he would not even think about crossing in the carriage.

Feeling strangely excited, Kate climbed down and dragged Edward in the direction of Saint Kevin's church. As they climbed up over the hill, they paused to look out over the tower and the flagstones and the other ruins. It had been a beautiful day when they left Enniskerry, but now a damp, chilly mist had descended. It was all rather grey and eerie. As she looked up at the tower and the little doorway about eleven feet from the ground, Kate felt herself shivering. The monks must have had a ladder to get up there which they pulled up whenever they were attacked. How could they have lived in those days, having to go through that every few weeks?

It was a remarkable sight, and as she got closer to the church, she realised it had been too long since she had said her prayers. Kneeling down, she whispered a few words to Saint Kevin, in case he was watching them. Further on they walked, eventually reaching a lake situated in a remarkably steep-sided valley. Below their feet, the water was black with peat, matching the colour of the hills rising on each side. With the mist sweeping in, the atmosphere was almost frightening. Trembling slightly, Kate hung on tightly to Edward's arm.

'Beyond here, there's nothing until you reach the other side of Lughnaquilla mountain. It's a part of Ireland virtually cut off from everywhere else.'

Looking around, she shivered and pulled her shawl closer around her shoulders.

'What do you think of all this, Edward?' she whispered.

For a minute or two, the man surveyed the scene. 'It's an incredibly atmospheric place, Kate, without a doubt. I don't think I can remember being anywhere similar. History seems to be hanging in the air all around us.' Gently, he patted her hand. 'And I've never seen so many ancient buildings. Where I come from, there's a number of churches going back to Norman times, but nothing as old as this. It makes you feel small, somehow.'

All of a sudden it began to rain, a few drops at first, but

quickly developing into a downpour.

'Céad míle fáilte, welcome to Ireland,' she shouted, as they dashed back to the church to take some shelter. 'This is more what I'm accustomed to. One minute sunshine, the next a torrential downpour.'

Hand in hand, they stood in the church for over twenty minutes, but the rain showed no sign of abating. At the same time it had started to get very dark outside. Rubbing his chin, Edward peered out through the door and up at the sky.

'Kate, I don't think this rain is going to stop. I suggest we make a run for the carriage and go back to that village we passed through. Laragh, I think it was called. I saw an inn there and we might be able to get some shelter and try to dry off.'

It took them no more than a few minutes to get to the carriage, and another few to reach the inn. The rain sleeted down incessantly and although they had found a blanket to cover up most of Kate's dress, her hair and face were soaked, and Edward's shirt and breeches were sopping wet.

As soon as they reached the inn, Kate rushed inside, keeping the blanket wrapped around her, while Edward went off with the landlord to see to the horses. Fortunately there were next to no customers around, so there was little chance of anyone seeing her with the water dripping out of her hair. A few minutes later, Edward returned with a lamp in his hand, and a bag and a dry towel over his shoulder. Kate could not drag her eyes away from him. His shirt and his breeches were sticking to his body, while his hair was plastered to his skull. In all her life she had never seen anyone so desirable. But what must he be thinking of her? After all the time she had spent brushing her hair and making sure it was pinned up and looking exactly right. And now it had to be in a terrible state.

'Right, Kate Brennan,' he announced, 'follow me. The horses are being looked after, I've got us a room and the landlord is filling a bath and bringing us some brandy.'

Before she could reply, he took her by the hand and led her down a dark hallway. At the bottom he unlocked a door, threw it open, and ushered her inside. Suddenly, she felt terrified. All that hugging and kissing they had done, all that touching and whispering, and now they were absolutely alone together, in a private place with a bed. It was probably only an ordinary sized bed, but it seemed to fill the entire room. For a moment she stood on the threshold, the blanket still wrapped round her middle, every muscle in her body frozen in apprehension.

Without preamble, Edward pushed her inside, closed the door, and casually kissed her on the back of her neck. It was nice, it was familiar, it was something that he had done a thousand times before. Turning slowly, she caught hold of his hands. For a moment she searched his face, and then they were kissing, hugging, laughing and giggling. It had been such a wonderful day, even with the rain.

'Shhh,' Edward scolded her. 'The landlord will be here any minute and he'll be wondering what we're doing if you keep making all that noise.' Scarcely had he finished speaking when there was a knock at the door. 'Do you see what I mean?' he demanded, trying to look fierce.

As he went over to open up, Kate scurried to the other

side of the room. In came the landlord with another man carrying a huge bath between them, half-filled with hot water.

'Here you are, sir,' the landlord spoke up. 'I'll be back in a few minutes with another jug of water and your brandy as requested.'

A few minutes later they were sitting side by side on the bed, drinking from huge glasses of brandy, gazing down at the bath.

'Who's going to be first?' Edward asked innocently. 'I always think that ladies should go first.'

'Ah, but you're the wettest,' Kate replied saucily. 'I'm dry except for my hair.'

Taking the glass carefully from her hand, he placed it safely on the nearby table. As he turned back, suddenly he grabbed her round the waist and wrestled her onto the bed.

'Do you want to fight for it?' he whispered in her ear. 'Loser goes first.'

He took her arms and pushed her back on the bed. For a moment she resisted, but she did not have the strength or the will. Instead, she wrapped her arms around him and kissed him passionately. She could feel his lips and his tongue exploring hers. Now his lips were nibbling at her breasts through her dress. God, she wanted him so badly. Slowly, his hand slipped slowly down her body and up under her skirts and petticoats. She could feel his fingers caressing her knees and her thighs. Was she going to be able to make love to him, and should she tell him she was still a virgin? Would it make any difference? Would he even notice?

Summoning up all her resolution, she pushed gently

against his chest and sat up.

'What is it, Kate, what's wrong?' he asked her anxiously.

'Nothing's wrong at all, Edward. I love you and I want to make love to you. But I'm not sure what to do.' She turned away so that he could not see her face, blushing scarlet. 'I've never done this before,' she whispered, so quietly that he could barely hear her.

Immediately, he sat up beside her. 'Oh, Kate, you're so beautiful, but you don't need to look so unhappy about it. Everybody starts off that way.' Again he kissed her with exquisite tenderness on the lips. 'But perhaps we will leave it till another day.'

Gently, he pulled her to the side of the bed. 'Right, I've decided. I'm going to have the bath first. I'm the wettest. And also,' he turned her face towards him and gazed into her eyes. 'You have the advantage in that you're accustomed to seeing me naked.'

Casually, he lay back on the bed. 'Imagine you're back at the hospital, Kate, when you removed all of my clothes. All you have to do is the same thing again.'

As he lounged back on top of the blanket, Kate looked at him under her eyelashes, trying to work out whether he was joking or not. He did look appealing. And he was certainly still wet. Leaning forward, she touched his shirt; it was easy to unfasten and pull out of his breeches. Carefully, she slipped it off his shoulders, aware that he was watching her, aware of his closeness. She could see the mark of the wound in his shoulder. Funnily enough, it seemed to be much smaller than she remembered, and it looked now as if it was almost healed.

But she remembered his chest and his stomach, by

God, flat and hard with delicate black curls lying against the brown skin. The longing to kiss his chest was so intense, but somehow she resisted, deciding she had better play the game now they had started.

'Just roll over slightly, Edward,' she ordered, 'that's fine, so I can slip this shirt off.' Now he was naked to the waist in front of her. But this time he was wearing boots instead of shoes. These were much more difficult to get off, but somehow she managed. Slightly out of breath, she leaned over and unfastened his breeches at the waist and at the knees. For a moment it was too much for her, and she had to kiss him on the shoulder. But somehow or other she managed to get her hands back on his breeches. She could see him looking at her, smiling slightly, the sly fox. He was enjoying this, watching her struggle.

Remembering what she had done at the hospital, she closed her eyes, and with one desperate effort she felt his breeches slide over his hips and down over his feet. Before she could do anything else, she sensed him sitting up and taking her hands.

'Well done, Kate, you've certainly proved again that you have no equal in knowing how to undress a man,' she heard him murmuring in her ear. Opening her eyes slowly, she realised he was sitting naked on the edge of the bed. Her knees trembling, she felt him pulling her towards him, his hands going easily around her waist. Very deliberately she lowered her head and kissed him again. She could see and feel his shoulders and his chest, and now she could feel his manhood thrusting against her stomach.

Still very deliberately, he stood up and turned her around, starting to unfasten her dress, then her bodice, followed by her petticoats and pantaloons. His lips were burning into her back as his insistent fingers caressed her all over. It was impossible to take any more.

'Edward, please do it. It's too much for me to wait.' Her voice sounded so plaintive. Everything seemed to be going so slowly. Again, he sat back on the bed, leaning against the bolster. By now, she could hardly bear to look at him.

'Come on over here,' he whispered. With her eyes closed, she crawled up on the bed beside him. Taking her hand in his, he guided it down across his stomach. She could feel him, hard and erect, brushing against the back of her hand.

'Hold me in your hand, Kate Brennan. That part of my body is going to be inside you. I want you to touch it and feel it first.'

Tentatively at first, she took him in her hand, stroking him nervously. Beside her, she could hear him breathing sharply. All of a sudden, a sense of immense power flooded through her. She felt incredibly aroused, but it was a shock to realise that Edward must be feeling the same. Suddenly, his voice was hoarse against her shoulder.

'Kate, Kate, you're too much for me.'

She looked at his face, his eyes closed, his breathing harsh. It was wonderful. Her eyes dropped to his chest, to her hand, holding him. For a moment, she felt an insane giggle in her throat. What were they trying to do, for God's sake? He would never go inside her. But at least he seemed to know what he was doing. If it had been left to her, they would never have got anywhere. Before she knew it, his hands were around her waist, arranging their bodies to his liking.

'Just kneel here and face me,' he whispered, holding her firmly. 'Move your thighs on each side of my legs – that's it. Now push your hips towards me, yes, just like that.'

Suddenly, his fingers slipped between her thighs. His smooth, cool fingers, caressing her, fondling her, teasing her. God, it was exquisite, incredible. His lips were on her neck and in her ear. 'Kate, you little beauty, I can feel you, I can feel your virginity. God, you are beautiful.'

All at once, he pulled her hips down towards him. For an instant, as their bodies came together, she experienced the most incredible, intense pain tearing at her groin. Frantically, she tried to pull away, but he held her firmly in his hands. And then, glory be, he was inside her. It was too much. She could feel him thrusting inside her body. His kisses were burning her breasts and her nipples, his hands caressing her back and her thighs. It was all she could do not to sink her teeth into his shoulder.

With his hands cupping her bottom, he began moving her slowly backwards and forwards. By this time the pain had almost disappeared, and little waves of sensation had started coursing through her body. But for some reason she felt clumsy and awkward.

'Kate, my baby,' he was whispering in her ear. 'Don't rush at it, just go slowly, breathe naturally, let your movements follow the rhythm of your breathing.'

At first she could not understand what he was talking about. Pressing herself against him, she tried to follow his lead. Somewhere, far away, she could hear herself breathing heavily. All of a sudden, the sensation was intense, starting to overtake her. It was so alarming, she could feel herself panicking. Edward's voice was still encouraging her, his hands incredibly secure around her. For one long moment, everything seemed to happen all at once, and then she was left hanging, helpless, gasping, crying.

Very slowly, she felt herself coming back, coming down to earth. Suddenly, with an almost guilty start, she realised that her eyes were still closed and that she was holding his shoulders in a fierce grip, her nails digging into his skin.

Opening her eyes, she was aware he was watching her, smiling. 'Well, Kate, did you enjoy that?'

Dumbly, she nodded her head. It had been wonderful. Inexplicably, she felt like giggling again. But Edward was still whispering. 'It certainly looked as if you did. And I enjoyed watching it, even being a small part of it.'

'Oh, Edward,' she made a face at him. 'I'm sure you enjoyed it all much more than that.' Leaning forward, she kissed him tenderly, luxuriating in the feel of her breasts pressing against his bare chest. 'And I love you.' She stopped and looked closely at his expression. 'But is that it? Is that it finished?'

Before she could say any more, he took her gently by the shoulders and turned her over on her back. As his knee pushed between hers, spreading her legs wide, she gasped involuntarily as he slipped smoothly inside her.

'No, my little Irish colleen,' he replied. 'It's not finished. It's only just beginning.'

Half an hour later, she was lying on her back, holding Edward's hand and looking up at the ceiling. It had been so beautiful. But it was just as well that he knew what they were doing, and had put the towel underneath them.

It had never occurred to her that she would bleed so much, but it seemed to have stopped now. In fact, she felt exceptionally good, except that she was suddenly ravenous. Was that what lovemaking did for you? Made you hungry? It did not appear to have the same effect on Edward. All it seemed to make him do was sleep – and snore! But it had been lovely – and why did she not feel any sense of remorse? If what everybody said was true, she should be feeling racked with guilt right now. Instead, she was thinking how nice it would be to do it again, whenever they wanted to. What a glorious feeling.

Putting her hands behind her head, she crossed her legs and relaxed. It was a strange feeling indeed. She had expected to feel different somehow after she lost her virginity, after she had become a woman; but she felt just the same. Opening her legs a little, she flexed her knees, letting her mind drift back over the last hour or so.

For some reason she started thinking of Mistress Jardine back in London. It would be lovely to be sitting now, with a glass of brandy, discussing men and how they made love. Mistress Jardine would enjoy that sort of conversation, she could be certain of that.

Turning her head slightly, she gazed at the man sleeping beside her. Now he had stopped snoring, he seemed much more like the Edward she recognised and loved. He had been so gentle, and so patient, and so tender. He must have thought her just a little girl. How could she have let herself get so carried away? She could still hear herself crying and sobbing and sighing. How could he have had such an effect on her? Suddenly, she remembered being back at the cottage, years and years ago when her mother and father sent her into the other room to play. Now she could hear it again. It was the same noise, the same cries. It must have been her mother. They had been making love, and she had thought her mother might have not been feeling well.

How stupid people were when they were young and innocent. Turning over, she studied Edward's face, so handsome, so calm. He deserved a rest right enough – but not all evening. Moving closer, she dug her elbow into his ribs.

'Wake up, macushla,' she whispered in his ear. 'Wake up and make love to me.'

An hour later, the two of them were sitting downstairs in the inn, enjoying a dinner of beef and potatoes. It was a pleasant enough establishment, and the landlord was certainly very friendly. So much seemed to have happened that day, she could hardly believe it was not yet seven o'clock in the evening.

Although it was a small room, at least compared to the Lord Chatham in London, a few more people had come in, and the inn was starting to get much noisier. Two musicians had set themselves up in the corner, with a fiddle and a bodhrán, and the sound of their music was enough to get the feet tapping. Against one wall, next to where Kate and Edward were sitting, the landlord had built up a huge fire to ward off the chill from the mist and the rain outside.

Then someone started singing, while everyone else stopped talking to listen. It felt so good sitting there with her man beside her that she almost felt like crying with emotion. Peeping around the room, however, she realised apprehensively that everyone was taking their turn to sing. Leaning over towards Edward, she whispered in his ear. 'Have you noticed everyone is singing a song? They'll expect you to sing as well.'

Edward looked at her, shrugging his shoulders. 'If they want to be afflicted by the sound of my voice, upon their own heads be it.'

Once again, she was amazed at his lack of concern at being in a strange place and a strange culture. This was her first visit to this village, and she was not too sure about the local customs. To make matters worse, the others were looking in their direction. The time must have arrived when they were expecting Edward to sing or do something. Panicking slightly, she caught him by the hand.

'Edward,' she hissed. 'It's your turn. I think you're going to have to sing.'

Pushing the table back to give himself more room, he called to the fiddler to come over, at the same time standing up on his chair. Kate was so embarrassed she could scarcely bear to look.

He began to speak. 'This is a song you might not have heard before. It's a song about what nearly was. It tells of a terrible tragedy. It's a song about a man who inspired thousands of people to give their lives, too soon, too young.'

As he sang about a bonny Stuart prince, about a prince who had very nearly reclaimed a throne, but had died in the attempt, Kate listened in rapture with the rest of the people in the alehouse. His voice was wonderful, with the fiddler catching the mood so perfectly that the others could do no more than sit in front of the fire with tears in their eyes.

After he had finished and sat down, she laid her head

quietly against his shoulder. 'I didn't know you could sing like that, Mister Tilbrook. Nor a song like that either.'

For a moment, he glanced at her with an amused expression, running his fingers through her hair. 'It's a good song and in keeping with the mood of the Irish. I don't think they'd be too appreciative of me singing a song about England. However, and I don't like to remind you of this, but I think, Kate Brennan, that it's now your turn and that you're being called upon to perform.'

Fearfully, she looked around the bar. They were all looking at her. She was going to have to do something. And it was no use singing – not after Edward had just captivated everyone in the room. What could she do? Suddenly, out of the blue she found the inspiration, or maybe it was the brandy and the strong Irish ale. But could she do it in this strange place? Could she remember the words? Glancing at Edward sitting beside her, she felt her confidence growing from his nearness. Oh well, she consoled herself, in for a penny, in for a pound.

Without waiting any further, she rose to her feet. 'Don't expect me to sing. Not tonight.' She spread her hands theatrically. 'Not unless you want to hear the sound of the banshee wafting through this house. Is that what you want to hear?'

She could hear some of those nearest to her muttering, 'No, no, anything but that.'

Out of the corner of her eye, she saw Edward winking at her. If he could do it, so could she.

'What I'm going to do instead is tell you a story. Does anybody here know the legend of Cuchulainn?'

She heard some voices assenting.

'Gather round,' she cried, 'For I'm going to tell you the story of how the boy Setanta, son of Dectera, and nephew of Conchubar Mac Nessa, High King of all of Ireland, came to be known as the hound of Culain!'

To her amazement, some people began pulling chairs over towards her, while others looked up from their tankards of ale. Whatever happened, she had to go on now.

At first, all she could feel were the nerves fluttering in her stomach. After all, she had never spoken to so many people before. The thought of telling them a story, something she had never told anybody previously, and which she knew only because her mother had told it to her, was nerve-wracking, but she had started now so she had to go on.

For some reason the tale came easily. When she spoke of Setanta, she found her words were the words of a boy. And when she spoke about Fergus McRoy, the Tánaiste of Ulster, her voice became low, gruff, and hard. And when she turned to Conchubar, the High King, her voice was proud and strong and rang imperiously throughout the inn.

Now she could see that she had everyone's attention. Even the innkeeper had stopped and come over to listen. For a moment, she glanced at Edward for support, only to see him open-mouthed, hanging on to every word. God, she told herself, if they were going to listen to Kate Brennan, they would remember this story all their lives. Growing more confident, she started to involve the others in the story.

'What do you think happened next?' she cried.

But they all shuffled their feet. 'Tell us, tell us,' came the response.

And when she told more of the story, she asked, 'And would you believe that?'

And someone shouted, 'Yes, we believe it!'

This storytelling was turning out to be easy after all.

And then she began speaking of Culain, chief of the black country of Ulla, watching the people in front nodding to each other. Finally, at the climax of her story, she stood up. Now she let her passion describe how Setanta killed the great mastiff of Ulla, and how Fergus McRoy acclaimed him with the name of Cu-chulain, the hound of Culain, the name he was known by forever after. To her amazement, every man and woman in the inn stood up with her, and together they drank deeply from their tankards, raising the roof with the great shout, 'Cuchulain! Cuchulain! Cuchulain!'

Gasping for breath, she fell back in her chair, desperate for a drink. Storytelling might be fun, but it was thirsty work. As she sat down, Edward squeezed her shoulder. 'That was incredible. You really do know how to get the people to listen to you.' For a moment, he looked around. 'And I think they want to hear more.'

'Oh, no,' she cried. 'One is enough. Perhaps another evening.'

Reluctantly, everybody went back to their tables, the musicians started up again, and Edward went off to refill their tankards. Kate sat back, watching him steer his way through the people in the inn, talking and laughing and joking as he went. It was impossible to believe what had happened that day. They had been standing up at the lake only a few hours ago. And she had made love today for the first time. Everything had changed, yet nothing had changed. She still felt the same; being a woman did not seem to be much different from being a girl. She squeezed her knees together deliciously. The best part about it was that they still had the room at the back of the inn, and they could go out there whenever they wanted and make love again.

Out of the corner of her eye, she saw the innkeeper coming over towards her.

'I hope everything is to your satisfaction, madam?' he enquired solicitously.

Immediately, she smiled to herself at the use of the word madam. 'Yes, thank you, you have made us very welcome here.'

The man leaned forward. 'That was a great story you told us there. You know, I've never heard anyone tell that story like that before.'

Unable to frame a sensible reply, she simpered like an idiot. But the innkeeper was leaning forward again. 'And your man there, your husband. When he came in here at first I was sure he was not from these parts. But would you look at him? And would you listen to him? For sure I don't know where I got that impression at all. He sounds as Irish as any man here.'

All she could do was laugh. 'Yes, he is that for sure.'

Chapter 12

————✦————

At dawn the next morning, Kate and Edward were making love. Under the covers together, he teased her breasts, tickled her tummy, her knees and her toes. If only it could have gone on forever. But eventually it had to stop. They had to get up early, to make sure she got back to Kilcarra. She had to speak to her mother again.

Outside the village, Edward dropped her off so she could walk the last mile to the church. After Mass, she spied her mother standing outside, about to make her way back to the cottage. Kate hurried after her.

'Mam, it's me,' she spoke quietly.

Her mother looked her up and down. 'Yes, I can see that. But I'm surprised to see you at church this morning. Have you come to repent of your sins?'

Trying to remain even-tempered, Kate let this welcome sink in. 'If you mean, Mam, have I decided not to see the man I spoke to you about, then the answer is no.'

'Let me tell you, Kathleen Brennan, that I have not discussed this with your father.' Her mother's voice was cold and distant. 'But when he finds out, he will be beside himself, and you can be sure he'll get to know about it. People have seen you, riding around in a fancy carriage, giving yourself airs, getting above your station. You're heading for a fall, Kathleen Brennan, you mark my words. And if I were you, I would not return here until you've given this man up.'

Without another word, she turned and strode up the hill, leaving her daughter looking helplessly at her back.

It was impossible trying to speak to her, Kate muttered fiercely to herself. Was there any point in trying again? Hesitating over what to do next, all of a sudden she felt a hand at her elbow. Startled, she looked round to see her brother, looking better than ever.

'Kate, hello, it's nice to see you again,' Declan began. 'But it's a pity about the circumstances.' As he finished speaking, he looked around furtively, as if concerned that someone might see them talking together. However, he carried on before she could reply.

'I don't come often to the village now. I've moved down to Arklow. I couldn't keep working here with Dad – it was driving me mad. Myself and two other fellows have managed to get together, and we've started to make a living down there.'

'Well, I hope it lasts,' she replied scornfully. 'But what's wrong with the circumstances?' she demanded. 'Are you talking about me seeing Edward Tilbrook?'

'Well, I didn't know that was his name,' Declan replied. 'I imagine this is the man at the sanatorium with the ball in his shoulder?'

'Yes, it's the same man. I didn't know his name either but he came to Ireland to find me.' Gingerly, she put her hand on his arm. 'And now I've fallen in love with him.'

'Kate, nothing's ever straightforward with you. I thought the scandal was going to be bad enough when you were seeing James Lavelle. But a Frenchman and a Catholic is not too bad, and at least his mother is Irish.'

'Is that all you've got to concern you?' she almost shouted. 'What your sister is up to and who she's seeing?'

Putting his hands out, he tried to placate her. 'Kate, your man's an Englishman. That's bad enough, but he's an English soldier as well. Don't you see? Mam and Dad will feel that you've brought disgrace upon the family. They'll not be able to face anybody when this word gets out. People are talking even now.'

Despite the note of concern in his voice, she could feel her teeth grinding together. 'Well, if they're talking about me, then they're leaving some other poor sinner in peace.'

In exasperation, she paced up and down. 'And what about you, Declan?' she demanded finally, her voice growing more shrill. 'Do you feel that your sister has disgraced you? Are you unable to look your friends in the eye?'

Taking a step forward, he tried to get her to stop shouting. 'Kate, my feelings don't come into this. You're my sister, and that will never change. And you helped me when nobody else would, and I'll always be indebted to you.'

As he tried to catch her eye, his voice took on a wheedling note. 'But don't you see? If you keep seeing this man, Mam and Dad will cut you off, and you might never see them again.'

She was enraged. 'I'm sorry, Declan. I told you once before, and I'll tell you again. I don't go around asking people their nationality or their religion, as if they have to pass some form of qualifying examination before I'm prepared to have any truck with them. For God's sake, I didn't know that Edward was an English soldier, and I didn't know I was going to fall in love with the man. Can't you understand the anguish it's given me?'

Alarmed at this onslaught, he tried to step back but Kate pursued him. 'I'm seeing a side of my mother and father, yes and you, Declan, and some other people too, that I didn't know existed. That they can condemn their own daughter without giving one single thought to what she is going through? I'm sorry, Declan, but it's not good enough.'

With that final word, she burst into tears. Pushing him away from her, she turned and ran down the road.

Two hours later, Edward found her, trudging along the track on her way back up to Mistress Delamere' house. Normally he called out whenever they met, but even from a distance the set of her shoulders showed all too clearly that something was wrong. Jumping down from the carriage, he ran over to find out what was the matter.

By this time, Kate had stopped crying, and for the last half hour had been giving herself a good talking-to. But catching a glimpse of Edward running towards her brought everything back all at once, and immediately she burst into a great flood of tears. Frantically, he took her in his arms and held her close.

'What is it, Kate, please tell me?' he pleaded, his voice soft in her ear.

'Oh, Edward,' she sobbed. 'It's not something you can

do anything about. It's been wonderful with you, and yesterday and last night and this morning, I was so happy. But my mother and father and some other people will not accept me seeing an Englishman. And I've had bad words with my mother and my brother about it.'

She pressed her face into his chest. 'They're not prepared to listen to anything I say.' Even as she spoke, she could feel herself drawing strength from his nearness. 'But they're going to have to like it or lump it, Mister Tilbrook, because I'm not going to give you up.'

Squeezing his arm as tightly as she could, she looked up at his face. 'You didn't realise what you were letting yourself in for, did you? You thought that you had met a nice little girl, that you might be able to take advantage of, didn't you?'

He began to protest, but Kate put her hand over his mouth. 'I'm sorry, Edward, I didn't mean that. I'm a little bit tense, that's all, I'll be fine now that you're with me.'

By the time they reached Mistress Delamere's house, she had regained her composure. Edward tried to get her to tell him more about her parents' reactions, but she managed to sidestep the issue, insisting that she had blown it all out of proportion. And they had little time to pursue the issue, as he had to leave immediately to get back to the house in Dublin where he was staying. However, they did manage to make their arrangements to meet again the following week. As she watched him disappearing down the driveway, she remembered the one question she had intended to ask, but had completely forgotten in all the excitement: how long was he going to be staying in Ireland?

As it turned out, she did not have to wait long for the

answer. On the following Tuesday afternoon she was with the children, when she was interrupted by the cook telling her she had a visitor. It was a pleasant surprise indeed to find Edward waiting for her in the library.

'What is it, Edward? Why are you here in the middle of the week?' It was impossible to keep the anxiety out of her voice.

Slowly, he walked across the room towards her. 'There's something I have to speak to you about. It will take only a few minutes, but it has to be today.'

Fearing the worst, her hand went to her breast. 'Give me a few moments, Edward, and I'll make sure the children have enough to keep them occupied for the next hour.'

Five minutes later she was back. 'Shall we walk round the garden?' she murmured. 'We can talk there.'

Edward did not say anything immediately. In fact, he was giving the impression of a man distinctly nervous about something. She forced herself to let him come out with it in his own good time.

Finally, he began. 'Kate, these last few weeks have been the most wonderful of my life.' He stopped, took her hands and looked down at her. Her heart dropped like a stone. It could mean only one thing – he had come to say goodbye.

'Without a doubt, you are the most beautiful woman I've ever met, and it breaks my heart to leave you, but I have to go back to England.'

Closing her eyes tightly, she tried not to listen. She was right; he was leaving.

'I've received a letter from Lord Cornwallis. The war with the rebels in America is not going well, and he wants me to work with the people in London to try and improve things. I have to leave immediately.'

Trying to forestall what he was going to say next, she turned her face to one side. 'Edward, please, don't say any more. I've told you I love you, and I'm sure I always will. But you need to go back to England. You can't be spending your time here with a foolish little Irish girl. Please, you don't have to make any excuses, I understand.'

Although she tried as hard as she could, she could not prevent tears welling up in her eyes. Bowing her head so that he would not see her crying, she tried to pull away. Instead, he gathered her closer, putting his arms around her waist.

'Kate, listen to me. It's not like that at all. I do have to go back to London, but I'll be back here to find you. And I have something to make sure you remember me, to stop you going out and seeing all these strapping young Irish fellows.'

He stopped and fumbled in his pocket. 'Here you are!' he exclaimed, taking a ring out of a small velvet bag and slipping it over the third finger of her right hand. 'There, it fits nicely. Keep that on at all times and remember me by it.' And then he kissed her.

For a moment, she was overwhelmed, waving her hand around stupidly, admiring the ring and the way it sat upon her finger. As she was about to make some reply, he put his hand to her lips. 'Kate, I have to go immediately, and you must go back to your class. But there's another question I'd like to ask before I leave. I know it's unfair with the other pressures you're under at the moment, and I don't need you to answer it now. I'm quite happy to wait for the answer when I come back in about three months or so.'

He stopped for a moment, obviously hesitating. Kate was intrigued. What was the question? Tearing her gaze away from the ring, she looked up at him.

'Well, ask me, Edward, whatever it is.'

'Kathleen Brennan,' he cleared his throat nervously. 'I know that I'm a lot older than you, and I could understand the answer that you may decide to give, but what I want to ask you is: would you marry me?'

He let her go and stepped back. 'Don't say anything now; just think about it until I come back. Here's my address on this piece of paper – write to me if you have a mind. I'll write to you.' Without another word, he rushed off. Stunned, Kate held the piece of crumpled paper in the palm of her hand, while the ring twinkled in the light. For once in her life she was speechless, as if every breath in her body had been knocked out of her. Had she heard him correctly? Had he really asked her to marry him? Was he sure he wanted her as his wife?

Slowly and carefully, she walked back into the house. It was amazing how unfamiliar everything looked. As she made her way through the library, she had to be careful not to knock anything over. Even the children looked strange. For the next hour or so, she tried to keep the lessons going, but it was impossible. After dismissing the class early, she soon found herself up in her room. It was too much to think about on top of everything else. With a sigh of relief, she lay down on the bed and closed her eyes.

Over the next few weeks, her moods seemed to swing

violently from one extreme to the other. In general, there were few problems with her work, she was pleasant and cheerful with the children, and polite and attentive in her conversations with Mistress Delamere. On occasions, she felt extraordinarily happy, more so than at any time previously in her life. Mostly, however, she found herself desperately depressed at the thought of how her family had rejected the man she loved, and because he was too far away to give her the support she needed.

She was not sleeping well – and she knew it must be difficult for the Mistress to ignore her red eyes and her drawn features on the other side of the breakfast table. Several times she recognised efforts being made to lift her spirits but somehow she could not respond. However, a letter arriving from England did cheer her up a little, enough to draw a comment from Mistress Jardine.

'So Kate, what news from across the water? Is it good or bad?'

Placing the letter down on the table, Kate smiled thinly. 'I suppose it's good news. It's from Teresa Ryan. Mister Boulton has given Patrick a job, and they're going to live near Birmingham. She and Patrick are going to have a baby, so they're getting married quickly before they leave London. She says they're blissfully happy and that she'll write again when they've settled down.'

'That's not good news, that's wonderful news!' remarked the Mistress. 'You should feel proud of the way you've helped them. Doesn't it make you feel good?'

In reply, Kate burst into tears. 'Yes, it does make me feel good,' she sobbed. 'I know I'm crying, but I really do feel happy for them. But it makes me feel miserable as well, because they're together, and no one's criticising them, yet there's people talking about my every move with Edward.'

'Have you had any letters since he went back to England?'

Blowing her nose, she wiped the tears from her eyes. 'No, I've not received anything yet. But I'm sure he'll write, when he has time.'

After a moment, she stood up to go to her room. 'I'm sorry to show my distress so publicly, Mistress Delamere. I think it might be better if I go elsewhere for a while.'

But the other woman jumped to her feet and took her by the hand, preventing her from leaving. 'Listen to me, Kate,' she spoke firmly. 'It's no good you spending all your time feeling sorry for yourself. We've spoken about this before. If you love Edward and he loves you, what does anything else matter? Look at Teresa Ryan and Patrick Nolan. Who do they have but each other? But this three months apart is a good test for you; use it wisely. If you love each other, a short time apart is nothing, and it won't have the slightest effect on the way that you both feel. But if your feelings are not there after three months, don't be afraid to say so. No one will think the worse of you for that, especially Edward Tilbrook, if he's half the man I think he is. And whatever you do, make sure you do it for love. Don't even think about doing anything just to be contrary, or to spite your parents or anybody else.'

Immediately, Kate began to protest, but Mistress Delamere cut her short. 'I'm saying this because I know how impetuous you can be at times, and also how stubborn you can be. Go and lie down if you must, but from tomorrow, I would like to see you starting to get back to the way you were a few weeks ago, at least on the outside.'

A short time later, Kate was thinking over Mistress Delamere's words. On the one hand, the woman obviously did not realise how much she and Edward cared for each other. But on the other, she was probably right in some ways. This was something she had to confront by herself, and there was no reason why everyone else should be dragged in. From tomorrow, she resolved, they would see a different woman completely.

The days that followed were a struggle, but not impossible. Through a combination of sheer concentration and strength of will, she managed to put her thoughts about Edward into a specific compartment in her mind, separating that from her normal approach to life and the people around her. She was determined to be less intense and more fun to be with, all of which made the children much happier. The Mistress was particularly pleased to see her getting her old spirit back, not least because it helped them to regain their former easy and informal relationship.

Unfortunately, the same was not the case with her mother and father. Although she had not said anything further to them about Edward, her mother somehow knew he had gone back to England. There was no more discussion about him, or about Kate's feelings. On Sundays, she still went to Mass at the church in the village, met her mother and went back to the cottage. And she still went walking with the dogs in the afternoon. But fewer and fewer words were exchanged, and her visits gradually became shorter and more strained. From time to time, Declan came around, and they were able to talk a little, but the joy was gone; they were not a family any more.

The walk back up to Enniskerry every Sunday evening had become the lowest point of her week. Time and again, she tried to rationalise her thoughts. What if she never saw Edward again? Would they all get back to normal? Would it be as if nothing had ever occurred? Somehow, she could not see that happening. Her family, the mother and father and brothers she had been close to, that she had shared a cottage with for nearly twenty years had withdrawn from her. The love and the bond that had once been there would never be the same again.

It was hardly any wonder that she started every week feeling desperately unhappy. Then, out of the blue, a letter from Edward arrived. What a difference a simple thing like a letter could make! Instead of having to work at being friendly, happy and smiling, Kate was in a state of continuous elation. This time everyone at Enniskerry could see it. Her sudden enthusiasm and zest was so infectious that everyone was caught up in the mood. The children were pressed into performing another play to mark young Arthur Wellesley's departure back to Dublin, while Mistress Delamere was persuaded to hold an Irish dancing competition, O'Brien having to hitch up the horse and trap and take Kate to Bray to buy new clothes. Meanwhile, Mister Grattan was pushed to the limit on the reforms that were urgently needed in Ireland.

Every night, she read Edward's words before she went to sleep. How he missed her, how he missed the

Wicklow countryside, how he missed his little Irish beauty. And at the end, how much he loved her, and how much he was looking forward to seeing her at the end of November. Over and over again, she read every line until she knew them off by heart. The intensity, the magic, the mystery – it was still there. Alone in her room, she lay back in the darkness and smiled quietly to herself. Everything was going to be so beautiful.

As the days became shorter, the weather closed in. The long, fine summer became no more than a passing memory. On one of the better days, Mister Grattan took Kate and Mistress Delamere out for a coach trip to an old inn by the river not far from Enniskerry. He had an idea of purchasing it and turning it into a place where he would live. And it was in a lovely spot, right enough.

But that was the last pleasant day of the autumn. In early November the rain set in, and did not relent for weeks. By the end of the month, Kate had barely set a foot outside the door, except for walking down to Kilcarra on Sundays, when she invariably got soaked to the skin.

She had received a few more letters from Edward, where he mentioned he would be coming across to Ireland around the end of November. But at the same time, he kept referring to his work and how busy he was, and never set specific dates for a visit. Since receiving his first letter, her outlook on life had vastly improved, and she was generally in a happy and optimistic frame of mind. But now, with the end of the month approaching and still no sign of him arriving, her spirits were beginning to sink. The visits to her mother and father were not helping either, as the black mood at the cottage enveloped her, dragging her down into the depths.

December came, with no let-up in the weather. Late on the first Sunday of the month, she was trudging along the path beside the Dargle river, back to Mistress Delamere's house. In the summer, it was a lovely spot, with the sunlight shimmering through the trees, but now on a cold, dark, wet, winter's day, it was frightening in places. It was not somewhere she liked passing through, but the only alternative was up over the hill, and that was like a bog from all the rain.

Keeping her head down, she hurried on. In her mind she was going over some of the letters she had received recently: from Edward, from Mistress Boulton in Birmingham, and even one that had arrived from her pupil in the summer, young Arthur Wellesley, who was now at boarding school. She had to start replying to all of these. Suddenly, without the slightest warning, a horse reared up out amongst the trees, scaring her out of her wits. At the same time, she heard the sound of a man's gruff voice. God! It had to be a highwayman. Instinctively, she thrust her right hand with her ring under her cloak. It was the only thing she had of any value, and she would be devastated if it was stolen.

As the man managed to get the horse under control, he approached her, blocking her way. From where she was standing, she could barely see his face. All she could make out was a long black cloak with the collar turned up and a black hat pulled low. He was a terrifying sight. For a long moment, she cowered in front of him, her back pressing hard up against a tree.

And then he spoke. 'Hello there, young lady. Would that be Miss Kate Brennan under all those clothes?'

It was Edward! How had he got there? What was he

doing trying to frighten her in such a dark place?

As he jumped down off the horse, she ran over towards him. 'Edward, I can't believe it's you. I've waited so long, and I've been expecting you, but I thought you'd tell me when you were coming.' All this came out in a mad gabble as she threw herself into his embrace. And then they were kissing and crying and laughing, as the rain poured down and the horse looked on mournfully.

Holding him at arm's length, she peered at his face in the dim light. 'It's so wonderful to see you. But you gave me an awful scare there, when you came rearing out at me on that horse.'

But Edward just laughed. 'I wrote you a letter saying I was coming but it must have got lost. I have a room at the inn down in Bray, and I managed to persuade the innkeeper to lend me this horse. But I don't think the poor beast is accustomed to having a rider on his back, and I've been finding it difficult to control him.'

Taking her in his arms, he embraced her again. 'I went up to Mistress Delamere's house, but O'Brien told me that you were over at your parent's cottage, and that you would be coming back about this time. So I rode down to meet you.'

Together they walked up the hill, with the rain, the cold, and the darkness now completely forgotten.

At the gate to Mistress Delamere's house, he stopped and took her hands in his.

'Kate, I'll have to leave you here. I'm going to go in to Dublin tomorrow for a few days. But I'll be back to see you at noon on Saturday, after you've finished with the children. Use your charm on Mistress Delamere to let her give you a day off on the Monday, and perhaps we'll be able to spend a few days together. But I must go back to England after that.' He kissed her gently.

Kate clutched at him. 'Edward, be careful riding around here in the dark. And I'll speak to Mistress Delamere about the Monday.'

As she turned to go into the house, she looked back over her shoulder, her eyes flashing mischievously. 'And make sure you have a place where we can go to bed together. I've thought of nothing else for weeks.' And then she ran up the driveway and through the doorway.

Their few days together were over far too quickly. Magically, the rain stopped and the weather cleared up. On Saturday afternoon, they went back up to the waterfall, and spent the entire time locked in each other's arms. That evening, Edward managed to smuggle her into his room at the inn, without letting anyone else see her. This was the centre of Bray and if they were not careful, someone was bound to recognise her. Kate was all for going in boldly through the front door, but Edward advised more discretion. He could see the agonies she was going through with her parents, and there was no need to make things worse.

It was the first time for years, other than when she had been ill, that she had ever deliberately gone to bed at six o'clock in the evening. But she had waited long enough. It was so wonderful to be with her man and to be able to make love to him.

Sunday at Mass went easily enough. Amazingly, she did not feel any sense of guilt at going to church after making love to Edward. She was half-expecting God to hurl a few thunderbolts at her as she crossed the threshold of the church, but nothing dramatic happened.

Perhaps Her Maker had more important matters to concern Himself with. After Mass, her mother and father were still as withdrawn as ever, but by now she was too impatient to listen to another litany of complaints about her behaviour, and the disgrace she had brought upon the name of Brennan. She had other things on her mind.

And so it came to Monday afternoon. They walked out over the rocks at Bray Head, passing the thousands of birds which seemed to be there all year round. Locked in each other's arms, they stood gazing out over the waves. Far away in the distance, out of their sight, lay the coast of England where Edward would be going the very next day.

Finally, he broke the silence. 'I don't want to go back, Kate, but I must. The war in America is not going well, and I have so much work to do. And there's always the possibility that I'll have to go there myself.'

For a moment she gazed at the sombre expression on his face. There was nothing she could say. They had already said it all. He knew she loved him, she knew he loved her. Their lovemaking had been so beautiful, so wondrous, so precious, it made her ache inside to think about it. It was only a few hours since they had been under the covers together. She could still feel the sensations deep inside her, how aroused she had been, and yet at the same time so tearful at his leaving. The experience had already left her emotional and more than a little weepy, but her spirits had been uplifted as well.

Placing his hand under her chin, he lifted her face to look into her eyes. 'My little Kate, when I came here at first, I thought that Ireland was a wonderful place. But I realise now that I was seeing it at the best season of the year. I'm not so sure that winter in Wicklow is a good idea.'

'I told you that when we first met,' she smiled. 'But we've learned to endure it.'

'Do you remember, when I was here the last time?' he murmured, brushing a strand of hair away from her forehead. 'I asked you a question before I left. Do you remember that, Kate?'

For a moment, she looked up at him with big innocent eyes. 'I don't think so, Edward. What can this question be that you say you asked me? I think that you'd better ask me again to remind me.'

Giving her a mock glare, he squeezed her waist. 'You're a little vixen sometimes, Kate. All right, I'll ask you again, but this time I would like an answer. Miss Kathleen Brennan, from Kilcarra in County Wicklow, will you marry me?'

For three months, she had been thinking about this moment. She did not need to wait a second longer.

'Of course I will, Edward Tilbrook,' she whispered, hugging him as tightly as she could.

After Edward's departure, going back to the house at Enniskerry and trying to establish a normal routine seemed something of an anti-climax. Particularly as she was bursting with excitement at the memory of being with him, and the thought of them being so much in love. Not to mention him asking her to be his wife.

Although she was desperate to tell somebody, she had nobody she could really confide in. Except, of course, Mistress Delamere. At first, she was afraid to tell her what had happened; after all, getting married would inevitably mean leaving the house at Enniskerry, and that would mean disturbing the children's education. Despite thinking long and hard about the problems that this might create, she could not see any easy answer. However, it was Mistress Delamere who raised the subject first, not long after Edward had returned to England.

The occasion arose when Kate and the Mistress were sitting in the drawing room making plans for celebrating Christmas. After they had agreed most of the activities to be tackled, the conversation turned to his visit.

'Kate, I hope you don't mind me saying this, but being with Edward Tilbrook appears to have been a wonderful tonic for you. I don't think I've ever seen you displaying such energy and enthusiasm. You're leaving the rest of us exhausted in your wake.'

'That's not so surprising,' Kate replied with a smile. 'You've no idea how marvellous it was to see him again, even for just a few days. And I need to thank you once more for giving me time off with him.'

The Mistress beamed with delight. 'Don't forget I was your age not that long ago. I remember very clearly what it was like when I fell in love with my husband, so I can understand your feelings.'

Before going on, the Mistress collected her thoughts for a moment. 'It sounds to me, however, that the enforced separation has done little to cool your ardour. Would that be a correct assumption?'

Almost afraid to speak for fear of shouting out with joy and excitement, Kate nodded her head.

'So, we have one of you in Ireland and one in England. What do you think is going to happen next?'

Pressing her temples with the tips of her fingers, Kate looked across the table. 'To be honest, Mistress Delamere, I've not thought so far ahead. Seeing Edward again and realising that we still love each other has been about as much as I could have coped with.' But then her suppressed excitement got the better of her.' However, there's one other thing I must tell you, Mistress Delamere. He's asked me to be his wife.'

Looking up at the ceiling, she closed her eyes. 'And I've said yes.' With some difficulty, she tried to compose herself and adopt a more normal expression. 'I'm sorry, Mistress Delamere. I had to tell someone. It's been so difficult keeping it bottled up inside. But we've not made any plans as yet, so I'm not sure what happens next.'

Before she'd finished speaking, the other woman jumped to her feet and went over to the sideboard, pouring out two large glasses of brandy. 'This is so exciting, Kate, let me be the first to congratulate you. I think it's wonderful news, and I'm sure you'll be very happy together.'

Closing her eyes again, Kate clasped her hands together. Thank God, that had not been too difficult, and the Mistress did not seem particularly displeased at all. Truth to tell, it had not been her intention to mention anything about Edward proposing, but she had been desperate to tell somebody.

But Mistress Delamere was thinking out loud now. 'From what you've said, it sounds as if Edward is busy in London, so it's unlikely that we'll see him over here in the near future. In any event, the weather is usually dreadful at this time of year, and it can be difficult to get across the water. So, it seems to me that the wedding won't be before sometime in the spring or summer.'

By now, Kate was sitting comfortably in her chair, drinking her brandy and feeling wonderfully relaxed. After all, this was a much more attractive topic of conversation.

'Well, at least you've given me plenty of time to find a replacement to look after the children, although where we'll find someone like you, God only knows. And Bernard will be starting at boarding school some time next year, so he should be all right. It seems it's only the girls I'll have to worry about. Am I thinking correctly here, Kate?'

'Yes, yes, Mistress Delamere. I'm sure I'm going to be in Wicklow for some time to come.' Suddenly, Kate realised she knew nothing about Edward Tilbrook's house. What if the Mistress were to ask where he lived, what the house was like, whether he had a man looking after things, or a cook or serving staff?

But the other woman was thinking of far more awkward questions. 'And what about your mother and father, Kate? They weren't very happy about you seeing Edward – how will they react when you tell them you're going to get married? And then there's the ceremony. I don't imagine your man is a Catholic. What will the priest at the church in the village say to this? And I expect this means you'll be moving to England?'

It was like being struck in the face by a splash of cold water. What was she going to say to her parents? And how was she going to raise the subject with them? And, yes, what about the priest in the church? She had not even thought about him. And of course, where were they going to live? In England? But how could she do that?

Lord, is this what happened when you fell in love? That you lost completely any sense you had, leaving you incapable of thinking about the simplest of questions?

Helplessly, she spread her hands in front of her. 'I don't know the answers, Mistress Delamere. But you're right. I have to find out, somehow.'

Later that evening, as she lay in bed, her thoughts of Edward were interrupted by Mistress Delamere's questions which kept spinning round in her head. She had to speak to her mother again, and her father, too. And she would need to tell Declan as well. It was not an attractive prospect, to be sure.

It took six weeks and another letter from Edward before she could pluck up the courage to speak to her mother. It was nearly the end of January, another cold Sunday morning, when Kate finally intercepted her after Mass.

'So, Kate Brennan, we don't see or hear much from you now. You come down here and you spend barely any time at all with your family, and then you rush off again. We barely saw you at Christmas, for God's sake.'

Kate struggled to keep her voice calm and even. 'I thought, Mam, that you wanted no truck with the likes of me, for consorting with an Englishman?'

For a moment, her mother looked down her nose at her. 'Well, the story is that he's returned to England, and he'll not be back.'

'Is that right now, Mam?' Kate asked quietly. 'And what blatherskite is telling you all of these stories? And how would they know anyway? I'm the only one that knows what the story is.'

'So, what is it you're saying, girl? Spit it out. Let's be

hearing what you've been up to now, as if it could get any worse.'

Taking a deep breath, Kate drew herself up to her full height. 'Mam, it's true that Edward Tilbrook has gone back to England. And you had better know from me, before someone else tells you, that not only is he English, but he's an English soldier as well!'

'The saints preserve us!' her mother shook her head in dismay. 'Is there no end to your mischief? How you have the audacity to visit the house of God after what you've done is beyond me. It's not just a disgrace to the name of Brennan, it's a disgrace to the entire Irish people.'

Despite her harsh words, Kate reached involuntarily forward to hold her arm.

But her mother wrenched herself free. 'How am I going to tell your father about this? The shock will probably kill him. It's just as well this Englishman has gone back to his own. If he ever shows his face here again, your father will be after him like a shot.'

Kate let the tirade come to an end. By now, she simply felt numb. Her mother, or perhaps it was her father's doing, was not prepared to listen to anything she had to say, or to soften her stance in the slightest. What was the point now? She might as well come out with everything.

'Mam, there's something else I have to tell you. It's true that this man has gone back to England. But before he left, he asked me to marry him. And I've said yes.'

Kate stepped back, her head held high. For one minute, she was sure her mother was about to strike her. But she refused to flinch, or cringe before her. 'I've fallen in love with this man, Mam, and I want to be with him, and nobody and nothing will stop me!'

Again, she thought her mother was going to strike her down. Instead, her face crumpled, tears streaming down her cheeks. Once more, Kate stepped forward instinctively and stretched out her hand. But her mother waved her away, sobbing and spluttering.

'Don't touch me!' she cried. 'You are lost to us. You are no daughter of ours any more.' And she turned away and stumbled off up the hill.

Having seen her previous reactions, Kate had not really expected anything less. It had taken all her courage to go and see her mother and their meeting had left her drained and depressed. But she was determined this was not going to affect her, not like months earlier when they had first spoken. Her life had to go on. She had made her choice, and she was gong to stick with it.

Through those next few weeks, somehow she kept to her resolve, although she could no longer face going to Mass in the village on Sundays. The thought of seeing her mother, yet being ignored by her was beyond anything she could cope with. And it meant the pain of giving up her beloved dogs, since she could not contemplate going back to what had once been her home. And then, to make matters worse, her brother Declan came up to see her at Enniskerry. Over and over again, they went over the same ground while he pleaded with her, but still she refused to be shaken.

After he had gone, she collapsed on the bed with exhaustion. At the same time, however, her determination was even stronger not to give in to the pressures being levelled against her. Somehow or other she would keep going.

Haunted by her mother's words, however, her heart

grew heavier as the days went by. Only the support of Mistress Delamere and the letters coming from Edward kept her resolve firm. By the time March arrived, she had reached a stage of near desolation. When she was not with the children, she spent virtually all her time reading Edward's letters, or writing to him herself. More than anything else, she wanted to reassure him she was fine and that he did not need to worry about her, so she tried her best to keep her letters light and carefree. But that belied the true feelings in her heart.

They continued to make their plans. Edward was going to travel to Ireland early in April, when they would decide how and where they would get married. And he wanted to meet her parents. Seeing him again was something she thought about constantly, although telling him about her parents was not something she was looking forward to.

In her innocence, she decided to go down to the village on the first Saturday afternoon in March, and talk to the priest about what they were intending to do. Even though Edward was not a Catholic, perhaps they could get some sort of blessing from the church. At first, she was encouraged by the priest's welcome, but as soon as she explained the situation he refused to listen to another word and ordered her out of the church, without a single word of sympathy or understanding.

This was almost the last straw. Surely, things could not get any worse. As it was, she was left devastated, wandering blindly through the village, the place she had lived for almost twenty years, but which seemed to have completely rejected her now.

Somehow or other, without realising it, she found

herself outside the forge where her father worked. He was there, right enough, she could see his familiar figure through the smoke, hammering away as usual. Despite her misery, she realised suddenly she had not spoken to him for over three months. Slowly, she walked around the side of the building, until she was standing opposite him where he could not help but see her. But not once did he look up to see who it was standing there.

'Dad, it's me, Kate,' she shouted above the noise. She saw him glance in her direction, but other than that, he ignored her. Deep inside, she could feel all the emotions of the past few months boiling up inside.

'Dad,' she screamed. 'Are you listening to me? It's Kate, your daughter, trying to speak with you, for God's sake.'

He stopped for a moment, raising his head, a sneering expression on his face. 'I'll not be hearing someone like you using the name of God in this place. You are no daughter of mine. And I'll thank you for keeping away from us.'

Raising his voice, he smashed his hammer down upon the anvil in front of him. 'You've brought nothing but shame upon our heads. It would be better if you went to England where you belong and never came back!' Without another word, he turned back to his work.

All of a sudden, Kate could feel herself choking. Whether it was the tension or the smoke, it was difficult to tell. But she had to get out of that place before she fainted. Standing outside, her chest heaving, she looked sightlessly at the handful of cottages, the church, Cormack's alehouse, and the dark green mountains in the distance. She could feel herself shivering. It was almost as if she was seeing them for the last time. How could this be? A year ago, she had been a happy, carefree girl, about to start work. Why was this happening to her? Bitterly, she looked up at the sky.

'Why, God?' she screamed in anguish. 'Why are you doing this to me?'

Again she shivered, as a sensation of dread began to overwhelm her. She was walking quickly now, faster and faster. She had to get out of this place and back to Enniskerry. Edward had been saying in his letters that he might have to go to the war in America. What if he went there and was killed? That would mean she would never see him again – it did not bear thinking about. By now she was almost running. She had to get back to Enniskerry, back to the big house.

It was O'Brien who caught her, as she collapsed on the stairs outside the door. In the kitchen, Mistress Delamere heard the noise and came rushing out to see what was wrong.

'In the name of God, what has happened? Has she been attacked?' Together, they pulled over a nearby couch, so that O'Brien had somewhere to lay her down.

'I don't think so, Mistress Delamere,' O'Brien replied. 'I think she looks more overwrought than anything else.'

Somewhere in the distance, Kate could hear their voices. Opening her eyes slowly, she tried to recognise who was speaking. She could see Mistress Delamere peering at her face, so she must have made it back to the house. For a moment she remembered the sheer dread she had experienced when she had started thinking about Edward. But now she was calm. Now she knew what she was going to do.

'I'm sorry, Mistress Delamere,' she attempted to speak, but her voice was so hoarse that the others had difficulty in understanding. Clearing her throat, she tried again.

'I'm sorry, Mistress Delamere.' That was better. 'I got myself into a bit of a panic there, and tried to rush around too much. But I'm fine now.'

By her side, O'Brien produced a glass of water. As she sat up to take a drink, she shook herself to bring herself back to reality. Yes, she did feel better now. Especially now she had decided what she had to do. For a moment, she glanced at the other woman.

'Mistress Delamere, do you think I could speak with you for a few minutes?'

The Mistress looked anxious. 'Well, if you're feeling up to it, Kate. We'll go into the drawing room and have some tea.'

In the other room, Kate sat down and put her hands squarely on the table. Thankfully she felt much more tranquil now. She gathered her thoughts before speaking, slowly and calmly, with hardly a trace of emotion.

'Mistress Delamere, I've reached a state of mind where I'm being driven crazy with anxiety about Edward. He's told me in his letters that he'll have to go to the war in America very shortly. But I have this terrible premonition he's going to be killed and that I'll never see him again. I would like your permission to have some time off to travel to London to be with him before he leaves.'

Taken aback slightly, Mistress Delamere shifted uncomfortably in her chair. 'Don't you think it might be better to wait until you've had a night's sleep to think about this?'

But Kate continued to speak positively and calmly. 'I've thought this through carefully, Mistress Delamere, and no amount of sleep will persuade me otherwise. I must go to London and I must go immediately.'

She could see the other woman thinking furiously. No doubt she wanted to try and convince her that this was a dangerous course of action. But she felt unshakeable. No one would be able to talk her out of what she was planning to do.

'Of course you have my permission,' the Mistress replied after a minute or two. 'And O'Brien will make the arrangements on your behalf. But I can't let you leave until after next Sunday. I must have your time until then to see to the children's needs.'

Kate stood up, only sorry that she could not leave for London immediately. Clearly, the Mistress had failed to recognise how distressed she was. There was no good reason for delaying so long. But rather than cause another argument, the following Monday would have to do. 'Thank you, Mistress Delamere. I'll not be a burden to you, and I expect to pay my own way this time. I've saved up some money which I'll use for the journey, and I'll prepare work for the children to do when I'm away. Now if you'll excuse me, I must go and lie down.'

Throughout the next week, her frame of mind did not waver. She remained calm, she knew what she was doing. No matter how much Mistress Delamere tried to dissuade her, she was also unshakeable. She had to go to England, and there was nothing that anyone could say or do that would make her change her mind.

And so it turned out that almost a year after her first trip, O'Brien took Kate up to Dublin to catch a ship to

England. This time, however, her mood was sadly different. This time, she was silent for most of the way, lost in her own thoughts. All the way through the sea crossing, she remained in the same state of inner calm, even on the coach to London. She spoke with no one and no one spoke with her, save the steward on the ship, and of course Mr Flynn at Liverpool. But even those conversations she kept to a minimum.

By nightfall the coach was approaching the inn where the horses would be changed and the passengers would be staying the night. As the driver pulled to a halt, Kate heard some sort of commotion outside. The last thing she wanted was to get involved in anything untoward that might be happening, and she shrank back in her seat. But the man beside her threw open the door to see what was going on. Outside, they could see a huge black carriage, with what looked like a driver and a bagman on top with two men accompanying them, both riding horses. The man turned round to the other people in the coach.

'I think they're looking for somebody. They appear to be armed to the teeth and someone has just said they're stopping all the coaches.'

Oh no, Kate muttered to herself desperately. It had to be some thief or murderer they were after. Please God, don't let this delay us, she prayed silently.

But the man was still speaking. 'Yes, they're asking for one person. It sounds as if the name is Brennan, or something like that. Has anyone heard of that name? Is it an Irish name?'

Her hand went to her heart. What was this? Were they looking for her?

Her voice squeaked. 'My name is Brennan.'

The man beside her regarded her in astonishment for a moment, before shouting over to the other carriage. 'Yes, over here. There's a woman called Brennan over here.'

A fierce-looking man, dressed in black and riding a black horse leaned low and pushed his head towards the door of the coach.

'I am looking for a Miss Brennan. I've been sent here by Captain Tilbrook in London. I don't want any trouble from anybody but we have to find her.'

Kate's heart leaped. Captain Tilbrook!

Her voice squeaked again. 'I'm Kathleen Brennan. I know Edward Tilbrook.'

The man outside the coach regarded her coolly. 'Can you take off your glove and show me your right hand, please, madam?'

Mystified by this, Kate did as she was asked. As she held out her hand, her ring flashed in the light of a hundred lamps.

The man immediately pulled out a letter from inside his coat. 'Would you be so good as to come with us, madam? This is a letter from Captain Tilbrook. Mistress Delamere from Enniskerry advised him that you were coming, and he's sent his carriage to take you to London with all speed.'

Before she could say a word, the other man had jumped off his horse and helped her down from the coach, picking up her bag, and escorting her to the other carriage.

'I hope you'll be comfortable here, Miss Brennan. We will stop whenever you wish, but otherwise only for refreshments and to water the horses. Just call out if you need to attract our attention.'

Kate pushed herself into the corner of the coach, still clutching the letter the man had given her in her hand. So, Mistress Delamere had written to Edward. That must have been why she had refused to let her travel for so long. Well, this arrangement suited her fine. The sooner they got to London, the sooner she would see Edward again. Suddenly, she realised that the following day would be her birthday. She was going to be twenty years old, and she had forgotten about it completely.

Thankfully, it looked like being a happy birthday, which for some time had seemed most unlikely, all things considered.

Chapter 13

Thank God, the nightmare was over. At least for the time being. Turning over on her side, she gazed at the man lying beside her. He would not be very pleased, she smiled to herself, when he woke up and found that morning had come and the sun was up.

Three days she had been in London, at Edward's house in Bracewell Place. Although they were almost inseparable, he had been most careful to ensure she had her own room, completely separate from his. When they retired in the evening, he joined her after everybody else had gone to bed, and then he returned to his own room before dawn. He had to be sure he was showing a good example to his housekeeper and her husband.

But today he had slept in. Reluctantly, she decided she had better wake him.

'Edward,' she murmured, shaking him by the shoulder. 'You're going to have to get up. Mrs Wallace will be up to serve tea any minute.'

Opening his eyes, he laughed at her concern. The swine had been awake all along, lying there watching her.

'Kate,' he whispered, making a grab for her at the same time. 'Today is Saturday. Mrs Wallace doesn't serve tea on Saturday mornings. Instead, we breakfast at nine, so we have an hour or two yet. What would you like to do till then?'

She jumped out of the bed, pulling the blankets with her and screaming in mock horror, while Edward chased her round the room.

Two hours later they were sitting sedately at the breakfast table, while Mrs Wallace waited on them. A major surprise had been finding the house every bit as large as Mistress Jardine's, with the same size of garden and surrounded similarly by a high wall. But the furnishings looked dreadfully old-fashioned compared to Connaught House. As she drank her tea, Kate made a mental note to take him round to meet the Jardines, and to show him what the interior of their house looked like.

And although it had not occurred to her previously, it was becoming abundantly clear that Edward must have a generous income to be able to run a house of this size in an expensive area of London, not to mention sending a carriage halfway across the country to collect her.

But now he was speaking with a serious expression on his face. That meant she had to pay attention.

'Kate, listen to me. When I received Mistress Delamere's letter I really expected that you were going to arrive here in a very poor state of health. But you seem to have recovered remarkably quickly.'

'For sure, Edward,' she smiled sweetly, 'it's being here with you that's bringing out the best in me.'

'Good, I'm glad to hear that,' he continued, taking her hand. 'Because if you feel up to it, I'd like to take you on a coach trip today outside London. There's a place I'd like you to see.'

'That's fine by me,' she replied, more serious now herself. 'The only thing I'd like to add is that we don't have much more time together. You say you have to go to America at the end of next week. You know my feelings on that. I know it's stupid, but I'm frightened I'll never see you again.'

As yet, she had not told him about the latest arguments with her parents and her brother and the priest. He had enough to worry him without that as well. Looking down at the table, her voice dropped to a whisper.

'You promised we could get married before you leave. Edward, please let's do that. It will make me so much happier, even though I have to return to Ireland to Mistress Delamere. It will be enough for me to know that my husband is out there, thinking of me.'

'My little Kate,' Edward rubbed her hand gently. 'I've not forgotten. And today is connected with that. You'll see what I mean later on.'

The coach trip turned out to be rather longer than she expected. Travelling out of London seemed to take forever – and they had gone east. Mrs Simpson's words came back all too clearly. 'God help any woman who travels east of the City of London!'

Although a little apprehensive, she saw nothing threatening; just more and more houses. Further on, the houses gave way to green fields and woods, the countryside being fairly flat and featureless. Beside her,

Edward had decided he was going to give the history lesson today.

'Look at this road, Kate. See how straight it is. That's because it's an old Roman road that leads all the way from London to Colchester.' He chuckled to himself. 'Conchubar Mac Nessa was probably king of Ireland about the time the Romans were building this road.'

Unimpressed, Kate gazed at the countryside around them. 'It's a little bit interesting, Edward, but very straight roads can become boring after a short time.'

Eventually, they turned off and followed a lane through the countryside. Crossing over a narrow river, with the horses splashing through shallow pools, they made their way past an old church and some ancient-looking cottages with thatched roofs, which Kate had only ever seen before in paintings in Mister Boulton's house. After a mile or so, he pulled up beside the riverbank and helped her down.

'Look, Kate, over there, across the other side and beyond those poplar trees. Can you see that house there?'

Trying to follow his pointing finger, she shaded her eyes. 'Yes, I can see it. It looks like a country house, a little like Mistress Delamere's. What's so special about that?'

Edward laughed out loud. 'It's special because it's mine, my dear Kate. This is the family house. All this land where you're standing and everywhere you're looking, all that is part of my estate. And Kate, if you wish to marry me after seeing this, you will be Mistress of this estate.'

He put up his hand to stop the question he could see forming on her lips. 'Not only that, you will be a Lady.

My title around here is not Mister, or even Captain. I'm actually Viscount Tilbrook, at your service, madam.'

For a moment, she clutched at the side of the carriage for support. In the name of God, was he serious? After everything else, it was just too much to take. Unable to stop herself, she burst out crying, tears streaming down her face. Immediately, Edward took her in his arms.

'What's the matter, did I say something dreadfully awful?' he asked anxiously.

'Oh, Edward, how can you have all this and a big house in London, and all these servants and coaches and horses and God knows what else, and still want me for a wife?' Between sobbing and blowing her nose, she could barely form any coherent words.

Taking out his handkerchief, he dried her eyes tenderly. 'I love you, Kate, that's why. And I'll always love you. If it makes you feel better, then we'll go and live in a small cottage somewhere. I don't mind. I never use the title and I barely make use of all of this; after all, I'm hardly ever here.'

Pulling her towards him, he held her close and looked into her eyes. 'But I did have this thought of one day settling down here as a gentleman farmer and getting to grips with all of these new ideas I keep reading about. And I'd like to have a wife to share it with me and children that we could bring up here in the countryside. And I'd dearly like you to be that wife.'

Slowly, her arms crept around his neck. 'Oh, Edward,' she wailed, which was about as much as she could bring herself to reply.

Releasing her from his embrace, he took her by the hand. 'See over here, Kate – do you see that little church we passed not so long ago? That's where we can be married. I've spoken to the vicar and everything is arranged. I know it's not a Catholic church, but it will be a blessing of a kind for you. It'll be difficult, but we might be able to find a priest at some time in the future who won't frown on our marriage. And we'll ask him to give us a blessing.'

Her reply needed about two seconds thought. 'Thank you for asking me, Viscount Tilbrook, and I will be delighted to accept.'

A week later they were man and wife. It was a short ceremony right enough, and the vicar was a very pleasant man. Some of the local people even turned up, presumably to see what this woman looked like who was going to become the Mistress of the estate.

The wedding party returned to Tilbrook Hall, where drinks were being served in the garden. As she looked around at the people who had come to celebrate with them, it was amazing to think that barely a year previously, she had not known a single person here, yet now some seemed like old friends.

Mister and Mistress Jardine had come, bringing Sister Mary Francis from the sanatorium. The Boultons had come down from Birmingham, bringing Patrick and Teresa with them. Henry Browne was there with a young lady she had not been introduced to as yet, as was the fierce-looking man who had escorted her down to London. His name was Sanderson, and he had brought a Frenchwoman with him. Kate did not yet understand the connection between him and Edward, except that they seemed to work together in some way.

And finally, there was Mr and Mrs Arrowsmith. He

appeared to be Edward's estate manager, while his wife ran the Hall. Kate had spoken to them for no more than a few moments, but she was determined to spend more time with them and get to know them better.

Smiling to herself, she looked across at Edward. He did look fine right enough. At first, she had been concerned that he might have wanted to get married wearing full military dress or something similar. But she need not have worried, as he had worn what seemed to be his habitual black jacket and breeches with a white silk shirt. Kate made another mental note to take him to some of those shops she had seen in Holborn. Perhaps she might be able to get him interested in something other than black.

But she did have to admire the way he seemed to be able to speak comfortably with everybody there, laughing and joking and putting them at their ease. And he appeared to be getting on particularly well with Mistress Jardine. As she cast her gaze around the group of people, she saw Sister Mary Francis standing by herself.

Going over to her side, she took the other woman's hands in hers.

'Sister, it's so nice to see you here. I wasn't sure you'd be able to come.'

'To be truthful, Kathleen,' the sister replied, 'I didn't think I would be coming either. But then I realised I've hardly been out of that hospital in almost ten years, and with Mister Jardine offering to bring me here, well, I couldn't refuse. But tell me, how does it feel to be married?' She stood back, her eyes twinkling.

'Not very different to being single. Perhaps when I'm

weighed down with worries and six children I may feel differently.'

The sister looked around and smiled. 'I don't think you'll have many worries here.' And then she saw Kate's face fall. 'What is it, have I said something wrong?'

Slowly, she shook her head. 'No, it's not something you've said. But I'm afraid my family haven't been able to accept the idea of their daughter marrying an Englishman. They've taken it very badly indeed. But I don't want to talk about that today.'

Taking the sister's arm in hers, they strolled through the gardens among the daffodils and tulips. 'I was also surprised to see you come to the ceremony, Sister Mary Francis, since it's not a Catholic church.'

The nun looked out over the flower beds and sighed. 'Kathleen, I've given up worrying myself about issues like that a long time ago. We're all people, after all, and some of these artificial divisions are not worth bothering about.'

For a few minutes, Kate told her about the reception she had been given by the priest in the church back in Kilcarra, while the sister sighed again. 'Wherever you go, you'll find that there's no shortage of priests getting involved in things they should have nothing to do with, and interfering in other people's lives unnecessarily. But when you've been working in the hospice for as long as I have, you realise what's important and what isn't. I have to pray every day, not just for my colleagues or for my patients, but also for myself. I have to pray for my faith. When I see the terrible conditions that some of these poor people have to live in, and the poverty and the disease, I find it difficult not to ask God why he is doing this. "Out of the depths I have cried to thee, O Lord." That's my daily prayer, Kathleen, I'm sorry to say.'

For a moment, the two women stopped. 'But why are we talking like this, Kathleen? We can't be making ourselves unhappy on today of all days. And I'll tell you some good news. Mister Jardine has really helped us. All the rooms have been cleaned up, we've new blankets and even some new beds, and we've recently had a kitchen built. So now we make soup every day and we can give the people something hot at long last.'

Kate squeezed the sister's arm. 'That's great news. He never struck me as being a generous man. It just shows you how wrong you can be.'

As they strolled on, Mister Boulton came towards them in deep conversation with the estate manager, Mr Arrowsmith. Kate looked at him and smiled.

'Mister Boulton, I see you've found someone else to listen to your thoughts on industry and engines and the like?

But the estate manager spoke up first. 'I'm finding many of these ideas interesting, madam. Mister Tilbrook and I have discussed in the past a number of projects which we would like to undertake on the estate, and we might be able to use some of Mister Boulton's engines to good effect.'

Before anyone else could comment, he carried on. 'We've been thinking of somehow using the river as a canal to allow barges to travel all the way up to Chelmsford. Coal and lime and foodstuffs could be transported very easily that way and make the price much cheaper. There's so many poor people living in Chelmsford and other villages who would benefit from that, as well as the extra work.' He looked for a moment at Kate. 'But perhaps, madam, coming from Ireland, you'd be more interested in the welfare of the Irish rather than the English people around here.'

'So,' Kate snapped impulsively, biting back at the man's words. 'Do you take me for some Irish harridan come here to grind the faces of the English peasants into the muck, is that it?'

Immediately, Mister Boulton put his hand on her arm, but Kate realised she had spoken too forcefully.

'Mister Arrowsmith,' she began, turning on all her charm. 'I imagine you didn't phrase that remark of yours in quite the way you intended. And I'm sorry for snapping at you like that.'

Lord, she had not thought about this part of the relationship. Now she was the Mistress, she had to keep a position with all these people. They all knew Edward and were sure to be loyal to him, but they did not know her. They were probably concerned that she would come and change everything – especially because she was not English. She would need to treat these relationships very carefully and find a way of winning them over. What a subject to begin thinking about on your wedding day.

Clapping her hands, she raised her voice so that everyone could hear. 'Come now, we don't want to be too serious. I think it's time we had a brandy or two, to make us all feel a little more relaxed.'

Drinks in the garden were followed by dinner, and then the chairs were moved back. To Kate's delight, Edward had found three Irish musicians to come and play, complete with fiddle and drum and tin whistle, to finish the day off in a whirl of jigs and reels.

Later that evening, after she and Edward had retired, leaving the others to their late night conversations, Kate sat at the edge of their bed, brushing her hair. What a wonderful day it had been, and how marvellous it was to have Edward next to her.

No, she had no regrets. Well, maybe one. How much better it would have been if her family had been able to accept Edward, in the same way as other people had. When he came back from America, if her family did not want her, it looked as if she would be spending all her time in England. For an instant she thought of her brother and Mister Grattan, at the opposite ends of the same fence. If only her family had not taken it so badly, she might have found some way to get them closer together. That would surely never happen now, and that might be another tiny regret.

As she looked across at her husband relaxing on the pillow with his eyes half-closed, she forgot those regrets as a little tremor of apprehension suddenly coursed through her body. It would not be long now till he was gone to the war. Without disturbing him, she put down her hairbrush and slipped to her knees beside the bed. Please God, she prayed, keep him safe. But her prayers did not make her feel much better.

All too soon the honeymoon had to end. It was time for Edward to leave, and Kate had to go back to her responsibilities in Ireland. All week they had spent every moment together, sorting out the details of Edward's will, what seemed to Kate to be an unnecessarily large income for her to draw upon, and the continuing management of the estate and the house in London. But now it had to finish.

After the goodbyes and the tears, Kate was determined that when she got back to Ireland she would adopt a philosophical approach to her life. It was a simple proposition, Edward had to go, she had to stay. Nothing would be gained by spending all her time worrying about her husband. The war could not last much longer, for God's sake, and Edward was not going to be in the front line. Perhaps he would even return to England by the end of the year.

Safely back in Mistress Delamere's house in Enniskerry, she immediately set about establishing the old routine. By now it was straightforward enough, but nevertheless still enjoyable to set out the lesson programme for the children. And it would be different this year, with Bernard going to boarding school in September, leaving only the two girls to look after in the autumn. After the plans for the children had been drawn up, Kate set herself a timetable of reading at least one book every week, and writing one letter every week. All she had to do was write thirty-five letters and by that time Edward would be back home.

By filling up her days in this way, she avoided making time for meeting her family. At some stage, she would have to travel down to Arklow to visit Declan, but she could not imagine herself going back to the village. It was easy to foresee how difficult a meeting with her mother and father would be, which would achieve nothing. No, most of her time was going to be spent at Enniskerry.

Of course, she had to be mindful of the estate in England, which she guessed would involve travelling there once every three months or so. Which meant perhaps three overseas trips for her before Edward would be back. Despite her misgivings about the journeys involved, the idea of travelling from Ireland to England to visit the estate was rather amusing. After years of complaining about the problems of absentee landlords in Ireland, for once the boot was going to be on the other foot.

Having an established routine helped tremendously, keeping her busy during the days, while ensuring she had no time to sit daydreaming or worrying. At first, going to bed by herself proved to be difficult, and she experienced many a tearful and sleepless night. Eventually she managed to control these emotions by banishing all her dreams and all her fears about Edward to a secret place hidden away in her inner mind.

In the early days after Edward left, Mistress Delamere continued to be her main source of support. This stemmed less from any specific actions on her part, but more because the older woman approached her life in a calm, organised way and was a perfect role model for Kate. And as well as the Mistress, various other people arrived from time to time who also helped to stimulate her mind and keep her from drifting into aimless thinking. Whenever anyone came to visit, Mistress Delamere always took great delight in introducing her as Lady Tilbrook, which Kate still found highly embarrassing. But at least it had the benefit of setting out her position right from the start and she did not find anyone patronising her, even unintentionally, unlike the conversation with Henry Grattan when they had first met.

While remaining a regular visitor, by this time Mister Grattan appeared to be involved in an inordinate amount of travelling between Bray, Dublin and London. Consequently, they were never sure when he would appear. He had presented his Declaration of Rights to Parliament, but had been bitterly disappointed when it was rejected. However, he was determined to keep trying, with Kate equally determined to keep supporting him at every opportunity.

He was also fond of talking endlessly about a dream to establish an Irish Parliament with total responsibility for the affairs of Ireland, answerable only to King George. She had heard him talking about this on a number of occasions, although she had only just become sufficiently confident to challenge his ideas about who should make up that government. This all made for great debates in the garden on Saturday afternoons. And of course, now she was a Lady everyone was extremely polite, giving her almost total freedom to put forward her own views.

Sometimes, she lay in bed on a Saturday night and shuddered at the things she had said. How could she have interrupted Mistress Delamere's visitors and challenged their points of view? People who had been in business or politics all their lives. They must think of her as some kind of naive half-witted girl. But then again, the more she deliberated, the more she knew she was right. These people were always talking about what was good for the country, but what they were talking about was good for no more than a small number of people who lived in Dublin or London. All she ever heard were the tired ideas of a few self-opinionated men. Not once did she hear the voice of a nation.

It was so continuously frustrating, particularly as there would never be a better opportunity to change the constitution, with England, fully stretched in America, lacking the will to resist a few political changes in Ireland. But there was nothing she could do except refuse to accept the status quo, and keep talking.

Meanwhile, time marched on. Before long, it was almost July and time to travel down to Arklow to see her brother. By this time, she had more than sufficient funds to hire her own carriage, which Edward would have insisted on, she knew. He was always concerned about her being held up by highwaymen and having her rings stolen, or her being kidnapped or even worse. But in the end, she took the mail coach. She could not face arriving in a place like Arklow and bringing out the locals to see who was arriving in such style.

Strangely enough, when they met at the inn where she had decided to stay for a couple of days, her brother seemed quite pleased to see her.

'Kate,' he greeted her with a kiss. 'It's been so long since we saw each other. And I understand that you've gone and got married, in spite of everything. But you didn't tell me your man was of the gentry in England; now I can understand why you were so keen to hang on to him.'

'Declan Brennan, that had nothing to do with it. I knew nothing about any of that until a few days before we were married.'

'So you say, my dear sister. Well, where is he now, and why are you still here in Ireland?' he enquired, ignoring her protests.

Gritting her teeth, she enunciated each word. 'He's gone to America with the war there. I've decided to keep on working at Mistress Delamere's until he comes back.'

'I see,' he replied, a quizzical expression on his face. 'But events are not going at all well for the English, I'm glad to say. Will your husband not be in some danger?'

For a moment, her spirits sagged desperately. 'Yes, he might be. But I'm praying he'll return safely. I don't like to think of these things, nor talk about them. Let's change the subject instead; tell me, how about yourself, what are you doing, how's life down here in Arklow?'

Declan rubbed his chin thoughtfully before replying. 'For most of the people it's a hand to mouth sort of existence. Rather similar to the way I was living in London when you came and found me. But I told you that we'd got hold of a boat. Well, that's beginning to work out really well.'

Kate tried not to look puzzled. But a boat? Declan had never been on a boat in his life other than to cross the water to England. 'I know it can't be for the fishing, Declan Brennan, but I don't understand what else you could want it for.'

With a slight smirk on his face, Declan sat back. 'Kate, or is it Lady Tilbrook now? If you'd been here just a few days ago you'd have met an old friend of yours.'

Her mind raced. Old friend? Who was he talking about? She could not think of anyone she knew here in Arklow. Before she could reply, he began smiling again. 'Do you remember James Lavelle? Your old friend in London? He was here until the day before yesterday.'

Despite herself, a tingle of excitement ran through her body. James Lavelle? Here in Ireland?

'What's he doing now?' she remarked, trying to sound indifferent.

'Kate, I'm telling you but not anyone else.' He looked

around, dropping his voice to a whisper. 'James fetches the goods across from France, you know, brandy and cigars and the like, and we bring it ashore here. And then we sell it to people in Dublin.'

'But that's smuggling,' she almost cried out. 'And is there anything else you're bringing in to the country at the same time?'

Her brother gave her a sideways look. 'Kate, whatever else could we possibly be bringing in?'

She shook her head vigorously, almost unable to comprehend this. 'And do Mam and Dad know you're doing this?'

Declan just laughed. 'Mam doesn't know, although I'm sure Dad does. But he turns a blind eye to it. In fact, I think he'd quite like to get involved himself.'

All of a sudden, she found herself getting irritated. Here was another example of different values. Declan could do anything he wanted and nobody seemed to mind. But every single action of hers was subjected to continuous criticism.

'And how are they keeping?' she decided to ask.

'I've barely seen them since I've been down here. However, I expect that they're still the same as before. But before we talk anymore, let me see if I can get us a drink here.'

Later that night, Kate lay in bed, thinking about their conversation. It seemed that her parents were still taking it badly and had effectively disowned her. But Declan did not seem to be anywhere near as concerned about her and Edward as he had been previously. Perhaps he liked the idea of having a Lady as a sister. But he also seemed to be adopting a different approach to life. He was more confident, more outgoing, and he had plenty of money in his pocket. That was it. Now he had money, he obviously did not feel so downtrodden. Perhaps now he felt he was more a master of his own destiny.

Suddenly, she remembered her thoughts about Declan on the night she had been in the Lord Chatham in London. Back then she had dismissed the idea of him being someone who could rally the others to a cause. But after seeing him tonight, now she was not so sure. This was worrying. Please God, she prayed, keep him to the smuggling and stop him getting involved in anything more sinister.

And then, despite herself, her mind turned to James Lavelle, whom she had not thought about for months. Why was she thinking of him now? She was a married woman after all, she should be thinking of her husband. But her mind drifted back to that night in the summerhouse. No, no, no, she told herself, as she forced the thought out of her head.

When she returned to Enniskerry, a letter from Edward had arrived. Her hands were trembling as she slit the envelope along one edge, but everything was fine. He had settled in, and he was thinking about her constantly. In his only comment about the war, he mentioned that it appeared to be more the French fighting the Germans, rather than the rebels fighting the British, so his language skills had been in demand almost immediately. At the end of his letter he left an address, allowing her to set about writing a long reply. But after that frisson of excitement, life settled back down into her self-imposed routine.

Later in the month, Mistress Delamere intended as usual to hold her annual garden party. Although difficult to believe, a year had passed since Edward Tilbrook had appeared out of the blue. No matter how long she lived, the sense of shock she had experienced on seeing his face that day last year would never leave her.

On this occasion, however, Mistress Delamere had not asked her to help, and with the date drawing closer, she could not help thinking she was going to be left out. A week before the big day, she decided to broach the subject while they were having tea and looking through the children's work.

'Mistress Delamere, now that we've reviewed the exercise books, there's something I'd like to ask you,' she began, a little hesitantly.

Engrossed in one of her daughter's essays, the Mistress was only half-listening. 'Yes, Kate, tell me what you want to know.'

'I know the garden party is next week but you haven't asked me to do anything and you haven't invited me either. I was wondering, that was all, perhaps you think that I've been too miserable and withdrawn to be good company?'

'Don't be ridiculous, Kate,' the other woman replied indignantly. 'Of course you're coming, aren't you? I hardly thought it necessary to issue you a formal invitation.' Then she smiled cheekily. 'But of course, now that you are Lady Tilbrook, you may wish things to be done differently. I'll go and write one out immediately.'

Now it was Kate's turn to laugh. 'Oh no, Mistress Delamere, I'm happy just to know that I'm invited. But you've not asked me to do anything, and last year I was serving the punch.'

This time the Mistress looked at her a little more closely. 'Are you serious, Kate? I mean, despite my little joke, you are after all Lady Tilbrook now, and I didn't feel I could ask you to help the way you did last year.'

Even Mistress Delamere was beginning to recognise her position, Kate muttered to herself. Was it perhaps because she had started to put on airs and graces without realising it? That was something she had to watch out for, especially here at Enniskerry.

She shook her head. 'Mistress Delamere, I've no worries about helping or serving the punch. If you can use me, I'll be more than delighted to do the same as last year.'

On the day of the party, she was glad to be serving the drinks rather than acting as a lady of the manor. With so much work to be done she was given little time to think. This suited her fine, it being such a poignant time, filled with memories of Edward and their first proper words to each other.

Throughout the day, the party went well, with crowds of visitors keeping her rushed off her feet. As the afternoon progressed, however, she detected a slight thinning in the ranks of people, allowing her a moment or two to see who she could recognise. She had seen Mister Grattan and a number of his friends she had met once or twice before at the house. She knew some people from the village and also Cathal's father and mother, although of Cathal himself she saw no sign.

As she turned to check the levels in the punch bowls, a small gap opened up in the crowd. She caught a glimpse of a woman's back, seconds before she disappeared amongst all the people. For an instant it could have been her mother. Hesitating a moment, she dashed out into the crowd to try and find her, but it was too late. The woman had disappeared. And behind her she could hear people becoming fretful and shouting for more drink.

Reluctantly, she turned back to her task, starting on a another series of mad charges backwards and forwards into the kitchen. However, the punchbowls had barely been filled to an acceptable level when she heard an unusual accent in front of her.

'Miss Brennan, it's so nice to see you after all these years.'

It was a voice she knew only too well. As she looked up to see her old schoolteacher standing beside the table, all at once memories came flooding back.

'Mister Hutchinson,' she began to say, uncertain what to do next. Should she be formal, and shake him by the hand, or should she embrace him? What was the done thing in these circumstances? While she was thinking, the man reached out and took her hand between his, squeezing it gently.

'Kathleen Brennan, when I last saw you, you were a pretty young girl. But now you are a beautiful woman.'

This made it easy for her. 'Mister Hutchinson, I think you're losing your sight in your old age. I've been serving this punch all day and I'm feeling excessively hot and bothered, and my hair is a disgrace.' Before he could reply, she carried on whimsically. 'However, I don't remember you offering me any compliments when I was in your class. In fact it was more the opposite. You were always telling me how lazy I was.'

The old man chuckled with pleasure. 'Those were fine

days indeed, Kathleen. But they're all gone now. You were such a difficult person to teach, always asking questions instead of giving me answers. But you know, I rarely had pupils with such a thirst for knowledge. I suppose it was a privilege having you in my class.'

Giving him her most devastating smile, she fluttered her eyelids in his direction. 'I probably didn't realise it at the time, but I was lucky to have you as my teacher. And I recognise that now.'

Shading his eyes against the sun, he looked around the garden. 'This is the first time I've been to Mistress Delamere's house for a few years. She always invites me but I don't like to be among too many people in one place.' Briefly, he glanced in the direction of the house. 'She tells me you're doing a good job with the children here, and that your work is very impressive.'

'Well, that's probably a result of all your teaching, Mister Hutchinson.'

But he was going on. 'And I've seen Henry Grattan here with some of his cronies. I had a few words with him, but he's always so pompous and pontificating all the time. I knew him when he was at Trinity, and he was the same there.'

This time Kate had to laugh. 'Mister Hutchinson, you're always so down-to-earth. Mister Grattan is a good friend of the Delameres, and I've talked with him a lot. And if you take the time to really listen to what he's got to say, much of it is very interesting.'

'Interesting, Kate?' the old man cried. 'You make it sound as if it's something you listen to for a moment, file away in your mind and then forget all about. He's supposed to be a politician, for God's sake. Shouldn't it be exciting, invigorating, even a little bit alarming?'

For a moment, she was back in the school with Mister Hutchinson as the teacher and her as the pupil. This had to be stopped right now.

'Mister Hutchinson, you're equally as bad. You're almost striking a pose there yourself. And I don't think I want to get into one of your discussions about Irish politics when there's far more important things to do like serving thirsty people.'

Dismissively, he waved his hands. 'Go and get them more drink, that will always keep them satisfied. I'll still be here when you get back.'

She rushed off to get the refills, and sure enough, when she got back he materialised out of the crowd once again. As he started speaking, for a moment it seemed as if there had been no gap at all in the conversation, except that he appeared to have adopted a more challenging tone of voice.

'I see you're moving in exalted circles now, Kathleen Brennan, if you're discussing politics with the like of Grattan and Langrishe and Daly, and those types. And have you forgotten your own background and upbringing?'

She felt herself bristling. 'Indeed I have not, Mister Hutchinson, and I'll thank you not to be making any more remarks like that which are totally without foundation. These people you refer to know my views well enough, and they are more than aware of where I come from.'

But her reply did not seem to have the slightest effect on him. 'And I hear that you've gone and got married into the English gentry and that we now have to address you as Lady somebody or other, and that you're taking on airs and graces.'

Now he was beginning to aggravate her. But at the same time she remembered the advice that he himself had given her years ago. Slowly, she counted up to ten, while he stood looking at her, waiting for her to reply.

'Mister Hutchinson, I believe you're trying to test me in your own devious way. However, I was not a pupil of yours for nothing. But let me say that, yes, you're correct, I have married into the English gentry. As for me putting on airs, well that depends on who I'm talking to. Or then, perhaps, who is listening.'

The man shook his head and laughed. 'Kathleen Brennan, I was merely interested in finding out if you were still a woman of her own convictions. It's been delightful talking to you. And there's so many other things that I would like to talk to you about, particularly now you have the ear of the likes of Mister Grattan.' All of a sudden, he stopped and looked around at the people still milling about the garden. 'But do you know that I've come here today with your mother?' he asked quietly.

Involuntarily, Kate gasped. So she had been right after all. 'I thought I saw her for a moment, but I wasn't sure.'

'Yes, your father wouldn't come. And I don't think he knows your mother has come or else there would be hell to pay.'

'So why has she come at all?' she demanded, her curiosity getting the better of her. 'She must have known I would be here. And she had terrible words for me when I told her I was going to be married.'

The old man screwed up his face, obviously mulling over his reply. 'It's difficult to tell. But she's a mother after all, and you're her only daughter. I don't think she could bring herself to come and talk with you, but perhaps she simply wanted to see you from a distance and be sure that you were keeping well.'

'She left me in no doubt what she thought the last time we met. But if you see that changing in any way, Mister Hutchinson, I beg you to come and tell me.'

'That I will, Kathleen. I'm positive you don't need me to tell you that in this life many things are said in anger and then repented over for years. But to me you'll always be my wee Kate, even though you're now Lady Tilbrook, or so Declan tells me. It's been wonderful to talk to you, and make sure you don't hold back with Grattan and his cronies. It's a frightening thing to have to say, but they're the people who've got the future of this country in their hands. Still, I'm absolutely sure that if anyone can convince them to look out for others rather than lining their own pockets, then you're the one. But I think you'd better see to your punch bowls again.'

As swiftly as he had arrived, he departed into the crowds. Dumbstruck, Kate stood motionless, looking at the space where he had been, disregarding the shouts of the people for more drink. For a moment or two she experienced yet again that strange sensation of being somewhere else, while she looked down at her body going through the motions. However, as the noise level intensified, she found herself firmly brought back to the present. So what would Teresa Ryan say to this lot?

'Would you ever just bide your time and you'll all be served,' Lady Tilbrook screeched at the hordes in front of her, as they brandished their empty tankards in her face.

That night she fell into bed, exhausted. Although she

had enjoyed herself, especially seeing Mister Hutchinson again for the first time in years, she was secretly glad that the garden party was over. It held too many memories that prevented her from getting back into her routine. Yet while she was tired physically, her mind was still racing. What had Peter Hutchinson really been saying? Had he been speaking in some sort of code? Did he agree with what Mister Grattan was trying to do, or did he think they should be pursuing a different approach? Was he perhaps in the same camp as Declan? That force was the ultimate answer? And what about this business with her mother? Should she go and see her or would she simply be rejected again? Still wrestling with these questions, she drifted off into a troubled sleep.

The following morning she realised another challenge still had to be confronted – the estate in England had to be reviewed. She had pushed this task to the back of her mind for too long. For sure, the estate would go on without her – the people in London and in Essex would continue as they had previously, but she would never win their confidence if she did not make the effort to visit them and demonstrate that she was interested in their future. So a trip to England it was, after she had agreed the timing with Mistress Delamere.

It turned out to be a long and tiring three weeks. To begin with, communicating with Mr Arrowsmith and his wife was a thankless task, taking considerable patience, tact and persuasion to win them over and start off some sort of relationship. The problem was that they had been accustomed to doing things in their own way for too long.

In London, however, Mistress Jardine was in sparkling

form, taking Kate out on shopping trips, to the theatre and to all the new hotels and restaurants to have dinner in the evening. Although eighteen months had passed since they had last seen one another, it seemed as if they had been apart for no time at all. For a few days, they were inseparable as they travelled around London, burning the candle at both ends. For most of the time, Mister Jardine came along too, not so much joining in, but more like some benevolent presence watching over them.

Although it was a wonderful release from continually thinking about Edward, the estate, and her family, not to mention everything else, four days was enough. There were only so many hours one could spend having a good time.

Moreover, she was determined to visit Mister and Mistress Boulton. Since her first visit to England, her life had changed in so many ways, and she yearned to go back to make sure it had not all been a dream and that her impressions had not been merely a result of her age or her naivety.

But, thank God, when she got there Mister Boulton was just as she remembered.

'Welcome, Lady Tilbrook, to our humble abode. It's not often we get the aristocracy coming to Birmingham to visit us.'

His eyes were twinkling as he spoke. And his good lady wife was every bit as welcoming and as comfortable as ever. Even though she had been there just the once, Kate felt immediately at home in their house. On the one hand, she was still confronted by the hotbed of his ideas, while on the other there was comfort and stability and consistency.

But Mister Boulton was not prepared to let her off lightly. 'So, Kathleen, do you remember the discussions at your wedding?' he began, almost as soon as she arrived. 'Have you built the canal, and is everything now moving apace in Essex?'

For a moment, she shifted uncomfortably. 'Well, Mister Boulton, we've not exactly done anything. My husband has had to go to America and I've been in Ireland.' She trailed off pathetically.

Pulling at his whiskers, he shook his head. 'Things are changing, Kathleen. Unless you move quickly, you'll be overtaken by events. If you delay for another twenty years, by that time we'll have the engines I spoke to you about travelling on rails around the country. And who'll want to use barges and horses then? Unless of course we can find a way to use the engines to drive the barges.'

Kate shook her head in amazement. If only there were more people like this in Ireland, full of ideas, ready to challenge the status quo, and not prepared to sit idly by while life went on as always.

As if he was reading her thoughts, he posed the question. 'And what about Ireland? I remember us talking about the industrial revolution here in England. Has it started yet in Ireland?'

Kate shrugged her shoulders. 'Mister Boulton, I don't know. I've not seen anything to indicate that the ideas you described might come to pass in Ireland. But you have to remember,' she snapped suddenly, 'that here in England, people have some responsibility for their own destiny. It's not like that in Ireland. People there are too busy trying to survive.'

Almost immediately, she felt guilty at replying so sharply. It was true but it was not Mister Boulton's problem. She had to change the subject. 'Can you tell me anything about Patrick Nolan, Mister Boulton? I believe he might have a position with you.'

'If I remember correctly, Patrick is the man you wrote to me about. All I can say is that if you have any more like him, send them over to me. He's my overseer now, responsible for turning our designs and ideas into something that can be built. I'll say this, he might not have the education, but he certainly has the aptitude.'

Thank God for that, she muttered to herself. If Patrick had turned out to be an idler after her recommendation and all her talk about Irishmen, she would have been too ashamed to show her face at the Boulton's ever again.

'And another thing,' he continued, while she tried to straighten out her thoughts. 'When you came here last year, my wife and I were taken by your charm and your beauty. But what impressed me most was your thinking. Well, let me tell you, that Patrick Nolan has a wife who's so sharp I have to be careful when I'm speaking to her. Someday, women will be doing the work that only men do now, especially if we can get people like Mrs Nolan.'

Kate let his comments sink in. So Teresa had been accepted as well. Good for her. Then she remembered Mistress Jardine talking about some of the other women at the theatre. 'They are not like us.' Those were the words she had used. And Kate had been amused by her apparent leap from the Irish bog into the London high life. Now, it seemed as if Teresa might have made a similar leap of her own. Good for her indeed – and even better if she could see them again.

'I'd like to visit them while I'm here,' she decided impulsively. 'Do they live far away?'

'That's a good idea, Kathleen. You must go and see them,' Mister Boulton said enthusiastically. 'Perhaps you can all sing songs together about the west coast of Clare or some other Godforsaken place. As it's Sunday tomorrow, you'll probably find them at home, except I suppose they'll be going to Mass, or whatever in the morning.'

That night, she lay in bed thinking about Mister Boulton's words. He seemed to be pleased with Patrick and Teresa, but equally, he gave the impression that he had expected more from herself. In some ways, it was not fair. Here was Mister Boulton trying to push her along, not long after Mister Hutchinson had been pushing her only a few weeks ago. And Mister Grattan and his friends never stopped pushing. And then Mr Arrowsmith at the estate. He had been almost insolent in the way he had kept looking at her for all the answers, as if running an estate came naturally, for God's sake. Even Declan had kept asking her what she was going to do next. Why were they all doing that? Surely, they had to realise she was going to settle down happily with her husband when he came back from America?

Around noon the following day Burton brought round the carriage and she set off to find the house where Patrick and Teresa were living. Mister Boulton had been right, it was not long before they came close to some of the factories that she had seen the previous year. This time, however, there appeared to be many more of the huge chimneys, all of which seemed to be competing to belch the most smoke into the atmosphere. Fortunately it was a calm day, and the smoke had risen high in the air, forming a long cloud that could be seen from miles away. At first sight, it looked like an eyesore. But then again, perhaps that was the price that had to be paid for this industrial revolution.

Not far beyond the factories came the houses. Unusually, they were laid out in uniform terraces interspersed with trees and bushes, with a roadway between each row. This was something that she was not accustomed to. Back in Wicklow people built their houses more or less where they had wanted, or wherever there was a piece of land that was not a bog. And it was possible to identify one house from another as they all looked different. But here they all seemed to be the same, and she soon lost all sense of direction. Fortunately, Burton seemed to know where he was going, and eventually they arrived at the end of one row where the tiny strip of land alongside one house appeared to be slightly larger than that of its neighbours.

'Here we are, madam, this is where the Nolans are living.'

For a moment, she took stock of her surroundings. Now she was closer, it was possible to see that the original row of houses must have been laid out to a standard design, but that many of the residents had personalised theirs by growing flowers and trees and painting the windows different colours. But no matter how neat and tidy most of the houses were, the same groups of small children with torn trousers and dirty feet that she had seen everywhere were playing in the road among the horses and the carts.

Burton came round to the side of the carriage but Kate

had already seen a small cot sitting outside the house with a baby inside.

'Thank you, Burton,' she said quickly, looking up at the house. 'I'll be all right from here by myself. Can you come back and collect me around six o'clock?'

The man touched his cap. 'That will be fine, madam.' A few moments later she saw him waving to her, as the carriage set off along the road with a dozen children chasing after it, all shouting and screaming at the tops of their voices.

As she walked slowly up the little pathway, Patrick Nolan came out to see what the fuss was about.

'Well, by God, we're certainly being graced here today,' he exclaimed. 'I can't believe that the famous Lady Tilbrook would be coming to a place like this.'

Kate caught hold of his arm and kissed him on the cheek.

'Would you ever shut up,' she said sternly, 'or for sure the neighbours will be round to see what's going on.'

'Teresa, come and see who is here,' he called in through the door. 'It's her ladyship, come all the way from London.'

His wife appeared, wiping her hands on her hips, a slightly uncertain look on her face, and her little daughter Marie clutching her skirts.

'Hello, Mrs Nolan,' Kate said with a twinkle in her eye. 'I've come to see you all and the new baby.'

'I don't believe it.' Teresa Nolan was smiling now. 'Lady Tilbrook! I never thought we'd see the day when you would come here.'

'For God's sake, call me Kate. And don't forget, I'm still the girl from Kilcarra village.'

Laughing together, Patrick took her arm and guided her up into the house. For the next few hours, she was able to forget everything as she played with the baby and Marie, swapping the latest titbits of news with her two friends. Eventually, however, the discussion moved round to Patrick's work for Mister Boulton and their move to Birmingham.

'So, are you satisfied here or are you still thinking about going to Ireland?' Kate wanted to know.

Looking across at his wife, Patrick Nolan frowned. 'That's a difficult question to answer, Kate. If I could get a job like this, I'd want to go back right away. But there's no chance of that, so I think we'll be staying here.'

Teresa was much more direct. 'Where we live now is a palace compared to the hovel that Marie and I lived in when we were in London. You might think it's tiny, but it's a home for us.'

A little overcome, Teresa wiped a tear away from her eye with the edge of her apron. 'The finest thing that has ever happened to me was getting married to Patrick here. But the second finest was you speaking with Mister Boulton about a job for him. We'll always be grateful to you for that.'

Kate tried to dismiss it as nothing but Teresa was still speaking. 'I miss being in Ireland as much as Patrick does, but I'd never let him go back while there's still talk of fighting and killing. After being here for so long I realise now that so many people back home still live in the past rather than thinking about the future. I remember what you said when you were in the Lord Chatham, and until that someone comes along who can make the whole country believe in what they can achieve together, then we'll be staying here. We've got two children now, and the way Patrick is going we'll soon have another two. And I want to be bringing our children up in a place where they have a future and where they can see their father when they want to.'

Kate looked at the two of them sitting on the other side of the table. 'I think, perhaps, your speeches are better than mine, Teresa,' she observed wryly. 'But I must say that while there's still plenty of talk, there's not much action. The Dublin people still have too much of a stranglehold over the rest of the country.'

Out of the corner of her eye she could see Marie staring at her. What must she be thinking about all this? 'But we might see some changes if the Americans win their independence, and that seems to be what's happening,' she continued. 'Perhaps someone will emerge who's capable of being a leader, but there's been no sign of that yet.'

'But your husband's in America with the British army,' Teresa exclaimed. 'If you say the war isn't going well, isn't he in some danger?'

Kate felt her heart lurching. 'Teresa, please don't remind me. I think about it and worry about it every single day.'

But the other woman's words had brought her back to reality. The few hours' enjoyment she had experienced had been no more than an interlude. She had spent too many days in England trying to forget about what was happening on the other side of the Atlantic Ocean. It was time to return to Enniskerry and get back into her routine. That was the only way she knew of keeping her thoughts and her emotions under control.

Chapter 14

———◆———

Another letter from Edward was waiting when she arrived back at Enniskerry. He loved her and missed her, but there was little mentioned about the war, and nothing about his return.

However, as that was no less than she was expecting, she was not deflected from working at establishing her planned routine. One surprise she did receive was a letter from Mister Hutchinson, who had written to say how pleased he had been to see her again. Curiously enough, he also mentioned that her mother was happy knowing her daughter was alive and well. Which immediately gave her some food for thought. Did it mean her mother was softening her attitude a little? Was there perhaps a chance they might be able to talk at some time in the future without recriminations? After weighing up the options, she decided that the best approach was a reply to Mister Hutchinson, offering an olive branch to her mother through any contacts the schoolteacher had with her.

The months rolled by, as autumn came and gradually faded into winter. Bernard went off to boarding school in September, amid a flood of tears and goodbyes. For the first time, Kate saw Mistress Delamere unable to maintain her normally calm and controlled manner. In some ways it was a surprise and a shock to see the woman who had been an example to her in so many situations suddenly experiencing such emotions, and it jolted Kate out of her own routine for quite some time.

As Christmas approached, Mistress Delamere slowly regained her self-composure, but Kate's own spirits were beginning to flag. The last letter from Edward had come at the end of August, and she had received no news whatsoever except that the war was still not going well for the British forces. More and more lonely nights were spent in her room, a premonition of doom becoming stronger and stronger. Her mind strayed constantly back to the previous winter, when Edward had surprised her on the road to Enniskerry and asked her again to marry him. Her memories were becoming inseparable from her dreams, and tears were never far away.

During November and early December, she tried to occupy her mind by writing Christmas greetings to some of the people living on the estate. Although she was not expecting any response from Essex, shortly before Christmas a bulky letter arrived from the Arrowsmiths. Inside she found a card and a short note wishing her the compliments of the season, and another sealed envelope addressed to her personally which had come to Tilbrook Hall a few weeks earlier.

Scrutinising the envelope, she placed it carefully on the table in front of her. With some difficulty she tried to compose herself. Although the outside cover gave no clue to the contents, somehow she knew what the letter would say without having to read it. Truth to tell, she had been expecting it for so long, and now that it had arrived, she knew her worst fears were about to be confirmed.

Slowly and deliberately, she picked up the envelope and slit it along one side with the letter opener. One loose sheet of embossed paper fell out onto the table. With a growing feeling of detachment, she reached out and picked it up. Strangely enough, her hand was perfectly steady. For a moment, she admired the ring on her fourth finger and the way it flashed and sparkled in the light of the lamps.

Turning the single page the right way up she started reading. The words were easy enough. She knew what they would say. In her premonition she had seen herself reading them over and over again. In fact, she was almost word perfect.

'My dear Lady Tilbrook,' it read, 'it is with great regret that I have to inform you that your husband, Captain Edward Tilbrook, is missing in action, presumed dead.'

There were some other words about glory and honour and service, but they were meaningless. At the end it was signed by Lord Cornwallis. Kate held the letter between her fingers, unable to feel anything. Should she be crying or consumed with grief? Perhaps, but she did not feel like that. She had carried the premonition of Edward's death with her for over twelve months. She had known she was going to receive this letter or something like it. In some ways she had been grieving all that time. It was a completely and utterly numbing sensation.

For some time, minutes, hours perhaps, she sat in the

chair holding the letter, her eyes sightless, her fingers numb. Very gently, Mistress Delamere prised the letter from her hand and put it down on the table. She had not read it, but she could see from Kate's face what it said.

'My poor, poor child,' the Mistress whispered as she knelt down beside the girl and took her in her arms. There was nothing more she could say. For a long time they remained in that position, the woman holding her, rocking her gently. Eventually, Kate struggled to her feet. The situation was so strange. Mistress Delamere was crying more than she was. Why was she not crying? Or was it simply that she had no emotions left to give?

Biting her lip, she looked at the woman beside her. 'I'm sorry Mistress Delamere. I must be such a burden to you. But don't worry about me. To be honest, I've been expecting this and it comes as no surprise. In some ways, it's better that it's come before Christmas. At least I won't go into the new year carrying foolish hopes.'

She could see Mistress Delamere crying even more now, but still her own tears would not come.

'I think I'll go and lie down. Please don't worry about me, I'll be fine. Make sure you go up to bed yourself and try and get some sleep.'

Sometime around the dark, dangerous hours before dawn, she sat up suddenly. At first she could not work out what had disturbed her. Then she realised what it was. Panic – sheer, blind panic, coursing through her body, rising in her chest, constricting her throat, making her head spin.

Ever since she could remember, she had been surrounded by people. Now, at the age of twenty, she was left with nobody. She had been disowned by her parents, her elder brother barely tolerated her, she scarcely knew her younger brother, and now her husband had been taken away. That dashing man, so strong, so sensitive, with a smile for everyone – now he was dead. She was never going to see him again, or hear the sound of his voice, or feel the touch of his hand against her cheek. What was she going to do? How was she going to cope without him?

Feeling more and more alarmed, she threw back the covers and swung her feet out of the bed onto the floor. For a short while she sat motionless, breathing deeply and counting slowly, as she tried to get her body under control. One thing was for sure. She could not stay here at Mistress Delamere's house. Christmas was only a few weeks away and the last thing she wanted was to be involved in a celebration. In any event, it would be unfair to the Mistress and her children to have a grieving widow moping around and ruining the atmosphere.

And the estate in Essex had to be ruled out for the same reason. They would be getting ready for Christmas now, and the appearance of the newly widowed Mistress of the estate would simply undermine her already fragile relationship with the Arrowsmiths.

Her thoughts roamed aimlessly. The attack of anxiety had left her feeling restless, and she stood up and looked blankly through the window into the shadows outside. If only she could go down to the church, and light a candle and spend a few hours praying. But the priest had told her never to come back. Would he change his mind now, if he heard about what had happened?

But she could not bring herself to walk down to the

village and beg for entry into the church. Nonetheless, as she sat contemplating, a glimmer of an idea crept into her mind, and she felt the panic recede and slowly melt away. Now she knew what to do, but if she was going to get there in time, she had to make her preparations quickly.

With her mind made up, she felt much more positive about her course of action. Climbing back into bed, she pulled the covers over her head. Two more hours rest, she told herself, then she would get up and make ready to leave.

Despite this positive approach, it took almost two weeks to reach where she wanted to go. Finally, however, three days before Christmas, she found herself at last walking up the familiar lane through Grays Inn in London, just as she had done some twenty-one months previously, looking for the Sanatorium of St John.

When she knocked at the door, it was Sister Agnes who answered, recognising her almost immediately. 'Kathleen Brennan, what are you doing here? And you look so cold. What has happened to you? Come in, come in.'

She went in through the door and shook the rain from her cloak. 'You are right, it's me, Kate, and I would like to speak with Sister Mary Francis if that's possible?'

A few minutes later, she was seated with the Mother Superior in her room. 'Sister Mary Francis, please listen to me for a few minutes. I'm almost at the end of my tether, and you're my last hope. It grieves me to say that my husband, God rest him, has been killed in the war in America. And now I've so many things to attend to, between the estate and the lawyers and the army.'

Stopping for a moment, she tried to catch her breath,

while the sister watched her impassively. 'All of those will have to wait until January. Right now, I'm in desperate need of finding a quiet place where I can have some peace to say a prayer or two for my husband's soul. And because of the local priest back home, I can't do that in the church at Kilcarra.'

She bowed her head slightly so that the other woman could not see her lips quivering while she was speaking. 'I would dearly like your permission to spend some time in the little chapel you have here.'

The sister reached out to her, but Kate had not finished yet, although she was finding it more and more difficult to speak. 'I could stay with Mistress Delamere or even Mistress Jardine over Christmas, but it wouldn't be fair on them or their children. Or I could go to the estate in Essex or even the house in London. But then I realised you would probably be very busy here with so many sick and homeless people with nowhere to go. So if you can find me a corner somewhere to sleep, I'd like to stay and help you until Christmas is over.'

Again, the sister reached out for her hand. 'You poor child. I'm desperately sorry to hear about your husband. Of course you can come to the chapel here. And the priest who comes in here now, Father Doolan, I'm sure he'd be happy to talk to you or hear your confession, if you want to do that. But there's lots of other churches in London now, where you can go without having to tell anyone why you're there.'

The nun looked round at the lines of beds and the people coming and going. 'And as for helping us over Christmas: if that's something that Lady Tilbrook is happy to do, there's no doubt that we'll be able to use all the help we can get. What I suggest is that you try it for a day or two and see how you feel after that.'

For the next week, Kate was rushed off her feet, fourteen hours a day, washing dishes and serving up bread and bowls of hot soup. Even the work at Mistress Delamere's garden party had hardly prepared her for this. Every night she collapsed into bed, exhausted, but with some sense of satisfaction at the numbers of people they had managed to serve during the day. Every morning, just after dawn, she had her time to go to the chapel, where for an hour or two she was able to have some peace, to sit or kneel by herself, and to pray for Edward and to thank God for the time they had spent together.

A few days before the New Year, she was busy in the kitchen serving a line of people. Outside, the weather was dreadfully cold, and all day long the queue had stretched around the room and through the door, giving her little opportunity to take a rest. Somewhere along the way, she had developed a kind of rhythm, where the person in the line thrust out a bowl, and without looking up, she filled it with a ladle held in one hand while handing over a slice of bread with the other, at the same time shouting for the next person in the queue to shuffle forward.

Around mid-afternoon the numbers had decreased a little, but she was still set firmly in her serving rhythm. As one customer approached, however, he appeared to thrust his bowl towards her more aggressively than the rest, and when she held out the slice of bread, he caught hold of her wrist with his hand.

Kate looked up, straight into the eyes of Mister Jardine. It was such a shock that she jumped back, almost burning her foot in the fire behind her.

'Mister Jardine, what are you doing here?' she exclaimed, her hand half over her mouth.

'And why shouldn't I be here?' his voice boomed out. 'I want to make sure that these people who are serving the food are keeping up to the mark and not slacking.'

Without warning, he pulled her close towards him. 'But Miss Brennan, more to the point, what are you doing here?' Lowering his voice so that no one else could hear, he leaned over so that his mouth was close to her ear. 'I did not expect to find Lady Tilbrook working in this place.'

Using all her strength, Kate managed to wriggle free from his grip. 'Mister Jardine, it's very nice to see you. But you are holding up the queue. If you would be so good to stand to one side so that I can serve the others, I will tell you as soon as I can.'

She smiled at him while she called the next person forward. 'Unless you were expecting another helping, was that it?'

Ten minutes later she had explained why she was there. At first she was not sure he had understood her. All he did was stand in front of the table, with every appearance of listening, but with his gaze fixed upon a spot somewhere in the distance beyond her head.

After what seemed like an age, he cleared his throat. 'Kathleen,' he began, hesitating. All at once she realised she could not recall him ever using her first name before. 'Kathleen, my heart goes out to you. If there's anything at all I can do, you know that you only have to ask.'

Amazingly, she detected a tear at the corner of his eye. 'So how long do you intend staying here at the sanatorium?' he asked her quietly.

For a moment, she let her mind drift. 'Mister Jardine, I know there's a host of matters to be sorted out. And I intend to face up to them in January once we are into the new year. But I couldn't cope with anything else before Christmas.'

'But what made you choose to come here?' He was looking at her quizzically.

'It's been good for me, Mister Jardine. I know I've been selfish, but it's helped me keep my mind away from all my problems, and I've been able to find some moments of peace and quiet to reflect on what's happened, and I suppose, on what might have been.'

Shrugging her shoulders, she rearranged the rows of serving bowls. 'Up to a few months ago, I believed that everybody had some opportunity to shape or change their lives, no matter how small. But now I feel so overtaken by events, that I'm not so sure.'

Gently, the man took hold of her hand. 'My dear Kathleen, I can understand you feeling like that at this moment. But things won't always be as bad as this. When we first met, what impressed me most was your single-mindedness and your positive approach to life. I'm not going to stand by now and let you lose that.'

Biting his lip, he gestured at the window. 'I have to go now,' he continued, letting go of her hand. 'But I'm sure I'll see you again in a little while.'

Not long afterwards, Sister Mary Francis came round to the kitchen to see how things were progressing. By this time most of the people had gone, and Kate was busy at the sink, washing up countless numbers of bowls and spoons. The woman surveyed the scene before saying anything. 'It would seem, Lady Tilbrook, that you're becoming quite an expert in matters of the kitchen.'

Kate was content simply to smile as the other woman continued. 'However, it must be about time for you to move on from here, unless perhaps you're after a permanent job?'

Frowning slightly, Kate studied the nun's expression. 'What's the problem with me staying for a little bit longer. It's been good for me here, and I think I've been able to help in a small way.'

But she could see the Sister choosing her words carefully. 'You can't stay here for ever, Kate. You have to start mixing with people you know outside of here, and get accustomed to talking to them again. I know that the next few months are going to be a difficult time, but you can't delay much longer.'

Suddenly Kate realised what had been going on. 'You've been talking to Mister Jardine, haven't you? Has he asked you to come and speak to me?'

'It's true,' the Sister replied slowly. 'I've been talking with Mister Jardine, but not behind your back, and only because we want what's best for you. He'd like to send his carriage round here tomorrow to take you back to their house for a few days. Of course you don't have to go, but I think you should.'

Reluctantly, Kate weighed up the proposition. 'I suppose you're right,' she conceded eventually. 'I could stay here quite happily another few weeks, and working in the kitchen has kept me occupied but at the same time let me be alone with my thoughts and my memories.'

She shook her head sorrowfully. 'You've no idea how desperately lonely I felt when I came here at first, and you've helped me get over that. All the same, for the last year all I've thought about was being with Edward again, and now he's been taken away from me . . .' Her voice trailed off.

'Listen, Kathleen, nobody's forcing you to do anything. And you can always come back here at any time. But you have to pick up the pieces sooner or later, and with the estate, you may find it has to be sooner rather than later. Many of the people there will be wondering what will happen next, and I think you owe it to your dead husband's memory to go there and let them know what you intend to do.'

'But I don't know what I'm going to do about the estate,' she exclaimed in frustration. 'I can hardly think about that now.'

'And for sure, I can't help you in these matters. But perhaps a few days at Connaught House will help you think about what you need to do.'

With a heavy heart, Kate forced herself to start thinking beyond the memories of Edward and the work at the sanatorium. But to go to Tilbrook Hall and deal with the Arrowsmiths and the rest of the people there? It was such a frightening thought. They would have hundreds of questions. How was she going to answer them all? She didn't have a clue about running a house and staff, never mind managing an estate.

And then there was Mistress Delamere. Kate had forgotten all about the children. What was she going to do about them? She could not keep going back and forth. It was too disruptive for everybody concerned, never mind the time it took and how exhausted she felt after every trip. Somehow or other, that was another thing she had to make her mind up about. Yes, she would write to Mistress Delamere and tell her she was going to stay in England. She would probably be desperately unhappy about that, maybe she would even be angry, but it was the best thing to do for everyone concerned. If she wrote immediately, Mistress Delamere could start to look for someone else to replace her. And she would need to write to the girls as well, to let them know what she was doing and why.

Feeling a little happier now she had made a decision, she looked up and realised that the sister was still looking at her, as if she was expecting an answer.

'Sister Mary Francis, as ever, I believe that you're right. I can barely bring myself to think about the things that have to be done, but I have to start sometime. So it might as well be now.'

As Mister Jardine's carriage pushed through the crowds of people thronging Holborn, Kate lay back uncomfortably on the cushions, looking sightlessly at the world outside, thinking about the bleak days ahead. Leaving the sanatorium had been a dreadful experience, and she was only going to Mistress Jardine's house. And that was with people she knew, people she was familiar with. What was it going to be like when she arrived at Tilbrook Hall, all by herself?

Stopping outside Connaught House in St Thomas' Street brought back an immediate flood of memories of her first visit. Sitting quietly, she closed her eyes for a moment, reliving those early days. Suddenly the door was flung open and she was seized by the hand and dragged out of the carriage into the embrace of Mistress Jardine.

'Oh Kate, you poor girl, how are you? And what a terrible experience! And what a way for you to spend Christmas!'

Despite herself, Kate had to laugh. 'You make it sound so dreadful, but it wasn't as bad as all that. And it was good for my peace of mind.'

The Mistress stepped back and looked at her. 'Well, I have to say that you look better than I expected. A little thin perhaps, but then you always were on the slender side. Still, I'm sure that a hot bath and some pampering with a few creams and ointments will not go amiss. Come inside and tell me everything. Never mind these bags and horses and things. Someone else will attend to all of these details.'

It was like a breath of fresh air meeting the Mistress again. She had almost forgotten the flouncing and preening, the expansive attitude, and the imperious and sometimes dismissive gestures. But all that was offset by her generosity and concern for Kate's wellbeing.

An hour or so later, they were standing by the sideboard, pouring out two brandies. Kate remembered all too clearly what had happened the last time she had sat in this drawing room drinking port, and she was determined that was not going to happen again. But Mistress Jardine was talking as she poured.

'Now, Kate,' she was saying, 'you can stay as long as you like. But I imagine you'll have so many different things to attend to. It's a terrible time in anyone's life when something like this happens, and there's always so many things that need to be done. If we can help you in any way, just let me know. But then, of course, there's the other side of the coin.' She rubbed her hands gleefully.

'I'm not sure what you mean, Mistress Jardine?' Kate asked, mystified.

'Why, you're now the most attractive, richest widow in all of England. Men will be flocking to your side from all parts of the Empire, and you'll need someone to help keep them at bay.'

'Thank you, Mistress Jardine, I'll remember that,' she replied evenly, sipping at the brandy and making a face. This was the first serious drink she had taken since April, since she had been with Edward. The memory brought another sudden rush of emotion, forcing her to stop for a moment to compose herself.

Swallowing hard, she looked over at the other woman to see if she had noticed anything amiss. But she appeared to be more interested in adjusting her cushions to make her armchair more comfortable.

'Thank you again, Mistress Jardine, and I might need to ask your advice. I've no experience of running a house, never mind an estate. I'll have to deal with all of that next week. But for the moment, I'm still living from day to day.'

The other woman leaned forward in her chair, waving her hand as if it all meant nothing. 'Kate, any help you need you can have. But you'll not have any problems, I'm sure of that. Running a house, or an estate, even the country, is not a difficult matter. What you have to do is make sure you have the right people, tell them what it is you want them to do, and then let them get on with it. But never, never accept at any time anything less than what you've told them to do. That's the road to disaster.'

Despite the enormity of the task, Kate smiled at the thought. In her mind's eye, she could see Mistress

Jardine discussing matters with the Arrowsmiths, and telling them in precise terms what she wanted them to do. The problem was she could not see herself doing that.

But the woman had already switched to another topic. 'I've noticed, Kate, and it's good to see, that you're not completely in the depths of despair. I can see you smiling about something – that's an unexpected relief.'

Squinting over the edge of her glass, Kate swirled the contents around and inhaled the heady aroma. 'Mistress, don't think I've not been close to despair a few times, where I've wanted nothing but to forget all about the house and the estate. But for some reason I can't do that. And then there's the memory and the thought of Edward, God rest him. I expected that my every waking moment would be consumed by thinking about him, but that's not really happened either. Somehow or other I've been able to function in a reasonably normal way, although for the last few weeks normal has meant living a very frugal life.'

With a flourish, Mistress Jardine raised her glass. 'The last time you were here, Kate, we had a toast to us. I don't think that today is a day for many toasts, but it will come again, you mark my words. Today we should drink to just one thought. Survival, that's the thought. You will survive this, just keep remembering that.' Clenching her fist, the older woman drained her glass in one gulp.

Taking a more tentative sip, Kate found herself drawing strength from the woman's words. The Mistress was right. She was going to get through this. Taking a larger gulp of the brandy, she convinced herself she could do it. She would take them all on, and she would survive. Impulsively, she stood up, raised her glass, and threw the rest of the spirit down her throat.

After that, the evening disappeared into a haze of drinking, talking, crying and laughing. Finally, she managed to let herself go, and the two women talked into the night about her doubts and fears, and her regrets and memories.

When she woke up bleary-eyed the next morning, she had a splitting headache, but the world did not seem quite as bad as it had previously. It was the first of January, seventeen hundred and eighty one. A new year and time for new resolutions.

Chapter 15

———◆———

Kate poured herself another cup of tea before walking over to the window and looking outside. It was almost midsummer's day and the garden was a blaze of colour. Mr Jones, the old Welshman, was doing a grand job with the flower beds. 'Dai the trowel', his lads might call him, but he certainly knew what he was doing. And he knew what the Mistress wanted. After all, they had discussed it often enough.

In the next room, she could hear Mrs Arrowsmith giving one of the housemaids detailed instructions about what she wanted done during the day. Outside, Roberts was getting the horse and trap ready, and the sound of the metal-shod hooves on the cobbles rang throughout the courtyard.

It was going to be a busy day at Tilbrook Hall. She had taken a leaf out of Mistress Delamere's book and decided to hold a garden party on the coming Saturday, and everybody who was anybody was invited. It would be the first social event at the Hall since the Master had died, and every person on the staff was working overtime to make it a success.

As she kept half an eye on the activities going on around her, Kate found herself thinking over the last six months. To the eye of a stranger, the estate would probably appear to be running like clockwork, but those first few days back in the depths of winter had been a terrible experience.

Initially, Mr Arrowsmith had been reluctant to discuss anything at all about managing the estate, but Kate had been so invigorated after spending a few days with the Jardines that she had been in no mood whatsoever to enter into any hesitant exchange of views. And she had made that clear right from the first minute of their first meeting. She was the Mistress and he was going to be reporting to her. And now, thank God, they seemed to have developed a much better working relationship.

Mrs Arrowsmith had been less of a problem, since Kate had simply expressed her wishes in the same way she had seen Mistress Delamere do so often, and they had worked well together almost from the first day. Without doubt that had helped her husband to come round to accepting the new Mistress.

What she had not considered but was now learning fast was the extent to which the management of the estate revolved around the seasons. The degree of forward planning that was necessary had quite staggered her at first, especially as she had arrived in January still living merely from day to day. However, as every week went past she was able to take a wider view of her surroundings, until she had become involved in all of the activities at the Hall and on the estate.

The other potential nightmare during the first few weeks could have been the dealings with the army and the lawyers. However, Mister Jardine and Henry Browne had been unstinting with their help and support, ensuring that her best interests were being protected at all times. And with Lord Cornwallis taking a close interest in her welfare, Kate was not short of powerful sponsors.

For sure, there had been some depressing moments, especially her twenty-first birthday, and the anniversary of her marriage in April. Her celebrations had gone no further than drinking herself half-stupid on brandy and reading all of Edward's old letters, getting herself thoroughly miserable. But things had improved remarkably since then. Perhaps it was the changing seasons, but every day she was more confident about facing the world. Now she was having the library extended, and Jones had created a completely new vegetable garden following closely to her instructions. After all those years spent working with her mother back in the village, that was something she did know about.

From time to time her thoughts turned to her mother. Since taking up residence at the Hall, she had received three long letters from Mister Hutchinson. These had been filled with news about events in Ireland and in Wicklow, but they also gave some inkling of her mother's thoughts. Faithfully, she had replied to every one, letting Mr Hutchinson know all the details of her life in England, in the hope that this might be communicated to her mother.

It was really such a senseless way for adults to behave.

But she was learning quickly that people were like that. More than likely her father's influence was preventing her mother from being able to speak more directly, although that was something Kate still failed to understand. How could her father have turned against her so forcefully, just because of her relationship with Edward? He had never met the man, yet he had taken so blindly against him. And all in the name of nationalism or patriotism or some other ill-thought collection of prejudices. How could her father have deserted her for that?

Shrugging her shoulders, she finished her tea. There was so much to be done, and no good would come from standing around depressing herself by thinking about the past. For some stupid reason she had decided to host this garden party, and the big event was only a few days away. With so many details still to attend to, it was all she could do to stop herself panicking – but at least it was a different type of panic now. Everybody knew what they had to do, and as long as they followed their instructions everything would be fine. Was that not what she had been told on New Year's eve?

How on earth had Mistress Delamere coped with this every year and still managed to look cool, calm and composed? Shaking her head in unspoken admiration, she crossed her fingers and offered up a silent prayer.

For once her prayers did not go unanswered. The big day dawned, warm and sunny. Kate and Mrs Arrowsmith had spent all week closeted together, planning the arrangements down to the minutest detail. She had observed Mistress Delamere taking this approach and it had always worked successfully. So why change now?

By nine in the morning, Mrs Arrowsmith's entire team of cooks, bottlewashers, housemaids, waitresses, marquee-erectors, punch-makers, tea-boys and meeters and greeters had been assembled. Kate, however, had decided that she herself had to stand back from the organisation. After all, she was Lady Tilbrook, Mistress of the Estate, and she could not be dashing around filling up punch bowls. Mrs Arrowsmith knew what to do, and she had to be given the opportunity to manage the day.

As things turned out, the meticulously-planned approach worked out wonderfully, and the event went off with scarcely a hitch. The vicar came and opened up proceedings with a mercifully short prayer, before downing a tankard of ale to start things off. Many of the neighbouring landowners came along, most of whom Kate barely knew, but it gave her a wonderful opportunity to find out who they all were. The estate workers and the tenant farmers came with their families, which again was a chance for her to meet people. Henry Browne arrived with his beautiful companion, the Lady Sarah Ffoulkes–Pollock, and announced that they were engaged to be married. Mister Grattan, of all people, turned up with his new fiancée, and declared himself to be most enamoured of the local society. And finally, Mister and Mistress Jardine arrived in a carriage fit to outshine everyone else, with a driver, a bagman, and various other attendants, all armed to the teeth. It would take a very brave and determined highwayman to go up against the Jardines.

All day long Kate mingled with the crowds, escorted everywhere by the ubiquitous Mr Arrowsmith, who seemed to know everyone. He also appeared to be relishing his role alongside the young Mistress. But this was not an unsatisfactory arrangement, as it helped her with the introductions and it also meant she could keep an eye on him as well.

The same rules applied as in Enniskerry. Seven in the evening was the finishing hour, and Sunday would be the cleaning up day. By seven, after everything had gone off well, Kate was even able to amuse herself by trying to assess who drank the most at these events, the English or the Irish.

After they had managed to clear everyone out of the grounds, she sat down finally on the terrace with the Jardines. Exhaustion was setting in, but also a great sense of satisfaction at the success of her first social event. It was particularly gratifying to know that Mrs Arrowsmith had managed everything so effectively, at the same time clearly enjoying the experience.

Mistress Jardine had been right. She had received so many informal invitations throughout the course of the day that her current non-existent social calendar would be full for months to come. And her advice about mourning for Edward had been absolutely correct as well.

'Some people will expect you to spend a year of your life moping around, dressed in black,' she had declared. 'You have to decide for yourself, Kate. But as for me, I would want to get involved in as much as I could. A month's public mourning, perhaps, and after that I would keep it to myself. Thank God she had followed that advice, Kate mused to herself. Otherwise she would still be wearing widow's weeds, with the estate gone to rack and ruin.

Stretching out comfortably, they relaxed over their brandies and reflected on the day's events. Suddenly Mister Jardine produced a sheaf of letters from a pocket inside his coat.

'Kate, I'm sorry, I forgot about these in all the excitement. These came to St Thomas' Street for you, and we collected them on our way out here.'

She glanced at the writing on the packets. One was from Mistress Delamere whose writing she could recognise anywhere, and one looked as if it was from Mister Hutchinson. The others were covered in more childlike writing and could have come from anybody.

By now she was almost yawning. 'Thank you for these, Mister Jardine. But I feel more like putting my feet up and relaxing. I think I'll read them tomorrow.'

'Ah, but I think one is from my cousin in Enniskerry,' Mistress Jardine declared. 'Just open that one and tell us what news she has of Wicklow.'

With a sigh, she slit open the envelope and started reading. Within seconds she was jolted upright in her chair.

'What is it, what's wrong?' the Mistress asked anxiously.

Kate looked up, her face drawn with anguish. 'It's my mother, she's been taken ill, and Mistress Delamere is very concerned about her.'

Feverishly, she opened the letter from Mister Hutchinson. It was the same message. Her mother was desperately ill with some sort of sickness and no one knew what to do. Another letter was from Declan, saying the same thing.

Holding her hands to her face, she looked across at the Jardines. 'What am I going to do now?' she whispered.

Mister Jardine spread his hands helplessly. 'Have you any choice? Don't you have to go there?'

For a moment or two, she paced backwards and forwards across the terrace. 'But my mother hasn't spoken to me since I told her about Edward. If I go there, will it help? Or will it make her more tense and cause the illness to get worse? And what about my father, will he let me see her? Another argument isn't going to help, is it?'

While she tried to get her mind to think straight, the Mistress reached out her hand. 'No one can know the answers to these questions. But you haven't asked the most important one. Now that you know your mother is dangerously ill, will you be able to live with yourself if you don't at least try and see her?'

Kate looked up. 'I know what I want to do, but I'm fearful of making a decision on the spur of the moment, especially after a day like today. I need to go to bed and sleep on it.'

Even after a night's fitful rest, however, she was still uncertain what to do next. Certainly, she could leave the estate for a few weeks. Mr Arrowsmith would probably be delighted to be in control again for a while. But she was beginning to have a home of sorts now in Essex, and the truth was she did not have a home in Ireland. Yes, she would be able to stay with Mistress Delamere, but that was not home.

But her poor mother, whom she used to spend so much time with in the garden, who used to go walking with her on the hills above the village, who used to come up to the school to make sure that Mister Hutchinson was not giving her too easy a time, and who used to sit beside the turf fire and tell her a different story every night. Could she stay in England knowing her mother was ill? Even if they had not spoken for such a long time? But if she did go back, what sort of reception would she get? Would it be simply another opportunity to open up old wounds, to vilify her as they had done previously? Surely, she had to go back. The thought of her mother being ill or even dying while she lorded it up on the estate in Essex was too much to take – she had to see her.

Ten days later she was in Dublin, getting off the ship, and looking around for O'Brien to pick her up. She could remember all too clearly arriving there before, overjoyed to be back, dashing across the quay, dodging the horses and the queues of people, and jumping up onto the trap beside O'Brien almost before he knew she was there. But not today. Not with the leaden weight of apprehension she could feel like a burden across her shoulders. Screwing her face up against the rain, she caught a glimpse of the familiar horse and trap, but the quay was too busy for him to get through. Calling to a nearby porter, she engaged him to carry her bags. As she trudged along the quay, she tried to judge the expression on O'Brien's face. Grim, downcast, unwilling to catch her eye. The closer she came, the heavier her footsteps became. It was obvious what he was going to say, and she was not looking forward to hearing his voice.

Eventually, he nodded to her, jumping down to pick up her bag and help her into the trap.

'Hello, Mistress Tilbrook,' he said, unsmiling. 'It's good to see you here in Ireland, but not so good at this unhappy time.'

Taking a firm grip on the handrail, Kate sat down without a fuss. Looking straight ahead, she spoke woodenly. 'Mister O'Brien, please tell me what the news is concerning my mother.'

Unable to look at her directly, the man took a moment or two to answer. 'Mistress Tilbrook, I'm sorry to say that your mother died a few days ago.' Turning slowly, he looked at her with tears in his eyes. 'It was a terrible shock. She was always so strong and healthy, but then she got sick with a fever and no one could do anything for her.'

Rigid with shock, Kate clung to the handrail. 'What about the funeral?' she whispered.

'They held it yesterday, Mistress Tilbrook. There was a big turnout of people from all over the area.'

So she was too late, even for the burial. For a moment, she felt like getting down and throwing herself under the wheels of the nearest carriage. That would be such a blessed relief from this continuous agony. And if only she could cry or weep or even rage against the providence that was responsible for all this suffering, but all she could feel was a detached numbness, little different from the sensation she had experienced on opening the letter from Lord Cornwallis.

O'Brien glanced sideways at her. 'Are you able to travel, Mistress Tilbrook?'

'Yes, I'll be fine, O'Brien. Just take me to Enniskerry, please.' Closing her eyes, she forced every single thought out of her head until her mind was a complete blank. Somehow, she had to get to Enniskerry without breaking down. Once she was there she could lock herself away in a bedroom, and let her feelings come out in solitary peace.

But seeing Mistress Delamere again was another blessing. Although there were few words that could be said, she drew comfort from being close to her familiar presence, which was more than she could have got from locking herself away.

Her first inclination was to do something. But what? Her mother had died almost a week earlier and the funeral was already over. People had gone back about their business. Who could she go and see? After much anguished soul-searching, she decided to walk over to the cemetery on the day after her arrival, to see the grave and to pay her respects to her mother's memory. It was a bright summer day, with the trees along the sides of the river casting huge shadows across the familiar road down to the village, a road haunted by still recent memories. She especially remembered those days when she had walked up to the house at Enniskerry, and the winter's eve when Edward had returned unexpectedly from England and surprised her.

Barely able to see where she was going, scarcely able to comprehend the events that had occurred, she trudged along the road. All she could think of was that there had to be some reason why this was happening. What had she done to deserve this?

Not far in front, through heavy eyes, she could distinguish the shape of the village, with the church over on the right behind Cormack's, and her old house on the hill up on the left. Her father was probably there now, by himself perhaps, or maybe with her brother Eamonn. For a moment, she thought of climbing up to see if she could find him, but almost immediately she was assailed by doubts. The last thing she wanted was any more bitterness. It would take all her courage to talk to her father, and she was not sure she was ready yet.

Instead, she turned in the other direction towards the church, and with some hesitation pushed open the iron gates into the graveyard. Slowly, step by step, she made her way past the rows of headstones, many so worn away that the original inscriptions were impossible to read. Generations of Brennans were buried in this place. Her grandparents' graves were there, and their parents before them. Further on she walked until she was some distance from the church, close to the stone dyke that separated the cemetery from the surrounding fields. It was easy to find the recent burials. The new headstones, the flowers and the freshly turned earth were all testimony to the latest bereavements.

On one side, she could see an old man standing by himself, leaning on a shovel. She had to peer closely at him before she remembered his name. It was one of the gravediggers, old Mr Tooley. As she came closer, he raised his hand to his cap and nodded his head.

'Miss Brennan, I'm sorry you have to be coming here.'

'I am too, Mr Tooley,' she replied quietly. 'Could you tell me where she is, please?'

The man picked up his shovel and walked over to the line of fresh earth mounds.

'Here you are, Miss Brennan, this is the one you're looking for. I expect you want to be alone, so I'll leave you in peace. If you want anything, just call me.'

Barely able to bring herself to open her eyes, she stood quietly beside the grave. Buried beneath this soil was a once beautiful, vibrant woman, who had spent so much of her life encouraging her only daughter to better herself. For a moment, Kate stared at her useless bunch of flowers, already wilting in the sunshine, before tossing them onto the pile in front of the headstone. Sobbing bitterly, she slumped to her knees on the wet grass. She could hear herself mumbling a prayer, but she was doing it automatically, the thoughts in her head more and more confused. Why had it come to this? What could possibly have been so wicked about what she had done that had made her mother turn against her? Why had they lost so much precious time together?

Bleakly, she gazed at the headstone. 'Anne Siobhan Brennan', she read, 'May she rest in peace.' All of a sudden, Kate realised that somewhere in America, at this moment her husband was lying, buried perhaps but with nothing to mark his going, and all because of some foolish war. How could people let that happen? As the rage started to build up inside her, she could feel her hands clenching into fists, while the desire to smash her forehead against the ground in frustration was almost overwhelming. All of a sudden, she sensed a presence behind her. Turning around, she saw the priest watching her, a baleful look in his eye.

'So you've returned, Kathleen Brennan,' his voice thundered. 'I thought I told you the last time you were here never to come back, that you were not welcome.'

Trembling with fright, she shrank back before his fearsome gaze. 'But Father, my mother has just died, God rest her, and I've come to pay my last respects. Surely you will grant me that.'

'You gave up all your rights when you consorted with

the English devils. You renounced your faith when you were married in an English church. And you've been living in sin ever since then, and I don't know how long before.'

As she listened to the priest ranting and raving, her respect and her patience began ebbing away. When he had started shouting, she had been terrified by his manner. But now that she could understand what he was saying, the nonsense he was mouthing, the bile began to rise in her throat as an incredible strength surged through her body. Scrambling to her feet, she stepped forward and brandished her fist in his face.

'God forgive me,' she screamed, 'I never thought I would see the day when I would threaten a man of the church with violence.'

She could hardly stop herself shaking with rage. 'You may be a man of the church but you are not a man of God. How can you be so bereft of compassion or common human decency that you would come between a daughter and the grave of her dead mother? Do you not have an ounce of thought in your head except to spout the same useless nonentities which do nothing but hold our people in fear?'

Bending down, she snatched up a rock which had been uncovered by the gravediggers, while the priest jumped back in alarm. But she was not finished with him yet, except that her anger and grief were combining to prevent her from being able to form any coherent words.

Holding the rock aloft, she advanced towards the priest, sobbing and shrieking at the same time. 'Get out of my sight and leave me in peace with my grief, or else I'll not be responsible for my actions.'

Unused to such aggression, the man put his hands up and backed off. 'Kathleen Brennan,' he shouted, 'you are no more than an agent of the devil.' Without another word, he ran off towards the church.

Her emotions spent, she tried to turn back to her memories of her mother. Instead she stumbled, falling forward across the newly dug earth, jarring her knees and her elbows. She barely noticed the pain. She hardly noticed anything, not even the rain which had started falling gently, mingling with her tears turning the earth that covered the grave beside her into dark brown mud.

With almost no recollection of time passing, she felt a hand upon her shoulder. Startled by the touch, and thinking it might be the priest coming back to abuse her again, she turned around, her features contorted by grief and fury. But it was only Mr Tooley. Seeing the expression on her face, he jumped back abruptly, taking off his cap and twisting it nervously between his fingers. He had obviously heard what she had said to the priest, and he was terrified of offending her as well.

'Begging your pardon, Miss Brennan. But the rain's getting heavy and you've no cloak on your back. I know it's difficult, but you'd better be careful with the wet ground and the damp getting through your clothes.'

Kate looked up at the leaden grey skies and the rain that was sheeting down. Putting her hands up to her hair, she realised that the man was right. She was soaking wet. 'Thank you, Mr Tooley, I had forgotten myself there for a moment. I think I'll go across to the village and see if my father is there.'

The gravedigger twisted his cap even more furiously in his hands. 'Miss Brennan, can I suggest that this is not the best time to do that? Your father is still in shock from the death of your mother, and you've had a very difficult day already. It might be better if you go and rest before coming back to see him tomorrow.'

She tried in vain to wring the water out of her hair with her hands. 'Maybe you're right, Mr Tooley. I don't know anymore.'

Kate took one last look at the grave and the headstone. Suddenly, a significance in the old man's words sank home that she had not noticed when he was speaking.

'Mr Tooley, has the priest gone to see my father? If you know he has, you must tell me.'

The man nodded dumbly. God, the priest would be up there now, planting thoughts in her father's head. By now, the two of them would probably be agreeing that she was some fiend come from hell to haunt them. No, today was not the day to try and see her father. Better to wait as the old man had said, until tempers and emotions had cooled down.

'Thank you, Mr Tooley,' she sighed heavily. 'I'll go back to Enniskerry and come here another day.'

And then another thought struck her. 'Do you know my brother, Declan Brennan? Is he here now, can you tell me?'

The man shook his head before replying. 'Yes, I know Declan well enough. I heard about you going to find him in London when he was dying over there, and you brought him home safe and sound.'

'Never mind all that,' she gave a small smile, but inside she could feel herself getting impatient. 'Did you see him at the funeral? Is he in the village now?'

'Yes, he was here,' the gravedigger replied cautiously.

'But I think he's gone back to Arklow. They tell me he has a house down there now.'

For a moment, she digested this before thanking the old man again and making her way out of the cemetery. In some ways it was a relief to be out of the place, and back on the road to the more welcoming prospect of Mistress Delamere's house.

By the time she reached Enniskerry, Kate had made up her mind that she would go down to Arklow to find Declan first, and then she would attempt to see her father. Who could tell what sort of welcome she would get. Besides the encounter with the priest had left her drained emotionally, and she did not relish going through something similar with her father.

Rather than take the mail coach and be cooped up with other people, she decided this time she would hire her own carriage to take her to Arklow. But Mistress Delamere would not hear of any such thing and insisted she went with O'Brien in the horse and trap. It was a good three-hour journey by coach, but O'Brien knew a quicker route which took almost an hour less. The rain had stopped the previous evening, and it was another fine sunny day as they set off. A lovely day for a trip to the seaside, in fact, if only she had been in a better frame of mind. Still, Mr O'Brien was good company for her on the journey.

'Do you remember the day we set off to Dublin, Miss Brennan? Your first trip there, as I recall.'

'Mr O'Brien, will I ever forget it?' she sighed 'And now I'm back and forward between England and Ireland every other week it seems.'

'Aye, a lot of water has passed under the bridge since then,' the man agreed.

Shifting uncomfortably on her seat, she looked off into the distance. 'If only I could get some good news for a change. Everything seems to be a desperate struggle all the time.'

The old man half turned, studying her expression. 'Perhaps it's just as well that we can't see into the future and what's going to happen. But maybe you'll get more of a welcome from Declan this time than you did when you went to visit him in London. I hear he's doing very well for himself and he's got you to thank for keeping him alive to see it.'

'I'm not looking for any thanks,' she exclaimed indignantly. 'But what is it you've heard? I've not seen my brother for almost a year.'

O'Brien cleared his throat and thought for a moment. 'Well now, he has his own house, so I hear, and he's always going up and down to Dublin. They say he has many contacts in France and with the rebels in America. And you know what the people are like in Arklow with their long memories; they've still not forgotten the Earl of Essex and his soldiers when they came here over two hundred years ago and slaughtered half the population. So they'll support anything that will antagonise the English.'

In a fit of annoyance, she thumped her fist against the wooden handrail. 'Is there anybody in this country who can think of something other than fighting and killing? Or is that always going to be what the rest of us will have to live with?'

'I expect, Miss Brennan, that if nobody ever listens to

the opinions of the people, then their only recourse is to violence, even if it's only to vent their frustration. Not everyone has had the benefit of an education or the good fortune to have Mr Hutchinson as a teacher.'

'Sometimes I wonder about that,' she replied thoughtfully. 'Would I be in the position I'm in today, would my mother still be alive, would Edward Tilbrook still be alive, if I hadn't gone to the hedge school.'

The man beside her answered immediately. 'You can't think like that, Miss Brennan. Then you could say that your brother might be dead, Patrick Nolan would not be where he is today, and the sanatorium in London might have had to close leaving hundreds of people with nowhere to turn to. Who knows? That's why I say it's better not to be able to see into the future.'

Raising his arm, he pointed off to one side. 'Look, Miss Brennan, here we are in Arklow. Your brother's house is that one over there on the right. I wish you good fortune in your journey, and I hope he can help you cope with losing your mother.'

The house was an old stone cottage similar to the one Kate had lived in up to the time she had gone to work for Mistress Delamere. Smoke curled lazily from the chimney, so clearly someone was at home. Picking her way around to the back, she lifted her hand to knock on the door when a girl appeared. For a moment, Kate looked at her in amazement. They could almost have been sisters, except her hair was black and she had blue eyes. She had obviously been cooking or making bread, her face flushed and her hands covered in flour.

Before she could introduce herself, the girl began speaking. 'There's only one person you could be. Declan has told me so much about you, and described you in great detail. You must be Lady Tilbrook, yes?'

Kate had to laugh. 'I'm astonished that my brother would be talking about me. I hope it's all been flattering. But yes, I'm his sister, although I'd rather you call me Kate. And can I ask your name?'

The girl wiped her hands on her apron. 'Yes, I'm Roisin O'Byrne, from up Roundwood way. That's where I met your brother Declan. But I expect it's him you've come to see. He's not here at the moment although I'm expecting him back later today. And I'm sorry to hear about you losing your mother – Declan was quite distraught about it. But what am I doing here standing on the doorstep? Come in and have some tea.'

In one glance, Kate took in the low roof, the smoky atmosphere, the heat from the fire, and the earthen floor. Once upon a time she would have thought nothing of going into such a cottage. But she had become too accustomed to living in more comfortable surroundings.

'Thanks for the invitation, Roisin,' she replied quickly, 'but I'll leave it till another day. I feel a little tired after my journey and I think I'll walk down to the Arklow Arms. I'm planning to stay there for the next few days and I'd like to drop off my bag and rest for a few hours. When Declan comes back, please tell him where I am. Perhaps I'll see you this evening.'

Some time later, the innkeeper's wife knocked on her door to tell her that Declan was waiting to see her. He was easy to find, being at the centre of a group of people in the bar with Roisin beside him. Although he was clearly telling them something, he stopped talking as soon as he saw Kate approaching.

'My beautiful little sister, hello,' he exclaimed, as she reached the table. Standing up, he embraced her for a moment, kissing her cheek while the others looked on.

'Listen, people, this is my sister Kate over from England,' he announced as he turned and looked at her. 'I'll always be indebted to her for coming over to London and helping me when I was in trouble. But she's a woman who knows her own mind, now, so be careful what you say to her!'

This for some reason made them all laugh. As they sat down with Roisin, slightly apart from the others, Kate caught hold of his arm. 'What did you mean by that comment, Declan Brennan? Were you warning them not to talk to me about the business you're into?'

'Not at all, Kate, it was just my little joke. Anyway it's good to see you, at this terrible time. It's so strange – I can scarcely believe it. She was always there, yet now she's gone. If only I'd gone to see her more often. What about yourself, how have you been taking it?'

Unable to catch his eye, Kate looked down at the table. 'I feel so desperately awful all the time and there seems to be no relief from it. Every night I feel like crying, but the tears won't come. It was the same when I got the news about Edward, God rest him. I don't know what's wrong with me.'

'I can understand a little,' her brother replied, putting his hand out to her. 'Events have taken such a desperate turn over the past few years that I'm only glad I've had so much to keep my mind occupied. I was also lucky to have Roisin here to comfort me when I felt really bad.'

Taking the other girl's hand, he pulled her towards him. 'You met my Roisin earlier today, didn't you? You and she have a connection which you might not know. Mister Hutchinson is her uncle.'

Her interest caught by the change of subject, Kate looked quizzically at the girl sitting opposite.

'He's not really my uncle,' Roisin explained. 'He was married to my father's sister before she died, but I know him quite well.'

As the girl was speaking, the noise levels in the bar had increased substantially. Kate looked around at the other people in the alehouse to see what was happening. They were a rough-looking crew, right enough. Was this the company that Declan was now keeping? She tried to imagine being left alone in the bar with this crowd – it did not bear thinking about.

As she watched, some other men began coming and going, dressed as if they might have arrived in off a ship.

'Kate, I'm going to leave you now. I have to go up to Dublin tonight to deliver some goods. But I'll be back tomorrow afternoon.'

Declan must have been reading her mind, or else the expression on her face was obvious. 'Please don't even think of asking me what they are,' he laughed. 'But you should wait here, because there's someone coming who'd like to meet you. And Roisin will keep you company, I'm sure, for the next hour or so.'

Who was he talking about: wanting to meet her? It could be only one person – James Lavelle. Despite her low spirits, she felt the familiar tremor of excitement at the thought of his name. Was he coming here? Was that why all these people were milling about? Perhaps he had just come from France and that was why Declan had to go to Dublin.

Suddenly, she realised that the other girl was watching her. 'I'm sorry, Roisin, I was away in another world there for a moment.' For the umpteenth time that day, she sighed heavily. 'I fear I'll not be much company for you. My spirits are at such a low ebb, and I can't see any signs of things improving. Perhaps a few brandies will help.' Signalling with her hand, she called over the girl at the bar to bring them some drinks.

Roisin smiled in reply. 'That used to be my work. I was serving in the Roundwood Inn when I met your brother Declan, and I followed him here.'

Picking up her glass of brandy, Kate leaned back in her chair. 'Is this how everybody meets these days? A friend of Declan's who comes from Bray, Patrick Nolan, he met his wife when she was serving in an alehouse in London.' She sipped at the fiery spirit, feeling the warmth in her stomach. 'But you say you followed him here. That's an unusual word to use, don't you think?'

Leaning over the table, the other girl kept her voice low. 'Perhaps you don't realise it, Kate, but Declan has a grand story to tell. And there's a few people around here prepared to listen to him and, aye, follow him, if that's what he wants them to do.'

Intrigued by Roisin's words, and taken aback slightly by the intensity in her voice, Kate sat up and folded her arms. 'And what's the story he's telling now?'

Over the top of her glass, she could see the girl collecting her thoughts. 'Only that the day is coming when we will be free of the English,' she replied confidently, 'and that we have to be ready to take our chances. Look at the Americans now. Not long ago they were the King's enemies, but soon they'll be free men.

413

Yet here we are, subjects of the Crown, and we're still to be kept as slaves of the penal laws?'

As she gripped the edge of the table, her eyes flashed with passion. 'Do you know, Kate, that the foundation of the English constitution, the pillar of their empire, for God's sake, is freedom for every man, and liberty to express his sentiments as to how he feels. Every man except the Irish! I'm telling you, Kate, if we all speak together, we will have a more powerful voice. And now that Lord Charlemont is allowing the Catholics to join the Volunteers, all the people here will be taking up arms and expecting changes to come about, sooner rather than later.'

She stopped abruptly, gasping for breath, giving Kate the opportunity to interrupt.

'I can see that you feel strongly about this,' she replied quietly, but her mind was racing. Was it Declan who had put these thoughts into her head? How many other people had he spoken to, and how many other people had he convinced? And what was he trying to do? Was he up to this on his own or with others? That James Tandy, for one, perhaps. He had said in London that they would have to use force, and it seemed now as if other people were of the same mind.

If only she was not so exhausted from her depression over Edward and the mother. Someone had to challenge what Declan was saying, otherwise the country was on the road to violence and bloodshed. All her talks with Mister Grattan and his friends, all those fine speeches in Parliament, they would be worth nothing if they did not achieve something that these people would recognise.

Why did all this have to be coming up now, on top of

everything else that had happened? Thank God, she could feel the brandy at work, warming her insides and dulling the edges of her grief. Maybe that was the answer. It had worked well enough on New Year's Eve. Perhaps it was Mistress Jardine she should be with, instead of listening to Roisin O'Byrne on her high horse about Irish politics.

As she mulled over the girl's outburst, she saw her look up over her shoulder and smile at someone behind her. Twisting round in her seat to see who it could be, she was immediately transported back to her brother's bedside in London and her first sight of James Lavelle. He looked little different two years later; if anything even better. Still the same long flowing hair, the jacket as beautifully cut as ever, and the off-white, immaculately pressed breeches.

With a gasp of excitement, she jumped to her feet, the brandy, the politics and the others in the alehouse all forgotten. But her voice deserted her. 'James,' she croaked, unable to manage another word.

At once he bowed, his same theatrical gesture. 'Lady Tilbrook. How delightful it is to make your acquaintance once again.'

Leaning forward, he took her hand and kissed it gently, exactly as he had done in London. 'And Roisin as well. I'm twice blessed with beautiful women this evening.' Taking the other girl's hand, he kissed it in the same fashion.

For the next hour or so, he kept them amused with hair-raising stories about his journeys to and from Ireland and his close calls with the English man o' war patrolling the sea routes to France. For the first time in weeks, Kate could feel her mood of depression lifting. Whether it was from listening to James or the effects of the brandy, or a combination of both, who could tell?

Scarcely had she begun to feel more responsive, however, when some people that Roisin knew came in to the bar. Making her apologies, she went over to speak to them, leaving James and Kate alone together.

'So, Mademoiselle Brennan,' he leaned forwards across the table, lowering his voice. 'The last time I saw you, if you remember, was in the garden at your Mistress Jardine's house.'

With a shiver, she recollected the scene. 'I remember it well enough, James. But that was some time ago. And so many things have happened since then.'

'Declan has told me all about the Brennan family circumstances. All I can say is that you appear to be bearing up remarkably well. I think there might be a certain fragility in you that I don't recall seeing before, but that simply adds another dimension to your beauty.'

As she listened to him speaking, inevitably her mind went back to those stolen moments in the summer house. Shaking her head, she forced herself to concentrate on what he was saying. But looking across the table at his fine features and his flashing smile, she could sense again that extraordinary madness in her head, the dizzy sensations of those distant days when he had met her outside the sanatorium in London. The feeling was so intense that for a moment she thought she was going to faint right at his feet. Pushing back her chair, she stood up a little unsteadily. She had to get out of the unbearable atmosphere and clear her head.

'James, I'm sorry.' Her voice was shaking slightly. 'I

have to go outside into the fresh air for a moment. It's too hot and smoky in here for me.'

Abruptly, she turned around, almost knocking over the glasses on the table in her rush to leave. Outside, it was such a relief to be in the cool night air. As she looked over the sea, shimmering in the moonlight, she breathed in deeply, suddenly aware that Lavelle had come out behind her.

'Are you feeling any better now, Kate?' he enquired anxiously.

Slowly, she turned and looked at him, standing so close beside her. 'Yes, I'm much better now,' she replied, her voice still trembling. 'The last year has been such an emotional time for me, with my husband and then my mother dying, and I'm not always in control of my feelings.'

Closing her eyes, she pressed her hands to her temples. 'I can remember my mother telling me over and over all the reasons for not going to England. Most of the possibilities she described had not even occurred to me. But never in my wildest dreams did I imagine that events would turn out as they have.'

She could feel the world pressing in on her again, and the panic building up in her chest. Glancing sideways, she saw him watching her, his expression turning to one of concern.

'I'm sorry to sound so miserable, James, but the last few weeks have been especially dreadful. I was in England when I received the news about my mother being ill. And it came at a time when I had just begun to readjust to living some sort of normal life after the death of my husband.'

At last, she began to feel the tears coming, although it was difficult to tell whether it was the thought of her mother or from feeling sorry for herself.

'And then I had a terrible journey coming over here, and I never got to see her before she died, and I was too late for the funeral, and then I had a horrible experience with the priest down at the cemetery.'

By this time, she could hardly stop herself sobbing and snivelling. 'Oh James, it was all just so awful,' she wailed, pulling out a scrap of cotton from the pocket of her dress to blow her nose.

As he reached out his hand towards her, without thinking she fell into his embrace. 'Kate, Kate,' he murmured against her hair. 'My little Irish sweetheart. It does indeed sound as if you've had a terrible time.'

Hesitating only slightly, Kate pressed her face against his chest. It felt so good to have his arms around her, so strong, so comforting.

'Oh James, just hold me,' she whispered. 'I've needed someone to do this, to hold me, to protect me.'

For a few minutes they stood on the side of the hill overlooking the sea, while he held her firmly in the circle of his arms. Gradually, she felt the panic recede, as he smoothed her hair and whispered against her ear and her neck.

All of a sudden, she sensed him moving one hand from her back and gently stroking her forehead. Slowly, she turned her head and looked up at him, her chin resting lightly against his chest. They were so close that she could feel the smoothness of his skin under his shirt, and the beat of his heart against her cheek.

It had been so long since a man had held her like this.

It had been so long since she had wanted a man to hold her like this. Her mind flashed back to the moment in the summer house when James had unbuttoned the top of her dress. That night she had wanted him so badly, and although she had barely been aware of what she had been doing, she had asked him to make love to her. She could feel herself wanting him again. What was the matter with her? Her husband was not long dead, her mother also, and now she wanted to make love to this man. Inexplicably, she felt herself starting to cry again, great sobs that racked through her body.

His voice was quiet, but she could hear his concern. 'What is it, Kate? For a minute there, I thought you were feeling a little better.'

'I don't know, James,' she sobbed, pushing him away and turning to one side. 'I don't understand my own feelings. I suppose I'm just too emotional. But I'm not crying because I'm unhappy.'

She turned back to face him. 'I think I'm crying now because when you were holding me I felt happier than I have in months.' Wiping her eyes, she tried to laugh through her tears. 'I'm just a strange person, James, that's all, and look at the state of me now, with my eyes all red and my nose dripping. I must look awful.'

James took her hand and kissed it. 'Kate, you look beautiful to me.'

Pulling her hand away, she slipped out of his reach. 'James Lavelle, you were a flatterer when I first met you and you're still the same. In spite of what you say, I'm going back to my room to wash these tears away and make myself look presentable.'

As she walked to the door of her room, she was

conscious of James close behind her. Nervously, she fished in the pocket of her dress for her key, unable to tear her mind away from the moment in Mistress Jardine's garden. All of a sudden, the door swung open and she straightened up, just as he put his hands on her shoulders and kissed the back of her neck. Without a word, she stumbled across the room next to the bed. Again he was behind her, again she could feel his hands unfastening her dress, slipping off her bodice. His lips were hot against her shoulders, his fingers fiendishly teasing as they danced across her stomach and fondled her breasts.

For a moment his hands stopped their caressing. And then Kate realised he was taking his clothes off. Then she could feel him again, hard, pushing against her back. Without realising it, her dress and her pantaloons had slipped to the floor.

'Oh James, please love me now,' she heard herself crying.

He swept her up on to the bed and almost with one continuous movement thrust into her. God, he was so different to Edward. No matter how excited or how aroused she would be, Edward had always found great delight in caressing her until she was unable to take any more. But James was much more abrupt, thrashing away against her hips in a hard and physical way that she had never experienced with Edward. Desperately, she tried to adjust her legs to find a more comfortable position, but this only seemed to spur him on to even greater efforts.

'James, James,' she gasped against his chest. 'Slow down a bit before you do me or yourself an injury.' But he was so engrossed in what he was doing that she could barely stop herself from laughing and giggling at his exertions. And then with a shout and a few strangled whimpers it was all over. As his dead weight pressed her against the bed, she could feel the breath being expelled from her body. 'James, for God's sake,' she whispered fiercely in his ear. 'You're crushing me to death.'

But he didn't take the slightest notice. With a superhuman effort, she managed to lever herself sufficient space to wriggle out from underneath him. Still taken aback, she glared at the naked man lying on his back beside her, already sleeping, and snoring heavily. Good God, was that the way that the French did their lovemaking?

For some minutes she lay on her side, resting her head in her hand, staring at the man beside her, a contented look spread across his features. Fleetingly, her thoughts went back to Edward. He had always gone to sleep as well after they had made love, but not before he had kissed her and told her how much he loved her. And she had always felt so warm and comfortable after they had made love.

Now she could feel nothing – well, that was not quite true. She had satisfied her curiosity, now she knew what making love to James was like. She thought again of that time in Mistress Jardine's garden. If he had made love to her first instead of Edward, she would never have known any different. She could hardly bear thinking about it. For a moment, she stared at the rings on her fingers. On her right hand was the ring that Edward had given her when he had first asked her to marry him, and on the third finger of her left hand, her wedding ring. Some widows wore their wedding ring on another finger, but it had never occurred to her to do that. Why was she thinking like this? It did not feel like guilt. But did it mean that she was never going to be able to make love to another man without thinking about Edward?

Briefly, she glanced at the man sleeping peacefully beside her. How wonderful it must be to lie there, happy and contented, without a care in the world. On impulse, she leaned over and tickled his chest. His skin was silky smooth and he had barely any hair on the upper part of his body, completely unlike Edward. Very slowly, she slipped her hand down across his belly and fondled him gently, until she felt him becoming aroused. His eyes flickered open, watching her. Sensing he was about to lunge at her again, she bent forward and whispered in his ear.

'Now then James, my little Frog, don't be grabbing at me or pummelling my body. Just lie back on the bed and keep calm. I have a nice little surprise for you.'

Before he could say a word, she rolled over until her legs were astride his hips, and very slowly took him inside her. She could see his eyes opening wide with the sensation, and then closing again as he felt the pleasure of her body.

'James Lavelle,' she spoke softly against his lips, 'you're not going to forget the night you made love to Kathleen Brennan.'

Again and again she took him, using his body, disregarding his pleas to stop. Finally, at long last, her frustrations and rage and depression were confronted and, in a glorious shout of triumph, overwhelmed. Gasping for breath, she fell back on the bed, physically exhausted, her emotions spent. Within minutes, she had fallen into a deeply satisfying slumber.

A few hours later, she was up and about, having taken a bath and changed her clothes. Standing beside the window, she was drinking a cup of tea as Lavelle began to stir.

'Kate, please,' he pleaded with her when the noise of her movements eventually woke him up and he saw her at the other side of the room. 'Come on back to bed for another hour.'

By this time, however, she had other things to do. 'Sorry, James, but I've a busy day today. Roisin and I are going up to Roundwood to meet her family. I won't be coming back to Arklow until tomorrow to see Declan after he returns from Dublin.'

'But Kate, I have to sail to France today. We'll not see each other until God knows when. Come back to bed.'

But she had already decided there would be no more lovemaking. After the initial shock of his advances, she had quite enjoyed herself. And it had helped to get rid of so many of the demons in her head. But it had not been the same as being with Edward. However, having James near, and having him comfort her when she had been so desperately depressed had been a wonderful boost to her spirits. Instead of the usual all-pervading mood of pessimism which had enveloped her for weeks, she felt much brighter and more hopeful about the future. Now she was really looking forward to the day ahead of her. Her night with James might not have turned out quite as she or he had expected, but without doubt she had come out of it with a much more positive frame of mind. And as for him going off to France, that was probably for the best. They were sure to see each other at some time in the future, although the prospect of them making love again was extremely unlikely.

Putting down her cup, she glanced at the man sitting up in the bed. With a flash of her most beautiful smile, she walked over and kissed him on both cheeks. 'Thank you for being there when I needed you, James, I'll never forget you for that. But you've had as much of Kate Brennan as you're going to get. So you might as well dress yourself and get on with your journey to France.'

Without lingering. she picked up her bag. 'I'm off to see Roisin. Have a safe voyage and I'll see you on one of your trips to England. You know the house where I live now. Just take the old Roman road from London to Colchester and turn right at Chelmsford. You can't miss it.'

Longingly, he reached out for her, but all she gave him was a wave of farewell before she closed the door. 'Au revoir, James,' she bade him quietly to herself, skipping along the corridor and out into the street.

Chapter 16

——— ◆ ———

After her night with James Lavelle, Kate found herself staying in Arklow for longer than she had intended, mostly getting to know Roisin O'Byrne. By the end of the week they were firm friends, although they had agreed to differ on certain points, in particular what was best for the Irish.

On a visit to Roundwood, she was surprised to find that Roisin was the eldest of seven sisters. Apparently her mother was desperate to have a son, and was determined to keep trying until she succeeded. At some point, every one of the older girls had been taught by Mister Hutchinson, and it was marvellous fun to exchange stories about the lessons and the tales he had told them all at different times.

On the other hand, most evenings ended in heated discussions at the inn in Arklow. Until this trip, Kate had spent scarcely any time in an alehouse or even a shebeen in Ireland, except waiting for her father outside

Cormack's in Kilcarra and the precious moments with Edward in Laragh and Bray. Being with a large group of Irish people was an unfamiliar experience, especially with Declan and Roisin taking great pleasure in introducing her everywhere as 'Lady Tilbrook, from across the water'.

Although the talk over the drink covered a range of topics, invariably the conversation turned to the revolution that many people were praying for. With the Irish Volunteers now better armed and Catholics being allowed to join for the first time, it was clear that a force had been created that represented the major section of the people affected by the penal laws. The mood of the town was militant in the extreme.

While she tried to say little at these sessions, she was surprised to see that Declan also contributed rarely, leaving most of the talking to the others and encouraging them only when the conversation dried up. At first, this did not seem to fit with Roisin's comments, until she realised he was operating in a similar way to James Tandy back in the Lord Chatham in London. It might be a slow process, but it seemed to be successful in stoking up the fervour of the people.

Sometimes, lying in bed at night thinking over the events of the day, she became more and more suspicious of Declan's motives in bringing her to these sessions. After all, he had no direct access to the people in power in Dublin. But she did. Had he recognised this? Was he trying to use her as a channel to find out what was going on? Or even trying to get some message across to the Dublin power base? And why was she so slow in the uptake? Everyone, even her brother seemed to be two jumps ahead of her in their thinking.

But despite the debate and the soul-searching, it was a delight being back amongst her own. Although they were argumentative at times, and poked fun at her for being an English Lady, they were always friendly and sympathetic. Even so, the time came soon enough when she knew she had to return to Enniskerry. She had to go and see her father, and she had to get back to the estate in England.

On her last day, as the coach pulled up outside the inn, Declan and Roisin came to see her off.

'It's a fine day indeed,' her brother remarked, 'when a daughter of the Brennans has a fancy coach to take her from Arklow to Enniskerry. Once upon a time she would have had to walk.'

Opening the door, he took her hand to help her up onto the step. 'I hear that James Lavelle is completely besotted with you and talks of no one else,' he shouted above the noise of the horses. 'What do you want me to say to him when he comes back here?'

For a moment, Kate smiled to herself. 'I'm sure he has a woman in every town, so it won't take him long to stop thinking about me. If he asks, simply tell him that I'll never forget our time together in Arklow.'

As she was about to close the door, she took one last look at her brother standing arm in arm with Roisin. 'On the other hand,' she smiled sweetly, 'if I happen to bump into Henry Grattan, is there anything you would like me to say to him?'

Declan smiled enigmatically, clearly squeezing Roisin's arm to prevent her saying anything. 'You must say what you think is for the best, my little sister,' was all he replied.

By the time she reached Enniskerry, Kate's head was a jumble of thoughts. Edward, her mother, the estate in England, her father's attitude, and her experience with James Lavelle were all mixed up together. But despite these emotional intrusions, her mood remained positive. She had a job to do, and she owed it to Edward's memory to get back to the estate and get on with it. Nonetheless, she could not tear herself away from the insistent sound of Roisin's voice, the strength and the urgency behind her words, and her plea for freedom and dignity for her people.

At Mistress Delamere's house, the news was all about Grattan. Not only was he exerting more and more power in the Irish Parliament, but he had been made a freeman of the city of Dublin for his efforts, and had taken the rank of colonel in the Volunteer Corps, the very same organisation that Roisin had been talking about. Apparently, the mood in Dublin was becoming more and more critical of any involvement with the English. Events in Ireland were on the move, there was little doubt of that.

After her conversations with Roisin in Arklow, Kate was desperate to speak with the man before she went back to England. In the end she had little difficulty in persuading Mistress Delamere to hold a dinner party in his honour. Sure enough, he was in fine form throughout the evening, and flushed by his recent successes, he went on at some length about his strategy for a declaration of rights, which he intended to present again to the Irish Parliament for their acceptance. While this met with the general approval of most of the others around the table, it was clear that he was not getting wholehearted support for his proposals from everyone.

'Lady Tilbrook,' his voice boomed out eventually, lingering over every syllable. 'Not for the first time, I must say, you don't seem to be in accord with everyone else's thinking here tonight?'

Shocked by the directness of his question, Kate sat up abruptly in her chair. Had she made it so obvious that she had different ideas in her head? She had been hoping to speak to him by herself, but he appeared to be expecting an answer from her right at this moment. If she muttered some inanities in agreement with what he had been saying, she would look foolish. She had been looking for her chance, and perhaps this was the best she was going to get.

'I fear, Mister Grattan, that the untimely deaths of my husband and my mother, God rest them, have diverted my attention away from events in this country.'

Pausing for a moment, she chose her words carefully. If this was going to be her opportunity, she had better make sure that she got it right. 'However, I know you've negotiated major changes in the relationship between Ireland and England, and I'm sure that the strategy you're proposing will build on these changes. But forgive me for saying this – I don't believe you're achieving as much as you could, and I don't believe you're carrying all the people with you.'

Around the table, the other dinner guests were putting down their glasses, some murmuring their disapproval at these comments.

'Wait, wait a moment, everyone,' Grattan implored. 'I've known Lady Tilbrook for two years and I know that she has the gift of being able to see things from a different perspective from the rest of us. Let's hear the good lady describe what we should be doing.'

In for a penny, in for a pound, Kate plunged on. 'Let me begin by saying that I have little personal ambition, other than perhaps the desire to see the people here at home given the same entitlements as anyone who lives on my estate in England. Through the swings of fortune in this life, I've been left a woman of some means, but let me tell you I would rather be in rags if it meant freedom for my brother and his family from the chains which still bind them.'

Around her, she could hear the sounds of chairs scraping against the floor, as some of the guests shifted uncomfortably in their seats. In the light of the candles she could see Mistress Delamere watching her intently, hanging on to her every word. This was a topic they had never discussed in the past. Moreover, this was something the dinner guests had not been expecting to hear, but nobody was interrupting her. They were probably giving her enough rope to hang herself. For a moment she was unsure what to say next, but then in her mind's eye she saw Mister Hutchinson and Roisin O'Byrne, yes, and even Teresa Ryan, urging her on.

'Mister Grattan,' she began again. 'The ways of parliament are certainly sure, but they are undoubtedly slow. You speak of meeting Lord this and Lord that, and making resolutions to the English government. You speak of free trade for our country and freedom for the judiciary in Ireland.'

Drawing breath, she looked around the table. 'Yet there are three million Catholic people in this country, still bound by the penal laws. Who among you is going to speak about freedom for them?'

One of the men on the other side of the table tried to interrupt her, but Henry Grattan put his hand on his arm to caution silence. Kate could see him watching her, a thoughtful expression on his face. Involuntarily, she looked down at her hands and realised they were clenched into fists. Her throat was dry and she had an intense desire for a glass of water, but she was afraid to pick up the jug in case anyone saw how much her hands were trembling. 'I'm saying that what you've achieved for this country in a few short years has been nothing less than remarkable. But the vast majority of the people of Ireland have not felt the benefits. Unless you move quickly to enlist their support, then I fear they'll take action into their own hands. Everything you've gained will ultimately be lost, not to mention the violence and the blood-letting that will ensue.'

'So, Lady Tilbrook,' Henry Grattan spoke quietly. 'I ask you again. What are you suggesting that we should do?'

For a long moment, she looked at the dinner guests around the table. Mister Delamere, the banker and entrepreneur, and his wife, from one of the grandest families in all of Ireland; three of the country's leading members of parliament; Mister Grattan, the most powerful force for change in the country; and his fiancée, Miss Henrietta Fitzgerald, from another of Ireland's greatest families. They were all looking in her direction, waiting for her answer.

Incredibly, she could feel Patrick Nolan's hand on her elbow, trying to restrain her, just as he had done in the Lord Chatham two years earlier. But this time she was not going to be denied. Again she stretched out her arms and put her hands on the table, breaking the shackles that were trying to keep her in her place.

'Ladies and gentlemen, now is the time for you to grasp the nettle firmly. I've heard you in the past, Mister Grattan, talk about your dream. Now is the time to make it a reality. You must press immediately for complete independence for the Irish Parliament from English control. Keep your allegiance to King George if you must, but only such extreme action will capture the hearts, the imagination and the support of the entire population of Ireland.'

'What?' Grattan cried. 'And if this action is unsuccessful, Lady Tilbrook?'

'If you go into this half-heartedly, the English will dismiss you out of hand. And then your Volunteers Corps, the organisation which you yourselves have created and set to arms, they will be waiting to take the country by force, and once again the might of the English army will be turned against us. But if you have the conviction of men who have right on their side, if you believe that the people of Ireland are by right an independent nation, then no power in the world will be able to stop you.'

Suddenly, she realised she had picked up a fork and was brandishing it in front of her, to emphasise her words. Sheepishly, she lowered her hand and place the implement carefully on the table. She had done it again. Now everyone around the table was looking at her as if she had two heads, but at least nobody was ridiculing her. No doubt they were marshalling their arguments to discredit her comments – well, she was not going to give them that chance. Only their actions would prove whether they were Irish at heart, or whether they were more concerned with protecting their own interests in Dublin.

Without realising it, she picked up the fork again. 'I'm sorry, ladies and gentlemen, but there's something more I would like to add.'

Mister Grattan smiled broadly at her fierce expression. 'Kathleen Tilbrook, you're a determined woman, by God. I thought perhaps we had already been given our orders. What else can there be?'

At the sound of his voice, Kate felt herself calming down. Without a doubt, her passions had been running away with her. She had felt she was in a minority of one at the table, forgetting she was among friends. Carefully, she put the fork down on the table in front of her.

'You must be bored listening to me, and I know these things are not easy. But the timing is so important, and now is the time. The English are fully occupied with the war in America, and the move must be made while their attention is otherwise diverted. Wait, and the opportunity will be gone. He who hesitates is lost, as my mother used to say.'

Suddenly, the thought of her mother and the level of passion which she had just expended became too much. Her eyes filled with tears, her vision blurring until she could hardly make out the others around the table. Before they saw her crying, she had to leave. Abruptly, she stood up, almost knocking her chair over in her haste.

'I'm sorry, ladies and gentlemen, you must excuse me,' she muttered, half to herself, as she rushed blindly up the stairs to her bedroom.

A moment later, Mistress Delamere knocked on her door, as Kate sat on the edge of her bed, wiping her eyes. 'Mistress Delamere, please, please forgive me, I've embarrassed you in front of your guests.'

'Don't be ridiculous, you've not embarrassed me in the slightest. In fact, I think that you're right, and now is the time for these people to seize the opportunity that presents itself. All they do is talk all the time. They may never get another chance like this. But I'm more concerned about your state of health. I think you might be trying to do too much, and you're going to make yourself ill if you keep on like this.'

With a struggle, she tried to get up off the bed, but the effort was beyond her. Thankfully, she fell back on the pillows. 'I do feel dreadfully tired, but I thought I might not see Mister Grattan and the others before I went back to England, and someone had to speak to him.'

Sighing heavily, she lay back and closed her eyes, almost immediately falling into a restless sleep, disturbed by constantly shifting images of Edward, her mother and father, Roisin and James Lavelle, mixed in with the guests who had been at dinner.

The next morning she awoke late, feeling dreadfully ill. Every bone in her body seemed to be aching, and the slightest movement brought on a feeling of intense nausea. And still she felt tired, despite having slept for over eight hours. It was midday before she felt well enough to rise from her bed and get dressed, and by the time she came downstairs the other guests had departed. As she was making her way slowly towards the kitchen, she bumped into Mistress Delamere.

'Well, good morning, how are you keeping after all

that sleep?' she enquired in a cheery voice.

'To tell you the truth, I didn't feel good at all earlier this morning, but it seems to have passed and I feel much the better for it now.' Kate looked around for a moment. 'Everyone else seems to have gone – did nobody else feel unwell this morning?'

Mistress Delamere frowned slightly. 'I don't think so. Why do you ask?'

'Only because I don't often feel sick, and I was thinking it might have been something I ate last night. On the other hand, it might simply have been all the excitement.'

The Mistress smiled. 'Their was certainly plenty of that. However, everyone left earlier this morning, leaving you their regards. Mister Grattan himself said you had given him great food for thought and that he was sorry you had to go back to England in these exciting times. I think you might have made a considerable impression on these people, Lady Tilbrook. Now, if you're up to it, Mrs Robinson will make you some breakfast. I have to go out for the rest of the day, but I'll see you this evening.'

'Don't worry about me, I'll be fine. I'm going to rest today. I've decided to go and see my father tomorrow, a prospect I'm not looking forward to.'

The weather matched her mood, dull, grey and foreboding, as she set off on foot towards Kilcarra late the following morning, her stomach churning, still suffering from the same tiredness and nausea of the day before. It was difficult to understand why she should be feeling so poorly, as she had eaten next to nothing the previous evening. The only explanation could be nervous tension at the thought of seeing her father again.

As she reached the outskirts of the village, she could hear the sound of rhythmic hammering in the distance. Her steps heavy with apprehension, she turned towards the smithy. Her last visit had been over a year previously, and on that occasion her father had virtually ignored her. This time, although the death of her mother was still a raw wound in her mind, she was determined not to be forced back into the mood of depression that had followed their last meeting.

However, he must have seen her, or someone must have warned him she was coming. As she turned towards the door of the smithy, he was waiting for her outside. Before she had a chance to open her mouth he started ranting at her.

'I see you coming, Lady whatever you call yourself now. I told you when you were here before that you're not welcome. You're no daughter of mine.'

Unable to think immediately of anything to say which might placate him, Kate reeled back before his onslaught.

'That sainted woman who brought you into the world, God rest her, the woman who was a true wife to me for over twenty years, worked her fingers to the bone to bring up her children. By all that's holy, she didn't deserve this – she didn't deserve to die at her age.' Ripping off his apron, he hurled it to the ground, while Kate looked on in horror. 'If it wasn't for you and the worry she would be alive to this day. It's you and your wild shenanigans that have caused her death. You're the one who's to blame, you and the English devils that have been conniving with you.'

Desperately, she tried to get a word in edgeways, but her father was in full flow and would not be interrupted.

'I told you before there was no place for you in Ireland – you're not wanted. All you've done is bring disgrace and shame upon our heads. Your type is no good. Why couldn't you have been more like your brother? He's prepared to fight for his country and his people, but all you're interested in is fornicating with the English devils and threatening a priest of God in his own church.'

As he continued to rant and rave, Kate could feel the fury taking over her body. How dare he speak to her like this? She had done nothing to bring on such righteous wrath. She did not have to listen to this nonsense. For a moment, he stopped to draw breath, and she saw her chance. Stepping towards him, she spoke quietly and coolly, controlling her rage, in contrast to his wild outburst.

'And what about my brother Eamonn, is he at the house now? And the dogs, are they still there?'

Her father looked at her with narrowed eyes. 'They've all gone, gone to my sister. You'll never see any of them again. I told you, your type is responsible for what's happened to the people here. You are not wanted, there is nothing here for you any more.'

This was the last straw. Almost apoplectic with rage, she stepped forward until she was forcing him back against the wall of the smithy.

'Have you gone mad?' she could hear herself shouting. Nearby, other people must have been able to hear, but she no longer cared. 'That you hold me responsible for the sins committed against our people? I won't stay and listen to this senseless rubbish. In the name of God, I vow that I'll not step foot in this country again unless you take back what you've said to me, your own daughter.'

Her father looked at her. 'By all that's holy, I've heard your vow and I'll never recant. You're not my flesh and blood. You are not welcome, don't you understand? Never set your foot here again.'

Kate was in such a fury that she scarcely noticed which direction she had taken to walk back to the house at Enniskerry. Before she knew it, she had climbed to the top of the hill where she used to spend her Sundays walking with the dogs and where she had first taken Edward. The view was as beautiful as ever but now it held little attraction for her. Even the spectacular sight of a storm coming in over the great black mountain of Lughnaquilla could not hold her attention. As she strode across the moor, yet again she experienced the sensation of being detached from her body. She could see herself walking furiously along the road and stamping in through the door of the big house, still in a state of high dudgeon, while Mistress Delamere stood at the other end of the hallway, wringing her hands and looking anxiously in her direction.

The sound of the other woman's voice brought her abruptly back to reality. 'Did you see your father, Kate? Did you manage to have a conversation with him?'

Suddenly, the awfulness of their meeting came back to her. She shuddered with the memory of their parting and the futility and the abrupt finality of their words. 'Yes, Mistress Delamere,' she replied wearily. 'Yes, I've spoken with him.' She turned away, her face ashen. 'I'm sorry, but I've nothing left to give. I have to go back to England, and I can never come back here while he holds the death of my mother against me. It's too much for me to stand up against. The hatred of my own father, for God's sake.'

For a moment, she pressed her fingertips to her temples. 'If only I didn't feel so desperately tired all the time. And I was sick again this morning.' She looked imploringly at the Mistress. 'What is happening to me?'

Taking her by the hand, Mistress Delamere led her into the drawing room and sat her down in a comfortable armchair.

'Kate,' she began nervously. 'I don't know how to say this, but you sound to me as if you could be pregnant. Is that possible? Being tired all the time and feeling sick, that's what happens when you get that way. Tell me, what about your monthly issue? Is that normal? Has anything changed?'

'It's not come so far, Mistress Delamere,' Kate whispered, suddenly reminded of her night with James Lavelle. 'And yes, it is possible. Is it true, then, is that what it is? Am I going to have a baby?'

Her eyes opened in wonder as she stared at the other woman's face, searching for some response, trying to sort out her thoughts. Surprised, yes, stunned more like, happiness perhaps, and even horror for a moment. All of these sensations, and yet none of them. In disbelief, she shook her head. All those times that she and Edward had made love without really thinking about the possibility of her having a baby. And nothing had happened. Yet just one night with James Lavelle had led to this. Could that have happened? Again, she shook her head. The world was indeed a strange place.

Opposite, she could see Mistress Delamere watching her pensively. 'Look Kate,' she spoke positively, 'you don't have to do anything immediately. Just sit there for a few minutes and let it all sink in. I'll ask Mrs Robertson to fetch us some tea, and you can tell me all about it.' She stood up and smiled. 'For sure, Lady Tilbrook, there's never a dull moment when you're around.'

After she had gone, Kate sat by herself, thinking quietly. This was dreadful. And what was it going to mean? How could she go back to the estate and suddenly produce a baby? They would be whispering about her behind her back. Lord, she would have to find some way of coping with this. Her mind tumbled over and over. But then, it was her life, her baby. She was the Mistress of the estate. She did not have to pay attention to anything anyone else said. They would have to like it or they could move somewhere else and hell mend them.

Suddenly, she had to laugh at herself. Here she was, in a house hundreds of miles away from Tilbrook Hall, before anyone had uttered a word of criticism, and already she was bristling with defiance and daring anybody to challenge her right to have her baby.

Scarcely had she relaxed a little and begun making herself more comfortable against the seat cushions, when the Mistress came back into the room. 'Well Kate,' she remarked, 'I'm glad to say that you seem to be taking all this rather well. I can see you smiling to yourself, so things can't be all that bad.'

With another laugh, Kate felt her stomach with her hands but it seemed to be little different from normal. Resignedly, she shrugged her shoulders. 'If it's true, it's not going to be easy, Mistress Delamere, but after everything else that's happened over the last two years, I'm sure I'll find a way to get by.'

As she was speaking, her words seemed to jolt Mistress Delamere's memory. Without warning, she jumped up and went over to the sideboard. 'Look, Kate,' she exclaimed, 'all these letters have come for you. I forgot about them in our excitement. You have a read through them while I find out what's happening about our tea.'

With the usual thrill she felt at receiving a letter from someone far away, she picked up the first envelope. The writing on the front was the childish scrawl she had come to recognise as Declan's. But the second envelope looked more interesting. It appeared as if it might have got wet at some point. The writing was smudged but it reminded her of Mrs Arrowsmith's. Opening it carefully, she discovered a note and another sealed envelope inside. Sure enough, it had come from Tilbrook Hall. Everything was fine, they hoped she was coping well, and they were all looking forward to her return. Well, that was a relief, at least.

Picking up the other envelope, she turned it over in her hands. It looked like one of the many army letters she received at regular intervals. Probably an invitation to some event or dinner, she muttered to herself, for wives of officers killed in action. Better just read it anyway. As she slit the envelope open, she noticed that the seal was that of Lord Cornwallis. That was interesting, because he was still in America. Quickly she scanned the single sheet of paper inside. As she finished, she realised she had got to the end without understanding any of the words.

Slowly, hesitating over every word, she began reading again. For some reason the house had become oppressively hot. And there was a sudden lack of air in the room, making it difficult to breathe. Without warning, everything around her turned to shadow, fading into black. Unable to move a muscle, she felt herself slipping off the settee and onto the floor, the letter still clutched in her hand. Half-conscious, she sensed a cushion being pushed under her head and a glass of water being pressed to her lips. Taking a sip, she felt her head starting to clear. As she opened her eyes, thankfully she recognised the person leaning over her.

'Thank you, Mistress Delamere,' she gasped. 'I don't know what came over me there, but I think I'm going to be fine now. It was this letter – it was such a shock.'

With some help, she struggled to her feet, finally managing to stand up. Reaching out, she grasped the other woman's hands, barely able to control her excitement. 'The letter, Mistress Delamere, it's come from Lord Cornwallis.'

'I know that Kate, I can see that from the seal. But what does it say?'

She glanced again at the piece of paper in her hand, to confirm what she had read the first time, to make sure she had not made some mistake.

'You're not going to believe this, but he's written to say that a French army officer has been found in a British military hospital near Yorktown. It seems he was injured in a skirmish and then captured He's been in different hospitals for the last six months or so.'

Mistress Delamere looked puzzled. 'Why shouldn't I believe that? There must be lots of Frenchmen out there.'

Her eyes shining, Kate stared at the letter. 'Because they've discovered he's not a French soldier after all. They're saying that it's Edward, Mistress Delamere – impersonating a French officer to get behind their lines. I can't bring myself to believe it, but unless it's some kind of horrible joke or misunderstanding, according to this letter my husband is still alive. Read it for me and tell me I'm not making a mistake.'

Snatching the piece of paper, the other woman read it quickly. 'Kathleen, nobody would write a letter like this if it wasn't true. They must have found him. She looked up. 'My dear Kathleen, I'm so delighted for you.' Grabbing Kate by the arm, she led her in a little jig of delight in the middle of the room. 'This calls for a drink,' she shouted, pouring out two large brandies. While she was at the sideboard, Kate picked up the letter and studied it again.

'Look,' she cried, 'this letter is dated in April. That's over three months ago, and it says that Edward will be on the next available ship to England. So he must be well enough to travel.'

Her mind racing furiously, she tried to work out how long it might take to get back to England from America but she was too excited to make any sensible calculation. 'It means he could be there by now. Mistress Delamere, I have to get back there straight away.'

'Will you not have time for a drink to celebrate?' enquired the other woman with a twinkle in her eye.

Kate laughed insanely. 'Well, perhaps just one before I go,' she replied, waving her glass triumphantly in the air.

The English coast was almost in sight before her excitement had abated sufficiently for the full realisation of her position to dawn. It was like being immersed in a bath of ice-cold water. Almost sixteen months had passed since she had last seen Edward Tilbrook. Would he still look the same? The letter said he had been injured in the war – what if he was wounded, or crippled even? Would he still love her? Would she still love him? She was going to have to tell him about Lavelle and the baby. What if he threw her out with only the clothes on her back? She had nowhere to go – especially after her vow not to come back to Ireland. And what about Mistress Delamere? In all the excitement she had not really told her about her disastrous meeting with her father and her solemn vow never to return. How would she explain that? And life without her mother or Mistress Delamere – it was too desperate to even comtemplate. And how was she going to support herself, with a baby as well? God forbid, she would have to do what Teresa Ryan had been doing.

But would he be there before her? Or was it indeed some form of horrible joke?

All the way to London these thoughts kept going round and round in her head. By the time she reached the city she was in such an extreme state of nervous tension that she almost called in at Mistress Jardine's house for some moral support. In the end, although she was exhausted by her journey, the excitement and the anxiety kept her going. Too determined to stop, she had to find out if the story was true.

By the time her carriage turned into the driveway of Tilbrook Hall it was early evening and Kate could feel the old familiar panic constricting her chest. Gasping for breath, she pressed herself against the seat and away from the windows, lest anyone should happen to see her. Ideally, she would have wanted to meet him in his house in London, but she had to go to the estate to make sure that the Arrowsmiths knew she was back in England, and in case Edward had not yet arrived.

As the carriage came abruptly to a halt, she shrank

back against the side furthest from the house. Outside, she could hear someone fumbling with the door. With a sigh of relief she saw that it was old Mr Jones.

'Mistress Tilbrook,' he greeted her gallantly. 'Welcome back. I hope your journey has not been too arduous?'

Hesitantly, she stepped down from the carriage and looked around. Everywhere appeared familiar, comforting. By the doorway she could see Mrs Arrowsmith, looking out cautiously. As soon as she recognised who it was, she came running down the stairs, curtsying and laughing like a madwoman at the same time. Before she could form the question, Kate knew what the answer was going to be.

'He is here, tell me, Mrs Arrowsmith? My husband is here, I'm sure of it.'

The other woman could barely contain her delight. 'Yes, yes, it's wonderful news, he's here. He came back only a few days ago, right out of the blue. It's a miracle, the master has returned from the dead.'

For a moment, Kate leaned against the wall to support herself, still refusing to believe, looking apprehensively up at the doorway. It was not a joke, he had really come back. Any minute now she was going to see him. All of a sudden, she realised she was desperately afraid. What had been between them before, would it still be the same? And what would happen when she told him about her condition?

Turning to the woman beside her, she grasped her arm. 'Tell me, Mrs Arrowsmith,' she insisted. 'How is he? Is he any different?' Although she was afraid of the answer, she had to know.

Another voice spoke. 'I'm not sure that you're asking that question of the right person.'

Kate reeled back in fright. He was there in the doorway beside her, with his cool, sweet voice, reaching out to her with one hand. Slowly, Kate forced herself to look up. With one glance, she took in the familiar white shirt and black breeches, the bandage around his head, the one hand leaning on a stick. But above all, she looked up at his beautiful, wonderful, smiling face and his twinkling blue eyes.

Almost simultaneously, she threw herself into his embrace, her arms wrapped tightly around him, sobbing, wailing, crying, laughing, all at the same time.

'Edward, Edward, Edward, my husband, my lovely man. I can't believe you're here. I thought I was never going to see you again.' Desperately, she pressed herself against his chest.

'Kate,' he cried, struggling to keep his balance, 'you're as sweet and as precious as ever. But be careful or you'll have me over. I'm not quite recovered yet, and if you throw yourself at me we'll both end up on the carpet. And in front of Mrs Arrowsmith as well.'

There were so many things to talk about, and so much lost time to make up. They were back together again, almost immediately recapturing the way they were in the days when they had walked along the hillside in Wicklow and been unable to stop touching each other. All evening she was in a another world, her tiredness and nausea forgotten – almost. But as the initial excitement began to subside, she felt herself dreading what she had to do. Eventually she could go on no longer. She had to tell him. There was no way of knowing how he would react, but she had to get it over with. Pulling over a chair, she sat up straight and erect, directly in front of him.

'Edward, my husband,' she began, grimacing at the curiosity in his face and his faint smile at her serious tone of voice. 'Please listen to me, there's something I have to tell you. I want you to know that I'll always love you. But I thought you were dead these eight months nearly. When I got the news of you being still alive, I was over in Ireland, and I'm sure Mr Arrowsmith told you why I was there.'

Edward squeezed her hand tenderly. 'Yes, he told me, Kate, and I'm desperately sorry for you.'

She could hardly bear to see the concern on his face. This was going to hurt him so much, but there was no way of letting him down easily. Nonetheless, he had to know.

'Edward, you have to know I was so completely distraught for a while that I scarcely knew what I was doing in Ireland. My husband had been killed, and my mother had just died, God rest her, someone I had been close to for almost twenty years, before she turned her back on me because of our love for each other.'

Standing up, she walked across to the window and looked outside at the familiar sight of the gardens sweeping down to the river. If only there was an easy way to tell him. Turning round again, she saw that he had followed her across the room. With a sob she fell against his chest, clutching his arms. 'Edward,' she whispered dully, 'Something has happened, which you have to know about.' Screwing up her courage, she blurted it out. 'Edward, my dear husband, I think I'm going to have another man's child.'

447

His stick dropped to the carpet as he stumbled, gripping her by the shoulders with both hands. She searched his face fearfully, but his features were expressionless. Only his eyes narrowed slightly.

'You've been sleeping with another man,' he said flatly. 'Is that what you're saying?'

Kate heard herself whimpering. 'Only once, Edward, in Ireland, when I had nobody left in the world and I was so desperately lonely and I needed someone to comfort me.'

Letting her go, he limped over to the sideboard and poured himself a glass of brandy. 'And do you love this man?' he asked quietly.

Kate held her head between her hands, trying not to listen to the agony in his voice, struggling to prevent herself from breaking down completely. 'No, Edward, I don't love him. I met him here in London just before I met you, when I first came here, and then I met him again by accident in Ireland a few weeks ago.'

Stumbling across the room, she stood in front of him, her head bowed. 'Whatever you say, whatever you decide to do, Edward, one thing will never change. I'll always love you with all my heart and soul. If you throw me out in the street with nothing, I could understand that, but it won't stop me loving you.'

Impulsively, she put her hand on his arm and looked into his eyes. 'I prayed every night for your wellbeing in America. I thank God that my prayers have been answered and that you've been delivered safe and sound. It's been the most welcome experience in my entire life to see you here, back in your own home. Everything else that's happened is a far cry from the hopes and dreams that we had once, Edward . . .' Her voice trailed off as she looked at the floor.

It was just too much. The excitement and then trying to explain had left her exhausted. Fighting to hold back her tears, she turned away. 'Think of me, Edward,' she mumbled, 'if only for a few moments.' Without waiting to hear any response, she rushed up the stairs to their bedroom.

Sometime later she awoke in the darkness, cold and stiff, still fully dressed. Swinging her legs off the bed, she walked slowly over to the table and poured herself a glass of water. As she stood looking blankly into the night air, she felt Edward's hands gently caressing her shoulders, his lips brushing her neck.

'Kate,' she heard him whisper, 'my little Irish colleen. Look out there at the moon. Isn't it beautiful? I remember how you once described Ireland to me, how the moon hangs in the distance over the green mountains. Every night when I was in America, I used to look out at the moon, and dream of you. I'd wonder if we'd ever be together again. But that's all over now. You're with your husband and that's where you're going to stay. Everything is going to be all right, and I'm never going to leave you again.'

Turning around in the half-light, she reached up to his neck with her arms, pressing her body against his, her eyes closed, her lips parted.

'Kate,' he whispered again, 'I've never stopped thinking about you and I never will. I love you no matter what. We will always be together – what you've told me tonight will not stop us.'

Anxiously, she looked at his face. 'But Edward, you

know that I'll not be parted from this baby. How will you be able to bring yourself to live with another man's child?'

'Kate,' he whispered, 'my beautiful Kate, this will be our child. No one will ever know that it's not ours.'

For a moment she stood motionless, her head against his chest, trying to grapple with the enormity of his words. 'I don't deserve this, Edward, and I'll never forget it. No man will ever have a more loyal wife, you'll see.'

Slowly, she looked up at the man beside her. Even in the darkness, he could see her eyes flashing. 'I'm sorry, but I have to ask you one more thing.' Her voice was quiet but firm. 'I will be eternally grateful to you if we can bring this baby up as ours, here in England, and we can keep what has happened to ourselves. But when the child comes of age, I'd like to tell him or her the truth. I know it's a lot to ask, but please, Edward, please promise me you'll let me do this.'

Smiling, he kissed her gently, sweetly on the lips. 'You're definitely still the woman I remember. Yes, Kate, I promise.'

As they looked at each other, at that moment they were the only two people in the world.

'Now, my wife,' he commanded, as he spanked her lightly on the bottom. 'We have to slip these clothes off and get you into bed with your husband where you belong.'

Chapter 17

———◆———

Unable to bring himself to look directly at her, Dominic shook his head in bewilderment. 'But that's an incredible story,' he cried. 'Are you expecting me to believe it? Or is it a way of diverting my attention or justifying your actions?'

Pursing her lips, Kate nodded in agreement. 'You're right, Dominic, it is an incredible story. But I've been completely honest with you, and it hasn't been embellished in any way.'

Watching him carefully, she could see emotions flitting across his face. But the pain was evident in his eyes.

'Let me be clear about this. What you're saying is that my real father is James Lavelle and not Edward Tilbrook. Is that it?'

Picking up a miniature from the table beside her, she rubbed the heavy silver frame with her fingers, something she had done a thousand times or more since Edward had died. 'Be careful how you use those words, Dominic. For sure, James Lavelle is your natural father, but it was another man who shaped your life, who brought you up as part of a loving family, who taught you to ride and hunt and fence, and who made you the man you are today. That man was Edward Tilbrook, God rest him, he was your real father. Now you've inherited his title – and it's your decision whether you take it up or not.'

Gritting her teeth at the thought of the pain she had caused him, Kate watched her son struggling to control himself.

'And what about James Lavelle?' Dominic asked finally. 'Do you know what has happened to him?'

Kate turned her head away, 'I have no idea where he is now.'

'I see,' he replied, his voice more puzzled than angry, 'But this story you've told me – I've scarcely ever heard you mention Ireland before, except for some ancient history or the fairy stories you used to tell. And as for all those people you seem to know, I haven't heard of most of them either.'

Again, she searched his expression, as he attempted to come to terms with her revelations and the changes in their relationship. As she assessed his reactions, however, it was clear that things were not turning out quite as she had expected. For sure, she had anticipated a hostile backlash, but it was obvious that her son's natural curiosity was taking over from the initial shock.

'Dominic, it grieves me to say this again, but I made a vow that I would never set foot in Ireland until my father took back his accusations against me. Keeping to that vow has almost broken my heart. Don't you see? When I left Ireland I was leaving behind my country, my people, and my memories. Over here, it was difficult to follow events in Ireland, not to mention keeping in contact with the people there. And all the while knowing I could not go back. Now you know why I threw myself so wholeheartedly into the role of Mistress of this Tilbrook Estate. It was at my insistence that neither Edward nor I ever talked to you or your sisters about how we first met, or what happened before you were born.'

But she could see he was only half-listening, as he tried to work out who he recognised from the story she had just told him.

'Mister and Mistress Jardine I know well enough, and also the Nolans and cousin Marie and her brothers. Mister Boulton I remember meeting once, although it's difficult to imagine him being as energetic as you describe. And Mister Wilberforce I've met many times whenever he's come to visit. But where is Enniskerry, and what has happened to the Delameres?'

Chuckling quietly to herself, Kate poured a small brandy. Now the secret was out, it did not seem all that important after all. 'What you have to remember, Dominic, is that as you grow older, the difference in age between people seems to become narrower. Mistress Delamere is not much more than six or seven years older than me, but she was married when she was only sixteen years old. At the time when I went to work at Enniskerry, however, she seemed so much older and wiser than I was. Even Mister Grattan was only thirty years old when I first met him. Now the difference in age is barely noticeable.'

Taking a sip from her glass, she fingered the silver-framed silhouette of her husband once again. 'And yes,

Mistress Delamere used to come here every year until you were about eight or nine years old, but then her husband's health deteriorated and she hasn't been able to travel much since. However, we still write regularly to each other, and she herself is in fine fettle, although her husband is still poorly.'

As Kate fondly recalled a long-distant memory, she found herself gazing into the distance.

'But I'm sorry to say that old Mr O'Brien died a few years ago. I said a prayer for him when I read about it, and I would have liked to have paid my respects at his funeral. He was a wonderful person and a great support to me when times were difficult.'

Pausing for a moment, she tried to make sure she had thought of everything. 'Mistress Delamere's daughters are now married and living in Dublin and she's now a grandmother. Bernard, her son, whom you might remember me mentioning, he's in India, an officer in the English army. My brother Eamonn went with him, but he was killed about five years ago, apparently in some local uprising. I was devastated at the time, but to be honest, he was someone I hardly knew. Also, you might remember me talking about young Arthur Wellesley. He's now Sir Arthur and a general in the English army, also in India. But he still finds the time to write a letter to me, his old teacher, every six months as regular as clockwork.'

Dominic must have seen the tear in her eye, giving away her innermost thoughts. 'I'm sorry about your brother. He would have been my uncle, but you never ever told me anything about him.'

His mind raced ahead to other topics. 'What about the politics, mother? From what you've said, it seems to me that events in Ireland were heading towards some sort of climax at the time you returned to England. It's a little surprising to me, especially with Ireland being part of Great Britain.'

For a moment, Kate sighed wistfully. 'Dominic, my son, I'm older and possibly a little wiser now, and perhaps I don't have the same passion I had in my youth, but I still get upset when I think of the events of the last twenty years. Over here, the people know next to nothing about what is going on in Ireland. All they think about is the French, and India, and the Empire.'

She gave her son an amused glance. 'When I talk about Irish politics I know I will get myself worked up into a rage, so I had better pour myself another brandy before I start.'

'Come over here beside me,' she began, 'where we can make ourselves more comfortable. Do you remember I told you about the night of the dinner party at Mistress Delamere's house in Enniskerry when Henry Grattan was present? The night your mother had the audacity to stand up, brandishing a dinner fork no less, and tell the establishment everything they were doing wrong?'

Her son nodded, trying to picture the scene.

'Well, in the spring of the following year Henry Grattan moved in the Irish Parliament for a repeal of the Act of George I asserting the right of England to legislate for Ireland. In other words, that Ireland should be completely free of any form of control or interference from England, the only condition being that the oath of allegiance to George III would be maintained. Ireland would be a country free of England, but sharing a common sovereign.'

Dominic was amazed. 'But that was what you said they must do. I didn't know that. Nobody ever told me about any of this. So what happened? Did the English dismiss them out of hand, to use your own words?'

Kate thumped the side of the chair with her fist. 'On the contrary, my dear Dominic, in fact the opposite happened. What Roisin O'Byrne and I had talked about previously and what I said that night turned out to be absolutely true. The English were exhausted by the war in America and were not overly concerned with making concessions towards a little impoverished country like Ireland. In April of that year, the Prime Minister of England granted full independence to the Irish Parliament, the only bond between the two countries being allegiance to the same king.'

'But that must have been fantastic news,' cried Dominic. 'Even though you were over here in England you must have been celebrating, surely.'

'Hardly celebrating, my son,' she replied dryly. 'I was lying on my back in agony surrounded by surgeons and midwives and God knows who else. Three days after the independence was ratified, I gave birth to my first child, a beautiful baby boy that Edward and I decided to call Dominic.'

Smiling a little ruefully, her son sat back in his chair. 'Sorry, I had forgotten all about that. I see, so I interfered again. That was a pity, but now that you mention it, why did you call me Dominic? Was I named after someone in your family or my father's family?'

She noticed that Dominic had still referred to Edward as his father. That was comforting at least. Looking at her son sitting beside her, she cast her mind back over his twenty-one years. The day he was born was still vivid in her memory, every detail standing out in sharp relief. The event seemed almost like yesterday, and it was all she could do to hold back the tears.

'No, Dominic,' she replied softly, still recalling those long gone days. 'You were named after someone who was a major influence on my life, someone who stood by me and offered help when I was really in the depths of despair. That was Charles Dominic Jardine, Mistress Jardine's husband. I know he's getting very old now, but you've no idea what a tower of strength he was to me in those dark days before you were born.'

Her son absorbed this for a moment, obviously slightly taken aback at the thought of being named after Mistress Jardine's husband. However, it was becoming clear that it was the political manoeuvring that was really intriguing him. 'I can understand that, mother,' he replied thoughtfully. 'But going back to the Irish Parliament for a moment. If everything you say did happen, how is it that less than twenty years later Ireland was made part of the Union? What did Henry Grattan have to say to that?'

Without realising it, Dominic had asked a particularly awkward question, and Kate found herself responding without thinking. 'Don't be so flippant about Grattan's contribution to the people of Ireland,' she snapped. 'He gave them an opportunity to take their country into their own hands and in the end they squandered it.'

Walking over to the sideboard, she poured herself another small brandy. 'It's a confused story. After parliamentary independence, Grattan was the leading politician and Parliament voted him a large sum of money in recognition of his services to his country. However, when the initial excitement died down, his political enemies started asking about his right to this award, and in the end he decided never to take office. But he was really the only significant person in power in Dublin who was inclined towards supporting the interests of the Catholics in the country. No one else came forward who was capable of articulating their cause, and sure enough the Government drifted into representing the interests of a small group of people in and around Dublin, and moved back towards the English camp.'

Dominic jumped to his feet. 'But mother, you knew that would happen, you told me in your story that you talked to Grattan and those other people about the dangers of that happening. How would it have turned out if you had stayed in Ireland? Could it all have been different?'

Shrugging her shoulders, she stared out of the window for a moment. God, she muttered to herself, after all the preparation she had gone through for this conversation, all the worry and the sleepless nights, and the nightmare where her son might turn completely against her when she revealed the secret of his father. How could she have foreseen that he would have taken all that in his stride? How was she to know that he would be more interested in the politics in Ireland? Perhaps, of course, this was because he was his mother's son after all.

'Dominic, how on earth do I know? I think in some ways I might have acted as the conscience for those people, constantly reminding them that they had wider responsibilities. Maybe, maybe not, I don't know.'

'So tell me what happened next,' he demanded, without giving her the chance to sit and reminisce. 'After the Parliament failed to maintain its representation of all the people, what happened after that?'

She collected her thoughts. 'Remember, Dominic, that I wasn't there. All I have to go on are the letters from Mistress Delamere and my brother Declan, and they were coming from completely different sides of the fence. What it seems happened is that someone did come to the fore who was able to argue the cause of the Catholic majority in the country. His name was Wolfe Tone, and funnily enough, he was not even a Catholic himself. But he managed to capture the imagination of the people throughout Ireland. Again, however, the problem was that he was not a real leader. He was a lawyer and a writer, but he was also a great orator, and he could work the people up into a frenzy of passion, but he didn't have the political grasp or stature to take what Grattan had achieved and build on it and maintain Ireland's independence from England.'

Her son scratched his head. 'But I can remember you telling me that you had spoken to your brother Declan about this, about the need for someone to stand up and represent the Catholics. If Tone did that, how did his efforts fail?'

'Let me say again, Dominic, that although we're talking about something that was close to my heart, I was reading the situation from a distance. He was aided and abetted by that man Tandy whom I first met in London The last thing you would describe him as being was a political reformer. He was no more than a man of violence, and the French had their own revolution which encouraged many people in Ireland to think they could do the same themselves. It was after that happened when Tone went to the French to enlist their aid, and I would not be surprised to find that James Lavelle was somehow involved.'

Taking a deep breath, she gave herself time to calm down. 'The French didn't care a fig for an independent Ireland. All that interested them was irritating the English, so everything they did was too little, too late. Wolfe Tone ended up committing suicide after the failure of one of the more ill-starred French expeditions to southwest Ireland. His death left the people frustrated and without any real leadership, and it all boiled over into the bloody uprising in seventeen ninety-eight, which left thousands dead and achieved absolutely nothing.'

Dominic raised his eyebrows in disbelief. 'What, all those people died for nothing at all?'

'Well, yes, I suppose it did achieve something,' Kate added dryly. 'It galvanised the English government into action and two years later Ireland lost whatever independence it had left and was taken back into the Union of Great Britain.'

'That is a fascinating,' Dominic declared. 'But I'm more convinced than ever that if you had been there, talking to your brother, and reminding the likes of Grattan who they were representing, that things would have ended up much differently.'

'Please don't speak like that, Dominic,' she whispered fiercely. 'It's hard to live with myself if I start to think about that. There's so many things I would have done differently with the benefit of hindsight. I never thought my brother Declan could arouse people politically until I saw him in Arklow after my mother had died. I should have tried then to persuade him to take a different point of view, and Roisin as well, but I was too distraught at the time. And then there was James Lavelle. I'm sure he would have done almost anything for me at one point, but again I had other things on my mind. So I never tried to get his support for changes to happen in the way I thought was best.'

Shrugging her shoulders, she sighed heavily. 'The time was right and I had my chance, but I never took it. God knows when that time will come again and when the Irish will ever get another chance.'

'I see,' her son replied, rubbing his chin thoughtfully. To Kate's relief, he seemed to have run out of questions, at least for the moment, and she was able to turn the conversation to other less controversial topics.

In an unusual departure from his normal outgoing personality, Dominic kept very much to himself for the next few days, and Kate saw very little of him. Two weeks after his birthday and their long conversation, however, he came to see her and announced that he was going up to London for a short while to visit some friends, and that he would be back in a few days.

When he returned, he seemed more thoughtful than ever. Eventually, her curiosity became too much and she had to ask him about his reactions to their earlier conversation, now that sufficient time had passed for him to have considered all the implications.

At first, he seemed amused by her concern. 'Listen, Mother, when you told me about father and my background, I swear my initial reaction was one of shock and bitterness. On reflection, however, there's not much

461

I can do about it now, so I don't think it's going to cause me many sleepless nights. But what I find so devilishly entrancing is discovering that my own mother is not quite the person I thought I knew, and finding out that she had such an exciting period in her life, even if it was only for a few years.'

Before he could protest, she threw her arms around him and given him a squeeze. 'My Dominic, you're a fine boy for sure. And you're indeed turning into a flatterer yourself. I'm not sure at all who it is you're taking after, whether it's Edward or James Lavelle, for they were both charming with the words.'

Her son was laughing as he struggled to release himself. 'I can't stop thinking about the life you led, and the passion and commitment which seems to have been part of everything you were involved with. Now, before she mentions it to you herself, I have to tell you that I've been up to London to see Mistress Jardine. I wanted to ask her about the times that you and she had together before I was born, and get another picture of my mother from a different perspective.'

'Aha, you sly child, Dominic Tilbrook. And did you find it entertaining meeting with Mistress Jardine?'

Dominic had to laugh again. 'Her stories are even more incredible than yours, if such a thing is possible. Some of what she says has to taken with a pinch of salt, but if she's done even half of what she claims, she must have lived an amazing life when she was young.'

Then he caught hold of her hand and looked intently into her eyes. 'But then, mother, you gave it all up. How could you live without the excitement of being at the centre of events, debating with the likes of Grattan, and talking into the night with your brother and Roisin O'Byrne about their plans for a revolution?'

For a moment or two, she could not reply. Instead she walked over to the window and gazed at the familiar view outside, a view she would never become tired of seeing. When she turned back to look at her son, she had to fight to keep her lips from trembling.

'What can I say to you about those days, Dominic? That I didn't find them exciting? That I don't miss them? That perhaps if I had stayed in Ireland that events might have turned out differently? You know it wouldn't be true if I said anything like that. But on the other hand, up until last year I had the happiest and most fulfilling life, with the best husband and friend a woman could ask for, and four wonderfully interesting children to keep me occupied and to make sure my mind didn't stray to what might have been.'

Although her son smiled faintly at her words, she could see he was itching to say something further. It took him a few moments to satisfy himself that he had found the right words.

'I have to ask you about something else, Mother,' he spoke quietly, but there was a touch of harshness in his tone. 'You've told me about your life all those years ago. But the woman you describe, she doesn't sound like someone who'd simply lose contact with her father and mother in the way that you did. In some ways, I find that hard to believe. Was that perhaps the actions of someone who was just being stubborn and headstrong? Don't you have any regrets about that now?'

She felt a senseless fury gripping her chest. 'How dare you say that, Dominic, how dare you accuse me of being stubborn. You weren't there, how could you possibly tell what it was like? I didn't plan to fall in love with an Englishman, but that's what happened. I went back to my parents so many times, I pleaded with them, but my father wouldn't listen. He was the one who was stubborn. And then he actually accused me of being the cause of my mother's death. That was so unbearable that I simply could not take it any more.'

Pausing for a moment to catch her breath, she felt her anger subsiding. 'Don't you think I've wanted to go back? The nights I've sat here, thinking about how it could all have been different?'

Unable to meet her son's gaze, she smoothed the back of a chair cover with her hand. Without realising it, he had discovered the thoughts that still haunted her, along with the feelings of guilt and remorse. But he had started speaking again and she forced herself to concentrate on what he was saying.

'Mother, there's something else that Mistress Jardine mentioned to me.' He stopped, hesitating.

'Well, go on, tell me, for God's sake.'

'She said that the United Irishmen, or the rebels as the English call them, have not all been defeated or captured. A group of them are still holding out in a place that you mentioned in your story, in the wild countryside in County Wicklow around Lughnaquilla mountain.'

Kate felt her heart sink. 'What else did she say?'

'I couldn't believe it, not five years after the uprising. But she assured me they're still there. Apparently, they're led by a Wicklow man by the name of Michael Dwyer. The English have done everything in their power to capture him, laying waste to the countryside and building roads to enable their army to move quickly from place to place, but so far they've failed dismally. Did you know about this, Mother?'

Kate sighed deeply, before nodding her head in reply.

Her son looked bewildered. 'How is it that a small group of people can survive for so long when the might of the English army is at their heels?'

Kate laughed thinly. 'It's not so difficult to understand. This is not rolling English farmland we're talking about. This is a fierce country of mountains, forests and boglands, and there's precious few roads there. The valley which leads up towards Lughnaquilla, Glenmalure it's called, was the fortress of the O'Byrnes for hundreds of years, and no one could ever flush them out. In fact my brother's wife, Roisin, is one of the O'Byrnes, which probably explains why she can be so bloody-minded when it comes to defending her own.'

Leaning forward in her chair, she emphasised her next point. 'But the real reason that Dwyer and his followers can stay one step ahead of the English is because they're getting support from the local people. And I know that one of their most prominent supporters is my brother.'

Dominic looked at her closely. 'So was your brother, my Uncle Declan, involved in the uprising?'

Kate sighed even more deeply. 'For sure he was. As far as I know he was in Wexford where the uprising began, and was even at New Ross where the militia finally got the upper hand. I believe he came back from there with Dwyer to Wicklow.'

'So tell me, mother, does that mean your brother is still there now?'

'Who knows, Dominic, I haven't had a letter from him

for at least a year. But to the best of my knowledge, yes he's still there.'

'Mother, I know you say that the reason the rebels are able to survive is because of the support of the local people. But Mistress Jardine believes that they're also getting support from the French.'

Kate gritted her teeth. It was all too obvious what was going to come next.

'Does that mean that James Lavelle could be in Wicklow as well?'

Unable to look her son in the eye, she stood up and turned away. 'Yes, Dominic,' she whispered, 'I believe he's involved somehow with my brother.'

'You knew, didn't you, you knew all along where he was but you wouldn't tell me.'

Pressing her hands to her ears, she tried to shut out his words.

'Mother, I have to try and find him. If he is with the rebels, he might be killed. Then I will never have had the chance to meet him. I want to go to Ireland to try and find him – and I would like you to give me your blessing to do it.'

A tremor of apprehension coursed through her body. These were the same words she had used herself when she had first asked her mother about travelling to London. But Dominic must have known what was on her mind.

'Mother, I'm older than you were when you first came over from Ireland to England. What I'd like to do is to go in the opposite direction. Yes, I'd like to go to Enniskerry and visit Mistress Delamere, find the church where your mother is buried and see the village where you lived when you were growing up. And I'd like to find that hill behind the village and look out at the view you describe so well.'

Closing her eyes, she felt herself dreading the thought of Dominic travelling over to Ireland by himself. He was still only a baby, he knew nothing about the world. What if someone tried to take advantage of him or he was waylaid by ruffians? Ireland was full of lawless bands of militia after the uprising. How welcome would a young Englishman be, wandering around by himself? It was easy to think of a hundred different reasons why he should not go.

Suddenly, the significance of her thoughts struck home. This was exactly how her mother must have felt when she had announced she was going to London. And she had been younger and even more immature than Dominic.

'I don't think you'll find it too grand a place, Dominic,' she replied hastily. 'We live in a much more affluent part of the world. And as an Englishman you'll stand out like a sore thumb wherever you go. I'm not sure how welcome you'll be.'

For a moment, her son considered her words. 'I don't think I'm too concerned about that, Mother. And it seems to me that you're determined to keep to your vow. If you'll not go to Ireland, then I must.'

Turning away, he looked over his shoulder and gave her a devilish grin. 'After all, I'm half-Irish, and I want to find out everything I can about my heritage, and what it's really like over there.'

She realised there was little she could do – what more could she say? She could not offer to go with him, she had the girls to think about, not to mention the vow. She had no arguments that would dissuade him if his mind was made up.

'I'd like to go down to Arklow as well, and find your brother Declan if he's still there. He's my uncle, and he should give me a welcome of sorts, I'm sure. But more than anything else, if James Lavelle is there, I would really like to meet him.'

Anxiously, Kate put her hand on his arm. 'Please, Dominic, for me, please don't do that.'

'Don't worry, mother,' he insisted, pulling himself away. ' I'd never tell him. Your secret is safe with me. But just because you don't talk to your father, don't deny me the right to speak to mine. After all, you've described him in impossibly romantic terms, and I'd like to see what he looks like in real life, and to find out whether I take after him in any way.'

Carefully, she studied her son's expression. 'But what about the rebels and the English soldiers and the fighting?'

'I'm going and that's that. Nothing you can say will stop me.'

'And when are you thinking of going on this journey?'

Throwing back his head, he laughed heartily. 'I can see that you're being very motherly and looking out for your little boy's welfare. You don't have to worry about me, I'll be fine. But since you ask, I think within the next few weeks. With the summer not far away, this is the best time to go.'

Although her heart was heavy, Kate did not attempt to dissuade him. What words could she use, what arguments could she deploy? She had seen this before and she knew it was useless. He was his mother's son, after all.

For the next few weeks, she tried to stand to one side and take no part as the arrangements were made. A place was booked on the coach to Holyhead, while letters were despatched to Mister Jardine's agent and to Mistress Delamere to let them know he was coming. Eventually, however, she could not resist his enthusiasm and anticipation of his first visit to his mother's homeland. As he was clearly determined to go and nothing she could say was going to change his mind, her only sensible course of action was to provide him with as much information and advice as she could.

The day before he was due to leave, she drew him a little map showing the relative positions of Dublin, Enniskerry and Kilcarra, and explained what he had to do.

'When you get to Dublin, take the mail coach for Arklow or Wexford and get off at the inn in Bray. You should be able to hire a hansom cab to take you from there to Mistress Delamere's house in Enniskerry. It's only a few miles and everybody will know where it is, as she receives visitors all the time. What I've shown here is Kilcarra village, with the church and Cormack's pub, and this is where I used to live. My father is still there, I believe, but he's an old man now and as far as I've heard has become very reclusive. I think it would be best if you didn't get too close, but simply had a look at the house from the hill behind the village.'

With a broad smile, Dominic looked at his mother. 'And what about your hiding place with the old cottage where you used to go with your first boyfriend? I'd like to go and see that.'

'What, am I to have no secrets left?' she demanded, drawing another little map. 'Please try and find this place, Dominic, and if it's still as beautiful as ever come back and tell me about it. But if it's been destroyed or someone has built another house there, don't tell me. I want to keep my memories the way they are.'

Her son tucked the maps into his pocket. 'And how do I get to Arklow and Glendalough? I'd like to see those places too, and the inn at Laragh.'

'There are different ways of getting there and Mistress Delamere will help. But for you probably the best way to Arklow is to take the mail coach from Bray, just as I did all those years ago. To get to Glendalough, you'll probably have to hire a horse and trap.'

'And what if I want to climb up towards that mountain of yours, Lughnaquilla? Can I get there from Glendalough?'

The thought of him wandering through rebel-infested countryside was horrifying. 'For God's sake, Dominic, don't try and go up there, you're sure to get lost. There's a road from Laragh over into Glenmalure, but that will be full of English soldiers and the militia trying to catch Dwyer and his people. Please don't go there as it will be dangerous. I believe there might be another way, from St Kevin's Church up over the hill, but it's a very difficult path to follow. I think it would be much better, Dominic, if you keep to the towns and villages, and gaze upon Lughnaquilla from a safe distance.'

'Don't worry, mother,' Dominic declared for the umpteenth time, 'I'll be fine. But you have to blame yourself for making me go. It was your vivid description of the countryside and the people that's whetted my appetite to see it for myself.'

'I only wish I could be with you, Dominic,' she confided, her eyes misting over. 'But I must stand by the vow. Maybe one day we can go together.'

Perhaps one day it would be possible. But that would almost certainly mean her father would be dead, releasing her from the vow. Even though she had not seen him for over twenty years and his last words to her had been so cruel and vindictive, time had softened the memory, and she could feel the pain in her chest of what might have been.

Vigorously, she shook her head to clear her mind. That was enough of that kind of thinking – she had someone much closer to home to worry about.

'Be careful, Dominic,' she repeated, hugging him tightly. 'And listen to whatever Mistress Delamere has to say. She'll know the current situation and you must take her advice. Write to me as soon as you get to Enniskerry and let me know you're safe and well.'

'I will, mother, I will.'

'And have you said goodbye to your sisters?'

'Yes, mother, indeed I have,' he assured her again.

'Then all I can say is go with God, enjoy yourself, and don't be breaking your shins on any stools that aren't in your path. But above all, don't be distracted by any doe-eyed Irish colleens, or your heart will be lost for ever.'

Chapter 18

——◆◆◆——

Following Dominic's departure, life continued at Tilbrook Hall but it was no longer the same. Although they had spent less time together as he had grown older, Kate was not surprised to find that her son's absence left a large gap in her life. He had been away for long periods of time attending boarding school, but she had always known where he was, and of course, Edward had been with her then. No matter how hard she tried, it was so difficult to come to terms with the uncertainty about where he was or what he was doing.

The weeks rolled by, with Kate becoming more and more anxious about his whereabouts, when at last his first letter arrived. He had reached Ireland safely and was staying at Mistress Delamere's house in Enniskerry. The countryside was beautiful but the weather was dreadful. However, it was possible to get around and he had seen many of the places they had talked about. Mistress Delamere was entertaining him greatly and was about to take him down to meet Mister Grattan who had bought a house not far from Enniskerry. After that he would be setting off for Arklow. Everything was fine, there was no need for her to worry.

These assurances set Kate's mind at rest for a short time, but a few more weeks with no sign of further letters soon brought back all the old worries. It was early July before she received another letter from Ireland, this time from Mistress Delamere. While this brought the usual news of the various goings-on in the country, it also confirmed what Dominic had said, mentioning that he had gone to Arklow but that was the last they had heard. Not unnaturally, this did little for Kate's peace of mind. Through July and August, her attention was diverted by the harvest, but after that spell of excitement life at the Hall slowed to a more languid pace. Towards the end of the month, a long spell of weather broke and the countryside was battered by fierce thunderstorms and torrential rain. Late one evening at the height of the storms, Kate was preparing to go to bed when she was disturbed by a tremendous banging at the front door, followed by the noise of Mrs Arrowsmith going to find out what was happening and the sound of loud voices.

In her worried state of mind, she had to find out what the commotion was. Throwing a dressing gown around her shoulders, she dashed to the end of the gallery, to be confronted by the sight of her housekeeper remonstrating with a stranger in the hallway. Even from some distance away Kate could see it was a young girl who must have been out in the storm for some time, as she was soaked to the skin.

'Mrs Arrowsmith,' Kate spoke firmly as she surveyed

the scene. 'Who is this and what is going on?'

'I'm not sure, Mistress Tilbrook,' the housekeeper replied, uncertainly. 'This girl has just arrived at the door and seems to be almost hysterical. I can't get any sense out of her.'

'Oh, the Saints be thanked, if you're Mistress Tilbrook, then I've come to the right place,' the girl exclaimed, before anyone else could utter another word.

Kate had to smile. As soon as she had opened her mouth, the girl's words had placed her background. She was Irish and no mistake. Then the alarm bells began to ring in her head. Irish, and she was over here in Essex – something had happened to Dominic. Reaching the bottom of the stairs, Kate could see that the girl was older than she first thought, about twenty years of age perhaps. Except for her large brown eyes, she was not unlike Roisin O'Byrne in her younger days. But she had to find out why she was looking for Mistress Tilbrook.

'Just calm down,' Kate spoke gently. 'Tell me your name and where you're from, and why you want to see me.'

But the girl was still in a state of high excitement. 'Oh, Mistress Tilbrook, I've been walking these last three days, trying to find this house, until I thought I was completely lost and I would have to throw myself on the mercy of a passing stranger.'

Kate forced a smile. 'Well, you're here now. Just start at the beginning and tell me who you are.'

The girl lowered her eyes as she appeared to calm down somewhat. In fact, she seemed to taking a few deep breaths, Kate noticed, something she always tended to do herself in times of stress.

'Begging your pardon, madam, I'm sorry to have disturbed you at this late hour. My name is Rachel Miranda, and I'm from County Wicklow in Ireland.'

With the mention of Wicklow, the alarm bells were now ringing louder than ever. 'You've come here to tell me something about my son, I'll warrant. Have you met him? His name is Dominic. Is he still all right? Has anything happened to him?'

'Yes I've met him,' the girl whispered. 'And yes, he was well enough, the last time I saw him.'

In her anxiety to find out more, Kate stepped closer to the girl and grasped her by the arm. It was only then she realised that the girl's teeth were chattering and she was trembling all over, from cold and fright and the effort of her journey. Kate turned immediately to her housekeeper.

'Mrs Arrowsmith, would you start filling a hot bath for this girl. We need to get her warmed up. She's about my size so I'll get her out of these wet clothes and into something dry.'

Upstairs, after she had dried herself and changed into another of Kate's dressing gowns, the girl tried to tell her story. 'Three days ago I got to London,' she began, 'but I had no money left and I was not sure where your house was or how far, and I started walking and it has taken me all that time and then it started raining and my shoes are worn through—'

'Just a moment, Rachel,' Kate interrupted, trying to control her impatience. 'You're starting at the end and working your way back. I know that's the normal Irish thing to do but it would be much easier to understand if you started at the beginning.'

Swallowing hard from the glass of brandy that Kate had given her, the girl took a deep breath and began speaking again, this time choosing her words more carefully.

'I'm sorry, I'm just relieved at getting here. But sure, you want me to start at the beginning. Two months ago I was working at the inn at Laragh. It's a little village near Glendalough in County Wicklow. Do you know where I'm talking about?'

'Yes, I know it well,' Kate replied with a wistful smile, as she thought of the moment in time she had spent there with Edward. 'Yes, it's a place I'll always remember, but go on.'

'Early one evening a young gentleman walked in and we got to talking, as I recall. He was asking about a Declan Brennan or James Lavelle and if anyone knew their whereabouts. I was really taken by him and when he told me he wanted to visit Glendalough, he didn't find it difficult to persuade me to take him there. I'm from Roundwood way and I know that part of the world well. My teacher told me all about the history.'

'Roundwood, you say.' Kate thought for a moment. 'My brother's wife comes from a big family in those parts, by the name of O'Byrne. Would you know any of them at all?'

'For sure, Mistress Tilbrook, that's one of the reasons why I'm here. Roisin is a cousin of my mother, God rest her, so I think that makes me a distant relation of some kind. One of her sisters taught me and my two brothers.'

'Well, that's a fine coincidence. And you say your name is Miranda. Forgive me for saying this, but that doesn't sound very Irish to me.'

This time it was Rachel's turn to smile. 'There's a few by that name, especially in Galway, for sure. Mi padre es español.'

The girl laughed at the baffled expression on Kate's face. 'My father is Spanish. Well, not really, he was a Creole, from a Spanish family but born in New Granada near Caracas in Venezuela. He was on a ship coming back from the Americas and they lost their way in a storm. Then they were fired upon by a British warship and forced into Galway Bay, where the ship sank. Most of the people on board eventually went on to Spain, but some stayed on, and my father was one of them.'

Before she could continue, Kate interrupted her. 'Miranda you call yourself, from Caracas? But my husband knew a man called Francisco Miranda. He came here to England from Caracas about ten years ago to try to convince the government to help them overthrow the Spanish. But it was too soon after the French revolution and the English didn't want to get involved.'

She thought again for a moment. 'And then he tried again in seventeen ninety-eight, when my husband was involved in looking at all the details of his plan. But by that time the English were at war with the French and were concerned about the uprising in Ireland. So they certainly didn't want to get into another war with the Spanish. Was he any relation to your father?'

Rachel brandished her glass in the air in front of her. 'Francisco Miranda is a famous soldier and a gentleman. And he is a cousin of my father. One day he'll be successful and his country will be free of the Spanish. Free, in the same way that Ireland will be free of the English.'

Kate stepped back slightly at this unexpected show of emotion. As if there were not sufficient things to think about without dragging in the Spanish and the Americas.

'I believe you Rachel, and we can talk about that some other time. But more importantly, please tell me about Dominic.'

Sheepishly, the girl took a sip of brandy before replying.

'This young gentleman ended up staying at the inn for near on a week, and then he went down to Arklow for a short time. Whatever he found out down there, it was probably from Roisin, and then he came back up to Laragh. But this time he wanted to find a way up to Lughnaquilla from Saint Kevin's Church. I should have told him it was impossible, but he has a way with words and I think he turned my head.'

She looked up at Kate, shaking her head. 'And I knew next to nothing about him. All he had told me was his mother was Irish from County Wicklow and that he was looking for his uncle. I believed him, but others didn't, and were suspicious of him asking questions. Some even took him to be an English spy, trying to find a way to where Michael Dwyer is hidden with his people.'

'But did you know at this time that he was my son?' Kate demanded.

'I only knew what he had told me,' the girl insisted, 'but he didn't mention this house or the estate; I knew nothing of that. And I didn't recognise your name, that meant nothing to me. It was only later when I went to see Roisin Brennan that I found out about any of this. But as I was saying, he wanted to go up to Lughnaquilla because he thought the men he was looking for might be in that area. And so he persuaded me again to take him there.' The girl stopped, uncertainty written large in her expression.

'I understand you so far,' Kate tried to encourage her. 'You showed him the path up over the hill. So what happened to him?'

'I'm sorry to have to tell you this, Mistress Tilbrook,' she blurted out, 'but he's been taken as a hostage by Dwyer and his people. I tried to tell them why we had come but they wouldn't listen, and all the time Dominic insisted that I meant nothing to him, and that he had paid me to guide him there. They had heard about him asking around for your brother and they were convinced that he was an English spy. And then he tried to get away and there was a big fight and your son got a bang on the head. He's recovering and he'll be fine, but I know he's acting as if it's much worse than it is.'

This was what she had feared most. Why had he not listened to her? She had told him not to go anywhere near Glenmalure or Lughnaquilla. Why had she not been much clearer about the dangers he might face? Why had she not been more strict with him?

Kate ran her hands through her hair. 'So he's well enough, you say. But he's a hostage. What are they holding him for, what are they expecting in exchange? A ransom of some kind?'

The girl held her head in her hands, sobbing quietly. 'I don't know, Mistress Tilbrook. I don't think they do either. I heard them talking and I think they may want to exchange him for a safe passage to America.'

Although Kate was dreading asking the question, she had to know. 'And what if nobody will trade with them?'

'Mistress Tilbrook, you must do something,' the girl beseeched her. 'You're the only person who can convince these people to give up your son. They don't have much food and they're being harassed constantly by the militia and the English soldiers. The last thing they need is a prisoner to slow them down. Please, for God's sake, if no one deals with them perhaps they'll kill him – especially if he tries to escape again.'

Unable to catch Kate's eye, the girl looked away. 'I pleaded with them but they took no notice of me. After that I went down to Arklow to see if I could find your brother, but they think he's in France trying to enlist support there. When I spoke to Roisin, she told me that Declan should have returned from France by now and she's not sure where she is. And then she told me about you. When I was there she was sick and couldn't do much, but we managed to get some money together that Declan had left and I came here as fast as I could.'

This time she looked up at Kate, reaching out for her hand, her voice pleading. 'Roisin has sent a message to your Mistress Delamere, to let her know what's happening. I couldn't think of anything else to do except come here. Please Mistress Tilbrook, you must come back with me to Ireland and save your son.'

Kate could barely look at the girl and the expression of despair on her face. Instead she paced up and down the floor, thinking furiously. What could she do, a woman who had been living in England for over twenty years? She could not just go to Ireland at the drop of a hat. What about the children, who would look after them? What would they do if their mother was away for several weeks? What would become of them if something awful happened to her? Who could she call upon to help her? Almost everyone she knew was English or someone that Dwyer and his United Irishmen would see as being part of the establishment. Declan was the only person they would listen to, and perhaps James Lavelle. And how could she go back to Ireland? Everything she remembered would have changed in that time. And then there was the vow. Her father was still there, still living, so the vow was still binding. How could she go back on that? But what was going to happen to her son in the meantime?

She could see the girl watching her, pleading for an answer that would make everything turn out right.

'Rachel,' her voice was hesitant, 'I can hardly bring myself to think about my son being held by these people. But what can I do? I can't think of anyone else who could help, and you've tried already, so what other options do I have?'

'Mistress Tilbrook,' the girl insisted fiercely, 'When I went to Roisin Brennan, she told me all about what you were like when you were younger. She said you would find a way, that you would come yourself and talk to Dwyer and his people and convince them to release your son.'

In exasperation, Kate threw her hands up into the air. 'How am I supposed to do that!' she shouted. 'I have three children to look after here. And more than that I made a vow over twenty years ago that I would not set foot again in Ireland. How can I break that vow?'

Her eyes flashing, Rachel stood up, her hands clenched into fists. 'Tell me this, Mistress Tilbrook, sitting here in your big comfortable estate in England.

Do you love this son of yours?'

'Of course I do,' Kate spat out, tossing her head indignantly. 'What sort of a stupid question is that?'

But the girl would not be deflected. 'So you've made a holy vow before God. What's the worst that can happen to you if you break that vow? That you will rot in hell for the rest of your supernatural life? Well, is that not worth it to save your own son?'

Abruptly, Kate sat down, bursting into tears. Of course it was worth it, of course the girl was right. She had to do something, anything. Her only other option was to stay in Essex and worry continuously for God knows how long. No, she would go; and the girls would be all right. There were more than enough people at the Hall to look after them for a few weeks. But what if something happened to her and they were left without a mother and a father? Instantly, she dismissed that thought; she had to think positively. She had to get to Ireland before anything else happened to Dominic, find Dwyer and persuade him somehow or other to free her son, just as Rachel had said.

By this time, the girl had calmed down a little, although she still had an expectant look on her face. Impulsively, Kate went over and took her hand. She seemed to resemble Roisin more than ever now, with her fierce expression and flashing eyes.

'Rachel, I'm sorry to have argued so much. You're right. I have to do whatever I can, and thank you for coming all this way and making such a journey to find me. I'll not forget that. You go and have your bath now, Mrs Arrowsmith will have it ready. Tomorrow we'll go up to London and make arrangements to travel to

Dublin. I'll need to tell my girls where I'm going, and write some letters and leave instructions for Mrs Arrowsmith for when I'm gone. I'm going to do all of that now. Sleep well and I'll see you at first light.'

Shortly after dawn the following morning, the two women set off for Cheapside to book their places on the mail coach north to Holyhead. Almost immediately they ran into a delay, discovering they would have to wait until the following day to get a seat. However, they decided to use the time to visit Connaught House.

Although Mistress Jardine's was delighted to see Kate for the first time in months, that soon turned to dismay when she learned of Dominic's predicament. The Tilbrooks and Jardines had often visited each other over the years and Mistress Jardine had admired the way Dominic was developing into a fine young man. As Rachel went back through her story, some mad impulse seemed to overtake her. Before anyone could protest, she decided she was coming as well.

'What, over to Ireland, and into the Wicklow mountains?' was Kate's astonished question when the Mistress made her announcement that she was intending to accompany them.

'Well, perhaps not quite as far as that,' the woman replied briskly, 'but certainly as far as my cousin's house in Enniskerry. I haven't been there for at least three years, so it's about time I went visiting. Also, you never know what support you might need over there, and if I can do anything to help that poor boy get out of his situation, then I will. And I know a number of people who might be able to help. I'm sure that Colonel Edwards is still in charge of the barracks in Bray, and that young lawyer Daniel O'Connell I met not long ago, who's making a name for himself here in London. He's the one who's been speaking up for the cause of the Catholic people in Ireland.'

But Kate was still not satisfied. 'Normally, Mistress Jardine, I'd be pleased to have the pleasure of your company and I'm grateful for your support, but Rachel and I are in a desperate hurry. We're taking the coach north tomorrow and I know how much baggage you like to take with you on every trip. Can you be ready in time?'

By now, the Mistress was indignant that anyone could doubt her determination to leave immediately.

'Kate Tilbrook, how could you say such a thing? Not only will I be ready at dawn tomorrow, but we'll travel in my own carriage. That means we'll get to Holyhead long before the mail coach, and we'll be able to get the best rooms on the boat. Now, how does that sound?'

'It does sound attractive,' Kate had to agree. 'I don't know why I didn't think of it myself. Till dawn tomorrow then.'

Just two days later, they arrived at Enniskerry. The journey had been a quiet affair. Mistress Jardine had tried to keep them in good spirits, but Kate and Rachel had generally kept to themselves with their own thoughts for company. As the coach drove the old familiar driveway and pulled to a halt outside the house, Mistress Delamere was the first person to come rushing outside to meet them. The shock of seeing Kate after so long, not to mention the sight of her cousin, appeared to overwhelm her at first, but the others had too much on their mind to spend time on greetings and hugs and kisses.

'Please tell me, have you heard anything?' Kate demanded, almost as soon as she managed to set foot on the ground. 'Has there been any news?'

But Mistress Delamere could not shed any further light on Dominic's fate. 'I've heard nothing, Kate. I've sent my man down to Kilcarra, and also to Bray and Wicklow, and even to your brother's wife in Arklow, but no one knows what has become of your son.'

As the coach driver unloaded the bags, the Mistress caught hold of Kate's arm. 'When I got the message that you were coming, I was going to send a man up to Laragh to find out if there was any news up there. But before I could do that, something else really dreadful happened.'

Dear God, Kate muttered to herself, what else had gone wrong that could be worse than her son's situation?

But the Mistress was continuing, her voice rising far beyond her normal calm tones into what was almost an hysterical scream. 'It's Mister Grattan, Kate, he's in terrible danger, they're going to kill him.'

Kate glanced over her shoulder at Rachel and Mistress Jardine, but they were equally baffled by the unexpected outburst.

'Mistress Delamere, calm yourself,' she snapped, in an instant reversing the roles they had been accustomed to for over twenty-five years. 'You're not making any sense. What's the problem and who's trying to kill him?'

Visibly shaking, the woman forced herself to speak slowly and intelligibly. 'Mister Grattan and his family live in a house not far from here. Ever since the uprising, we've had these bands of militia men roaming around, almost a law unto themselves. Once before, they threatened Mister Grattan and accused him of supporting the United Irishmen and of being a rebel, as they put it. But he stood up to them with his pistols and sent them packing. But this time he's a sick man and he can't defend himself or his family, and I'm afraid that some madman will try to be a hero and kill him.'

Her fingers clutched at Kate's arm even more fiercely. 'We must do something to try and save him.'

Kate looked blankly at the woman's face, her role model, the person she remembered as being in control of every situation. What was she suggesting? That somehow two middle-aged women should confront a group of restless, undisciplined and probably well-armed thugs, masquerading as some kind of peacekeeping militia? For the last two days all she had been thinking about was how to persuade Dwyer and his United Irishmen to give up her son, if she could ever find them. Now Mistress Delamere was expecting her to come up with a completely different argument which would convince a militia group opposed to the rebels. Had the woman completely lost her reason?

Frustrated by this turn of events, she shook her head. Why did everything always happen at the same time? If she went to Mister Grattan's house, she would lose time that could be better spent trying to find Dominic. But if she did not attempt to do something, she would run the risk of alienating Mistress Delamere. She could hardly ignore Mister Grattan's plight, not after the time they had spent together, the encouragement he had given her, and after everything he had achieved for so many people.

Out of the corner of her eye, she could see Rachel watching her, afraid to say a word, pleading silently not to be diverted, not to waste any more time. Equally, she could see Mistress Delamere, an anguished look on her face, racked with worry about both Dominic and Mister Grattan. Expecting the worst, she turned to Mistress Jardine, but thank God she had already moved into action, waving at the footman who was hovering nearby.

'Mr O'Brien,' she could hear her saying, 'get these bags off the coach if you please, and into the house. Kate, we can't achieve any more at this late hour, so we need a good night's rest and then we can decide on our course of action first thing tomorrow morning. Right everybody, into the house. After that abominable journey, we need a drink to wet our throats.'

Secretly, Kate smiled to herself. Thank God Mistress Jardine had come after all. There would be no shilly-shallying allowed while she was around. Decisions would be taken and that would be that.

Over breakfast next morning, she felt in a much more positive mood. Perhaps she had been wavering slightly the day before, but that had been in the face of yet another seemingly intractable setback. However, she had been tired and irritable after the journey. Now, she felt refreshed after her first night in Ireland for a long time. Yes, she was back in Wicklow. Breaking her vow had not caused her to be struck down by a thunderbolt – at least not yet. But God could deal with that. At that moment, she had more to worry about than incurring the wrath of Himself up above.

'Rachel, you go off this morning to Laragh and find out if there's any word. I'm sure that Mr O'Brien's son can take you. When you get there, pick up as much information as you can, but stay there until I join you. I must go over to Mister Grattan's house to see if there's anything I can do to help.'

Immediately, she could see the disappointed look on the girl's face. 'Please don't be too despondent, Rachel, it won't delay me for more than a day or two.'

Turning to the other women, she tried not to sound as if she was issuing orders. 'Mistress Delamere, you're going to have to come with me. I don't know Grattan's house or where the different parties are located.'

The woman gritted her teeth. 'Yes, I'm ready. Do you think we should take my husband's pistols with us?'

Despite the seriousness of the situation, Kate could not stop herself from laughing. 'What, are we going to do battle with them? I don't know about you, but I barely know one end of a pistol from another.'

With a heavy sigh, the Mistress had to admit she was somewhat short of experience with these weapons also. 'But how else are we going to get them to leave, Kate?' Her voice was plaintive. 'Force is the only argument these people listen to.'

Trying not to give too much away by her expression, Kate frowned slightly. 'I hope you're not right, Mistress Delamere, otherwise we'll have had a wasted journey.'

By now the Mistress had a puzzled look. 'If we can't use force, what are you going to say to them?'

Shrugging helplessly, Kate turned her head away. 'Who knows, Mistress Delamere, we'll have to think of something. All I know is that if you put your hand in the mouth of a mad dog, always make sure you withdraw it gently.'

Without waiting any longer, she got up from the table. They had to get going, or else they would spend all day discussing the situation, and end up convincing themselves there was no solution. As Rachel went off to get her bag, Mistress Jardine drained her cup of tea, stood up, brushed down her dress in a most businesslike manner, and looked Kate straight in the eye.

'I'm coming as well,' she declared. 'Don't start telling me it's not safe, or that I'm not involved. I know that, but it won't stop me. If you're going, so am I.'

There was no point in arguing, Kate decided, not with that look on her face.

An hour later they could see the house. Tigh na Hinch, Mistress Delamere said it was called. Originally, it had been an old inn by the river, but Mister Grattan had bought it and converted it into a comfortable family dwelling. It was a bright autumn morning, with the leaves on the trees just starting to turn a soft golden yellow. In the distance, they could hear the sounds of the river splashing against the rocks on the other side of the house. It was such a peaceful scene it was difficult to imagine that violence could erupt at any minute.

As the three women approached the house, a slovenly looking individual materialised out of the hedgerow beside them. He was wearing a grubby military-style coat and had a musket slung over his shoulder.

'Good morning, ladies,' he rasped, while they were still a few yards away. 'And what might you be after around here?'

Mistress Delamere was the first to respond. 'We've come from Enniskerry. I've a house near there and my husband is Richard Delamere of Stephen's Green in Dublin. We'd like to see Mister Grattan and his family.'

'Well now,' the militia man replied hoarsely. 'This

Mister Grattan of yours is in some trouble. He's been seen consorting with the rebels, that Wolfe Tone in particular. Some say he should be installed in Mountjoy prison rather than enjoying his comfort here in this house.'

Stepping forward, he tipped up the brim of his hat with the barrel of his musket and leered menacingly. 'There's even some who say he should be dancing at the end of a rope for the crime of treason, if you know what I mean.'

Heavens, it was even worse than Mistress Delamere had feared, Kate muttered to herself. They had to get into the house to see if Mister Grattan was well enough to defend himself. Taking a step forward, she spoke firmly to the sentry, trying to disguise her nervousness.

'Good morning to you, I'd like to speak to the officer in charge, if you would be so good.'

'Well now, madam, he's probably having his breakfast now, and would not thank me for disturbing him,' the militia man replied with a smirk.

Opening her bag, she pulled out a letter from Lord Cornwallis that she always carried, prominently displaying his seal, and stating that she could count on his support at any time.

'My good man,' she spoke quietly, 'as you can see from this letter, I'm sponsored by Lord Cornwallis, Commander-in-Chief of all of the forces in Ireland, including the militia. If he is given to understand that I've been obstructed from going about my business for no good reason, I know who'll be passing time in Mountjoy prison, and it won't be Henry Grattan.'

It was obvious that the soldier could not read very

well, but he fingered the seal reverently. While he considered what to do next, Kate fought hard to conceal her impatience. Every second that they spent with this gatekeeper was another delay in her getting to Dwyer and her son. They had to press on.

Somehow, she managed to flash her most devastating smile. 'Mister Grattan is a sick man, I believe, and for sure he can't escape. We've come merely to see how he's keeping. I'm certain you've nothing to fear from us, three women on our own.'

Eventually, the man seemed to make up his mind. Grinning eagerly, he made a half-hearted effort at a salute.

'For sure you're right, madam, and for someone from Lord Cornwallis I believe we can make an exception.'

Ten minutes later, after much undoing of bolts and barricades at the front door, the three women gained entrance to the Grattan household. It was the first time Kate had seen Grattan's wife since the dinner party at Enniskerry over twenty years previously. But she had aged well, still recognisable as the woman she had met that day, except that now she was visibly trembling with fear. As soon as she recognised her visitors, however, she rushed over and grasped Kate by the hand.

'Lady Tilbrook, I can't believe it's you. Thank God you've come. Every moment we're in terror of our lives. Either these men will break in or else they'll set fire to the house. We can't sleep for the worry and we've hardly any food left.'

'What about your husband?' Kate asked quietly, trying to keep the woman from getting too excited. 'I heard he was ill – how is he now? And have these people outside issued any specific threats?'

The unhappy woman could barely speak for stammering. 'Yes, yes, they are outside all day long, shouting for his head. And poor Henry's too ill to move a muscle.'

The situation did seem desperate – somebody was going to have to do something to avoid a confrontation, there seemed little doubt about that. Kate's mind raced. Gripping the woman's hand tightly, she tried to get her to concentrate.

'Think hard, please. How many men are out there?'

'I don't know for sure, Lady Tilbrook,' the woman wailed. 'Perhaps ten or twelve, maybe?'

Again, Kate thought fast. She had nothing to offer, except possibly a few words. If that were not enough, they might precipitate even more extreme actions by the militia men. But if they did nothing but wait, eventually the men's impatience would boil over and Mister Grattan's life would be seriously in jeopardy. Facing up to the facts, Kate made her decision. It was not going to be easy but she knew what she had to do.

'Right,' she announced firmly. 'I'm going outside to speak to these people.'

But before she could move, Mistress Delamere caught her arm, pulling her back. 'For God's sake, Kate, it's going to be dangerous out there. You've nothing to defend yourself with.'

Impatiently, Kate wrenched herself free. 'I'm only going out to speak to them. Standing here will get us nowhere and it's wasting precious time. I'm going to do what I can, and if it's not good enough at least I know I'll have done my best.'

Drawing herself up to her full height, the Mistress looked her directly in the eye. 'I'm not going to stand by while you go out there by yourself,' she declared firmly. 'If you're going, then so am I.'

Immediately, she linked her arm through Kate's to prevent her going by herself. At which point Mistress Jardine stepped forward, waving a clenched fist in their faces.

'And so am I,' she cried. 'We'll all go together.'

Through the window, Kate could see the militia men's camp in the orchard about fifty yards away. Some men were lounging around, clearly bored and awaiting developments. Taking a deep breath, she crossed her fingers and looked at her two companions. Her immediate reaction had been to persuade them to remain indoors. But one glance at their faces was enough. She was not going anywhere by herself.

'Right, ladies, whenever you're ready,' she declared. 'Let's go and find out what these men are made of.'

Glancing around apprehensively, they approached the camp. When they were no more than a few yards from the first tent, one man detached himself from the others and came forward to meet them. He looked as unkempt as the rest, but his voice was not as harsh as that of the soldier who had spoken to them earlier.

'Yes, ladies, what can I do for you?'

Immediately, Kate spoke up, trying to sound much more confident than she felt.

'My name is Lady Tilbrook, and I would like to speak to the officer in charge of this band of men.'

The man spoke again, quietly. 'That's me, Lady Tilbrook, why do you want to see me?'

Holding her head high, she forced herself to keep her voice firm. 'I've been married to Captain Edward Tilbrook for over twenty years,' she began. 'In that time I've learned how they do things in the army. And they certainly would not countenance skulking in a man's garden for days, issuing empty threats and generally disturbing the peace. The way that your platoon of men is behaving is an absolute disgrace.'

Out of the corner of her eye, she could see Mistress Jardine staring at her, a horror-struck expression on her face. But the man merely sighed and shrugged his shoulders.

'You're probably right, Lady Tilbrook, but they no longer listen to me. Most of them have nowhere else to go and this is almost an entertainment for them, although it could have a deadly serious outcome. I'm trying to prevent anything tragic happening, but I've very little influence left, I'm afraid. If only someone could offer them an alternative or give them some hope for the future, then perhaps they would lay down their arms.'

In reply, Kate smiled as sweetly as she could. 'And do you think you might be prepared to let me talk to them about this situation?'

The militia man shrugged his shoulders again. 'What harm can it do? But I tell you, Lady Tilbrook, they'll not be as pleasant-natured as me and you had better be prepared for some terrible abuse.'

A few minutes later, the officer had managed to gather the remnants of his troop together, but they were clearly a reluctant lot, many of them still lounging against nearby trees and openly smoking pipes. As he made his announcement that a woman wanted to speak to them, he was greeted by a chorus of whistles and catcalls. Kate was reminded of her first visit to the theatre in London, and how the actors had managed to cope with the unruly behaviour of the spectators. That was it, she muttered grimly to herself, it was going to take some acting to get a resolution here. And perhaps one of her mother's old stories might provide her with some inspiration.

Taking another deep breath, she stepped forward. For a moment she surveyed her audience, bellowing and brandishing their muskets.

'Just give me a moment,' she shouted at the top of her voice. 'I want to ask you men a few questions. First of all, are you Irishmen? Or are you subjects of the English?'

'We are Irish,' they bayed indignantly. 'But we are loyal to King George.'

'If you are really Irishmen,' Kate almost screamed, 'then you will know of the day when Fionn MacCumhail came to the great palace of Tara?' Some of the men answered and looked at one another.

Again she spoke, this time more quietly, trying to draw them in closer.

'And you will know of the terrible powers he used to smite down the evil son of Midna? And how he saved Tara and the Kingdom of Ireland from fire and destruction?'

'Yes, we know about Fionn,' some of the men admitted, muttering among themselves.

By this time, she knew she had their attention. 'Let me ask you something else,' she demanded. 'As military men, I'm sure you will all know the answer to this. Who are the three finest generals in your army today?'

For a moment they were nonplussed by her question

and the sudden change of subject. But thankfully she got part of the answer she was looking for.

'My Lord Cornwallis, madam, he is surely the finest,' shouted one man, with the others nodding in agreement.

'I know, I know,' another man spoke excitedly to his colleagues around him. 'Sir Arthur Wellesley, he has to be the finest general in the army.' Again the others nodded in recognition.

'And the third?' Kate asked them quietly. They all turned to look at each other but no one could think of a name.

'Let me give you a hint,' Kate said to them. 'Who led your forces against the rebels five years ago at Wexford, and then won a great battle at Vinegar hill, saving the country from a desperate revolution?'

'I know that,' one man stepped forward. 'I was with him at the time. It was Sir John Moore, madam.' The others chorused their agreement.

Kate chose her words carefully. 'And do you think that these men are loyal to King George?'

'Of course they are,' came the shouts. 'That's a ridiculous thing to say.'

'Well, let me ask you something else,' she screamed above the tumult, 'would you say that these men might be consorting with the rebels?'

One man stepped close to her and waved his pistol in her face. Beside her, she could sense Mistress Delamere flinching in fear.

'How can you make such an insulting statement?' he shouted. 'What do you know – you're nothing but a bloody woman. Those men are the greatest leaders and the finest generals in the British army.'

'I agree with you,' Kate replied, her voice as harsh as his. 'These men are the finest in your army and their allegiance to King George is without question.'

Without warning, she lowered her voice to a conspiratorial whisper. 'Yet not six months ago, all three of these men were at this house, discussing matters of the world with Mister Grattan, and Mistress Delamere here beside me.'

At this the men stopped and looked at one another, fierce expressions being replaced by baffled looks.

'How do we know this to be true?' one demanded.

Smiled pleasantly, Kate pressed home her advantage. 'I suggest that anyone who's concerned enough should go and ask Lord Cornwallis in person. He happens to be in Dublin this very week.'

As she spoke, she pulled the letter out of her handbag again. 'And should anyone doubt my acquaintance with that good Lord, I have a letter here addressed clearly to me, with his seal on the outside, plain enough for you all to see.'

Craning their necks, they tried to see the envelope that she was waving in her hand.

'But let me tell you this, my brave body of men,' she shouted again. 'The great powers that Fionn MacCumhail used to free Tara were as nothing compared to the vengeance of Cornwallis, which will surely be inflicted on those people who this day threatened an innocent man for no reason other than rumour and supposition. This, I promise you.'

As one man they fixed their eyes on her, their mouths open, suddenly speechless with fear. Carefully, she studied them one by one.

'Is that what you want?' She kept her voice low, but there was no answer, except a mumbling and a shuffling of feet.

'Is that what you want?' she screamed, at the top of her voice.

This time the officer stepped forward. 'No, Lady Tilbrook, nobody wants that. We would not offend Lord Cornwallis, for God's sake. If you insist, we'll move from here and leave Grattan in peace.'

Suddenly she was aware of the hoarseness of her voice, the perspiration trickling down her forehead, and her hands, trembling so much from tension that she had to grip the sides of her skirts to prevent her feelings becoming too obvious.

'Thank you, my good man,' she croaked weakly. 'That's all we can ask.'

'But, Lady Tilbrook, please listen to me,' the man begged. 'Despite what you probably think, these are willing men, but most of them have nowhere to go. Their farms, their work, their livelihoods have been taken away from them. What will they do now? Go begging for a crust on the streets of Dublin?'

Her voice still husky, Kate looked over the officer's shoulder at his men. 'I'm sure you're right,' she agreed. 'Some are sure to be good workers at heart. In fact I think I recognise one of them.'

Although she tried to get a closer look, most of them steadfastly refused to catch her eye. Suddenly, she remembered where she had seen one before.

'Michael Potter,' she cried, 'I believe it's you, is it not?'

The man shuffled his feet but he could not bring himself to raise his head. 'Yes, madam, it's me.'

Before replying, she walked over to where he was trying unsuccessfully to conceal himself. 'Michael Potter, I remember you at Mistress Delamere's garden party years and years ago. You were helping your father to mind the horses, as I recall.'

At last, the man smiled. 'You've a good memory, Lady Tilbrook. I remember you when you used to be called Kathleen Brennan and all the young lads were besotted by you. But you ignored us all. And I remember Mistress Delamere as well. That was a long time ago, Lady Tilbrook, a different world from today.'

'Not as different as you might think,' Kate laughed, turning to face the others. Now she was with them, rather than confronting them. 'And who is this here, skulking at the back? I think it might be Mattie Quinn, if my eyes don't deceive me, although it's difficult to tell under all that dirt.'

The man grinned at her. 'Yes it's me, Kathleen Brennan. I didn't think you would remember me, but I recognised you immediately. It's been a long time since Mister Hutchinson's class at the school, but you've barely changed at all.'

'It was a long time ago, Mattie,' she replied dryly. 'But now we have to think of the future.'

Abruptly, she turned and walked to the front, rejoining Mistress Delamere and Mistress Jardine who were still watching in amazement. Linking her arms with the two women, she began to speak. The group of men hung on every word.

'Personally, I can offer you little. But a man named Patrick Nolan from this village is now the overseer in a factory near Birmingham. He's always looking for men who are prepared to work, and he likes to employ some of his own. I can persuade him to take four or five of you, should you wish to go. It's not an easy life in England, but you can earn a living for yourself and your family.'

Thinking about her offer, the men began muttering amongst themselves. Before anyone could respond, Mistress Delamere stepped forward. 'And I'll take two men if they prove they can work, one for the gardens at Enniskerry, and one for the mill at Bray.'

At that Mistress Jardine put her hands on her hips and regarded her two companions coolly. 'I'm not going to be outdone here,' she murmured. Turning to the men, she raised her voice. 'Our business is in London. But if any man can work hard and prove himself, my husband will employ him or find work for him.'

With a sweep of her arm, Kate turned to the officer. 'There is your answer. Now it's up to you. I suggest that you move on from here to Bray and decide among yourselves if you wish to take up any of these offers. Potter here knows where Mistress Delamere lives. Once you've decided, let him come to Enniskerry and tell the Mistress.'

Pulling off his cap, the officer replied earnestly. 'I'm truly sorry about the troubles that have been caused here, Lady Tilbrook. And I can't thank you enough for the generous offers you three ladies have made. We'll be on our way now, but one of us will come to Enniskerry tomorrow as you suggest.'

Slowly, the three women walked back to the house. Again the bars and the bolts had to be drawn before the door could be opened. One by one they filed silently into the hallway and closed the door quietly behind them. At the entrance to the dining room, Kate stopped and looked around at the others.

'Someone tell me I'm not dreaming,' she whispered.

Mistress Jardine walked over to the window. 'It's not a dream, Kate, they're taking the tents down even now.'

For a moment they stood at the window, watching the activity on the other side of the garden. Suddenly they were whooping and cheering, hugging and kissing each other.

Henry Grattan's wife regarded them in astonishment. 'What's going on? What's happened out there?' she gasped.

With a triumphant shriek, Mistress Delamere thrust her fist into the air. 'It's all over, don't you see?' she shouted 'The men are leaving, they're packing up now. Lady Tilbrook here was wonderful, the way she spoke to them.' Turning to Kate, she shook both her hands. 'But what was all that business about the army generals meeting here with Grattan? Was that true?'

Kate put her finger to her lips. 'Of course not. But they weren't to know – and I had to make up something to impress them.'

As she was speaking, Grattan's wife peered through the window to see for herself what was happening. 'You're right,' she exclaimed, 'they are going. I would never have believed it. Lady Tilbrook, I don't know how we'll be able to thank you enough for today. It must have been so difficult for you to come here, with your son missing, and you wanting to find him. I don't know how you did it, but what you've achieved here is beyond words.'

Blushing furiously, Kate shook her head from side to

side. If only they knew how terrified she had been, they would not be speaking like this. She was just good at hiding it, that was all. For a few seconds, while the others were celebrating and searching for the brandy, she closed her eyes and offered up a silent prayer of thanks. Maybe God was watching out for her after all. Perhaps, just perhaps he would be looking after Dominic as well.

Suddenly, she remembered Mistress Delamere's words. She had almost forgotten her son for an hour or so, while they had been out in the garden facing up to the militia men. Immediately, she could feel the tension building up again in her chest. She had to get to Laragh to find out if anything had happened. Perhaps Mr O'Brien would have dropped off Rachel and returned by now. If she ran back to the house at Enniskerry, it might be possible to get up to the inn before darkness fell.

'I'm going to have to dash off now,' she muttered to the others. 'I want to ask O'Brien to bring me up to Laragh this evening if we've got time.'

Before she could move a muscle Mistress Jardine caught hold of her by the arm. 'You're not going anywhere this evening, Kathleen Brennan,' she declared. 'I know you must be desperately concerned about your son, but you've been through a lot today already. If you rush off somewhere else you'll be exhausted. I saw how you dealt with those men just now and it was absolutely marvellous. I can hardly believe that the shy little girl who came to stay at my house all those years ago could do something like that.'

Holding her arm even more fiercely, she looked Kate straight in the eye. 'But you may have to do something similar again, perhaps tomorrow or the next day, to free

Dominic. And you won't be able to manage that if you don't eat something substantial and get some rest. It will be dark in an hour or two, and even you won't be able to achieve anything significant tonight. We'll go back to Enniskerry this very minute, you can have a bath, then some dinner and a few drinks. Tomorrow you can set off for Laragh at first light, fully refreshed and ready to take on the world, if needs be.'

For a moment, Kate struggled before giving in. It was true enough, she did feel exhausted.

'Yes, Mistress Jardine,' she agreed meekly. 'As ever you are right. Tomorrow will be the best time to start. I'll stay in Enniskerry tonight.' Picking up her shawl, she wrapped it carefully around her shoulders. 'In which case,' she remarked as lightly as she could, 'I would be obliged if you would lead me back to this bath, and especially to those drinks I think you mentioned.'

Chapter 19

———— ·•·——

The next morning, Kate was up and about shortly after dawn. Despite the hour, O'Brien had been to Mister Grattan's house and come back to report that the band of militia had gone and that everything was calm.

This good news helped her to start the day on a positive note. Although neither Mistress Delamere nor her cousin had risen, she had decided to leave before either of them came downstairs. After the previous day's success, she was more than aware that the others might feel compelled to come with her to Laragh, if only to provide some moral support. But she did not want that. A pleasant trip by coach from Enniskerry up through Roundwood and on to Glendalough was one thing, but a two or three day hike through the boglands and into the fastness of Lughnaquilla was quite another. How long it would take to find Michael Dwyer was impossible to tell. They might have moved on since Rachel had last seen them. And there were English soldiers to contend with as well. They were everywhere, the girl had said. But at least they would be easy to pick out in their redcoats.

Rubbing the sleep out of her eyes, she peered out at the early morning sky. It looked like it was going to start off a clear day, but the threat of rain was in the air. At some point, she was sure to get wet, but she had come prepared. Dominic's old riding clothes, last worn ten years previously, made the perfect outfit. Wearing a smaller version of what had once been Edward's favourites – black breeches, a thick black jacket with a heavy silk shirt underneath, sturdy leather boots and gloves, and a three-cornered hat to top it all off, she was ready for the mountains. Although this ensemble had received some decidedly odd looks from the cook, it was definitely much more suitable for the wild country ahead than any long skirts and parasol.

Again she looked out of the window. It really was time to go. The coach was outside, ready and waiting. Draining the last of her tea, she turned towards the front door. All of a sudden, Mistress Delamere came flying down the stairs, still in her dressing gown. Kate could see her trying to recognise the unfamiliar figure in the hallway.

'Lady Tilbrook,' she muttered doubtfully. 'Is that you?'

'Yes, it's me,' Kate smiled thinly. 'I'm off to Laragh to find Rachel. Then I hope it's Dominic next.'

'You look so different, dressed like that. But it's probably for the best. Do you want me to come with you?

Shaking her head, Kate opened the door. 'Thank you for that kind offer, but the answer is no. You've too much to do here. You must enquire after Mister Grattan's health, and you need to be here to meet these militia men should any of them turn up to see you. God willing, Rachel and I should be back within five or six days. But if we have not returned to Laragh within two weeks, then by all means come and find us. Please tell your cousin where I've gone, tell her not to worry, and that we'll all be celebrating in a very short time.'

Before she could get into the coach, the other woman reached forward and embraced her tightly. 'Go with God, Kate,' she whispered, 'and take the luck of the Irish with you.'

As the coach drew closer to Laragh, Kate found herself becoming more and more apprehensive. If only she had left Enniskerry when Rachel had suggested. Now they had lost almost forty-eight hours. What if something awful had happened in that time? Without doubt, the previous evening had been an occasion of quiet triumph after the stress of dealing with the militia men. But now, in the cold light of day, events had taken on a different perspective. All that time she had expended trying to get those soldiers to move on might have been better spent trying to find her son. Crossing her fingers, she prayed fervently that he was still alive, and moreover, that Rachel would be able to find him.

As they reached the crossroads in the village, young O'Brien squinted up at the sky and spat on his hands.

'I don't like the look of those clouds, Lady Tilbrook. It's pleasant enough now, but there's a lot of weather in a Wicklow day. I think we might see a storm later. It'll be cold and wet where you're going. You're dressed for it, madam, but I'd make sure your companion is well wrapped up as well.'

Trying to allay her fears, Kate examined the sky herself. Since it invariably rained around these parts, O'Brien's forecast did not signal any particular local insight. But the weather was the least of her worries. Her main concern was Rachel's whereabouts and the latest news, if any.

But she did not have long to be concerned. As the carriage pulled up outside the inn, Rachel came running out to meet her.

'Mistress Tilbrook, thank God you're here,' she shouted, her voice strained. 'I didn't recognise you at first dressed like that. I've been waiting here for so long, I was beginning to think you weren't coming.'

Although she scarcely felt like it, Kate laughed, more to ease the girl's tension than anything else. 'I've come prepared for the mountains,' she declared. 'But first, tell me, is there any news?'

The girl's face was crestfallen. 'I've heard nothing new at all about Dominic. And the talk about Dwyer is not good. The English soldiers are here in strength and they're getting closer to the place where the men are hiding.'

While O'Brien was getting her bag down off the coach, Kate mulled over her words. 'That's doesn't sound good. It could mean that the English will find them and kill them all or take them as prisoners. And they might not recognise that Dominic is a hostage. Or it could mean that Dwyer will be forced soon to trade Dominic for their free passage.'

Making her mind up, she looked at the girl. 'Whatever way, I think we have to move as quickly as possible.

Have you heard anything more about my brother?'

'Yes, I have, Mistress Tilbrook,' Rachel replied eagerly. 'He's arrived back in Arklow, and apparently he's going to try and get up to Dwyer's place as well. Should we wait for him to get here?'

It was a tempting thought. If Declan arrived, perhaps accompanied by some of his people, maybe even James Lavelle, there would be some protection in numbers, and he would probably know the most direct route. But who could say how long it would be before they got there? And although it was more than likely that they would come through Laragh, she could not be sure of that. No, she could not wait any longer. She had to go now, and if it had to be the two of them, then so be it.

'We can't wait for my brother,' she announced, keeping her voice crisp as she could to make sure the girl would not see her doubts. 'We must leave now. When can you be ready?'

'I'm ready to leave whenever you are, Lady Tilbrook,' the girl replied immediately.

Kate contemplated the girl's bare head, long skirts and worn and scuffed shoes. 'Have you nothing better to wear?' she enquired. 'It's going to be wet up there.'

But the girl could only shake her head in reply. 'I've brought a shawl for the cold, madam, but nothing else. But I've been up there before and I managed to survive then.'

'Well, you're still young,' Kate replied dryly, 'so I suppose you can cope with it. At least we'll be travelling light.'

Picking up her bag, she slung it over her shoulder and looked up the valley. 'Right, let's go. And Rachel, please

stop calling me madam and Lady Tilbrook. My name is
Kate, just call me that if you would.'

Rachel thought about that for a moment. 'All right,
Mistress Tilbrook, I mean Kate, but perhaps not when
others are with us.'

Reaching the top of the hill above Glendalough
involved a long walk followed by a tough scramble
through difficult countryside. On another day and
another occasion, Kate would have lingered at the top of
the ridge to admire the glorious views across the
countryside, all the way down to the sea. But she had too
much on her mind to stop for long, They had to get as far
as they could before nightfall.

However, she soon realised that climbing up the hill
was quite an effort. 'Rachel,' she puffed as they reached
an outcrop overlooking the adjoining valley of
Glenmalure, 'how far do we have to go from here?'

Motioning with her arm, the girl stopped in front.
'Down there to the left, Kate, away in the distance.
That's where the Englishmen have set up their barracks.
They've also built a new road that goes up to
Aghavannagh over the other side of the valley from here,
and on this side goes all the way over to Glencree near
Enniskerry.'

Suddenly, she pointed at somewhere down below.
'Look there, Kate, right down at the bottom of the valley.
Can you see those redcoats of the soldiers between the
trees? They look like little dots from here.'

Squinting her eyes, Kate tried to pick them out. Then
she detected a slight movement. 'Yes, I can see them, but
what are they doing there?'

Her lips pursed, Rachel turned with an anguished

expression on her face. 'It's a tragedy we are witnessing. All the way from where they are there, almost down to the sea, that valley was once filled with trees that have been here for hundreds of years. But that meant cover for Dwyer and his people. So the redcoats are chopping down every tree all the way up the valley. Another few months and there won't be a single tree left.'

Looking fiercely at Kate, the girl clenched her hands into fists of rage. 'There's no limit to what these devils will do to this country. Once it was a beautiful place but when they're finished it will be like a desert.'

Although she sympathised, Kate decided she better change the subject of the conversation. Otherwise, they ran the risk of Rachel being diverted from their real task.

'Where do we go from here?' she demanded again, to get the girl's mind back to concentrating on what they were doing.

Dragging her gaze away from the tiny figures in the valley below, Rachel indicated towards the green mountains in the distance. 'First of all, Kate, we have to get below the skyline, so it will be more difficult to see us should anyone look up.'

Doing as she was told, Kate clambered down the side of the hill, this time stopping a few yards further on to wait for Rachel to catch up. Now she was becoming accustomed to the effort. And wearing the jacket and the breeches had been a grand idea, she muttered again to herself, as she scrabbled through the clumps of ferns and grassy hummocks. Her clothes were still dry and it was relatively easy to climb down the hill, but the girl was clearly finding the descent hard going. The lower edges of her skirts and petticoats were already soaking wet and tattered in places from snags on the bushes and thorny trees that were dotted around the hillside.

'Look up there, Kate, that's where we have to go,' Rachel gasped, pointing to the other side of the glen and up towards the dark mountain beyond, whose summit was already obscured by angry black clouds.

'What?' Kate exclaimed. 'Up to the top of Lughnaquilla?'

This time Rachel had to laugh. 'Not to the top. I don't think that even Michael Dwyer could survive up there for very long. No, we go over the shoulder of the mountain and into the glen on the other side. That's where we'll find them, I hope, near a small village which is close to the head of the valley. It's a long walk, Kate, and I hope our legs are up to it.'

Turning to the girl beside her, Kate smiled grimly. 'I hope so too. But standing here won't get us there. Let's keep moving now so we can give ourselves the target of being there tomorrow.'

By early afternoon the following day they had almost reached the place Rachel had described. Both women were tired after a poor night's sleep in an old deserted hut near the edge of the tree line. Kate was still going reasonably strongly, but Rachel was in a sorry state. Her clothes were wet through, she was cold and uncomfortable, and her shoes had split in several places. At some point she had scratched her ankles and feet and they were hurting her more and more. Although she had managed to tear some strips from her petticoats as makeshift bandages, she was limping badly and falling behind.

They were spurred on, however, by the distant sounds

of explosions and musket fire, which they assumed must be coming from some sort of conflict between Dwyer and the English soldiers trying to capture them. As they drew closer to the noise, without warning Kate lost the path she had been following and found herself balanced precariously at the top of a steep, rock-strewn hillside. Somehow or other, Rachel managed to catch up and took a grip of her arm to hold her back.

'Down there,' the girl hissed. 'Just behind those trees at the bottom of the hill, there's an old cottage. Where we are now is the place where one of Dwyer's men found your son and I when we came up here first. He was hiding among the rocks, watching over the house down below.'

For a few minutes, the girl scrutinised the area around them. 'It looks as if is no one is here today. Perhaps the noise of the muskets means the soldiers are very close and everybody's needed to fend them off.'

Kate wrenched her arm free. 'That means that we have to get there quickly, Rachel. If the soldiers get there before us, they may kill everybody. We have to keep going.'

With her heart in her mouth, she inspected the hillside below. It was terrifyingly steep, with loose stones and mosses everywhere. It would be a dangerous place to try and negotiate, for sure. With a grimace, she turned to the girl.

'How did you and Dominic get down here the last time with Dwyer's man? Is there a path down there?'

Shuddering slightly, Rachel pointed far to one side. 'No one could get down there in one piece. There is a path, but it goes the long way around. That's why they picked this place. They're safe from a direct attack from behind. Although the cottage is not far from here as the crow flies, following the path adds to the journey and it took us almost two hours to get down.'

'Two hours,' Kate cried in frustration. 'How could it take that long? If it takes us another two hours to get there, the English could have arrived and wiped out everyone.'

As if to support her words, a sudden rattle of musket fire echoed below them, no more than a mile from the cottage.

'Rachel, we have to get down this hill, whatever it takes – we'll lose too much time otherwise. Are you game for it?'

As if seeking inspiration, the girl gazed at Kate for a moment, before nodding her head weakly. 'You go first, Mistress Tilbrook. My feet are so painful I might not be able to keep up with you.'

Without waiting any longer, Kate set off at a reckless speed over the edge of the hill. Under her feet, loose pebbles bounced and tumbled crazily down the slope. Clutching desperately at the thorn bushes, she managed somehow to keep her balance. Above her she could hear Rachel gasping with pain. Not only were the girl's feet bleeding, but she had no gloves to protect herself, and the thorns were raking across her bare hands. Suddenly, the girl cried out in agony, as a barrage of stones hurtled past. Kate glanced round frantically, only to see that she had slipped and fallen, unable to get back to her feet.

'Rachel, are you all right?' she called urgently, her teeth clenched with the strain.

'Yes, Mistress Tilbrook.' The reply was barely audible

between muffled sobs. 'But I think I've twisted my ankle. I can't put any weight on it.'

'Sit there,' Kate whispered fiercely. 'I'll try and climb back up the hill and help you.'

Suddenly, another fusillade of musket shots rang out below them.

'Kate, please,' the girl cried. 'Don't wait for me. I'll be fine here for the moment. You get down to the cottage and find out what's going on.'

Torn between going back for the girl, and carrying on to see if her son was there, she hesitated for a few minutes. She had to make her mind up and it had to be now. Reluctantly, she decided she had to go on.

God must have been with her that day. She stumbled, fell, rolled over, got up, fell over again, but somehow she got to the bottom in one piece, with a hail of stones accompanying her. Thank God she had been wearing Dominic's old clothes, otherwise she would never have managed.

For a moment, she stood up at the bottom, trying to get her bearings. Behind her was the steep bank she had just come down. Now she was standing on a flat strip of land which appeared to jut out over a very deep valley. To her left the hillside was thickly wooded, with what appeared to be high bogland over to her right. Dusting herself down, she looked back up the hill for some sign of Rachel, but almost immediately another series of musket shots goaded her into action.

On the other side of the trees, the girl had said. Quickly, she dashed across the clearing, thrusting aside the low hanging branches that barred her way. Sure enough, over on her left, she could see the crumbling walls of a decrepit old building. Taking a deep breath, she stopped for a closer look. The walls appeared to be made out of mud and straw as much as stone, and at one end the roof had fallen in. That must have happened a long time ago, because she could see clearly an assortment of weeds and wild flowers growing out of the wall where the roof should have been. As she got closer, it became obvious that the windows were no more than rough-hewn gaps, with what appeared to be pieces of sacking stretched across to keep out the worst of the elements.

However, the cottage was certainly located in a commanding position, and it was obvious how difficult it would be to dislodge anyone who was determined to defend it.

By now she had reached the side of the building, tiptoeing through the shadows towards the nearest window. Nervously, she peered through the gap between the hessian and the wall, but it was so gloomy inside that she could hardly see a thing. As her eyes became accustomed to the darkness, it became obvious that she was looking into the part of the cottage where people had been sleeping. But at the moment the room was empty.

Silently, she crept along the back of the building until she reached the window at the other end. Again, she had to wait until her eyes adjusted to the light, but this time she could distinguish one man standing on the other side of the room with his back to her, looking out of the doorway and down into the valley. On his right stood another man, leaning against the wall and looking in the same direction through a window.

Fearfully, her gaze swept slowly around the room.

Dear God! She had to clutch her chest to prevent herself being overwhelmed by a rush of emotion. Sitting on a rickety old chair beside a table was her son, his hands tied behind him. He was so close she could almost reach in and touch him. For a moment she nearly forgot herself and called out his name. In the same instant, she thought of signalling to catch his attention, but he was looking in the same direction as the other two men. Moving out of sight of the window, she leaned against the wall to recover her composure. What Rachel had said about his injuries appeared to be true, if the rough bandage around his head was any indication. But he appeared to be alert enough.

Now she was here, now she had found him, what was she going to do next? The only way she could get into the room would be to climb in through the window, and that would not be easy to do quietly as the bottom edge was some distance off the ground. The only other route was in through the door. Perhaps there was something she could do to divert the attention of the two men, but she could think of nothing that might create a distraction. Even if she did somehow manage to get them to leave the cottage, what would she do then? She did not know if Dominic could walk, and then there was Rachel to think of. She would certainly not be able to move quickly, which meant they would probably be captured again very easily.

No, there was simply one thing for it. Her only hope lay in Michael Dwyer being in the cottage and that she could convince him to release Dominic. That had to be her plan. Taking some deep breaths, she stood up, straightened her hat, and set off around the corner of the cottage towards the doorway. As she came out of the lee of the building, suddenly she felt the wind and the rain driving into her face. God almighty, she hoped that Rachel was all right up on that hill, and that she had managed to drag herself somewhere out of the worst of the elements. It would not be long before evening would set in, either. Rachel, it seemed, was going to be spending another night uncomfortable and sleepless, the poor girl.

By this time, she had reached the corner of the building where she could see the nearest man's head protruding out of the doorway. Quietly but firmly, she cleared her throat.

'Good afternoon, gentlemen,' she began, her voice low and harsh with tension.

'Jesus God!' the man shouted, rearing up, startled by her sudden appearance out of nowhere. The second man, who had not seen her, came running out of the house with a pikestaff in his hand to see what had given his companion such a fright.

'Don't move,' he screamed, ' or I'll smash this pike into your chest.'

'You can put that weapon down,' Kate stood her ground and spoke firmly. 'You've nothing to fear from me.' Taking off her hat, she tossed her head to let her hair fall loosely to her shoulders.

'I don't believe it,' the first man muttered. 'It's a woman, if my eyes don't deceive me.'

Staring at her as if she was an apparition, he gasped out, 'How did you get here? Are you real? Why are you dressed like that? Are you some spy sent by the English to distract us?'

His manner was so demented that Kate had to laugh.

'No, I'm real enough and I've nothing to do with the English soldiers down in the valley. I've just walked over the hill from Laragh with my companion, a girl by the name of Rachel Miranda.'

The man regarded her suspiciously. 'Don't be ridiculous. How could you do that? Two women by themselves, coming down that hill? It's not possible.'

Kate began to feel impatient with this conversation. Again she breathed deeply to calm herself. It was essential to keep her wits about her.

'How else could I have got here?' She tried to keep her voice as reasonable as possible. 'Desperate people can do desperate things. But my companion has hurt her ankle and can't get down. She's still on the hillside above this house.'

The second man peered at her. Shaking his head in amazement, he shrugged his shoulders and smiled.

'If you came down that hill it was a brave thing to do. But why did you do it, why have you come to this godforsaken part of the world? This is a wild place with wild men, not to mention the English soldiers snapping constantly at our heels. We've no time to be entertaining casual visitors.'

In reply, Kate pointed through the window. 'I've come here for the best of reasons, my good man. You've taken my son there as a hostage, and I want him back.'

Again, the man stared at her incredulously. 'But he's English,' he cried. 'How can he be your son? You're from Bray or Enniskerry or somewhere close from the way you speak.'

Kate could feel her impatience growing again but she fought hard to keep herself under control. 'What does it matter where I come from?' she snapped. 'It's a long story, but I assure you he is my son. His name is Dominic Tilbrook and he came here to Ireland to see the countryside where his mother lived when she was a child. He did not come here to be taken as a hostage by a band of desperate men.'

As she drew breath to launch another onslaught, the man stepped back, startled by the ferocity in her voice. Before he could reply, she pressed on. 'I understand that Michael Dwyer is here somewhere. If so, I'd like to speak to him to ensure there are no misunderstandings.'

Rubbing his chin thoughtfully, the man looked at Kate, then over at Dominic. 'Come into the house,' he murmured, 'let's see if your so-called son recognises you.'

The two men walked in through the door of the cottage with Kate following close behind. As soon as she crossed the threshold she looked over towards the table where Dominic was sitting.

'Mother!' he exclaimed. 'How did you get here? How on earth did you find me? And why in heaven's name are you dressed like that?'

The man who had done most of the talking spoke up again. 'At last, something seems to be true around here. It appears that you might be mother and son after all. So who exactly are you?' He directed his question at Kate.

Carefully, she put her hat down on the table. 'My name is Kathleen Tilbrook and this is my son Dominic. I live in England now but I was born and brought up in Kilcarra. Declan Brennan, who lives down in Arklow and who I'm sure you know of, he is my brother.'

Struggling against his bindings, Dominic tried to

interrupt her, but she put her hand out, bidding him to be quiet.

Pushing her hair back with one hand, she allowed her gaze to sweep around the room. 'But I would still like to speak to Michael Dwyer, before any mistakes are made here.'

The second man scrutinised her for a moment or two before replying. 'You've met the man you're seeking. My name is Dwyer. And what leads you to think we might be making a mistake?'

On the point of answering, she was rudely interrupted by the sound of loud voices outside the cottage. This time, to Kate's amazement, her brother appeared, followed closely by James Lavelle, as recognisable and as fresh-looking as ever, despite the fact that he had probably just walked more than twenty miles.

As he came through the door, Declan stopped so suddenly at the sight of Kate that Lavelle walked into his back and nearly knocked him over.

'Jesus,' he gasped as he recovered his balance, but still unable to believe his eyes. 'Kate, is it really you?'

'Yes, Declan,' Kate replied, smiling wryly. 'It's true, I'm real, I'm your sister, and I'm here. Do you remember me saying that once before, in London, a lifetime ago?'

'I do indeed and I'll never forget it,' he cried, rushing forward to take her in his arms.

For a moment, she held him tightly, trying to draw strength from his touch. But over his shoulder she could see Lavelle continuing to stare at her, his mouth still open in astonishment. Disengaging herself from her brother's embrace, she looked up at the Frenchman standing a few yards away.

Although more than twenty-two years had slipped past since she had left him behind in Arklow, he was still clearly the same James Lavelle. The hair was shorter, lighter in colour, flecked with grey, and the laughter lines were etched more deeply into his face, but there was no doubting it was the same man.

'Hello, James,' she said quietly. For a moment she was convinved that this time, surely he would be too taken aback to be his normal self. But no, within seconds he had recovered his poise, bowed as theatrically as ever, took her hand and kissed it.

'Madame Tilbrook,' he intoned, as if he had been in discussions with her only the previous week instead of so long ago. 'How nice it is to see you again. And how ravishing you look in those clothes.'

The man Dwyer stood back from these pleasantries, an amused expression on his face. 'That looks like something else is settled,' he declared. 'You are who you say you are, and this is indeed your brother. And clearly you know our Frenchman here.'

Suddenly, Kate remembered Rachel. She was still somewhere up on the side of the hill – they could not leave her there all night. Immediately she put out her hand to interrupt Dwyer and turned to her brother.

'Declan, I'm sorry to break in here, but Rachel Miranda is lying injured up on the hill just above this house. She was the one who showed me the way here but she's twisted her ankle and can't walk.'

Forgetting Dwyer and his companion for a moment, she pulled at the sleeve of his jacket. 'It will be dark in a few hours and we can't let her lie there all night, or she'll catch her death from the cold. Come with me, please, and you too, James, we have to fetch her down.'

Before anyone else could move or say a word, she picked up her hat and rushed out of the door. Immediately, Declan and Lavelle ran after her with the other man following close behind. Over his shoulder her brother shouted his apologies to Dwyer, who by this time had been left standing by himself in the middle of the room, looking nonplussed by the sudden frantic activity.

The hill that Kate had scrambled down in only a few minutes took over an hour to climb up. Somehow or other they managed to find the girl, and as gently as they could, manhandled her down the slope. But by the time they reached the bottom it was so dark that some oil lamps had to be pressed into service to enable them to see.

Eventually they got the girl into the cottage. As they carried her in and tried to make her comfortable on a makeshift bed, Dominic, appalled to see her in a such a state, began shouting frantically at Dwyer to cut his bindings so that he could go to her.

But the Irishman was not someone to be rushed. 'Just you calm down there, young man, Dominic Tilbrook or whatever you're called. The girl is not as bad as she looks and your mother can attend to her if needs be.'

As some sort of gesture he took his pistol out of his belt, cocked it and placed it on the table. Sitting down on an old stool next to Kate, he looked at the gun and then at Dominic.

'Nothing I've heard here today changes the fact that you're an Englishman, the son of a well-known English soldier, and a person of great value to us.'

Kate opened her mouth in a cold fury, on the point of

hurling abuse at the man, when some inner sense told her to keep quiet, just for a moment. Somehow or other she managed to cover her rage by turning it into a coughing fit.

On the other hand, Declan spoke up immediately, his voice harsh with emotion. 'Don't be ridiculous, Michael. You're talking her about my sister and her son. He's part of an Irish family, for God's sake—'

Without warning, he was interrupted by the other man, whom Kate had learned was called Cummings, who jumped up and pointed at Dominic. 'Are we indeed?' he shouted. 'I hear tell that this woman here has abandoned her family and won't speak to her father. And she's given up her faith as well and married an Englishman in a Protestant church.'

Dwyer sat back in his chair, his eyebrows raised. 'You've always been a great support to us in our struggle, Declan, but you must admit that this doesn't sound like someone who is part of an Irish family.'

With these words, Kate was transported instantly back to the cemetery in Kilcarra, the day after her mother had been buried, listening to the priest ranting at her without any knowledge of what had happened, except through listening to idle gossip and hearsay. And now this man beside her was speaking the same way. All over again, she could feel the same burning rage inside her. Clenching and unclenching her fists, she tried to concentrate on what Dwyer was saying, but it was becoming more and more difficult to think clearly. In vain, she looked for support from the other side of the table, but Declan seemed to have slumped into silence after his initial outburst.

As the red mist descended across her vision, she realised that Cummings had started speaking again, and she tried desperately to listen.

'If we have an Englishman as a hostage, the son of an army officer who was a friend of Lord Cornwallis and well-known in London, he will without doubt be someone the English will want to rescue, and we'll have a powerful negotiating position. Declan, despite your sister being here, and this man being your nephew, this is a fight to the death. I say we keep the Englishman and barter with him, just as we planned. What do you think, Michael?'

Uncertainly, Kate looked at her brother shifting uncomfortably in his seat but saying nothing. For a moment she willed him to get up and shout and scream and smash the man to the ground, but all he did was sit there with his head bowed. Even Lavelle had nothing to say, his expression suggesting that this was entirely a matter for the Irish, and nothing whatsoever to do with a Frenchman.

By now, her jaws were clamped together with tension as she tried to restrain herself, but it was impossible to take it any longer. With a tremendous thump, she crashed her hands down on the table, making the candle holders rattle.

'Why is it,' she forced out through gritted teeth, 'that whenever I come to this country I have to be confronted with people who are rooted in the bog and who have not the slightest vestige of foresight or common sense?'

Standing up abruptly, she pointed angrily at the man sitting beside her at the table. 'You, yes, you, who calls yourself Michael Dwyer. I had heard of you before I came here. Some people told me you were a hero and a man of vision.'

With a derisive sneer, she turned and spat on the floor. 'All I can ask is, do you have any sense at all? Or do you prefer to listen to the chatter of fools and village idiots?'

At this, Cummings reared up and tried to interrupt, but Dwyer motioned to him to sit down on the floor and listen. Flicking her fingers dismissively at the man across the table, she looked directly at Dwyer. 'Is this the kind of person that you listen to? Someone who opens his mouth and says the first thing that comes into his head? Who carries nothing but gossip, tittle-tattle and lies?'

Out of the corner of his eye, she noticed that Declan had sat up in his chair and was watching her intently. Even Dominic had forgotten his concern for Rachel for a moment and was staring at her, his eyes open in wonder. Only James Lavelle stood back unconcerned, leaning against the wall, a slightly amused expression on his face. Despite her rage, Kate almost smiled to herself. This was not new to him, this was not the first time he had seen Kathleen Brennan stand up and lecture people, whether they wanted it or not.

Tearing her gaze away she forced her mind back to what she had been saying.

'This man here, who you listen to. Do you think he knows anything? Perhaps that's why you and what remains of your gallant band of heroes are cooped up in this hut in the back of beyond, and probably about to die a most unpleasant death.'

Again she glanced briefly at Cummings and curled her lip contemptuously. 'What does your friend here know, Michael Dwyer, I ask you that? He says that this

Englishman,' she gestured at her son, 'is going to be a valuable pawn in your negotiations with the English army when they get here.'

Pausing for a moment, she drew breath. 'I say that the English will not be interested in him in the slightest when it comes to negotiations. In fact he might even be one of the first to be killed. And why do you think I say that, Mister Michael Dwyer?'

Again she stopped and looked him straight in the eye, daring him to speak, but all he was able to do was spread his arms helplessly.

'I can say that because he is my son, the son of a Wicklow woman and proud of it, but not a drop of English blood runs through his veins. Rather than being a well-known English soldier, his father is a Frenchman, a sworn enemy of the English. And if you doubt me ask his father yourself, because it is that man sitting there, who has supported you for over twenty-five years!'

Dramatically, she pointed her finger at James Lavelle. As the Frenchman's jaw dropped, everyone in the room turned to look at him in astonishment.

'What!' he stammered, trying to recover from the shock. He stared unbelievingly at Kate and then at Dominic.

'Do you mean that time at Arklow . . .' his voice trailed off.

'Indeed I do, Mister Lavelle,' Kate interrupted, smiling thinly. 'Let me introduce you to your son, Dominic. And in case you're wondering, he knows all about it, for I've already told him about you.'

Turning to Dwyer, she pressed home her point. 'So much for your English hostage, Mister Dwyer. He's no use to you now, especially as you're so dependent on this Frenchman and he'll hardly want his son bartered, I'm sure of that.'

Kate could see clearly the emotions flitting across Dwyer's face as he tried to think of some possible response, but no words came. Gazing around the room, she scrutinised the expressions on the other faces. Now the secret was out in the open – all of these people knew. Soon those in Wicklow who knew her would hear about it, and somehow they would find out about it in England and that would mean everyone would know. For a moment, she thought about the twenty-odd years that had passed since the fateful meeting in Arklow with James Lavelle, and the secret she had carried all that time.

All at once, she realised she didn't care. Let them think what they liked. She had achieved what she had set out to do – she had found her son. To hell with everyone else and what they might be thinking.

Again, she looked across at Michael Dwyer but he had nothing left to give. In fact, he was the one who now sat slumped. To her amazement, Kate suddenly found herself assailed by doubts. This man looked as if he had just seen the last throw of the dice. The great adventure that had started in May five years previously, the struggle for the cause, the change that was going to create an Irish nation once again, this is what it had come to. Their last chance, their way out to somehow start again had been snatched away from them by this woman.

In sympathy almost, she reached out towards him. Suddenly, without the slightest warning, the door burst open with a resounding crash, a blast of cold air whistling through the room. Fearfully, Kate twisted round, half-out of her chair, horrified to see a red-coated English soldier charging through the doorway, brandishing a musket in front of him. Across from her she could sense Dominic trying desperately to get out of the way but he was hampered by his bindings and fell awkwardly against the table. For an agonising moment the makeshift structure tipped dangerously on two legs, and then righted itself and slid to one side, trapping Dwyer and Kate against the wall of the cottage. Despite the shock and the panic, Kate distinctly felt the thump against her thigh from Dwyer's pistol as it slid across the wooden surface with a horrible scraping sound.

Rooted to the spot in shock, she watched the soldier swing the musket up towards her son and pull the trigger. With a roar and a blinding flash, the weapon went off, in the same instant that her brother leapt out of his chair, throwing himself at the redcoat. As the two men fell in a heap the soldier pulled a gun from his belt and aimed it unwaveringly at Dwyer. With a scream of defiance, Kate snatched up the pistol on the table in front of her with both hands and somehow managed to get it pointing in the direction of the vivid red coat.

'Shoot, woman! Shoot, for God's sake!' she heard Dwyer imploring her. Crash! The pistol went off in her hands with a tremendous shock, throwing her back against the wall and temporarily blinding her. Almost immediately, she heard another shot. With a struggle, she managed to stay on her feet, trying desperately to rub her eyes and clear her vision. But all she could make out were dancing lights and indistinct shapes.

There was a momentary deathly silence.

'Mon Dieu, Kate, you nearly killed us all there.'

That was James Lavelle's voice. Did he mean she had hit the English soldier? My God, how could she have killed someone? And what about Dominic and her brother? Had Declan been struck by the ball from the musket?

'How did he find this place? And is there anyone else with him?' Dominic's voice – so he must be all right.

'He must have seen the light from the lamps when we brought in the girl. But where there's one there's bound to be others not far behind.'

That was definitely Dwyer's voice. She rubbed her eyes again, closing them once or twice, as her vision started to return to normal. Things were still blurred but she could definitely see again, thankfully. Turning her head slowly to the right, she was confronted by Dwyer's face, no more than a few inches away from hers.

'Mistress Tilbrook,' he remarked calmly. 'The next time you fire a pistol, I suggest you hold it a little more tightly and a little further away from yourself. That way you'll not have to wait for weeks while your eyebrows grow again.'

Her voice was shaking so badly she could barely speak. 'Did I kill him?'

'I think not, Mistress Tilbrook,' Dwyer replied, as he pushed back the table to release his legs. 'It was Lavelle who got him. But you certainly managed to give the rest of us a fright.'

On the other side of the room she could see Dominic and Lavelle clustered around her brother, who appeared to be half lying on the floor, half against a chair that had been knocked over. Oh no, he had been hit after all.

'Declan,' she screamed, 'Declan, please.' Stumbling across her chair, she pushed the table to one side in her desperation to get to him. But before she reached where he lay, she knew it was all over. The ball had taken him square in the centre of his chest, and his clothes and the surrounding floor were saturated with his blood.

Helplessly, Dominic knelt beside him, cradling his head, tears streaming down his face.

'That ball was meant for me. He knew I couldn't move to get out of the way and he threw himself in front of me.'

He looked at Kate, his face crumpled in grief. 'He did it deliberately, don't you see, he saved my life.'

Slowly, Kate knelt down on the floor herself beside her son, her breeches stained with blood from her brother's wound.

'Oh, Declan,' she whimpered, holding his head as gently as she could. 'My beautiful, brave, wonderful, brother. Please don't die.'

For an instant, his eyes flickered open. 'Kate,' he whispered, so quietly she could barely hear him. 'Is it really you?'

She leaned forward to try and make out his words. 'Kate,' he whispered again, so very faintly, 'I think the debt is repaid.'

She felt rather than saw the life go out of him. It was too dark to see, but she knew the moment it happened. As she knelt among the blood and the tears, her son by her side, her brother drew his last breath. She pulled over an old piece of sacking and laid it carefully under his head. Very gently, James Lavelle picked her up and comforted her in his arms for a moment. Her eyes closed, she turned to her son and held him close.

'I'm so sorry, mother,' he whispered, the tears still running down his cheeks. 'It's all my fault – that it should have come to this.'

'Don't be sorry, Dominic, don't blame yourself,' she murmured as he clung to her, a child once again. 'From the time he started to recover in the hospital in London it was always going to end in sorrow. It was just twenty-three years in the coming, that was all.'

For a moment, she studied her son's face, wiping away his tears. 'Don't weep long for him, Dominic. If you'd known him better, you'd realise he wouldn't have wanted that. He would have wanted us to live for the future and not in the past. The journey he started out upon has not yet come to an end – but now someone else will have to finish it for him.'

Chapter 20

The warmth of the day still lingered, but the evening chills of the autumn were not far away. With only her thoughts for company, Kathleen Tilbrook stood under the shade of the willow trees by the river at Enniskerry, idly casting pebbles into the swirling, peat-stained water.

Thank God it was all over, she sighed inwardly. By tomorrow she would be travelling back home. It was strange to think her home now was so far away from where she had been born and brought up. Only her father was alive, the last family link with the old country – but still steadfast in his refusals to have any contact with her whatsoever.

With a shiver, her thoughts turned to Michael Dwyer and his people, and James Lavelle with them, still holding out in that godforsaken place in the wilds of Lughnaquilla, with the cold winds and the rain of winter sweeping in. How much had they given for their cause and their beliefs? How much had their friends and loved ones given? And had their way achieved anything?

Again, she shivered as she thought of Declan, sacrificing his life for the nephew he had never known. At her insistence they had buried him high on the hillside beside the English soldier, close to the trees and the shade, where the rain could fall softly on his grave. With her own hands, she had marked it with five stones in the shape of a cross, so that Roisin might be able to find it after the troubles were over. Her sons would be the ones who would carry the family name now, and for sure their mother would not let them forget their father. Or the cause he had lived with for so long.

It had taken them almost five days to get back to Laragh, half-starved, with Dominic having to carry Rachel most of the way, watching out for the English redcoats all along the route. Now they had recovered, at least physically, although the mental scars would live with them for years to come.

With a tear in her eye, she picked up a larger rock and hurled it with all her strength into the fast flowing water. If only it would make her feel better. As she bent down to pick up another stone, she heard a familiar voice behind her.

'It's a lovely place indeed, Kathleen, but you seem bent on destroying it.'

With a guilty movement, she dropped the stone immediately, the tension broken by the sound of the man's voice. For a moment she made no reply. Then she laughed, sweetly and easily.

'Mister Grattan, I'm sorry. It's a beautiful garden you have here, and I shouldn't be throwing all these pebbles into the river. I've been standing here thinking about the events of the last twenty-odd years and generally feeling sorry for myself.'

Seeing the concern on his face, she smiled again. Without doubt, he appeared to be much more robust than their previous meeting, when the militia had been camped in his garden. He was still a trifle shaky on his feet and he needed a stick to support himself, but it was good to see him up and about. Who would have thought that one of her Irish stories would have helped save him – one that he had encouraged her to write down in the first place. The world was a strange place right enough.

But there was nothing wrong with his voice. That was as rich and mellifluous as ever. 'I hope you enjoyed our little celebration today, Kathleen. That was my wife's idea as a way of expressing our gratitude for your assistance a few weeks ago.'

Stopping by her side, he reached out his left hand towards her. 'I was really sorry to hear about the tragic death of your brother up on the mountain, and about the sad loss of your husband last year.'

Those few words were all it took to strip away the protective layers that she had built up resolutely over the previous eighteen months. Tears stung her eyes as the memories overwhelmed her. Twenty-two years together had been all the time that God had given them. Such a short time with that wonderful, humorous, tolerant man, the man who had been her friend, her confidante, her lover. The man who knew everything about her and still loved her.

And now he was gone. That fateful moment came back yet again, as her daughter came running into the house, screaming hysterically. It had been impossible to believe that he had died so simply. One minute he was there, and the next he was gone. If only the weather had not been so cold, if only the river had not frozen up, if only the dog had not gone through the ice, Edward might still be with her. If only . . .

Those were the same words she had hurled at her mother all those years in the past when she had been desperate to go to London to find Declan. If only. That was what she had said to old Mr O'Brien on the day he had taken her down to Arklow after her mother's death. If only.

Shaking her head furiously, she brushed her cheeks with the back of her hand. Edward was gone. There was no going back. She had her son and her daughters to think about, they were her life, they were her future. With a supreme effort she forced herself to concentrate on Grattan and what he was saying.

'Life has dealt you some bitter blows, my dear. But I want you to know that I'll always be indebted to you, not so much for myself, but for what you did for my family.'

Kate blushed with embarrassment, overcome by the compliment.

'Sure, it was nothing at all, Mister Grattan. And thank you for your condolences. At least I have my memories, and I know they'll never leave me. But now, I did want to ask you about something different entirely.'

Linking her arm in his, they strolled back across the lawn. 'I haven't been very close to events in Ireland over the past few years,' she began. 'But I understand that you've resigned your seat in the Parliament in London since the Union with Great Britain. Does that mean that you're no longer interested in politics? Have you given up working for the future of this country?'

Grattan stopped and looked at her impassively. 'Do you remember that night all those years ago when you stood up in Mistress Delamere's house? With your eyes flashing, you spoke so passionately about a vision for Ireland, a vision that you convinced us was achievable?'

Her mind turned back the years, a lifetime into the past, although she had a slightly different picture in her head of her performance. Before she could answer, however, he carried on.

'Do you know, Kathleen, that everything you spoke of we achieved in the following year. We were going to have a people's parliament, except it never came to pass in the way we dreamed.'

Quizzically, she looked at him, as he waved his stick vigorously to support his words.

'But I don't understand what went wrong. Why did it not continue?' she wanted to know.

'For many different reasons, my dear, but mainly because of that one key issue that you yourself had identified. There were not enough powerful voices in Dublin representing the majority of the population.'

Breaking off, he turned and looked at her squarely, an animated expression on his face.

'Enough of the past, Kathleen. We have to learn from our mistakes and think of the future. Now at last there is a powerful voice prepared to speak up on behalf of the Catholic people all over this country, one Mister Daniel O'Connell. He may be just the man who can achieve the emancipation that so many people have waited for. And let me tell you, if I ever recover from this wretched illness, I'm going to get back into that parliament in

London and support him myself.'

His excitement brought on a coughing fit, and Kate had to wait patiently for a few minutes while he calmed down and recovered his composure.

Before she could comment, however, he was off again. 'I expect you'll be going back now to your fine house in Essex, Kathleen. What will you be doing there for the next few years?'

For a moment or two, she mulled this over before replying. 'I'm not really sure, Mister Grattan. My son appears to have found his feet and this trip seems to have given him a taste for adventure, never mind romance. I don't believe I'll see much of him in the near future. But I still have three daughters to marry off and an estate to run, so I don't imagine I'll be short of things to do.'

'I'm sure these activities will keep you occupied,' the man replied, 'but will they keep you satisfied? Ask yourself that.'

Pausing for a few seconds, he gave her a long hard look. 'Now that Ireland is part of the Union, any changes in this country will have to be achieved through the government in London. There are more than one hundred members of parliament representing Irish interests, but those who want to change things for the better for the majority in the country are few. We're going to have to work very hard to achieve anything. For sure, we will need all the help we can get, especially from someone like yourself, someone who is a woman of great influence.'

For a moment, Kate pondered on this. 'And what exactly are you saying, Mister Grattan? That a girl from the bogs should be walking the corridors of Westminster?'

The man laughed, but his voice had a persuasive edge. 'Kathleen Tilbrook, you may smile and try to sell yourself short, but you could be a force for change if you were really interested enough in the future of your country.'

Immediately, she gripped his arm fiercely, her eyes blazing. 'Because I'm the Mistress of Tilbrook Estate doesn't mean that I've forgotten where I come from. So many people have given their lives because they believed in freedom and equality for everyone in Ireland. For over twenty years I did not come to this country because of my stupid vow. Now that Rachel Miranda has made me see sense, if I can help I'll do whatever it takes. Please don't forget that.'

Again, Mister Grattan laughed. 'Now that's a lot better, Lady Tilbrook. I was beginning to think that the last few weeks had left you so exhausted that you had lost your appetite for confrontation.'

Leaning on his stick and holding one of her arms for support, he looked at her out of the corner of his eye. 'There's a number of people I think you should meet. Daniel O'Connell I've mentioned to you, and William Wilberforce whom you know already. And I must make sure that you meet Matthew Buckley. He's a lawyer who lives over in London, but he's Irish born and bred, so he's not all bad. And he's been a great help to us recently. He's here somewhere, so if I see him I'll introduce him to you.'

Thank you, Mister Grattan, Kate muttered to herself. That was all she needed today, to meet some dry stick from the Dublin establishment, and be on the receiving end of a lecture about Irish and British politics. Trying to hide her feelings, she smiled wanly. 'Perhaps, Mister

Grattan, perhaps. Let's see what happens in the future.'

Like a schoolteacher admonishing a small child, he gave her a reproving look. 'I'll not stop pursuing you on this matter, Kathleen. We may yet have another chance and we must try and take it this time. However, that's probably enough talk of politics for today. I think it's time perhaps we rejoined the others.'

As they parted company, Kate found herself left with a group of people she barely knew. One gentleman, a farmer by the looks of him, was holding forth on the problems of rearing cows and how to improve milk production. Somewhat less than riveted by this conversation, she found herself looking around idly at the other people in the garden to see who else she knew that she had not already met that afternoon.

Turning her head slightly, she observed a group of people nearby. At the same moment, a man she did not recognise turned towards her, in lively conversation with the woman beside him. For a second or two he stopped speaking and looked up, directly into Kate's line of sight. Even from so far away, she felt the shock as their eyes met, like a kick in the stomach. For a few seconds, she managed to hold his gaze, before she had to look away. What had happened there? she wondered. She was accustomed to men watching her, but this was different. Again, she glanced quickly in his direction. He was tall, probably about the same height as Edward, dressed similarly in black, and perhaps about the same age as herself.

Quickly, she turned her head away, in case he caught her staring at him but not before she had noticed his conversation with the woman appeared to be finished.

God only knew what made her react so quickly. Without thinking, she slipped away from the group she was with. All of a sudden, they were so close she could almost reach out and touch him. What was she to do? Her clear-thinking, decisive mind had been transformed into a mass of confusion.

Without warning the man turned and looked in her direction, unnerving her even further. In an act of desperation she did the only thing she could think of and dropped her bag as if by accident. Awkwardly, she bent down to pick it up, closing her eyes and hiding her face with the sheer embarrassment of it all. How could she have done something so obvious, and been so clumsy about it as well? It was like being nineteen years old all over again.

Blindly, she groped around, trying to collect together the contents of her bag. And then, he was down on one knee beside her. As he started to pick up her belongings she stole a glance sideways. Close up, he was slightly older than she had first thought. His hair was flecked with grey, and his face was creased around the eyes, perhaps by laughter lines. And then she realised he was smiling, the devious man.

'Madam, are you all right?' Her head was spinning, but she could hear his voice clearly enough, low and firm. She did not trust herself to utter a word. Slowly, she got to her feet.

'Lady Tilbrook,' she heard his voice again, slightly more anxious. 'Are you feeling unwell?'

Kate could see his face, his smile replaced by a look of concern. Swallowing hard, she forced herself to speak.

'Sir,' she croaked, 'you have the better of me. How do

you know my name when we have not been introduced?'

'Lady Tilbrook, I'm sorry,' he apologised immediately. 'Mister Grattan and some of the other guests have told me so much about you. I was hoping we might meet, but I was being careful, for I've been told that you can be a strong-willed woman.'

On the point of making a sharp retort, she looked at his face and realised he was teasing her. Unaccountably, her heart jumped under his steady gaze.

'Well, sir, are you going to tell me who you are, or are you going to keep me in suspense all afternoon?' she demanded, flashing her most devastating smile.

'Certainly, Lady Tilbrook,' he replied with a flourish. 'My name is Matthew Buckley, at your service.'

So this was the dry old stick of a lawyer she had been concerned about meeting? Kate glanced again at the faint smile, and the cool, level gaze. As she took his hand, all her anxieties seemed to melt away. Perhaps the world was not such a bad place after all.

Epilogue

The late eighteenth and early nineteenth centuries were a time of major change in Great Britain and Ireland. Both countries were affected by the huge political and social turbulence of the time, including the French Revolution, the American War of Independence, the Irish Uprising and the all-pervading Industrial Revolution.

This upheaval continued until 1815, when the defeat of Napoleon at Waterloo ushered in a period of peace and stability for both countries. The general who masterminded the victory over Napoleon was none other than the boy who spent a childhood summer at Enniskerry, Arthur Wellesley, by that time better known as the Duke of Wellington. Some years later, he became Prime Minister of Great Britain and played a prominent role in the struggle for the rights of the people in Ireland, eventually signing the Catholic Emancipation Act.

The prime mover in Ireland for Catholic emancipation throughout the early nineteenth century was Daniel

O'Connell. He was one of the first Catholics to enter the legal profession in Ireland after the rules of entry were changed in 1792. He then became involved in politics and saw his work rewarded by the signing of the Act in 1829.

Henry Grattan, the man who had done so much for independence in Ireland, returned to politics in 1805 as a Member of Parliament for an English constituency, Malton, and also campaigned vigorously for equal rights for the people of Ireland until his death in 1819. He wanted to be buried in his beloved Wicklow but his wishes were not granted and he was buried in Westminster Abbey.

Michael Dwyer, the leader of the United Irishmen who held out in Wicklow for almost five years after the initial uprising, finally surrendered in December 1803. He was kept in prison in Ireland for over a year before being transported to New South Wales. His wife and children joined him some time later and he became a farmer and a pillar of the local society. He died in Australia in 1825.

One of the leaders of the Industrial Revolution in Great Britain was Matthew Boulton, who supported James Watt for many years in his work to develop the steam engine. He died eventually in 1809.

William Wilberforce became the champion for the abolition of slavery and the protection of human rights, and fought tirelessly throughout his life for the emancipation of Catholics in Ireland.

And finally, what happened to Lady Kathleen Tilbrook, her family and friends, and even James Lavelle? Well, that is another story . . .